Henry Kingsley

Oakshott Castle

Being the Memoir of an Eccentric Nobleman

Henry Kingsley

Oakshott Castle
Being the Memoir of an Eccentric Nobleman

ISBN/EAN: 9783337778910

Printed in Europe, USA, Canada, Australia, Japan

Cover: Foto ©Raphael Reischuk / pixelio.de

More available books at **www.hansebooks.com**

BEING THE

MEMOIR OF AN ECCENTRIC NOBLEMAN.

BY

HENRY KINGSLEY.

A NEW EDITION.

London:

CHATTO AND WINDUS, PICCADILLY.

1876.

CONTENTS.

CONTENTS.

OAKSHOTT CASTLE.

CHAPTER I.

THE PUBLIC-HOUSE.

THE weather had been dim and wild all day, and the sea
had begun to tumble in heavily from the south-west; but
when the fishermen had gathered round the fire inside the
screen, there was one matter of congratulation among them
all: there was not one single boat out; the catch had been
good, the hucksters had been ready, the fish were gone, the
money was paid, the women were seeing to the nets, and
each man had in his pocket a sum of money allowed him by
his wife for liquor. If he chose to spend it that night, he
could spend it; if not, he could leave some of it for another
night: but so long as he did not come to bed with his boots
on, every married man there was as free as if he were a
bachelor. As the head lady of the place, Mrs. Price, said,
"They have arnt their money, God bless 'em, and arnt it
hard; let 'em have some good company together." And so
these wicked women, not having the fear of the League before their eyes, had made their husbands strip and dry, given
them their suppers, taken their money from them, given them

half-a-crown apiece, and sent them off to the Oakshott Arms
for a gossip, while they turned to hanging out the nets.   A
most reprehensible body of women, doubtless, but certainly
with a set of hard-working and affectionate husbands.   The
bachelors, it may be remarked, stayed and helped the unmarried girls with the nets, and a kiss or a squeeze of the
hand from a handsome young sailor is much the same,
whether he be as dry as a dandy or as wet as a shag : and a
saunter home to the house with him may be made as pleasant in a furious south-westerly gale on a dark night, as in a
bright June day under towering elms, with flowers round
your feet at every tread ; at least it would seem so, for a
great deal of honest love-making went on that night, both on
the beach and in front of the cottage-doors, until the bachelors were driven away through the rain and wind by mothers
to join their seniors inside the screen at the Oakshott Arms,
down on the beach.

How it blew, and how delightful it was to hear it blow !
How it roared in the chimney, and blew at the door like a
hungry wolf wishing for their blood !   That morning they
had been all out together, not ten miles between any of them,
and nearly all over-loaded.   Captain Joyce, at the windy
Preventive Station on the Point, had looked more than once
at his barometer, and then had fired a gun every five minutes
until they turned and came home, the last of them in a heavy
tumbling sea, which got up with wonderful rapidity, for a
strong wind had met the tide.   They were very deep, and
it had been a question with the last of them whether they
should part with their fish or no, but they had held by their
fish.   Between the walls of ugly green water which broke
audibly on the rocks in the lee, only being able to show a

rag of sail, these last men had held on, keeping the boys baling, with two oars out to leeward, and had won the harbour: sometimes upon the top of a wave, when they could see the women grouped upon the beach watching them, and Prout the landlord, with his apron, looking on from the public-house door, which they might never enter again ; sometimes deep in the trough, when they could only see the mast of the next boat like a brown spike above the wind-driven foam :—these men had held on and won, though death was a little nearer to them than usual. Now the fish were sold, the boat was safe, the nets were out to dry, the wives had the money, and they were inside the screen with their grog and their tobacco, while the wind was impotently getting up outside. Where is the man who will look one in the face and say that they had not earned a little innocent pleasure, and that they were not better there than anywhere else ?

Mr. Prout, the landlord, was a very sensible man ; he knew perfectly well that the married men would have their supper before they came there, and that the bachelors would want some when they came, so he had it ready for them ; and the young men, when they had torn themselves away from the young women, found themselves in the presence of a large hot pie which the landlord had cut open. The moment a young man smelt that pie as he came in, he called for a pint of beer, drew a stool, and sat down without any further questioning. The steam out of the pie mingled with the steam of the undried clothes of the young bachelors, and made a scent like a mixture of haunch of venison and bromine, with a *soupçon* of tobacco. The elders, who had been dried, looked on approvingly.

"Cut away, boys," said the landlord; "cut and come

again. That cost me nothing but the pie-crust and the fuel to cook it, and it shan't cost you anything. No charge for supper to-night."

"What is it?" said one young man who had helped himself and was looking at his plate with a pleased expression.

"Venison, my lad," said Mr. Prout; "my lord's own venison, sent by his own hand."

"It's too good for the likes of me," said the young man, laughing; "but here goes."

"Nothing is too good for the likes of a man as brought his boat in as you brought yours," said Mr. Prout. "Why, you are wet now, my lad; take a drain of this. Take drains all round, you lads, and pay when two Fridays come in one week. You sleep single and cold now; here's to the time when you may all sleep double and warm."

There was no resisting the landlord : the venison pie disappeared very rapidly; the dish was moved away by the maid, and the wet young men settled themselves among their drier elders, and steamed before the blazing fire until they too were dry.

At first it was too delightfully comfortable for conversation; they were packed close together, like herrings in a barrel, and each man could feel his neighbour's body, which is a sort of company. Then everybody knew what anybody else would say, which was also very comfortable. So they sat and smoked, and drank warm liquors for a little while, and no one said anything. At last Mr. Prout, standing before the fire beaming, thought that he would start the conversation by saying exactly what he was perfectly sure any one else would have said.

"It's blowing hard, Master Dixon."

Master Dixon moved a polite amendment to this by taking his pipe out of his mouth and saying—

"It's blowing darned hard."

Old Horton ought to have been addressed first, as the oldest man in the company, and he let them know it. He took his pipe from his mouth and looked round; there was a general attention.

"It's blowing," he said, "at this present minute as hard as it's blown for forty year, and it's going to blow harder." Then he put his pipe in his mouth again, and there was silence.

It is noticeable that whenever it blows, it blows harder than it has done for forty years.

But only for one moment, a quiet voice from the end of the screen said—

"You think so, do you, Horton? I am very much of the same opinion myself."

Every one rose and looked, while a man came forward to the fire, and, taking a chair, sat down and warmed his hands by the blaze. His figure was tall and athletic; his face very brown, with a light yellow beard; his expression dreamy and inscrutable; his dress like that of a sailor.

"Sit down, my dear people," he said : and they sat down in silence.

"Are all the boats in ?"

"All, my lord."

"I think," he said, dreamily, "that we ought to give thanks to God for that, each one of us, before we go to bed. I do not see how we could do otherwise. I think that it would be only decent. Not that I wish any man to give thanks to God on my account ; I only make the suggestion." And then the conversation flagged.

"I wish, Mr. Prout," said Lord Oakshott, "for a glass of warm beer, and I shall smoke my cigar here among you all. I am not easy in my mind. My cousin wrote to me from Cherbourg to say that he would be with me to-day, if the weather served ; now the weather *has* served, and I am very anxious. Make room for me by you, Horton ; I am keeping the fire from every one."

He sat down quite contentedly among them, and now that the ice was broken they were not a bit afraid of him.

"When was Sir Arthur to sail, my lord?" said a young man.

"That I cannot tell you," said Lord Oakshott ; "he said he would be here to-day. Here is his letter :—'I will be in harbour with you on the evening of the 15th.' I am very anxious."

"What is Sir Arthur's new yacht like, my lord ?" asked old Horton. "I have never seen her."

"Oh, one of these 250-ton American-fashioned schooners ; a keel ship ; a rare sea-boat ; weather anything. He is going to sail her across the Atlantic, he says."

"Has he spare spars on board ?" said Horton.

"He always carries them," said Lord Oakshott ; "and he is under-sparred as it is. He is not in racing trim."

"A good thing for him," said old Horton.

There was a crash overhead at this moment, and Mrs. Prout was heard screaming upstairs. Prout ran out, and soon came back, saying that it was only one of the chimney-pots, and that Mrs. Prout was quite quiet again. The conversation went on :—

"What crew had he, my lord ?" said Horton.

"I suppose a common crew," said Lord Oakshott.

"Sir Arthur is too fine a sailor to make this little harbour to-night," said old Horton. "If he sailed at all, he has run under Portland; make your mind easy, my lord."

"I cannot quite do that, he is so desperately rash; and I could not have anything happen to him for fifty thousand pounds."

A dead silence showed that sentiment did not meet the views of the company at all. Sir Arthur was next in succession, and Lord Oakshott was unmarried. If Lord Oakshott had been looking at his tenants' faces, he would have seen that there was not one of them would have given fifty shillings or fifty pence to save Sir Arthur from drowning.

"Well," said Lord Oakshott, "I shall stay here to-night; I could not get a wink of sleep up at the Castle in this howling weather, and Arthur at sea. Prout, get me a bed ready. I will sit here with you men and talk. I must have company; that Castle would drive a man mad."

"It *is* lonesome," said old Horton, "but it would be lonesomer still if you were to leave it; your study window in the tower, my lord, makes a beacon for us, as good as Eddystone. When we are far out at night, in all weathers, we see your lonely light burning up there, and we think my lord is up there at his books; and however wild the weather may be, it makes us feel homely and comfortable."

"I should comfort some one," said Lord Oakshott, "for I am little comfort to myself."

"You are some to us in bad winters, my lord; but, as I was saying, we make a beacon of that reading-lamp of yours. I and my grandson were out in the little yawl one night, and it came on from the south-east, and I couldn't tell where we were, and I kept the spritsail only on her and let her drive, as I thought, to kingdom come : and all of a sudden my boy sings out, 'Get the foresail on her and luff her : there's my lord's light in the tower ; we are all right.' And so we were. You little thought, while you were up there with your books, that we were blessing you for not having gone to bed."

"Shall I always keep a light burning?" said Lord Oakshott ; "always, until the sea gives up its dead?"

"The sea will never give up its dead, my lord, until the day of judgment," said old Horton, very solemnly.

"I suppose not," said Lord Oakshott ; "I think that I will build a lighthouse in the park, and leave funds to keep the light burning ; for when I am dead the light in my study window will be dark for ever. Arthur will never go there."

There was more talk on indifferent matters, principally about the gale, which was certainly doing itself justice. One by one the tired fishermen went out into the wild wind to their homes, and at last Lord Oakshott went to bed, with the wind howling at his window as if it would tear his flesh.

CHAPTER II.

THE SHIPWRECK.

In the very early morning there was a great cry and a hurrying to and fro. Prout was in Lord Oakshott's room, shaking him by the shoulder, and he bounced out of bed. "What the devil is it ?" he cried. "*Is it Arthur's yacht ?*"

"No, my lord. It is the poor *Albion*, the Poole and

Cherbourg steamer. Lost her place in the night, my lord, and fighting for her life so bravely. Oh, poor Jeffreys ! poor Jeffreys !"

Lord Oakshott ran out with his clothes put hurriedly on, and stumbled over in the blast which met him. When he was ten yards from the door, he saw that all was over, and that that ship would sail no more for ever.

Beyond the surf, which raged and rushed at his feet, there were walls after walls of green sea-water following one another inexorably, and combing over in the expectation of their hideous death. Among these walls of water was the *Albion*, fighting them stoutly and bravely to the last, without the slightest hope of mercy or of safety. Her steam-pipes were roaring, and her wheels were tearing into the grim sides of the waves; she knew she must die, but she was dying fiercely, like a true English ship. At one time, as her bows lifted, you could see the whole of her bare deck, two men at the wheel, and Jeffreys steadfast on the bridge ; the crew and apparently three or four passengers huddled under the forecastle,—thank God, no women ! Then you only saw her stern as it rose over a wave, and then her deck again. It was maddening, but there was nothing to be done but to walk wildly up and down.

" Where will she touch ?" said Lord Oakshott, shouting into old Horton's ear.

" On the outer land in one minute."

Almost as he spoke she touched it with her stern and broached to ; three or four green seas leaped over her and hid the deck, which was towards them, from their view. The larboard paddle-box, the one in the air, burst with a noise like thunder, and then everything was utter ruin and confusion : men struggling amidst the broken ruin of the ship in the leeward of the hull.

Half-a-dozen ropes had been ready, and half-a-dozen young men were in the surf with the ropes round their waists, at once : one of them was Lord Oakshott ; a floating companion-ladder struck him heavily on the chest, but there were two wild, clutching, sinking hands before him in the horrible hell-broth, and he dashed on and seized one. In another instant he was thrown down badly bruised and half-stunned, but he held on by that hand, swearing to himself that his grip should only be loosened by his own death. He felt the rope tighten round his chest, and he knew that they were dragging him on shore. In a few moments he was lying half dead upon the sand, on the body of another man, the man he had saved. He rose, staggered, and then looked into the man's face. It was Captain Jeffreys, the man of all others he wished to see.

Jeffreys was soon himself again, though very badly hurt ; they had told him the name of the man who had saved him, and when Lord Oakshott came to him he sat up on the land and put his hand towards him feebly. Lord Oakshott knelt by him and said—

" Jeffreys, I want you to listen to me. When did you sail from Cherbourg, old man ?"

" Yesterday noon."

" Had Sir Arthur sailed ?"

" Yes ; three hours before. I passed him about mid-channel."

" How was the wind ?"

" Northern-by-west, *then.*"

" Was he making good weather ?"

" There was no weather in particular, my lord ; he altered her course after he spoke me. He was tacking to westward when I saw him last. Then it came on to blow ; and here I am. I have something more to tell you about Sir Arthur, but I am terribly knocked about. What men are drowned ?"

" There are four."

" Give me your arm, one of you, and let me look at them."

They went to look. The dead men were lying quietly on the sand, with groups of women round them. The women parted as they went up to the first one, and they looked at him : a young man lying on his back, looking like other dead men who lie on their backs, the face quite calm, and the slightly parted feet turned up to heaven (those who have been among these later carnages will know what I mean). There was nothing to remark about this man ; he had been the steward of the steamer. The next man was lying on his face, and was dressed in uniform. At Jeffreys' request two old women turned the body on its back. Jeffreys sighed, and said—

" That is all I wish to see : that is a man who could have told much ; how much I cannot say. Do you know who he is ?"

" No," said Lord Oakshott.

" He was Sir Arthur's sailing master. I brought over nearly all the rest of his crew. He discharged all but four, and paid their passage home."

" But what crew had he then ?"

" All the scum of Cherbourg. He took two refractory French sailors from the Isle Pelée."

"Were his crew of any use at all?"

"They were very good sailors—but the people are listening, and I am very weak. Take me somewhere where I can lie down."

Lord Oakshott took him along and put him in his own bed at Prout's, after which he gave him hot brandy-and-water, and Jeffreys told him all that he knew.

"There were terrible works at Cherbourg, my lord. Sir Arthur was always bullying Mr. Clough, his sailing master, and Clough has come on board my ship and told me that he would send his engagement to the devil. I have told him that if he thought of his wife and child he should do nothing of the kind. I have spoken to Sir Arthur more than once, and I came to the conclusion that Sir Arthur's object was to pick a quarrel with Clough and the best hands among his crew. Anyhow he did it. He insisted on bringing aboard a woman of bad character, and Clough would not have it, and told him so. There was a general row, and the main of the crew sided with Clough, and were discharged and sent home, and he filled up with such as he could get, all foreigners."

"There is nothing very remarkable in all that," said Lord Oakshott. "He expected to be here last night."

"He wrote to that effect, did he, my lord?"

"Yes."

"Then you may entirely depend that he did not mean to be here. Did you ever know him do what he said he was going to do?"

"Not that I remember. But we all have our eccentricities."

"Now, you saw that young steward who lay drowned?"

" Yes."

" Clough knew something, but he knew more. I heard Sir Arthur offer him ten pounds a month to stay with him, and the young man refused. I saw a look in Sir Arthur's eyes when he refused, which made me advise him quietly to come on board my ship at once. He wanted to go on board the yacht for his kit, but I persuaded him not, for she was out by the Digue, and I thought it was quite as well that he should claim his kit in England."

" Well ?"

" Well, my lord, Sir Arthur sailed, and the two men who knew most about his plans are drowned."

" What do you conceive has become of my cousin ?"

" He is possibly in Portland."

" Thanks ; I will send high and low to find him. As a matter of detail, did the lady you mention sail with him ?"

" Yes."

" Do you know her name ?"

" You must know it, my lord."

" Madame d'Espérance ?"

" Exactly."

" Then you were scarcely justified in saying that she was a woman of bad character."

" She was another man's wife," said Jeffreys.

" She was nothing of the kind," said Lord Oakshott ; "she was as pure as your sister."

" Then why was she Madame, my lord ?"

" She was an actress, and she took that name. Why, good heavens, man ! she was my cousin's wife."

" Why did he not acknowledge her ?" said the bluff sailor.

"He never did anything like any one else," said Lord Oak-shott. "Why, I wanted to marry her myself, Jeffreys, but she preferred him : and I was going to welcome them at the Castle yesterday."

"Well, my lord, in my opinion it will be a very long time before you welcome them there. I have my opinions."

"Go to sleep now, at all events," said Lord Oakshott ; "I will go and search for them."

His search was a long and a weary one, but he never found them, never got the least trace of them, save one : the captain of the *Jumna* had seen a schooner very like the *Petrel* lying to, clear off the Lizard, with her mizen topmast gone. From fishermen and pilots on the tumbling seas, in the chops of the Channel, from keen-eyed Preventive-men on windy capes, he learnt nothing more at all. There was no doubt that this cousin Sir Arthur and his wife were gone to the bottom of the sea ; one waif of them only remained.

Wearying of all hope, he borrowed a friend's yacht and steamed across to Cherbourg, taking Jeffreys with him. Jeffreys was immensely popular, and the people had neither forgotten the loss of his ship nor the rather strange behaviour of Sir Arthur with his crew. Madame Mantalent was ex-tremely garrulous on the subject. She discussed Jeffreys' mishap, and then, utterly unaware that Lord Oakshott was Sir Arthur's cousin, began railing at him.

"Savage and barbarian !" she said ; he beat and cursed his crew so that no honest Englishman would stay with him. And he had designs, that man—oh yes, he had designs. And look once more at his treatment of Madame—for she *was* Madame, Captain Jeffreys, as sure as your mother was Madame, though he would not call her so ; I saw the ring on her finger, and the writing from the Protestant minister in the Rue Auguesseau. Ah, she was Madame, though he says she was ballet-girl, lorette, I know not what, to make quarrel with Clough. And he makes quarrel with him, and all the respectables depart and go with Jeffreys. And before she sailed she went down on her knees to him in the room by the shore, that he should let her take her child with her, and he r-r-refuse—the barbarian !"

"What child, Madame?" said Lord Oakshott, quietly. "I was aware that Sir Arthur was married, but I was utterly unaware that he had a child."

"Do you know Sir Arthur, then?" said Madame Mantalent.

"He was my cousin. He was next in succession to my title and my estates. Is the child a boy or a girl, then, Madame ?"

"A beautiful boy, and they are going to send him to the *enfants trouvés.*"

"You perceive, Madame, that if he can be proved legitimate he is my heir ; and as I shall never marry, the boy's life is of importance to me."

"The child is legitimate," said Madame Mantalent, looking a little puzzled and elevating her eyebrows. "I can give you one hundred, two thousand proofs of that. But why then did Sir Arthur leave him behind ?"

"It is evident that poor Arthur thought the crossing would be too rough," said Lord Oakshott.

"Then why did he take Madame ?"

"Marie was used to the sea, Madame. She had lived at Morbihan."

"You know her Christian name then, Milord ? Why did

you allow that dog to blacken it?   I also am from Brittany, and I would often have put a knife in his heart if I dared, when he taunted her about Edward."

" Did he do that?" said Lord Oakshott, very quietly.

" Always.   He said that the child was Edward's."

" God forgive him that lie, Madame.   When he left her in Paris, I found her, and treated her as what she was ; in fact, my own sister.   And I loved her still, Madame."

" Then you are Edward?"

" I am Edward.   But they are drowned now ; my life is ruined, and it is all over.   We have at least the boy saved from the wreck.   You must remember, Madame, that the child is the son of a woman I wooed and of a man whom, with all his faults, I loved.   He will be dear to me.   Can you fetch him for me ?"

Ask a Frenchwoman to do a good-natured thing when her domestic sympathies are aroused ; you will not ask twice. She had on her bonnet and shawl at once, and was away, leaving Lord Oakshott with his head buried in his hands. Captain Jeffreys sauntered out on the quay down by the Arsenal, to smoke, and he met a comrade there, as true a salt as himself.   This skipper hailed from Weymouth, and knew Lord Oakshott well.   Jeffreys explained to him what had happened, and concluded by saying—

" I have not a word against a man who saved my life. My lord is a good man, but he wants more of the devil in him. Why, if a man had served me as that dog Sir Arthur and that woman served him, I'd have started them both overboard some dark night, and sent the kid to the *enfants trouvés*.   But my lord is a sentimental fool."

Then he returned to Lord Oakshott.   The child, a beautiful boy of three had been fetched and was on his knee, with his handsome head buried in Lord Oakshott's yellow beard. Captain Jeffreys heard Lord Oakshott say, as he bent and kissed the boy: " My darling, nothing shall separate us but death."

Possibly Captain Jeffreys was right.

CHAPTER III.

THE OAKSHOTTS.

THEY say in Dorsetshire that the human race is divided into men, women, and Sturts. Now, the Oakshotts always deny this, and say that they are an older and more important family than the Sturts, inasmuch as there is no mention made of Sturts in the Old Testament or the Apocrypha at all, whereas their family tree is distinctly mentioned in the history of Susanna and the Elders, under the name of Holmoak. The Oakshotts declare that Daniel married Susanna, and that they are the lineal descendants of the marriage.* Be this as it may, and leaving the Sturt question aside, they claim to be the oldest family in England ; and if purity among women and shrewdness among men are the tests of an old family, the Oakshotts may fairly claim to be the oldest in the land.

The Mostyn pedigree begins with Adam and Eve, and the devil is represented in a lawyer's way tempting Eve. Everything seems to have gone well with the Mostyn family down to the comparatively recent creation of Adam and Eve and the appearance of the devil in the form of a lawyer. It was

* Another pedigree is quite as ambitious, so I am well within bounds.

very much the same with the Oakshotts. Early in this century the direct line of the family failed, and for the first time a nephew, and not a son, was heir to the estates and title. The nephew and his brothers had been brought up as men who had to make their way in the world. The eldest was made a soldier, the youngest a barrister. The soldier was a colonel in a King's regiment in India, and the lawyer was already Q.C., when their cousin, the heir, was drowned in the bay, and Colonel Oakshott found himself next in succession. He left the army and assumed that position in the county to which his vast expectations entitled him, and to which he very soon succeeded.

This made but little difference to the younger brother. Lord Oakshott would have had him retire from the law, and gallantly offered to make him comfortably rich. He accepted all that his brother gave, but told him that he was too used to work to do without it. He did not even take the title of Honourable, which he might have had for asking, but remained plain Mr. Oakshott, having determined to found another branch of the family by his own exertions.

He was a man of astonishing abilities, an iron constitution, and most unwearied diligence. He married the daughter (and heiress) of the head partner in one of the most famous firms of solicitors in London. It was a splendid match for the Brogdens, as well as for himself, for Lord Oakshott, the soldier, had lost two children in India, and had buried his wife there. Should he not marry again, only one boy—the Lord Oakshott with whom you have already made acquaintance—stood between him and the title; to that boy he conceived a violent dislike.

He made a vast fortune; he made so much money that he

used laughingly to say that he could not afford to be a judge. People behind his back, however, used to say that he had better wait until he was asked. He had enemies. His private character was not very good, some hinted; others said that his extreme violence in politics rendered it quite impossible for either party to do anything for him. Be this as it may, he ended his days as Sir Richard Oakshott, of Shepperton, a splendid estate which he had bought, not twenty miles from his brother's.

The brothers, though extremely different in character, were very great friends. Lord Oakshott (our friend's father) was a singularly amiable and simple man, who looked up to the talents of his younger brother with the profoundest faith. Sir Richard despised and disliked the Earl entirely, considering him a milksop both in politics and in religion. Only his brother and his brother's son stood between him and the Peerage. The Earl's health had suffered greatly in India, but the wretch of a boy was horribly healthy and gallant; exactly the sort of boy whom his sentimental fool of a father would allow to marry at nineteen,—nothing was more likely.

There are some lawyers—nine-tenths, ninety-nine hundredths, we believe—who wade year after year through the miserable filth and brutality which are necessary in courts of justice, and who come out clear, unspotted, honourable, and innocent. Now and then you find one, very rarely, who assimilates the horrible wickedness which must of necessity be his daily *entourage*, and his daily bread. Such cases are extremely rare, as any one who knows many retired lawyers of eminence will testify; but there are such, and Sir Richard was one of them. He saw things done every day which he

would have done himself had he dared.   He could, however,
do much.

Lord Oakshott, his brother, had learnt how to keep
accounts and manage affairs, firstly by having been a little
extravagant himself when he had his own way to make in
the army, and secondly by having had to manage an extremely economical marching regiment, in which every one
had to see that two and two made four.   He found it not so
very difficult to manage a splendid unencumbered estate,
the revenues of which he could not, as a widower, spend.
Sir Richard had no chance whatever of getting his fingers
into his money matters.   Although Compton and Brogden
were the Earl's solicitors, they were, as all the world knows,
the souls of honour, who had been trusted by great houses
for generations.   Sir Richard (we call him by his title,
though he was plain Mr. Oakshott still) could do nothing
here, but as he grew older, and as he believed wiser, the lust
for wealth grew upon him,—he began to want his brother's
possessions as well as his own.   As Lord Oakshott, he
would be one of the richest men in the kingdom, and with
his talents one of the most powerful.   The boy stood in the
way, certainly, and he did not see his way to getting rid of
the boy.   His own boy, his only son, was of the same age,
and he asked him sometimes about his cousin, with whom
he was at Eton.

His son Arthur gave a most favourable account of his
cousin : he was idle and often wild, but he had good abilities,
could write good poetry, and was a great favourite with the
masters.   Was he a healthy lad?   Yes, he was one of the
strongest lads in the school ; he was very lazy at all sports,
though he could beat most if he chose ; his cricket generally

was not good, and his batting was atrocious, but when he did get hold of a ball he could send it over the Castle. Was he a milksop? Yes, he was spooney over Whybrow's sister, where he went last holidays, and the best of everything was not good enough for Whybrow.

It was perfectly evident to such a very acute knower of the world as Sir Richard, that a fine-grown, strong, and innocent boy like this, who could fall in love with his friend's sister at sixteen, was uncommonly likely to live unless he broke his neck, which Sir Richard devoutly wished he might do. He must trust to the chapter of accidents about him. One thing, however, could be prevented—his brother should not marry again.

Sir Richard was not happy in his wife. She was highly educated, religious, and conscientious, and no use to him at all. He was profoundly civil and affectionate to her, for old Brogden, a most resolute man, was not yet dead, adored his daughter, and had the disposition of sixty thousand pounds, besides what he had given her. He could not use her at all, except by utilizing her profound respectability; so he used that.

At the time that old Lord Oakshott began to go more into the world, which was ten years after his return from India, a certain very beautiful widow, Mrs. O'Brien — *soi-disante* Duchesse d'Avranches—put her claims into the hands of Compton and Brogden; and Compton and Brogden retained Sir Richard. Her character was spotless as snow, but she had enemies. To have her case taken up by Compton and Brogden was to win it; *they* never took up doubtful cases. It was a will case, of undue influence, and the villains on the other side said worse. Compton and Brogden were in a state of holy heat at this woman's wrongs, but the heat did not on this occasion communicate itself to the leader on her side, Sir Richard. He spoke to the Court, not to the groundlings, so judiciously and well, that she won her cause and twenty thousand pounds with it. It was entirely impossible to avoid taking up a saint of this kind, who had brought into the office a sum of money large even for them. Mrs. Compton took her up; Mrs. Brogden took her up; and Lady Oakshott had her down to Shepperton at Christmas, at the particular request of her husband.

Lord Oakshott met her there, and fell in love with her. Her enemies saw what every one else did. Lady Oakshott, Sir Richard's wife, knew nothing, and, as the woman had always been represented to her as a wealthy saint, let matters go as they chose. They went very fast indeed. Lord Oakshott proposed to her and was accepted before Sir Richard had returned from Scotland, where he had been shooting with the Duke of Aberfeldy.

When he heard what had happened, he was furiously angry with his wife first, and then went to his brother's dressing-room. "George," he said, suddenly, "what madness is this? Have you actually proposed to Mrs. O'Brien?"

"Yes."

"Why, man, she is——" and I will spare my readers the details.

"But you defended her, Richard."

"I have defended a murderer who has told me the truth, and I have brought him off free. I am proud of it: I love my profession."

"But this is horrible. Have you no principle, Richard?"

"Thus much, if you offer to speak to that woman again,

I will say a few words to her which will send her to America pretty quickly."

"You asked her to stay in your house with your own wife," urged Lord Oakshott.

"My wife is such a pillar of virtue that she can do anything. Besides, my father-in-law did so first, and I am not going to risk sixty thousand pounds by offending him. My wife's mother received her, and I could not let her fly in her mother's face."

"What shall I do, Richard? I love her."

"Well, as you perceive that you cannot marry her, it is a matter of indifference to me, only I do not want to see my brother disgrace himself with what he knows will be a bitter shame to his son. Go home, and I will send the woman away."

Lord Oakshott went into his bedroom, and Sir Richard heard him packing. "I think," he said, with a sneer, "that there is an end of your love-making for a time, my sweet brother. By heavens! I'll ransack Newgate before you shall marry."

Lord Oakshott bid good-bye to Sir Richard in the hall with a bent head. Sir Richard was almost sorry for him until he remembered that the boy was still in his way. Then he went to break the news of Lord Oakshott's departure to Mrs. O'Brien. Mrs. O'Brien said very quietly, "I thought it never would do ; but I fancied that your wife had told you about it, and that you would let it go on. Well, I am sorry for it, for I was very fond of him, and he loves the ground I walk on. There need be no *esclandre*, for no one knows it but your wife." And Mrs. O'Brien ate a most excellent dinner, while Lord Oakshott was driving broken-

hearted over the hills towards his melancholy home. He
never used more than common civility to any other woman
in his life : and so far Sir Richard was successful.

CHAPTER IV.

A FEW OF LORD OAKSHOTT'S INDISCRETIONS.

LORD OAKSHOTT was the first who died of the two brothers,
leaving behind him the name of the good Lord Oakshott.
His son succeeded him at the age of twenty-two, having
been to Eton with moderate success, and to Cambridge with
very little more. He was one of those young men who have
the credit of being able to do anything they choose, and he
chose to do nothing, except write poetry and speak at the
union, both which things he did very well. On his succession to the title, he left Trinity without a degree, and went
abroad to Italy and the Nile. We will, for a short time, dismiss him, to write a most excellent and admirable volume of
poems, and to make the intimate acquaintance of the Carbonari and Cammoristi, who first gave him that extraordinary
bias which has never since entirely left him.

Shepperton, the purchased estate of Sir Richard, was
hardly less grand in its way than Oakshott. It was very old,
the "keep" being, in point of fact, Norman or older. It
lay low, under towering hills so high that the summits of
them could be seen above the dense woodlands which surrounded it. On the east the façade was very fine Tudor,
into the midst of which some seventeenth century Cockney
had built a gateway with a real portcullis. This was not,
however, the grand front ; that stretched for three hundred

feet, and was mostly modern, though handsome and in good taste. The whole atmosphere of the place was profoundly gloomy and dark, and was not very much enlivened by a great piece of artificial water, fifty acres in extent, which lay in front of the house among the trees, and nearly on a level with the house. It was not at all a nice place, and Lord R—— had sold it, with the consent of his son, as they both agreed that if they lived there they should drown themselves in the lake, or hang themselves on the boughs of one of the immemorial elms.

Inside the house was as handsome and as gloomy as the best house in Russell Square in a November fog. It was by no means a pleasant place to live in, for every window was darkened by trees ; and it was certainly a most unpleasant place to die in, though some say that one place is as good as another for that purpose. However, Sir Richard had selected to end his days there, and there he was about five years before the wreck of the *Albion*, described in our first chapter.

He was in the great drawing-room, propped up on a couch, with a reading-lamp, surrounded by blue-books, law reports, and papers. A great case had come on, and his wife's cousin, young Brogden, had posted down to him for his advice, and was with him as the autumn evening set in.

" I am very sorry to see you so ill, Sir Richard," said he.

" Bah ! I shall be dead in a week, but I will do this for you. Hand me the fourth book there on the table."

Young Brogden did so.

" Yes, I see. Tell Mr. Compton that it will go against us in an English court, but for us in a Scotch one. These are the memoranda all bracketed for him ; run your eye over them."

The young man did so, and looked up with an appearance of amazement.

"Have you done all this single-handed since I came in the morning," he cried, "and say that you are dying ? Why, this is the most dexterous and rapid work I have ever seen in my life."

The old man raised his heavy white eyebrows, and his white beard shook with laughter.

"I can work and I can hate till I die," he said. "I am only sixty, and have the constitution of a horse yet. But do you know what is the matter with me ?"

"No, Sir Richard."

"Cancer, young man. I must go ; I can't stand the paroxysms of pain. I can't wait to see this trial out ; I shall be gone in a week. Just hand me the morphia, will you ?"

He took his dose, and lay back.

"Post to me, or come at once if I post to you. I may see something more for you. I owe your house something. What with your poor uncle's money and the fees I have had from you, I must have made over a hundred thousand pounds out of you, first and last."

"My cousin, Lady Oakshott, has never been happy since her father's death," said young Brogden.

"No," said Sir Richard. "While her father was alive I did not disagree with her, but since I have the money all safe we have not been quite so friendly. Do you know where she is ?"

"At the house in town."

"If she marries again, she will only have fifteen thousand

pounds," said he; " so I suppose she will not. Good-bye. I expect Arthur from Paris every hour. You had better go straight to London with my opinion, and not stop even for dinner."

Young Brogden, when he got into the dog-cart outside with his precious papers, looked round at the cold, melancholy-looking landscape, and thought that it was at all events more pleasant than the well-furnished, well-heated drawing-room where the godless old sinner lay dying. He missed his train, and had to stay for three hours at the railway hotel, so he ordered dinner and made himself comfortable. He was a talented, amiable young fellow, with that love for his profession which was engrafted in his family and that of the Comptons. He was determined to master these papers once more before he laid them before old Mr. Compton and the other partners. As he turned over the blue sheets he was more and more entranced by their marvellous acumen; at last, between two of them, he came on a document which put the whole case out of his head entirely.

It was a sheet of foreign note-paper, which had evidently come by post, and had been folded in an envelope. It ran as follows :—

" I have the honour to inform you that Lord Oakshott did not attend the rendezvous made by a mysterious young lady in the Coliseum on political grounds. The young lady was the son of Petruchio Bellini, dressed in his sister's clothes, of quite sufficient personal strength for the object, the other party being totally unarmed. It is suspected that he told the design to his sister, and that she betrayed him to the Cammoristi, who warned Lord Oakshott. My lord is a member of one of their clubs, which will account for it.

Nothing can now be done in the kingdom of Naples, and his lordship has departed for Switzerland, as I understand from his servant, to Chamounix.

"BORICHI."

Young Brogden thought about this on his way to town, and the moment he was in his office he wrote—

"DEAR LORD OAKSHOTT,

"Go suddenly and quickly to Paris, to the Hôtel Meurice, and don't be out after dark much. Your dealings with the Carbonari and Cammoristi have brought you into great personal danger. Pray be more careful.

"LOUIS BROGDEN."

He was alone in the office, and was just going home, when there came a knock at the door, and in came a young man.

A very fine-looking young man, of dark complexion, with intensely black eyes, and a look like a pirate ; somewhat like his mother in features, but so utterly unlike her in expression, that it forced itself on young Brogden's attention more than it had ever done previously : yet it was he, Arthur Oakshott, his cousin.

"Why, Louis," said Arthur, catching him warmly by the hand, "I called at your house, and they said they thought you had come straight here. What news of the governor ?"

"Sir Richard," said Louis, putting his back to the fire, "told me this afternoon that he should not live a week, but I don't believe it."

"Is his cancer worse ?"

" Then you knew of that ?"

" Of couse I did,—did not you ?"

" Not I."

" By-the-by, he told few.   I must go and tell my mother, and take her down.   Poor old governor !"

" I would go to her," said Louis.   " Where have you been ?"

" I have been on the Continent generally, but six months in Paris, perhaps the luckiest, perhaps the most unlucky, I have ever spent."

" Have you been playing ?"

" Yes, in the money market, and winning.   But, Louis, can I tell you a secret ?"

" I never betrayed one."

" I know, and so I will tell you.   I am married."

" Without the governor's knowledge, I suppose."

" Of course."

" Well, I will keep your secret, Arthur, most sacredly, and I should advise you to keep it yourself.   Who is she ?"

" An actress."

" Whew !"

" A most excellent and noble girl.   She did not get on with her mother, the Duchesse d'Avranches, and she went on the stage sooner than live in the house.   The Duchesse d'Avranches is most charming to every one except her daughter.   A most charming woman."

" She is one of the most charming women I ever met in my life, though it is some years since I saw her, and I am not yet thirty-six.   I remember her when she was Mrs. O'Brien.   What is the Duc d'Avranches like ?"

"Oh, he is older than she is."

"He is a lucky man," said Louis Brogden. "Now, Arthur, I want to ask you if you have seen your cousin."

"What, Oakshott? No. But he is getting a name all over the Continent. He has joined the Carbonari: he is capable of any folly in creation. He will end his days in a Neapolitan prison if he don't mind, and I shall be Lord Oakshott. By Jove, I have half a mind to go to Naples and denounce him."

"Do you know Naples?"

"Well."

"Do you know one Petruchio Bellini there?"

"Rather: he is rather a famous man. At one time Cammoristo, at another Carbonaro, then a Government spy, he knows so much that all are afraid of him. He is a masterly rogue, for all his secrets are known to his rather numerous family, and so it would be necessary to assassinate the whole family to do any good, otherwise he would have had a knife in his ribs long ago. I wish Oakshott neither good-will nor ill-will; but if he is in with that man, he ought to be warned at once."

"Do you know Borichi?"

"Borichi the policeman? Yes, I know him very well. He is the man who arranges assassinations in that happy kingdom: he gets them done by ex-convicts at so much a head. Is this the kind of company my cousin has been keeping?"

"I fear so."

"It is lucky for him that I am less unscrupulous," said Arthur, laughing. "But I must go. Good-night."

"You are innocent, at all events," thought Louis; "but

it is appalling to think of that miserable sinner, Sir Richard,
going to his grave like this."

CHAPTER V.

SIR RICHARD OAKSHOTT'S WILL.

IT was late the next day when Lady Oakshott and Arthur
arrived at the grand door of Shepperton. When the door
was thrown open and the servants stood upon the steps, Sir
Richard's valet was at the carriage-door before they could
get out, and he said in a whisper—

"My lady, let me speak to Mr. Arthur before you go up
to Sir Richard. He is very bad, my lady, and the doctor is
with him."

"I ought to go to your father, Arthur," she said.

"Let me talk with Jamieson first, mother," was the quick
reply : and he hurried into the hall with the valet.

"Sir Richard is very ill, sir. The pain has been on him
very bad ; and he has been swearing, and cursing, and calling out for you. I said I felt sure that her ladyship would
come when she heard from Mr. Louis Brogden, but he swore
that if she came into the room he would jump out of the
window."

"Did he give any reason ?"

"No, he said that he would die alone with you, for that
she would hear something she should not, and tell it to the
first old woman she met."

"Is he quiet now ?"

"Yes, sir; the morphia has quieted him."

Arthur stepped back. "Mother," he said, "do not

come till I bring you :" and the patient lady submitted, weeping.

The old man was lying quite quietly on his couch beside the fire as Arthur approached him over the soundless carpet; he looked for an instant, and then said, " Father !"

" Is that you, Arthur ? Come here, my boy. Are we all alone ?"

" We are quite alone, father; I have closed the very farthest door."

" Come here, then, my darling, and let me feel your hair. Sit on the ground, my pretty boy. I am going to die and leave you."

" Not yet, sir."

" Don't you want me to go, Arthur ?"

" Why should I wish to lose a father who has never done anything but spoil me. Ah, sir ! spoilt children love their parents."

" I think so ; I would have done more for you if I had lived, but I cannot endure this pain and this sense of inaction. I have worked to the last for you, but if I could have lived I would have done more."

" What more, sir, could you have done ?"

" What more, puppy ! Why, if Oakshott was out of the way, you would be one of the most powerful men in England —ay, and in Europe—and here you are left with a beggarly fifteen thousand a year."

" I know, sir, that if Bellini, Borichi, and Co. had had their wicked will of him, I should be Lord Oakshott."

" Did you know of that plot, then ?"

" No, sir, I knew nothing."

" Wise boy,—never know anything. I know nothing. But

remember always that Oakshott is between you and everything which makes life dear. Always remember that. Is your
mother here ?"

" Yes, sir."

" I can't see her to-night. Give her my love, my dearest
love, if you will; for she has been a good wife to me, and
she is *your* mother. Take care of her, Arthur, and don't
grumble, my boy. Remember Oakshott. Leave me to
sleep."

From the leading morning journal we get the following :—

" DEATH OF SIR RICHARD OAKSHOTT.—This eminent
lawyer died last night."

Then follows an able account of his legal career, which
had been written with infinite diligence by a briefless barrister on the staff a month or so previously and pigeon-
holed. The notice concluded :—

" Sir Richard had suffered long from cancer under the
arm, but the immediate cause of his death was an over-dose
of morphia administered by himself in the night during the
temporary absence of his valet. In the unsteadiness of his
hand, arising from the violence of the pain, it is perfectly
evident from the state of the bottle that he must have un-
consciously poured out far too large a quantity."

Serjeant Hulker met his brother Bulker the next day in
Westminster Hall, and they had a talk about the deceased
Baronet, which may be worth writing down.

Said Bulker : " So Dick Oakshott is gone to his place."

" Yes," said Hulker ; " Old Nick has got his due."

" He was a sound lawyer," said Bulker.

" None better," said Hulker.

"And an honest man," said Bulker.

"He never cheated any man that I am aware of," said Hulker. "But he was not a gentleman. He never treated his wife well after her father died and he got the money, and that was utterly mean."

"Well, I don't say anything about that," said the gentle Bulker; "that was wrong."

"He was an unscrupulous old blackguard," said the vehement Hulker. "He kept briefs which he ought to have thrown up. He knew, for he told me that he knew, all about Mrs. O'Brien, now the Duchesse d'Avranches, and he knew from the man's own lips that Barret the murderer was guilty."

"If the man frankly put his life in Oakshott's hands, he was right to do his best, Brother Hulker. And he was a good father," said Brother Bulker.

"Yes, he was mad about that gambling young pirate," said Brother Hulker. "I believe he would have murdered Lord Oakshott, and got himself off afterwards by acting as his own counsel, if he could have got the young villain the title. There was one spark of honesty about the man : he stuck to his Radical politics to the very last ; but that was only because his character was so bad that neither party would have anything to do with him. He gave the best dinners in London ; I made it a rule to throw over every one for him. He has left a good bit of money—fifteen thousand a year."

"Yes, he left a deal of money—a vast deal of money, Hulker. Have you heard anything about the Eaton Bay pier, lately?"

"No," says Hulker; "I haven't got any money in it."

"Nor I," says Bulker; "but Sir Arthur Oakshott has."

"It don't much matter," said Hulker. "What is far more important is that he has above one hundred thousand pounds in this new Mining Company. I don't like the business."

"Well, his estate would stand *that*," said Bulker. "He *is* awfully dipped over the General Cornish Mining Company. I have seen some of the papers, and they must wind up."

Serjeant Hulker looked at Serjeant Bulker steadily, and then did a very odd thing—a thing which few men can do. He took a sheet of paper and wrote his own name backwards. "Is that what you mean?" he asked.

"Not quite," said Serjeant Bulker.

Serjeant Hulker took another piece of paper, and wrote on it the name of Serjeant Bulker.

"*That* is what I mean," said Serjeant Bulker.

"*Ex-actly*," said Serjeant Hulker. "Will he—— ?"

And Serjeant Hulker drew his hand across his throat.

"I should say not," said Serjeant Bulker. "What is that thing on my door below the lock ?"

"Bolt," said Hulker.

"That will be about the size of it," said Bulker.

CHAPTER VI.

THE FIRST GLIMPSE OF THE LUNATIC.

I HAVE seldom seen finer surf than that which breaks against St. Andrew's Head : I say seldom, for the surf at Ilfracombe in Devonshire, and at King's Island in Bass's Straits, is certainly heavier : yet the surf never wins ; it has done all that it can, and the chalk walls remain like ramparts. One sees on the north coast of Kent how the sea wins some two feet a year : on the coast of the promontory which contains Oakshott Castle it never wins an inch.

That promontory of St. Andrew's Head is in its way a remarkable one. It contains 18,000 acres, every acre of which belongs to Lord Oakshott, though he would not be an astonishingly rich man without his Warwickshire and Yorkshire estates, near which he never goes. The highest point of the promontory is that next the sea, probably 300 feet, as high as the sources of the Thames; and from St. Andrew's Head the whole estate trends inland, so that a spring rising close to the summit of the "head" grows into a trout stream before it passes into the sea at Oakshott Haven. To Oakshott Haven you have been already introduced. It is a low-lying village on the east of the neck which joins St. Andrew's Head to the mainland. Oakshott lies to the east of the isthmus ; Lulworth lies to the west, within how many hundred miles I decline to say. I dislike being close about localities, but Oakshott Castle may be distinctly seen from Bournemouth on a fine day, but it must be a very fine day. In point of fact, it lies between Swanage and Poole; and if you inquire at either place, they will give you quite as much information about it as I can. If you take the trouble to write a note to Lord Oakshott at the Athenæum, he will promptly give you an order to go over it ; but casual visitors are not admitted from the neighbouring watering-places, because Lord Oakshott swears that the scarlet-fever was introduced into the establishment by a party of tourists' children from Swanage, who were brought there to improve their minds by looking at the astoundingly classical collection of pictures gathered

by Alured, the sixth Earl, at one time accredited to the
Court of Louis XV. He attributes the illness of Dickie (our
hero, if it mattered) to the fact of these children having
come there : whereas Father James, from a *certain great
house in the neighbourhood,* declares that the illness of Dickie
arose from the sin of Lord Oakshott in permitting the pictures to remain one hour in the house, and also from Lord
Oakshott's obstinate refusal to listen to the teachings of the
only true Church. Lord Oakshott and Father James continue their friendly war to this day, but Lord Oakshott is
still of opinion that the scarlet-fever was brought in by the
children from Swanage, so he generally objects to tourists.

You can get no notion whatever of Oakshott from the
sea. It lies in a deep dell, and the principal part of the
building is touched by no wind of heaven : it lies down in
a hollow, sheltered by oaks, by the banks of the little trout
stream which we have mentioned before. Let us approach
Oakshott Castle in the tourists' fashion ; there are many
worse fashions. Let us take a fly from Poole, and see it
like this.

Ha ! we have left the sea now ; we have left the fishing
village, and clatter over the stone bridge which spans the
little trout stream. Now we are in a dell following the brook,
surrounded on all sides by straight growing oak timber, not
in any way affected by the sea wind. At last we come to a
wall spanning the dell, in the centre of which is a Norman
gateway barring the road.

(This ancient Norman gateway was built in 1732, by the
sixth Earl, who lived to the age of ninety-five, to the intense
exasperation of his family. He was the man who collected,
rather late in life, the classical pictures before alluded to.

He was of a patriarchal turn, in more ways than one, and always insisted on every available member of his family dining with him on Christmas Day. On one occasion eighty-six sat down, and the Duchesse d'Avranches says, in her witty Irish way, that "there wasn't the divvle of a pennorth of poison among the lot." In fact, Lord Oakshott says himself, that he was the greatest blackguard, morally and artistically, which the family ever produced, except himself.)

Passing the abominable iniquity of the sham Norman gateway, the dell or glen opens out, and you get to meadows, narrow indeed, but with a very fine avenue of studded oaks, like those at Fulford in Devonshire. Rise here and look over the driver's shoulder, and you will see that the avenue is finished by a dark cave : it is the porch of the great house ; a deep Tudor porch, the only part of the house which you can see. At this point get out of your fly, telling your driver to follow slowly, and walk on. It is ten to one that you see a picture. You will see the great brown porch under the branching oaks, and under the shadow of it will be standing Mrs. Prout, sister of our friend the landlord, in lavender silk and a white cap, waiting for your arrival. If you can find a prettier picture than that in the three kingdoms, I am puzzled.

Having made acquaintance with Mrs. Prout, and given her half-a-sovereign, she will show you everything. All round are woods leaping up to the sky, and below them gardens filled with all kinds of flowers. The bright chalk water of the brook has been utilized, and there are pools of it amidst the short shaven grass, well fenced with carved stone, in which Mrs. Prout will show you scudding trout, as large as small salmon.   Then you turn and look at the house, and then, if you are standing to the westward and are at all an impressionable man, you are pretty sure to say, " Ha !" or " By Jove !" or something of that kind.

For, rising out of a mass of short turf, bright water, and gaudy flowers, are two Tudor quadrangles at different levels ; you must conceive Balliol as it was with Exeter as it was, placed the one fifteen feet higher than the other ; then you can get a notion of the main building.

But there is something else at Oakshott which makes you take Mrs. Frout's arm suddenly ; a thing astonishing and awful.   Behind and above the higher quadrangle, rising from it, there goes soaring up to the sky a tremendous Norman keep, one hundred feet high, which rising nearly to the zenith casts its creeping shadow over the smoothly-shaven lawns like the index of a sundial.

"That," says Mrs. Prout rather proudly, "is the lord's tower.   It was built by Sir Denys of Coutances to defend the promontory of St. Andrew's, which was granted to him in 1067 by William.   The Bishop of Lisieux and he had a dispute about it, and quarrelled.   The Bishop said that the succession would fail as long as the owners of Oakshott could not look on two seas.   But Sir Denys outwitted him, for he built that keep, and can look at the Solent and the Atlantic."

You ask : " Can you see the Solent ?"

Mrs. Prout says : " Yes ; the tower tops the hill, and you can see the Needles.   Then you can see Lulworth Cove, which *is* the Atlantic.   I wish that was all."

You let the old lady go on, but she gets petulant :—

" I am sick of the rubbish myself, but it is the talk of the neighbourhood, and my brother at the Oakshott Arms would tell it to any bagman.   My present lord has got the legend into his head, and nothing will get it out."

" And what is the legend ?"

" Why, rubbish," says Mrs. Prout.   " The Bishop of Lisieux told Sir Denys that unless lights were kept burning every night in that tower for the benefit of poor mariners, the heir to the estates should be drowned in sight of them. Much he knew about his business, rabbit the man (that I should say so about an anointed Bishop).   And since Sir Arthur has taken so much to yachting, my lord has taken his books up there, and sits night after night.   When he is away he makes me sleep in his bed with a maid, or else he makes two of the grooms sleep there, for fear the light should go out.   Even now that Sir Arthur is drowned he goes on with his fancy : even now, when we have Sir Arthur's own son in our possession, he has still a notion that Sir Arthur may come back from the sea.   He is doting over it, and mopes up there all night."

" Could not Lord Oakshott marry ?"

" No, Sir Arthur married the only woman he ever cared for.   As he could not get her, he has got her child, deserted by Sir Arthur when he bolted last year and was drowned in trying to escape."

" Escape ! from what ?"

" This is the blue drawing-room, sir," says Mrs. Prout, throwing open a door, but closing the conversation.   " In this drawing-room, sir, our mad Countess Henrietta murdered her own little girl.   The deed was done, sir, just behind that sofa in front of the fire : the poor little thing was found dead on the hearth-rug, and the mother kneeling and singing over it. A pretty golden-haired child with blue eyes : I will show you its portrait by Memling as it lay dead. The poor broken-hearted Earl would have it done."

At this point Mrs. Prout, my excellent gossip, uttered a wild scream and clutched my arm. I was very much scared also, for most certainly a pretty golden-haired child with blue eyes looked at us from over the sofa and disappeared.

My fright was very soon over, however, for a very handsome young man, dressed very much like a sailor,—a man with a splendidly formed head, and a light beard and moustache,—rose from behind the sofa with a living child and not a dead one on his shoulders.

It was a remarkably pretty sight, and I forgave the child the fright he had given me. I thought that the man was one of the sailors who swarmed here and who was nursing his child, until Mrs. Prout called out—

"My lord, I beg pardon. I did not know that you were here. It is show-day, and I thought you were out."

"It is I who have to beg this gentleman's pardon for being here," said Lord Oakshott. "Sir, I hope that Mrs. Prout is doing her duty by you in showing you over this old crow's nest. I hope you like it; I do not. As a Republican myself, I should like to burn it down, or turn it into a home for my tenantry; but then I should have to destroy the pictures, every one of which represents something either brutal or superstitious. Mrs. Prout will show you the degradation of my family as far it can be shown by pictures and legends." And so with a bow we parted, and I went to the picture-gallery.

"I did not know that Lord Oakshott was a Republican," I said.

"*He!*" said Mrs. Prout. "He is one of the stoutest Tories and one of the best Churchmen in Dorset, but he took a fancy to a young man called Garibaldi down in Italy, and he got away. He is always up to some mischief with the Carbonari and other Italian Radicals; and since he has been with them he has talked like this. Mind you, he is a Republican in one thing. You injure a widow, a child, or a poor man, and see if you dare face him after! You had better face a tiger."

"He has forgiven Sir Arthur?" I asked.

"This is the picture-gallery," she answered. "That is a copy by a young man of the famous 'Ecorchement' from the Museum at Bruges: observe the quivering of the muscles of the thigh as the skin is being removed, and the guilty look of another unjust judge in the background, who knows the same horrible fate may be his if his malpractices are discovered;—Martyrdom of Dame Dido Oakshott, who took up with the Reformed religion in the reign of Queen Mary, after her desertion by Sir Æneas Howard;—Fourth Countess undergoing whipping by the hands of the common hangman, for harbouring her brother the Jesuit during the reign of Elizabeth;—Murder of Sir Anthony Oakshott by the Irish; —Child of the Fifth Countess murdered by herself, attributed, but it is supposed falsely, to Memling;"—and so on.

I got no more out of Mrs. Prout at all, and left Oakshott Castle under the impression that it was by no means a cheerful place with all its beauty, and a particularly unhealthy place for a poet of the gloomy school, like Lord Oakshott himself. He says—

> "I would God would sever
> These memories from me:

> I hear only for ever
>   The rush of the sea ;
> The rush of the surges
>   By creek and by shore ;
> But of all the bay's verges
>   I see thee no more.
>
> " I would I were dead
>   By the shore of the sea:
> Thou hadst a fair bed,
>   But it was not for me.
> I would I were lain
>   In the wild driving sand ;
> Thou might pass me again,
>   And might kiss my dead hand."

Now, that may be beautiful, pathetic, and powerful, but it is not by any means cheerful. We shall see that Lord Oakshott was not a cheerful person, and that Oakshott was by no means a cheerful place. I was glad that I had seen Oakshott Castle, and also that I had seen the great poet himself; but I was also uncommonly glad to get back to the village, and smoke after supper among the fishermen. I did not on the whole envy Lord Oakshott; and though many years are passed, I am not sure that I envy him anything now, except his temper, his virtues, and his personal appearance.

Like all great poets (the above well-known verses prove him to be one), Lord Oakshott will manage his matters differently to any one else. I thought that my readers would like to know that I had had one personal interview with the great man himself: it was the first, and it shall be the last. It is odd that Louis Brogden, a very sharp lawyer, says that he is not only the best, but one of the shrewdest men he ever met.

Shrewd he certainly is to the extent of knowing that two shillings do not make half-a-crown, and that if you have £100 a year and spend £150 you will get into debt. Sometimes I wish he had been a little less shrewd; some of the things he did are apt to take the edges off his poetry very much indeed.

CHAPTER VII.

A LETTER FROM A SCOUNDREL.

A few months after Sir Arthur's death by drowning in the chops of the Channel through the sinking of his yacht, the *Petrel*, in the gale in which the *Albion* was wrecked, it so happened that Lord Oakshott got the following letter from him, which, as it will take a load of explanation off our minds, I will give *in extenso* :—

"Dear Edward,

"I declare to heaven that if virtue was ever properly rewarded in this world, I ought to be K.C.B. I left Cherbourg intending to cross the Atlantic to this place, telling you that I was coming to you. Will you believe it? I lost my foretopmast almost as soon as I started, and my rascals mutinied and refused to go on. I shot down one of them, hit him most dexterously in the deltoid, and the saintly way in which Marie nursed him got the rest in order. To tell the truth, the one-half of my crew were under police surveillance in France, and, as I pointed out to them (whether rightly or wrongly, {I neither know nor care), could not possibly land in England in consequence of the extradition treaty for criminals. This had as much effect as Marie's nursing. I liquored them up well, and got up a spare foretopmast in the first possible weather. After which I hung a young man over the stern and made him paint the ship's name out. I also at this time took the liberty of altering my signal number and making it the same as that of Lord Kampion Segramour, who was just going to sail to New York in the *Witch*. It will rather astonish Segramour when he hears that his yacht was spoken by the *Arabia* in the mid-Atlantic, just as he was putting his champagne on board at Cowes. He will not be the only person astonished over this matter. You are yourself astonished even now. You always, from a boy, had the power of being astonished more than any one I ever saw, but just wait, will you have the goodness?

"I got my crew into excellent order. I pointed out to them that as the main part of them were convicts, they could not possibly go to the United States or British America, and they took it in. All rogues are credulous. I therefore sailed for this place, and we had splendid weather. I have my men well in hand here too : there is pretty sharp police, and no chance of their running : my *forçats*, when they see the convicts working with the irons on them, are pathetically reminded of old times, and, as none of them speak English, are as humble as need be. There is no place like Bermuda for making a sailor civil.

"I sailed here for three purposes : I wanted provisions, I wanted to write to you, and I most particularly wanted to avoid the United States, because, if all is discovered, no less than three steamers must have anticipated me. I must be lost to sight—to memory dear."

Lord Oakshott paused. "'If all is discovered?' *I* have heard nothing." And indeed nothing ever *was* actually heard to the outside world, but the letter continues—

"From here I shall sail to another port, then I shall pay off my crew, and if possible get a crew of Lascars, who will sail me to where I want to go, not one of them understanding a word of English more than the words of command. My present crew could get easily from Aspinwall to San Francisco with the money I shall give them, and nothing more would be heard about me. I could get a crew of Lascars or foreigners of some sort at Aspinwall easily. Then my plan was to wreck the yacht on a certain reef and get ashore: but the fact is that I cannot do that. I have a great sum in gold, and Marie, neither of which things can I afford to lose. Marie is young enough to give me a child of my own, not of yours. You have got your child: if he is as great a fool as you, you will make a good pair."

Lord Oakshott put down the letter again. "My God!" he said; "and poor Arthur believes that I wronged her. What devil has possessed his heart? And why," he continued, "has Marie not spoken more boldly and contradicted this monstrous assertion of his? Has he made the assertion to her? for Madame Mantalent said that he had at Cherbourg. Oh, Arthur! Arthur! how could you believe such a horror of me and of her? Can you trust no one?"

It would appear that Sir Arthur could, in one way, trust some one, for Lord Oakshott, taking up the letter, again read:—

"I know that I can trust you. I think that you behaved badly to me in one way, but I know your sentiments of family honour, and I do believe that you have some queer kind of personal affection to myself. You may conceive that I cannot particularly like you : you have been an utter villain to me : you came between me and all hopes of better things.   Marie and I were Bohemians, possibly, but we loved one another until you sundered us, not for ever, as you thought, for she loves me again ; ay, and I can put a dagger in your heart by telling you that she will bear me a child.   You did me a wrong which I can never forgive, but I can trust you.   I know your canting ways, and the power that your position has over you.

" You will have to pay £60,000.   If I had only forged your name, I would not care : you are fool enough to forgive that : but I have forged young Brogden's and Sir Hilary Beaudesert's.   I suppose that the four great speculations are burst by now, or nearly so.   Pay that money, and hush it up, or I'll tell you what I shall do.

" I shall take that boy from you.   He is mine in law, but yours in fact.   If you don't save my name and your own, I'll have the boy, and I'll make him worse than myself.   I have ways and means to do it.   " ARTHUR.

" P.S.—You will hear no more from me for a long time. I know where to make money, and I am going to make it. I don't think that it would be wise to risk England again until every bit of forged paper is behind the fire. ' Why did I do it?'   Well, I was heavily dipped, but I did it principally to annoy you.   Mind, I have heard of your getting the boy from Cherbourg."

CHAPTER VIII.

A START FOR LONDON.

It was on an early summer's afternoon when this letter was received, and Lord Oakshott after a few minutes rang his bell and asked where Mr. Dickie Oakshott was.

" He was bathing with the rest of them," was the answer.

Lord Oakshott went down to the Cove at once to the bathers. It was just the time of the day when every one bathed, and so Lord Oakshott, going down through the stunted fir-trees, saw through their stems a line of white, which was not surf, for there was none ; nor a flock of geese, for they had been driven out of the water, and were nibbling and pecking on the short grass far from the shore ; but the clothes of the bathers, who were disporting themselves as much out of the water as in it, who ranged in age from thirty to three, and of whom the younger portion yelled quite as much as they bathed. The heir of the house was supposed to be somewhere among these *sans culottes*, learning the great lesson that one naked man or boy is very much like another, all told.

On inquiring of one of his grooms, just emerging from the briny deep, where the heir was, the young man, touching an imaginary place where his hat would have been, had he had his clothes on, pointed out to sea. " Tom Horton has got him on his back, my lord, teaching him nerve."

" Swim out for me, Sanders, and fetch him in."

It was rather a long swim, for young Horton seemed bent on carrying the heir to Cherbourg, but Sanders returned with the pair in tow, and Richard—or, as we shall call him in future, Dickie—was hoisted off the great shoulders of young Horton and set on the sand, where he stood laughing, with his little stomach stuck out, as proud as if he had been swimming himself.

"Horton," said Lord Oakshott, "please don't go so far out at sea with the child. I thank you very much for teaching him to swim, but it makes me nervous. If you drown that child, you drown me."

Horton, while wiping himself, promised to be more discreet.

"Sanders," said Lord Oakshott, "put on your clothes.—Dickie, run and dress yourself.—Sanders, I must have the dog-cart as soon as it can be got; you must come to London with me by the six o'clock train from Poole."

Dickie was dressed as soon as Sanders, and had his hand in his cousin's hand. Sanders, passing the pair, and hurrying on, heard Lord Oakshott say—

"You will promise not to leave Mrs. Prout while I am away."

And there was some confusion at the Castle too. My lord was suddenly going to London, and was taking one of his grooms instead of his valet. His valet had orders to pack, and was a trifle sulky (as sulky as any of the Oakshott servants ever were) at being left behind. But it was so. Sanders was a most excellent young man, but a clever rider, and profoundly stupid and forgetful.

It so happened that Lord Oakshott *wanted* an excellent young man who was profoundly stupid and forgetful, and who also could ride with safety a London hack.

This young man Sanders was very modest at appearing before my lord without a rag of clothes on his back; he might have been more modest if he had known that my lord, while eyeing him admiringly, was saying to himself: " Yes, this is the fellow, the greatest fool in the stables. If he does hear a word, he'll never remember it. In body he is just like Sir Hercules Ajax, the Irish boy at Eton, who, when he was stripped in the Brocas, was the best-made lad among us, with a little snake head on his shoulders. *He* couldn't tell off his sisters' names, if you took him in a hurry. Now Jenkins" (his valet) "is big-headed and narrow-shouldered; and though I have never seen him without his clothes on, I am absolutely certain that he is like Parker, the College boy, who could remember the names of every Ministry since 1780. I want a fool, and in Sanders I think I have got one. Jenkins reads my poetry also, which shows a little too much discrimination in a valet."

The dog-cart was ready; and there were a few last words :—

" Dickie, dear, you will be good, and never leave Mrs. Prout till I come back."

" Let me go too ; I want to go."

"Why, my man ?"

" I want to go with Sanders."

"Not with me ?"

" I want to go with Sanders," said the child. " I want to go to the horses."

It was nothing. The child loved him better than ten thousand Sanders', but the child was petulant, and inflicted one of those wounds which only women and children can give. Sanders, the shock-headed groom, could no more have inflicted such a wound than he could have stabbed Lord Oakshott; only women and children do these things.

As they drove off, while they were in the avenue, the shock-headed groom, with the sea-water still in his hair, said—

"Master Dickie don't mean it, my lord. He don't care for me not three fardens. Don't think of it."

And Lord Oakshott began to doubt whether Sanders was such a fool as he looked. He thought perhaps that the business he was going about had better be kept more carefully from Sanders.

Sanders was a typical Englishman of a certain kind. Scotch and Irish think them fools because they don't talk. The fact is, that they never talk unless they have something to say, and have made up their minds about it. Scotch, Irish, and French more particularly, have just now a habit of speaking first and thinking afterwards. Many English do the same thing also, but the typical Englishman never does; he is the most proud, the most suspicious, and the most silent of men.

CHAPTER IX.

OAKSHOTT SHOWS HIS METTLE.

LORD OAKSHOTT, accompanied by the bull-headed Sanders, arrived at Comfrey's Hotel by ten o'clock. There was no one there except the King of Belgium, Count Orloff, Prince Alexis of Russia, and King Otho of Greece : the place was as dull as ditchwater. He met the great peacemaker, King Leopold, on the stairs, and then, after a mere interchange of civilities with the King, started off in a cab to the House of Lords.

He went in and took his place, and at once he saw that he was the object of great curiosity; why he could not think. The Archbishop was speaking very well, though rather sententiously, on the subject before the House. The question was, whether the Houses of Parliament had the right to take into their hands funds left by private testators and divert them into fresh channels. His Grace argued that they had legally no such power, and his Grace argued very well. The matter in hand was Dulwich College, and the Archbishop allowed that in that case there had been *nearly* a malversation of funds. But he went on to argue that private bequests for the purposes either of education or religion were absolutely and for ever sacred. He spoke well, and to an attentive and large House; and when he sat down to the House found, to its great astonishment, that Lord Oakshott, the yellow-bearded young poet, a man seldom seen and still more seldom heard in that assembly, was on his legs, and looking savage.

Lord Oakshott looked around him, and saw that something was amiss. He could see six or seven intimate friends, but they all had their heads bent down, as if refusing to look at him. What was it? He glanced at the Lord Chancellor, and the Lord Chancellor appeared to be trying to find out in what part of the roof α Cygni might be. Lord Oakshott got angry, and the Archbishop looked so provokingly Christian and forgiving, that, with the hot temper of a poet, he went in at the Archbishop as a terrier goes at a rat; and the more the Archbishop folded his hands and forgave him, the more savage he got.

To give his speech *in extenso* would be, of course, impossible. He wished to ask his Grace, it seemed, "From what

source are the revenues of our cathedrals, our principal col-
leges, ay, and our principal grammar-schools, derived? Why,
from the bequests of Roman Catholics. Did his Grace stand
there and deny the fact?" (His Grace was neither standing
nor denying, but was folding his hands, forgiving Lord Oakshott for every word he said, and hoping that the roof would
not come down on the young man's head.) We were not to
use the revenues of Dulwich for an extended system of
education. Well and good. What, then, became of the
revenues of Balliol, New College, and Brasenose? What
became of the revenues of Winchester, Westminster, and
Salisbury? Those revenues were left by pious Roman
Catholics. Does his Grace imagine for an instant that
William of Wykeham would have founded such institutions
as Winchester and New College, had he dreamt that the
funds would pass into the hands of a Protestant archbishop?
His Grace was too honest to believe such a thing for a moment. The funds, however, of pious Romanists were diverted
at the Reformation. He (Lord Oakshott) entirely approved
of that act. But here was a Primate of the English Church
trying to draw a line *now*. He (Lord Oakshott) acknow-
ledged fully that the Primate was his spiritual father, and
would obey him in all things. He therefore regretted the
more that the Archbishop should try to re-institute a rule
grossly violated by that Reformation which rendered it possible for him to take the chair of St. Augustine.

Then Lord Oakshott sat down, having spoken well as far
as voice and presence went, but far too hurriedly. Lord
Howard of Lipworth (an old Catholic) got up, and also
agreed with every word which Lord Oakshott had said
against the Reformation ; and the Archbishop, laughing be-

hind his pocket-handkerchief, said, "Heaven save us from all poets !"

But the speech had a very good effect. Lord Howard of Lipworth came over to Lord Oakshott and sat beside him. "Oakshott," he said, "you spoke splendidly. I know you too well to dream that you will ever come over to the real Church, but I am heartily sorry for your ruin."

"My ruin !"

"Yes. All the world knows it now. It was so good of you to show : do come up and speak. Face the world, Oakshott : be with us more, and your character will carry you through."

"My dear Howard," said Lord Oakshott, laughing, "I am not ruined at all. What *have* you heard ?"

"Well, that you were dipped to the tune of £750,000, through your cousin, Sir Arthur."

"My dear man, sixty odd thousand will clear everything. Pray, Howard, don't believe these old women's stories."

"You are perfectly sure ?" said Lord Howard of Lipworth.

"Perfectly."

"Then I may put it about ?"

"Certainly."

"I will do so, then."

"Everything will be paid," said Lord Oakshott. "My cousin's death balances all things. I will pay, and keep the boy."

Lord Howard of Lipworth (now Father Augustin) looked at him, and said—

"Then your cousin was drowned ?"

Lord Oakshott shook his head.

"I thought so," said Lord Howard of Lipworth. "His wife is a Catholic."

"A Romanist, yes," said Lord Oakshott.

"You were in love with her?"

"Yes."

"And you have the child?"

"I have my cousin's child."

"Not yours?"

"Howard, how dare you suggest it?"

"I beg your pardon. Only the world says so."

"The world lies. Marie is as pure as your mother."

"So I thought. I thought that I could trust you. I *knew* I could trust you. Come and see me, Oakshott, when I am gone."

"When you are gone—whither!"

"Into the Cloister. I can't stand the world; it beats me."

"I'll come to you as often as the men into whose keeping you are going to give your life will let me. Why on earth can't you face God like a man? God is more merciful than these priests."

"The Church teaches," said Lord Howard of Lipworth——

What Lord Howard of Lipworth went on to say, or what wicked words Lord Oakshott said in reply, can never be written down, for the Archbishop was in another mess, and was making uncommon bad weather of it; in fact, it was a very evil night for the Archbishop. Lord Wargrave aired the audacious theory that Dissenters ought to be allowed to bury their dead in country churchyards, without the Established ceremonial. The Archbishop notoriously agreed with him, but defended the Establishment in a very lame manner. Lord Oakshott, hitting Lord Howard of Lipworth a dexterous smack on the inside of his thigh, rose to defend the Archbishop. "You have lost your money and are reckless," said Lord Howard of Lipworth; "you will do him more harm than good." But Lord Oakshott went on for all that:—

"My friend Lord Howard of Lipworth tells me that I shall do his Grace more harm than good by my advocacy. That is quite possible. I have been hard on his Grace to-night, and I wish to put some words in his mouth in extenuation. I wish him to ask the Dissenters to what part of our Burial Service they object, and then to ask his Grace to get them altered. Surely the *odium theologicum* need not be carried into the churchyard. I am, however, speaking now with a purpose other than that which appears to your Lordships. Lord Howard of Lipworth tells me that your Lordships believe that I am a ruined man: I beg to inform your Lordships that such is not the case, and that I am one of the richest men in England. Perhaps we don't get quite as much lying in this House as we do in another place, but we seem to get our share."

Lord Howard of Lipworth said to him—

"How horribly indiscreet you are; I never heard such a speech in the House."

"You'll never make anything of me," said Lord Oakshott. "Come and dine with me to-morrow."

Lord Howard of Lipworth took out a little book. "I can't," he said; "it is the eve of St. Cecilia, and a fast."

So Lord Oakshott went to his hotel thinking of many things; and on the stairs he met Count O——, and went into Count O——'s room, and they agreed over their cigars that the world was rather mad.

" Madder than ever," said Lord Oakshott.

" Why, no," said Count O——, " not madder, but just the same. Do you know that at Boston the other day there was a man who said to me that we were the most enlightened nation in the world ; that the future means of locomotion would be entirely by balloons ; that his were the only balloons which would go against the wind, and that he would sell me the secret ?"

" Did you buy it ?"

" No ; as I knew that the air could not, under any circumstances, offer sufficient resistance for any balloon to go to windward, I refused to have anything to do with him."

" Pitched the humbug overboard, in fact," said Lord Oakshott.

" My dear lord," said Count O——, " he was not in the least degree a humbug ; he believed in his own theory. Do you go to church ?"

" Yes."

" Well, and so do I. Do not think that a man who believes is of necessity a humbug, or a fool. Am I a fool ?"

" I fancy not."

" Yet I am a member of the Greek Church, and, what is more, an entire believer. What do you make of that, for example ?"

" That we shall both sit together in the Radical paradise of fools," said Lord Oakshott ; " for I am an Anglican, and an entire believer also."

" I thought you were Republican," said the Russian.

" I am not exactly Republican ; I am socialist."

"And you make that fit with Christianity?" said the Russian.

"No, I do not make it fit with modern Christianity, but you will allow that the early Christians were the first Socialists?"

"Yes, but then I disagree in that matter with some of the Apostles. No one will have the face to deny that St. Peter was never in Rome at all."

"I am very sleepy," said Lord Oakshott, "and I wish to go to bed." So he went to bed; and that is the best thing a man can do when he gets in hot arguments on certain subjects, either with a barbarous Russian or an intelligent Kaffir. Had a good and virtuous Bishop gone to bed and kept there on one occasion, what a deal of trouble would have been saved.

CHAPTER X.

A CHAPTER OF FIASCOS.

SIR RICHARD's affairs were certainly in a terrible strait. Compton and Brogden went through them very carefully, and then came to Lord Oakshott with the result.

Young Louis Brogden came to him.

"It is worse than we thought," he said.

"Well, let us know the very worst."

"It is very strange," said young Brogden, "but he has made this *fiasco* without any visible reason. *We* cannot understand it at all. His own estate would pay everything twice told. But he seems to have done—well, you know what—with your name in sheer recklessness."

"*I* know why he did it," said Lord Oakshott. "He did it to annoy me."

"He has taken a singular way of annoying you," said young Brogden. "If he were caught, he would have two years' penal servitude at the least. Your name is in this matter for a very large amount. His estate must go into the Bankruptcy, and you will have to swear that these signatures are yours."

"I can't perjure myself," said Lord Oakshott.

"Of course you cannot ; you would be in a worse position than he is, and I, knowing these signatures not to be yours, should, as an honest man, be obliged to say what I know."

"You would denounce me, then ?"

"How could I do otherwise? There has not been one spot or stain on our professional character for a hundred years. I should be making myself party to a fraud."

"That is evident," said Lord Oakshott. "I would not commit perjury even to get the boy. Yet I don't know ; I wish I had told you less."

"I am glad you told me so much," said the lawyer. "I can prevent your making a fool of yourself, you see."

"Well, I don't see," said Lord Oakshott, "because I am going to do it in spite of you."

"To swear to the forgeries ?"

"No. What are the total liabilities of the Company ?"

"One hundred and sixteen thousand pounds."

"Good. See every creditor paid in full."

"Oakshott, are you mad ?"

"No; quite sane. I can sell Drumston for one hundred and thirty thousand pounds, and the odd money shall go for educating the boy."

“ This is intolerable folly,” said Brogden, furiously ; “ I will be no party to it. Don't you see that you have the boy now, and that he is not likely to be reclaimed ? You have only to keep absolutely quiet, and the boy is yours for ever, without the least trouble.”

“ If I let things go,” said Lord Oakshott: “if I let this Company go into bankruptcy, this boy would start in life as the son of a fraudulent bankrupt and forger. I won't have that. What is Drumston to me ? I ask you that.”

“ Well, Drumston is close on four thousand a year.”

“ Do you think that I would not give up four thousand a year for *her* son ?” said Lord Oakshott angrily.

“ I think,” said Brogden, now utterly angry, “that a poet is fool enough for anything. When there is a woman in the case every man is a fool ; but a poet and a woman together are enough to send all Lincoln's Inn to Bedlam. Are you resolved on this ?”

“ I am.”

“ I will have nothing to do with such an act of folly,” said young Brogden.

“ What fools you lawyers are !” said Lord Oakshott, laughing.   “ Don't you see that you can't help your-self ?”

“ I can.”

“ Hardly. How long have you known of these forgeries ?”

“ Well, for some time.”

“ And have not yet denounced them ?” said Lord Oak-shott, merrily.   “ Come, let us have no more baby's talk. I want the boy, and I want him to start well in the world. Also, I don't want a hound or a horse called Oakshott to go before the world as a scoundrel. We live in different circles, Brogden : I am a nobleman, you are a solicitor : but answer me as a man. If one of your family had done what my cousin has done, would not old Mr. Compton or old Mr. Brogden have sold the coat off his back to do as I am going to do ?"

When it came to a matter of family honour, the young solicitor was the equal of the young nobleman ; his face flushed up, and he said, " Yes, yes, you are right : I see it now. My uncle or Mr. Compton would sweep a crossing sooner than not do what you have done. Why the devil did you not put it in that way at first ?"

" Because I wanted to show you what a fool a lawyer was compared to a poet."

" Mind, Oakshott, I do not allow that," said Brogden.

" Never mind what you allow. Pay twenty shillings in the pound, and hold your tongue. I had better stay in town until the matter is finished, I suppose ?"

" As much as you can."

"You will go to the gallery of the House of Lords to-night. I shall go to the lobby of the House of Commons first," said Oakshott.

" Why ?"

" I shall meet Granby Dixon, the best gossip in Europe. The smash is known, and I shall give him my own account of it. What becomes of Arthur's estate ?"

" Unless you know where he is, I am at a loss to say. You had better see to it, in an amateur way, and wait for events. Now tell me, Oakshott, shall you communicate with him as to what you have done ?"

" If I can find him, I shall."

"And lose the boy ? He has the whip hand of you

there. *If you want the boy, say not one word. Hold those forgeries of his in your hands, and he will never come back.*"

"I see," said Lord Oakshott, thoughtfully. "Well, I shall go down to the House."

"Shall you speak?" said Brogden.

"Yes, I am going to speak."

"On what subject?"

"I have not the wildest idea," said Lord Oakshott. "I only know that the first man who says anything with which I disagree will have me at his throat like a bull-dog. Brogden."

"Yes, Oakshott."

"If you get those papers for me, I can hold them over him and keep the boy?"

"Certainly. But you are such a spooney about the boy that I can't trust you. You might destroy those papers in the boy's favour, and then Sir Arthur would get hold of the boy, and plague you about him."

"He does not care for the boy. He believes that the boy is my son."

"There is no truth in that, is there, Oakshott?" said Brogden..

"Not the ghost of a word," said Lord Oakshott, looking kindly and frankly at him. "I am no more to her than I am to your sister. I *love* her, and the boy has her eyes. Aha! lawyer, do women ever bring work into your office?"

"Well," said young Brogden, good-humouredly, "our profession would go to the deuce if it wasn't for the women. My father says he has never, in forty years, had a case in the office but what a woman was at the bottom of it. Now, I'll see this thing through for you. We have got the title-deeds of Drumston, and we shall want power of attorney, or something of that kind, from you to-morrow, so you had better look us up. Meanwhile go down to the House of Lords and blow off your steam on the first subject which comes to hand. Whatever you do, *make a noise and keep before the world.* Let us see you in the *Times* to-morrow."

Lord Oakshott left his friendly young lawyer, and went down to the lobby of the House of Commons. There was Granby Dixon, faultlessly dressed, as usual, who soon came up to Lord Oakshott.

" Hallo, Oakshott ! I thought you were out of town."

" Not I. I am not likely to be. This infernal Company having smashed will keep me in town till August. So I shall amuse myself by being personally disagreeable in the House of Lords, instead of venting my spleen on my house-keeper."

" They say you are dipped," said Granby.

" Dipped !" said Lord Oakshott; " dipped is not the word. Drumston is gone."

" Nonsense !" said Granby Dixon.

" Fact," said Lord Oakshott.

" The devil !"

" Ah, and it is the devil," said Lord Oakshott; " you would say so if you had lost it. Drumston is in the market for, say, a hundred and twenty-five thousand pounds. Why don't you buy it ?"

" His losses have made him bitter," said Granby Dixon. " I have but twenty thousand in the world, for I sold out three to pay for my last election. What will the Company pay ?"

"Twenty shillings in the pound, and half a year's interest," said Lord Oakshott.

"Well, I have only two five-pound shares, but ten pounds is ten pounds. Is Sir Arthur dipped?"

"My lunatic cousin has taken uncommonly good care of himself, as usual. He is out of it; he was the son of a lawyer."

"And has left you in it," said Granby Dixon.

"Well, it would be hardly fair to say that," said Lord Oakshott. "None of us will be in the week after next. The shop is shut."

"And your cousin was drowned?" said Granby Dixon.

"That has not been proved," said Lord Oakshott, quietly. "I beg you to remark, Granby, that his death has not been proved. I am left with his heir, and I wish to consult you about Eton: you were there yourself."

So Lord Oakshott went to the House of Lords, and Granby Dixon to the House of Commons. A remarkable thing took place in both Houses of Legislature that night.

Granby Dixon was at that time Under Secretary to the Admiralty (and he will tell you, with the calm pride of superiority, that no one ever made such a mess of it as he did), and he had to answer a question in the absence of the First Lord, in consequence of gout, family affliction, and urgent private business. There is not a nimbler man in the House than Granby, but he was a little too nimble on this occasion. The fact is that his hat and his pockets were stuffed with papers containing details, and he mixed up one private letter with his facts and figures.

The member for Bolton (of those times) had asked the First Lord of the Admiralty whether it was not expedient to substitute bunks for hammocks in the Royal Navy. It was an easy business to answer him, and Granby Dixon was quite up to the occasion.

He gave the number of men in each of her Majesty's ships. He gave the number of cubic feet per man, and proved that it was nearly as great as that of the Middlesex Hospital. Then he went on to prove that the hammock system was infinitely superior to the bunk system. He had proved his case in a canter, and the House cheered him when he ridiculed the (then) member for Bolton. When he asked whether the hon. member was prepared to entirely give up an appeal to nautical experience, the House was certainly with him, almost to a man. *Then* he made his terrible *fiasco.* Granby Dixon is now called Oakshott Dixon, and the name will stick to him.

Granby Dixon had a rather heavy matter in hand. The question put by the hon. member for Bolton was only a war-whoop, leading to a general attack on the Admiralty. The House seemed to resolve itself into a debating society, and was certainly out of order for more than three-quarters of an hour. Granby very soon saw why it was convenient for the First Lord to be confined to his bed by the gout. Question after question poured in on him without notice. The Opposition thought naturally that the First Lord would have been in his place : the First Lord knew better ; so did the First Secretary. Granby had to fight it out single-handed, and he did it like a little lion. He was never petulant when he was called to order, and the House was delighted with his wit and his pluck. The House knew perfectly well that he was being made a victim of, and Granby by his sheer power of nimbleness and dexterity was carrying all before him ; he was palliating every mistake; he was boldly denying facts, or demanding their proof; he was doing everything, in fact, which an unsupported junior in the House should do; he was gaining golden opinions from both sides of the House, when Admiral Blofus rose and took leave to ask the Under Secretary, in the absence of his two chiefs from indisposition, whether the Admiralty were prepared to adopt iron cables entirely in her Majesty's ships, and to dispense with cocoa-nut and hemp.

Granby was perfectly ready. He knows a little of everything. He told Admiral Blofus that the Admiralty were thinking about it, and then he made his grand *fiasco*.

People who are used to speaking in public, or to lecturing, know how easy it is to read a wrong document. Granby was immensely excited, and he saw he was winning. He confronted Admiral Blofus, thinking that he was the last of his attackers. Granby was faint with his long and unsupported fight. Blofus finished, he might go to his dinner. He said: "With regard to cocoa-nut cables, I hold in my hand " (here he took a letter out of his hat) "a communication from a gallant admiral, who at one time represented Southampton. I think that his decision will be taken as final, or nearly so. I am not a nautical man myself, but I think that Admiral Cumberwater knows something of his profession. He is emphatically against the cocoa-nut cables. However, I will read you his letter." And the unhappy man, who was nearly in a state of coma, read the following letter to an astounded and puzzled House :—

"DEAR GRANBY,

"Buy at once every share you can lay hold of in the

Cornish Mining Company *below par*. Oakshott, like the sentimental ass he is, is going to pay up every penny. He has got a fantastic fancy for the cub, who is probably his son. Buy in, whatever you do.

> "Yours very truly,
>> "ABRAHAM MOSES."

Granby Dixon had only time to read this, and to say that he thought he must have read the wrong letter, when the laughter of the House came down on him.

He went to Brighton for three weeks; but if he had gone for three thousand months or years, it would have been the same thing. The nickname of "Oakshott Dixon" will stick to him for ever.

As for office, no one would have given one shilling for his chance. He had once made himself transcendently ridiculous; people said that men with half his brains, and a tenth part of his debating power, might get office, but that no reasonable Minister would ever trust Granby Dixon to his dying day.

By the decrees of Providence it so happened that while Granby Dixon was making this illimitable mess in the House of Commons, Lord Oakshott was doing very little better in the House of Lords.

Lord Roversdale was making a very long, very clever, but transcendently dull speech about the new Winding up of Companies Act. Lord Oakshott was very much disappointed; he knew nothing on earth about the matter, and he wanted to fight somebody. His chances seemed to be infinitesimally small, but Providence favoured him in a most remarkable manner.

Lord Roversdale, probably nearly the best man of business in England, is not an orator ; he has, on the contrary, a pestilent habit of telling the plain truth, and of backing his truth up by the most inexorable facts and figures.   He went slowly on through the affairs of several Companies which had gone to ruin lately, giving arithmetical details of their finances, which very few of the Lords followed ; at last he came to the Cornish Mining Company, and, wiping his spectacles, said that he would quote that as the very worst case of all.

Those who watched Lord Oakshott saw him advance his chin and look dangerously quiet.   Noble lords who knew the two men were immensely interested.   Roversdale the arithmetician and Oakshott the poet were supposed to hate one another like poison.   Roversdale had the best command of facts, but Oakshott had a bitter tongue.   Oakshott, cousin of Sir Arthur, had been chairman of this Company.   It was evident that there would be a scene, and that Lord Roversdale's figures would be a little enlivened by Oakshott's temper.

To every one's utter surprise Lord Roversdale began it. He went slowly through the accounts of the Company, and certainly they looked terribly bad.   They had certainly suspended payment since Sir Arthur's disappearance.

"I speak in a rather feeling manner of this particular Company," said Lord Roversdale, "because I am a shareholder to a heavy amount.   The names of the late Sir Arthur Oakshott, a most excellent man of business, and of Lord Oakshott, were quite enough for a simple man like myself.   I took one hundred ten-pound shares : any one may have them at five shillings a share, if any one is foolish enough to buy them.   As far as I can see, there are no assets whatever."

The gentle Lord Doughton said, "There is Sir Arthur's estate."

"Sir Arthur had sold out every penny," said Lord Roversdale, "before he went abroad. In the present state of the law, the principal culprit escapes."

"Do not speak so of a dead man, my lord," said Lord Doughton. !

"*Is* he dead?" said Lord Roversdale ; "perhaps Lord Oakshott can tell us."

Then the row began. Oakshott rose with fury in his eyes, and every one sat silent.

"My lord," he said, "you abuse your position as a senator and as a gentleman."

The Lord Chancellor and the Archbishop both rose, but they sat down again. They had been at a public school together, and thought that the two noble lords had better "have it out," which the noble lords proceeded to do.

"I repeat, my lord, that you abuse your position as a senator and as a gentleman. You assert that you were induced to join this Company by the power of my cousin's name and my own. Did you not carefully examine the prospectus before you joined us?"

"No ; had I done so, I should not have joined you."

"You are a careful man of business, my lord," said Oakshott, with a sneer. "Now, you assert that my cousin Sir Arthur sold out every penny before he was—before he—went on that voyage. Such is not the case. He holds—I should say held—very heavily. You assert that there are no assets in this case ; I will send your lordship a cheque for the amount of your shares at par before I go to bed this night. That Company will pay up every farthing with half a year's interest, and the shareholders may invest their money elsewhere under your lordship's direction, not under mine. Had it not been for my cousin's death, it would have been done before now."

"You use the word 'death,' Lord Oakshott. Is your cousin dead?"

For one instant Lord Oakshott felt inclined to lie. But he was a man whom a lie would choke. He thought for half a minute, and then addressed himself, not to Lord Roversdale, but to the Archbishop, in a voice of suppressed passion.

"Will your Grace be good enough to inform Lord Roversdale that my cousin is *not* dead, but that there are family matters of the most delicate nature with regard to his disappearance which a costermonger would have respected, but which he has not grace to respect?"

Lord Roversdale held up his hand and cried out, "Oakshott! Oakshott! don't say such horrible things. How *could* I know?"

But Lord Oakshott, with his hat over his forehead, strode out of the House into Parliament Square, where he met Granby Dixon, walking up and down, and cooling himself.

Lord Oakshott said, "What have you been doing?"

"Making an awful ass of myself."

"So have I. Where shall we go?"

"Let us jump off Westminster Bridge," said Granby Dixon.

"By no means. What would become of the boy without me?"

"You are mad about that boy," said Granby Dixon. "I say, Oakshott, *are* you going to pay?"

"Every penny," said Lord Oakshott.

"Then I'll tell you what I shall do. Hi! here—hansom!"

A cab rattled up to him at once.

"Where are you going now, you lunatic?" said Lord Oakshott.

"To Dulwich, you lunatic," replied Granby Dixon.

"What for?" said Lord Oakshott.

"To see my stockbroker, who lives there," said Granby Dixon.

"The man will be in bed," said Lord Oakshott.

"He won't be there long after I get hold of his door-knocker," said Granby Dixon.

"What are you going to do?" said Lord Oakshott.

"Order him to buy up every share in the General Cornish Company to-morrow morning. By-the-by, how *are* the shares?"

"Decimal 333 below par, I think. Be quick, Granby; collar them before people have time to read their *Times*. I have let the whole cat out of the bag in the House of Lords in a row with Roversdale."

"I wish," said Granby, "as the lady in Kingsgate Street says to Mr. Pecksniff, that you had chosen some other time, but it is always the way with me. The fact is, that I have also let the cat out of the bag in the House of Commons."

"How on earth did you do *that?*" asked Lord Oakshott.

"In the debate on the Admiralty."

"Well, you are a very clever and ingenious man, but upon my word I don't see how you could have managed that," said Lord Oakshott.

"If we are to remain friends, Oakshott, you must never

allude to the circumstance again. I am positively ruined, but, *en revanche*, I think that by raising (if necessary) a cry of fire at Dulwich I can arouse my stockbroker, and put eight or nine thousand pounds of your money into my pocket by Tuesday afternoon."

"You are welcome to it, old boy," said Lord Oak-shott.

"Listen to me a moment more, old fellow," said Granby. "Attend to the last of my political acts. Old Poulter is dead."

"Any relation to old Poulter's mare?"

"No; don't be silly: you know whom I mean—the member for Lipworth."

"I know. And so the old fool has gone to his place at last."

"Ay; and we want your influence in the borough to get our man in."

"Now, Granby, I can put any man in for that place, or I can keep any man out of that place. I am as powerful for that one seat as Lonsdale is for his five. But I must have a first-rate man, sir; and a man who cares for the people. I will not disgrace my influence (which I think unconstitutional) by putting in a useless man. Who is your man?"

"Young Brogden, your own connection."

"But he told me nothing of this to-day."

"No; he would not speak to you, and the mere fact of his being your connection will probably, with his absurd notions, prevent him from standing for the place. If we can get him to do so, will you back him?"

"God bless his dear heart, of course I will. Why, you could not have got such a man as that."

" He opposes you strongly on some points, Oakshott," said Granby Dixon. " He is no patient nominee."

" *I* know him," said Lord Oakshott. " He called me an ass this morning, when he must have known about Poulter's death. I am with him, forty-horse power."

" I want to speak a word more to you, Oakshott, out of earshot with the cabman. Come here." And they went together into the shadow.

" Oakshott," said Granby Dixon, " we have always loved one another. Tell an old friend the truth. *Is* this boy for whom you are sacrificing Drumston, your own son ?"

" No, Granby !" said Lord Oakshott. " For the last time, no ! He is his mother's son, and that is enough for me."

Granby gave a long whistle.

" Do you think that I would let *her* son come before the world under a cloud ? You know me better than that," said Lord Oakshott.

" I know you, my dear old fool, as well as you know yourself. But, Oakshott, remember that I am not rich, and that I am risking at least seven thousand pounds by saying these words. Pause before you sell Drumston for the sake of this child. In God's name, think ! The boy, on the father's side, comes of a bad stock ; the boy may turn out as thundering a rip as his father, and break your heart. Pause, Oakshott, I pray you to pause in your course of sentimental folly."

" Get into your cab and go to your stockbroker, my dear Granby," said Lord Oakshott. " The boy is the son of his mother ; that is enough for me."

So Granby, without one word more, called his cab.

" Will you kill me ?" said Granby Dixon. " Lost as I am

to all political preferment, from this day forward, I feel that I am not fit for death."

"What have you done, you dear little man?" said Lord Oakshott. "You seem always to come when one wants to be put in good spirits. Give me a laugh, and let me go home."

"I had better get into the cab first."

"Very well."

Granby Dixon got into the cab and shut the doors to.

"Now," he said, "I am safe, and will tell you.—Cabman, on the slightest attempt at violence on the part of his lordship, drive off like fury.—Why, Oakshott, in the heat of debate with old Blofus, I read aloud a letter from my stock-broker by mistake, and then let it all out. You must have been speaking to some one."

"Drive to Dulwich, sir," cried Lord Oakshott to the cabman. "Drive like the devil, sir : do you hear ? Here is half-a-crown for you. Good-night, Granby. Pull the fellow out of bed by the ears." And away went the cab over Westminster Bridge, leaving Lord Oakshott musing.

CHAPTER XI.

OAKSHOTT GETS SENTIMENTAL OVER THE WRONGS OF THE POOR.

MANY members of both Houses were coming out now, and Oakshott walked away through the quietest streets, thinking, until he lost his way.

"Some one will get my money. Why not that kind and gentle little fellow as well as another? I'll warrant he does no harm with it. I don't think I should have done as he has done, but he is not rich, and poverty must be a fearful temptation. I will write to Jinks about that election to-night. I don't think that it is constitutional, but Brog is a very good fellow. Hallo! Here, young one, you will hurt yourself."

A little wretch of a boy, with a ragged shirt and trowsers, flying for his life, had cannoned against his legs and thrown himself heavily on the ground. Before he could rise, the policeman had him. Lord Oakshott addresses the policeman.

"I am Lord Oakshott. I am walking home from the House of Lords. Here is my card. What has this child been doing?",

"Stealing potatoes, my lord."

"Poor little beggar! Do you know where he lives?"

"Yes, my lord, down this court."

"Can you show me the place?"

There was no difficulty at all. The policeman told him that he was not going to charge the boy, but only to shake him and warn his mother. Oakshott followed him and saw where the boy lived; and, having left the court, said to the policeman—

"These things should not be, and by heaven they shall not be!"

"What would become of us if they didn't exist, sir?" said the policeman. "Get rid of those places, and you would have no use for us."

"I suppose not," said Lord Oakshott. "Meanwhile, here is half-a-sovereign for your trouble. Look round on me to-morrow morning, and help me to mend matters *there*, at all events.   I have a boy of the same age myself; would he become like that if he were lost ?"

"You can't tell, sir.   Some come through it all, and some don't.   I hadn't more clothes to my back at his age than he has, and here I am with a stripe on my arm.   There's black sheep and white sheep in all classes, my lord.   I have seen black sheep in yours."

"God knows it is true," said Lord Oakshott.   "But are not our temptations as great as yours ?"

"That I can't say, not being a rich gentleman," said the matter-of-fact policeman.   "Here is the end of my beat— this is Parliament Street, my lord."

Parliament Street.   Yes.   He would write about that election before he went to bed.   The great clock boomed twice before he turned to go home.   Could Dickie ever turn out, under any circumstances, like that ?   Quite an impossible thing.

He wrote this letter that night to his agent.   It was not exactly the letter he meant to have written :—

"DEAR JINKS,

		"Will you tell the people that Mr. Brogden is my man ? Every one may vote as they like, but I am in favour of Brogden. I only want one pledge from him, which he is certain to give.

									"OAKSHOTT."

Mr. Potter, of Comity, Dixon, and Potter, on hearing that Lord Oakshott was going to support Brogden, went down and had a look at the borough.   It was no use, and he told the Tory party so.   Lord Oakshott, so long eccentric, had now utterly ratted, and was going to send in a Radical.

It was a seat lost to the Conservatives. But Brogden's pledges had been entirely satisfactory to Lord Oakshott, and he nobly redeemed them.

CHAPTER XII.

TWO FOOLS.

THOUGH Granby Dixon went away to Dulwich at eleven o'clock, cursing all poets as sentimental fools ; though he paid 7*s*. 6*d*. for his cab, and though he had to sleep in the same room with Mr. Elias Moses, a high-flavoured young Jew, who snored like a grampus ; though Miss Moses was more polite to him than he liked, and though he had to go to town in a hansom cab the next day with old Moses (which made him, as he said, smell of Jew for a fortnight), yet he never regretted his journey. Mr. Moses paid him no less a sum than eleven thousand pounds. What Mr. Moses did on his own account the deponent sayeth not. It was extremely honest of him to write to Granby Dixon at all, and his wife bullied him for doing so. But good Moses said: " My dear, for one time you can give the office to a Parliament man, he can give it to you fifty times. Granby Dixon is a clever little chap, and knows which way the cat jumps. If he asks me to buy in fifty pounds for *himself*, I always buy in five hundred for *myself*. I got the office about Oakshott paying this morning from one of Brogden's clerks, and I naturally gave it, as one gentleman to another, to Granby. That Oak-shott is an awful fool. He might have made a composition for five shillings in the pound, but he says that would be robbing the shareholders. Where should we be, Rebecca, if

there were no fools like *him?*" After which, Mr. Moses
went to sleep, and dreamt that a Parliament man had given
him the office to a job which brought in fifty thousand
pounds.

When everything was over and done, and every one was
paid, Lord Oakshott got the following letter :—

"DEAR OLD FELLOW,

"I dearly like a little stockjobbing and a little betting.
I made £11,000 out of you the other day, *but I could not
swallow the money.* I have been down and paid it into your
account at Hoare's. I suppose it will go into the boy's
breeches pocket. Hang the boy! I hope he won't take after
his sainted papa.

"Yours ever truly,

"GRANBY DIXON."

Lord Oakshott, who would die sooner than do anything
like anybody else, at once took his hat and his umbrella,
stepped round to Mr. Moses, in Chancery Lane, and showed
him the letter. Mr. Moses said very little to Lord Oakshott,
but in confidence and bed he told Mrs. Moses that, as regarded Lord Oakshott and Granby Dixon, he did not know
which was the "hangedest" fool of the two. Mrs. Moses
emphatically declared in favour of Granby Dixon.

CHAPTER XIII.

A COMMITTEE OF THE HOUSE OF COMMONS.

A COMMITTEE-ROOM in the House of Commons is not
exactly lively at any time ; but when the subject in hand is

a matter between two railways, about an extension, nothing can be more dull, unless the counsel fall out, or a witness is fractious under cross-examination, or the chairman falls out with the counsel, or the counsel go to the limits of parliamentary privilege with the chairman. The law-stationers tell me that you very seldom get any fun at all unless there is a female witness, in which case there is generally some " hay " made by a clever counsel; and the law-stationers ought to know, because they have to wait till the stroke of four, to see how many folios they have to put in hand before five.

Lord Oakshott had never been on a committee in his life. He knew, however, that Granby Dixon was on one; and as he wanted to see him very much he sauntered down to the House of Commons, and asked one of the policemen in the lobby to tell him where Group 7 was located.

The policeman knew him, and took him up to the board. The Salford extension was in Room 8. Lord Oakshott, taking off his hat, passed in, perfectly uninterested in the business, but wanting word of Granby Dixon.

There was a rather large crowd of outsiders. Lord Oakshott pushed in among them, and looked round, rather wondering where Barry had got his upholsterers. Eversdale, M.P., came up to him, and entered into conversation.

" I say, Eversdale," said Lord Oakshott, " where the devil did Barry get his upholsterers? I can't get *my* beggars to give me such colour as this. Look at this olive green with the gold wandering all over it. It is superb."

" You should see my new house at Bolton," said Eversdale. " I left the furnishing of it to my wife, and it is like an everlasting toothache. She always consults me, and she came to

me about the pictures. She said that the upholsterer wanted
to know whether she was going to furnish the dining-room
in oils or in water-colours—at which I swore. She, being a
religious woman, pulled my hair, and we made a compromise;
I have filled the rooms with chromo-lithographs. It appears
to me that they are as good as anything else. Well, and so
you have paid up. I should not have done so myself, but
you know best. The reason why I should not have paid up
is that I don't happen to have any money. My wife has
plenty; she gives me a thousand a year for petty cash, and
sends a large proportion of the remainder spinning among
the parsons. Do you believe in converting Jews at six
hundred pounds a head?"

"It seems dear at that price," said Lord Oakshott.

"Are you a witness?" said Eversdale.

"Not I. I want to speak to Granby Dixon."

"Here he is," said Eversdale, M.P., "fast asleep."

In fact, the good and excellent Granby *was* fast asleep,
though to those who did not know him he appeared only
wrapped in thought. The Committee consisted of four, one
being absent (on private affairs, gout, or family affliction).
On the extreme left of Lord Oakshott sat Captain Turn-
over, R.N., who could have sailed his ship to any port you
liked to name, but who knew nothing of Salford. Then came
Granby Dixon, wrapped in a placid slumber. Then came
Mr. Dereham, Q.C., the chairman, who knew all about it;
and beyond him, Colonel Beckers, who knew nothing about
the matter, but who insisted on pretending that he did. Such
was the Committee upon which Lord Oakshott looked. And
he at once began composing a short poem on it in a satirical
vein, before the face of the unconscious Granby. But that

poem was never finished. It stands exactly in this way in
Lord Oakshott's MS. :—

> " When senators sleep at their duties,
>   When our children are dying in heaps,
> .   .   .   . beauties,
>   And our .   .   .   . sleeps,
>
> Then our .   .   .   . forgather,
> .   .   .   .   .   . old.
> .   .   .   .   . wind and weather,
>   All is damned* for their gold."

That is the very way in which the poem stands in Lord
Oakshott's MS. I am of opinion that he will never complete it now. He says that what took place in that Committee-room was extremely disagreeable to him, and we all
know what geniuses are.

He was composing, as we see above, and Eversdale was
getting interested in the Committee. Eversdale said, "Oakshott, I will bet you three to two that the defence gets it ;"
and Oakshott said, "What rhymes to weather?" when
a new witness was called, who put all poetry out of his
head.

The promoting counsel asked the chairman if he might
now call the lady of rank who was one of his principal witnesses, as she had waited for a long time. The chairman
said, " Certainly ;" and he called the Duchesse d'Avranches.
Lord Oakshott was now in the front row of spectators, and
he saw that the woman who came in was Mrs. O'Brien.

---

* Lord Oakshott's secretary says that the word is not
"damned," but "indeed." Now, in the first place, that would
not scan, and the word is written "d———d." It is as certainly
"damned" as Lord Oakshott's only farce was.

He pushed back, but she had seen him. She sat down, perfectly dressed, perfectly gloved, perfectly shoed, perfectly cool. She knew that Lord Oakshott had seen her, and she let him know that she had seen him. Face to face as she was in cross-examination with the cleverest parliamentary lawyer of the day, she had pluck and dexterity enough to stab Lord Oakshott to the heart in nearly every word she spoke.

Her evidence in chief (given in French : the Committee were all good Frenchmen ; Granby, who was asleep, was the best of them) was nothing.' She had simply to give evidence about a road in Salford, by the side of which she had a little property. The adverse Company were foolishly disputing over a few hundred pounds about the re-making of the road. Her examination was of the most innocent character. Then she was cross-examined. She looked like a woman difficult to cross-examine, she was so wonderfully self-possessed.

She was dressed in pearl-grey silk, with cream-coloured gloves. *That* the cross-examining barrister could have stood without a tremble of the nerves, but he, as a man of experience, saw that this was a dangerous woman, *because she could sit down.* He argued in his mind that no English or Scotch woman ever sat down and kept quiet in the history of the world ; whereas a Frenchwoman or an Irishwoman could put herself upon a chair and remain there in a perfect pose, without disarranging one fold of her dress. Yet this woman was sitting there, with her cream-coloured gloves folded in her lap, looking perfectly ready for him ; not in the least like an Englishwoman or a Scotchwoman. She was described in his brief as an Englishwoman ; and he, though an

Englishman himself, saw some foreign element in her, and took his own course. He addressed her in English.

"You have only a life interest in that property, Mrs. O'Brien," he said, suddenly.

And she, thrown off her balance, said—

"Only a life interest."

"I think that we may dispense with French, then, Mrs. O'Brien?" said the counsel.

"You can examine me in German or Italian if you choose; all languages are alike to me. I spoke French because it is most familiar to me."

At this moment Granby Dixon was awakened by a thrust in the ribs from his neighbour; and the cross-examination went on.

"I have twice called you Mrs. O'Brien, and you have not challenged me," said the counsel. "You are now the Duchesse d'Avranches. Well, we will not quarrel about that. How did you become possessed of this property?"

"Ask Lord Oakshott, who is standing behind you and prompting you," was her sharp reply.

The counsel looked behind him rather dazed. A handsome and well-dressed man was standing behind him, and he said—"Are you Lord Oakshott?"

"Yes."

"I have to tell you, Mrs. O'Brien, that although I have read Lord Oakshott's poetry, and admired much of it, I have never seen him to my knowledge until this moment; he has said no word to me. I am in utter ignorance, on my honour as a gentleman, as to what he has to do with the matter. My lord, what is the meaning of this?"

"She will tell you if you leave her alone," said Lord Oakshott.

"This is extremely irregular," said Granby Dixon, now entirely awake, and irritable with that irritability which comes of irregular sleep. "The counsel for the defence is holding a confidential conversation with a member of the other House. The least which can be said of it is, that it is a shameless breach of privilege. You must order Lord Oakshott to withdraw at once."

Lord Oakshott withdrew without giving any further trouble, and the counsel went on.

"You have, then, only a life interest, Mrs. O'Brien?"

Granby Dixon interrupted:

"I can tell you all about it; if I am wrong, the Duchesse d'Avranches can contradict me."

"Who is irregular now?" said the chairman.

"Not I. Lord Oakshott made over this property in Salford to the daughter of the Duchess, Lady Oakshott, the wife of Sir Arthur, Lord Oakshott's cousin. She made over her life interest to the Duchesse d'Avranches, the lady who is sitting here. Is not that so, Madame la Duchesse?"

"That is precisely the state of the case," said Mrs. O'Brien, without moving one muscle. "Lord Oakshott had long planned his cousin's death, and he wished to buy my daughter by gifts. My daughter would have nothing to say to him, and made over her life interest to me. Men like Lord Oakshott, however, occasionally miscalculate in their villanies. Lord Oakshott planned the drowning of Sir Arthur, but my daughter was faithful, and was drowned with him."

Sensation!

"May I be allowed to say," said Granby Dixon, "that

Sir Arthur is *not* drowned, and that in all probability he will be exhibiting his old hospitality in England in about a year, with a new son or daughter."

" That is very singular, Mr. Dixon," said the chairman, hastily. " Duchess, we only want to know this—Will this railway deteriorate your property ?"

" I think so," she said quietly. " It will most seriously deteriorate all property there. The tunnel is thirty-three feet below the roadway, and I cannot see how the foundations of my houses can stand in that gravel.

The cross-examining counsel was by this time all abroad. He was not in possession of facts, and was inwardly and with a calm countenance cursing his instructing solicitors up hill and down dale. He made one more dash at the Duchess, however, to save his character.

" You are aware, Madam, that it is proposed to drive a railway underground in London ?"

" Sir," she replied, " London is not Salford."

That absolutely meant nothing whatever, but it finished the Committee, and moreover the opposition counsel. A smashing truism of this kind is awfully dangerous in any argument. It takes all the half-tones out of an argument. You may have given in the question about space being filled with matter, but may be arguing successfully that space is of necessity illimitable, when a man may suddenly say, " But, my dear sir, you cannot deny that six times seven are forty-two." It takes the wind out of your sails : perhaps you do not remember what six times seven makes ; but the argument is stopped, possibly for ever. People who suddenly introduce irrelevant truisms into an argument ought to be burnt alive.

Mrs. O'Brien did it. She said merely, "London is not Salford," and then, with the air of a woman who had finished the matter, she rose, and bowing to the chairman, asked if any one wished to ask her any more questions. The chairman asked the opposition counsel, and the opposition counsel forgot himself so far as to say, "Oh, Lord, no !" Then Mrs. O'Brien bowed and withdrew.

She passed into the corridor outside the Committee-room alone. But at the door she found a man's black arm held out to her, and she laid her pretty cream-coloured glove on it. "I know you, you fool," she said to herself, and then she looked up into the face of Lord Oakshott with an air of surprise.

"Come and let us have our quarrel out in the Abbey," she said. "There are too many people here. Let us be discreet in our anger."

"You were very discreet in the Committee-room," said Oakshott.

"Ay, but I chose to think Arthur was drowned, and my daughter with him. Is it true that they are alive ?"

"I think it right to tell you, Mrs. O'Brien, that Arthur is alive, and his wife also."

" Tell me also—a fool like you cannot lie—have you paid Arthur's debts ?"

" Every farthing."

" I wish you were dead, Oakshott ; I have sold out every farthing at ten and three-quarters."

" My dear Mrs. O'Brien, you have actually ruined yourself. The shares are at par."

" You might have told me," she said sulkily.

"You might have trusted me," said Lord Oakshott. "Have you actually sold out?"

"Actually."

"What sum?"

"Eight thousand."

"I'll go to Moses and see what I can do," said Lord Oakshott. "I will see you through it. You shall have your money."

"Ay, that is the least you can do. Will you give me my daughter?"

They were now in Westminster Abbey, leaning against Chaucer's tomb. They had come to have their quarrel out here, and they had it.

"What is your daughter to me, Mrs. O'Brien?"

"Always Mrs. O'Brien," she said. "I am the Duchesse d'Avranches."

"You know that you are not Duchesse d'Avranches, Mrs. O'Brien. You have been shamefully deceived; but you know that the Court received the real Duchesse d'Avranches yesterday."

"The Court would receive any one," said Mrs. O'Brien.

"I think not," said Lord Oakshott. "I do not mean to say that there is one word against your character. I fairly tell you, that, although I am a peaceable man, I would hit any man between the eyes who said one word against Lady Oakshott's mother. But I want to know what I have to do with your daughter, Lady Oakshott."

"Oakshott," said Mrs. O'Brien, "our family has always been respectable."

"I wish I could say the same of mine," said Lord Oakshott. "Still, we have kept pretty well in the ruck of the great race of respectability, and we are no worse than our neighbours."

"I allow that," she said. "You were the first scoundrel of your family."

"My dear Madam," said Lord Oakshott, "I think that your reading in history is deficient. I should be inclined to say that I was the most respectable member of my own family, with the solitary exception of my father."

"Who is the father of the boy Dickie, then?"

"Arthur."

"You are not speaking the truth; you are his father."

"I will go round to the altar, Madam, and swear that your daughter is as pure as yourself. Dismiss these monstrous notions. I am utterly incapable of the thing you charge me with, certainly not with the woman I love best in the world."

"Listen to me, sir. As for your going up to a Protestant altar, and swearing before an empty shrine, that to me, as a Catholic, is nothing. I ask you this—When did the child sleep last with you?"

"Dickie never sleeps with me, Mrs. O'Brien. He sleeps in my dressing-room," said Lord Oakshott.

"Then the story I have heard of your valet coming into your room, of seeing the child's cheek in your beard, of his calling Mrs. Prout to look at the pretty sight, is all wrong?"

"No," said Lord Oakshott, "that is all true enough. The pretty little fellow had a childish fright in the night, and he ran into my bed; and when my valet came in in the morning, the pretty innocent little fellow had his cheek in my beard. Now, Mrs. O'Brien, we are both of us grown up, and are too old to talk nonsense. You are a very clever woman, and I am a very clever man. Let us understand one another. I write poetry, but it is so very bad that I am still considered among my friends as a man of business. The case stands simply in this way. I wanted to marry your daughter, and did not ; Arthur had her. I want something to love, and, like a sentimental fool, I have taken the boy—this boy Arthur believes to be my son. Leave me the boy, Mrs. O'Brien, and I will make your shares right for you."

" Thank you very much," said Mrs. O'Brien. " Now we can part friends, as you think. One word more, Lord Oakshott. May I remark to you that, as a general rule, men like you do not absolutely nurse children as you do that baby, unless they are their fathers ? Do you think that you can blind *me?* I give you my scorn and defiance ; and, mark me, you shall not have that boy."

" I do not see how you can interfere," said Lord Oakshott.

" I will have him and pull him through every degradation sooner than a prig like you shall have him."

" You have no authority, Mrs. O'Brien."

"I have the authority of an angry woman, whose daughter's life you have ruined," said Mrs. O'Brien. " An angry woman knows no law, no mercy. I'll have the boy."

Lord Oakshott was very sorry to do it, but he did it. He was a perfect gentleman, he was determined to have his little cousin, and this woman was perfectly inexorable to reason. He took out his pocket-book.

" Mrs. O'Brien, I am very sorry that we should part enemies. I am determined to have the boy. I think that I shall do better by the boy than Arthur, who does not love him."

"You are the scoundrel who deceived my daughter," said Mrs. O'Brien, "and you shan't have him."

"Mrs. O'Brien, that is not true. Will you have the goodness to look at this paper? Softly, Madam,—in my hands, if you please."

She saw what it was, and made a clutch at it. Oakshott caught her arm like a vice. "*Now* will you be quiet about the boy, Madam?" he said.

The answer astounded him ; he had played his last card. Mrs. O'Brien said quietly, "No, you smooth-faced villain ! you shall *not* have the boy. You have ruined my daughter's domestic peace, and I am your enemy. I know what you hold in your hand, and I was a fool to clutch at it, because a man like you would never use it. I *did* forge your name. Am I worse than Arthur?"

"Why, no ; but I might deal differently with you."

"Well, you have done the worst that you could do to any woman. Do your very worst to me ; but watch your boy night and day."

"I will do that, but I must put your shares right for you first. Good-bye."

CHAPTER XIV.

LORD OAKSHOTT'S WILL.

LORD OAKSHOTT got Mrs. O'Brien a cab, and then he went home, and wrote his celebrated poem of "Thanatos and Mnemosyne." When asked by Granby Dixon why he wrote poetry at a time when his whole life's happiness was in the balance, he confessed that he did so because the poetry had nothing to do with the matter in hand; which was scarcely satisfactory. He went to his solicitors, made Mrs. O'Brien safe at a cost of £8,000, and then he went home and deliberated whether he should make his will or write a poem. I rather think that he was going to make his will, but he altered his mind and wrote a poem instead, for the original MS. stands thus on a sheet of foolscap :—

" I, Earl of Oakshott, do hereby will and bequeath the whole of my personal property to——" The will goes no further; the poetry begins :—

> Thanatos and Mnemosyne
> Sat on a high cliff over the sea :
> A hundred fathoms under their feet
> The ocean surges clawed and beat ;
> And the gulls, as white as the sea-driven foam,
> Perched on each porch of their rock-bound home.

> A hundred fathoms down below
> They saw the great waves come and go ;
> Come and go, advance and flee,
> Like the waves of a great democracy,
> Advancing ever eternally.

> The mermen who swim in the shallow waters,
> To catch the eyes of frail fishermen's daughters,
> Were a hundred fathoms deep in the brine,
> Watching the great waves darken and shine,
> As they passed to their death on the cruel shore,
> Where they burst and died, to live no more.

> And the mermaids who watch for the fisherman's son,
> In the lonely creek when the day is done ;
> Whose song is so sweet that the fisherman's boy
> Puts his breast to her bosom, and dies for joy :
> These mermaids were still, for the word had gone forth,
> That the Demon of Tempest was out in his wrath ;

So they twined their hair with the dank sea-weed
Which the sailor clutches in death's dark need.

    One man was there, and only one,
    Come down since the rising of the sun ;
    And the youngest mermaid stroked his hair,
    Kissed his cold lips, and said he was fair.
    " Sisters sweet," this mermaid said,
    " Look, my sailor is not dead :
    I will warm him into life ;
    He shall be king, and I his wife."
But the cruel mermaids under the sea
Smiled at their sister sarcastically ;
They said, " He is dead, and you know that we
Cannot wed the men of the sea :
And if a man of the shore is found,
We drag him down, and he is drowned.
We are all maidens under the sea.
      Let be, let·be."

The youngest merman loved the girl
With hair like amber and teeth like pearl :
But she loved the dead sailor better than he,
This cold, cruel maiden under the sea.
The young merman went through the bursting surf ;
He climbed the high rocks to the short sweet turf
    Where Thanatos and Mnemosyne
    Sat in the shade of a juniper-tree.
And Thanatos said, " Art thou come from the dead,
   And what message bringest thou me ?"
And Mnemosyne said, " Hold up thy head :
   Wantest thou aught of me ?"

    The merman told his story
    While the sunset's glory
      Came lighting up the sea ;
    And his story was so plain
    I might tell it once again,
      Of you or me :-—

> " I loved a maid beneath the sea,
> But that sweet maid cared nought for me :
> We cannot wed beneath the waves ;
> Our gardens are the sailors' graves."

Here the poem unfortunately comes to a sudden end and finish, as so many of Lord Oakshott's poems do. Witness his " Fragment about the State of the Soul in the Next World," in which piece he leaves off suddenly just as we all thought he was going to begin and tell us something. It is a fearful pity that the poem quoted above was never completed. Lord Oakshott says that he was going to make the merman ask Thanatos for his gift of death, and Mnemosyne for loss of memory. I wish he had. Exquisitely beautiful as the fragment is, it would have been far better for him to have made his will instead of writing it.

This is all the will Lord Oakshott ever made. He was, however, a most marvellously methodical man in his way. Before he wrote one word of it he took three sheets of foolscap, folded them in a way which would have satisfied young Brogden ; docketed the document as the last will and testament of Lord Oakshott, deceased ; then he unfolded the paper, wrote as much of the will as appears above, and walked up and down the room. Then the divine afflatus came on him, and he wrote off the above beautiful poem. Then he tells Brogden that he went to sleep in his chair, and finding the document before him when he woke, got up, and under the firm impression that he had made his will, called up the steward and housekeeper at Comfrey's, and made them witness it.

I should like to have seen Mrs. O'Brien's face when she *did* get hold of it ; but it was denied me. Mrs. O'Brien was such an extremely clever woman that she could not believe in a fool.

CHAPTER XV.

MRS. O'BRIEN.

THOSE who remember Miss Dora Martin of Connemara must be old now; but any one of them will tell you that she was the most beautiful girl in that county, which claims equality with Devonshire and Lancashire in the matter of female beauty and virtue.

Dora Martin was only a distant connection of the great family, and only such by marriage. She had no right to sing—

> " Place me amidst O'Rourkes, O'Tooles,
>   The ragged Royal race of Tara ;
> Or place me where Dick Martin rules
>   The pathless wilds of Connemara."

She was a Lancashire lass, and she did not like the Irish of Connemara. They bored her. She liked them at first because they flattered her ; but she used to tell her friends that she could not trust them, they lied so. One thing, however, they could not lie about, and that was her wonderful beauty.

Mr. Martin, her father, had been in Lancashire for many years : he would probably have been angry had any one called him an Irishman ; he had made an Englishman of himself, had married an Englishwoman, and dropped his accent entirely. I do not think that he had improved himself much by doing so, but as he thought so we ought to respect his belief. When his daughter was only fourteen years old he accepted an agency in Connemara for Lord Mersey, who held large estates in that district, and for whom Mr. Martin had done much electioneering work. Mr. Martin had been an attorney, with no great practice, in Liverpool, and the place was a perfect godsend to him. It was a permanent post of £600 a year, with an interest as great as that of Lowther Castle to back him. He moved into Connemara at once.

Mrs. Martin was a perfect nonentity, an Englishwoman who could adapt herself to anything, everything, or nothing. Dora, on the other hand, had her opinions, and in the five happy years which she passed in Connemara, she came to the conclusion that she did not like the Irish at all. Her dislike for any man calling himself an Irishman is so terrible now, that those who still speak to her never mention the name of that nation. I am not here to uphold her in any way. If you drive a woman mad, why, mad she will go. I don't defend her in any way ; I only write down two facts in her life.

When she was nineteen she was quietly sitting at supper with her father and mother. Without the slightest notice the door of their house was broken in, and six men in crape masks entered the room and asked for her father. He stood up and declared himself, saying hurriedly to her, " I knew this must come : take care of your mother." In two minutes after he was beaten to death before their eyes by sticks. In the midst of it she ran in and tore one of the young men's mask off. She recognized him, and he was put on his trial ; but the jury would not convict ; they knew what their lives were worth.

Lord Mersey behaved very well over the matter, though

possibly, if he had resided more in Ireland, or if the Irish had allowed him to do so, it might all have been different. He allowed the widow and daughter of his agent the same sum which their father had taken. Dora took her nearly idiotic mother back to Liverpool, and tended her carefully until she died, a year after the murder of her husband.

Lord Mersey at this time most certainly made a great fool of himself about her. He came to see her, and, looking at her wonderful beauty, offered her what is called in polite circles protection, but which ordinary people call prostitution. She would have nothing to do with the matter at all. If any one could hate her, it would be Lord Oakshott; but Lord Mersey and he are prepared to swear that she acted well up to this point, and in one way always well. The girl and woman was cold, hard, and cruel. Many women have fallen away from all grace and virtue for a time, who are less sinners than the inexorably virtuous Mrs. O'Brien, or, as she calls herself, Duchesse d'Avranches.

In every woman's life, however hard she may be, there comes a time of *tendresse*. I don't care who the woman is —she may be the mother of the Gracchi for aught I care— but every woman has one *tendresse* in her life. Mrs. O'Brien had one. It left her without hope, without heart, almost without God. But the woman was in love once, and it is necessary that we should give the details.

She refused to have anything to do in any way whatever with Lord Mersey. The murder of her own father before her eyes had chilled her, and she hated men, with their cruelty and brutality. She said to herself, " I must go among women and children, or I shall go mad." Can you follow her thoughts, or must I explain them more fully?

After the murder the woman was on the verge of madness. I believe that she was only saved from it by her solitary love adventure, tragical and lamentable as it was. The child saved her possibly.

She threw aside Lord Mersey's pension, and then she took a situation as nursery governess with Lady Killshannon. It would be a vain and idle thing to speak of Lord Killshannon, fifth Earl, who died in 1830 from injuries received at a prize-fight. Lady Killshannon, I say, was of the most virtuous, and respected Miss Martin's virtue. She took her into her house at thirty pounds a year, and set her to educate her children.

They were all very kind to her, and the children would have liked her very well, but unluckily Miss Dora Martin was not quite like other young ladies. The children told their mother that sometimes she sat and stared without saying one word for a long time. And one night, when Lord Killshannon was in bed with his wife, and was "catching it" for having been out too late at a dog-fight, Miss Martin appeared in the room with a candle in her nightgown, and said, "I am sorry to disturb you, my lord, but the Irish have broken in, and are beating my father's brains out."

As her father's brains had been beaten out two years previously, Lord Killshannon naturally suggested to his wife that the young lady was not exactly in her right mind. When she came back from her interview with Lord Hill, however, there was no trouble at all. She told Lady Killshannon that she had ceased to love. She had certainly ceased to hope.

During the time when she lived with the Killshannons there used to be very much about the house a certain Honourable Captain O'Brien, the brother of Lord Killshannon. He was a grand Galway giant, well-born, well-bred, well-looking, but having the character of being rather unprincipled. From the first moment of his arrival at Killshannon she was attracted by him, and by degrees he began to be attracted by her. He got leave more and more often from Dublin, and both Lord and Lady Killshannon said that he was in love with her. The good-natured couple consulted about the matter in this wise.

"Kate," said Lord Killshannon one night, "George seems to me to be sweet on the governess."

"Killshannon, you smell of smoke," was the only reply which her ladyship gave.

"That is not an answer to my question," said Lord Killshannon.

"You asked no question; you only made an assertion."

"Well, my dear, be it so. I do smell of smoke, for I have been smoking. I will reassert my fact. George is sweet on the governess."

"I hear you," said the lady.

"What do you think of it?" said Lord Killshannon.

"I will give my opinion when it is asked," replied the lady.

"But, the deuce take the woman, her opinion has been asked," said Lord Killshannon.

"There," said the lady, "you need not lose your temper and twitch your pillow away like that. I'll tell you what I think of it if you will be quiet."

"I'll be as quiet as a lamb," said Killshannon. "But you see, he might marry her. And she is extremely flighty, so much so that I am afraid of her."

" I don't see why he should not marry her," said the good lady.

"A penniless governess !" said my lord.

" You had no money with me," said the lady, " but I have kept you from bankruptcy."

"That is true, Kate," said the wild Earl, "and God bless you for it."

" You know as well as I do how well she behaved in the affair of Lord Mersey. The girl is a good girl. Our boy being dead, unless I should have another boy, a matter utterly unlikely, George will be head of the family ; he must marry and have heirs. The girl is as good as another girl ; and George might any day bring us back some horrible woman whom I could not receive."

"George is capable of any folly," said Lord Killshannon. " Two years ago——"

" Pray spare me," said the lady. " We want a good wife for George, and with his character he is not likely to find a better one than Miss Martin. I advise that we do not put our fingers in the pie at all. George is now as apparently irreclaimable as you were before you married me. Look how wild you were, and what a good husband you have been to me. Surely there is a hope for George if we do not interfere."

" That is said like your own true self, my darling, but——"

" But what ?"

" George is not like me. I was very wild, but I never was a blackguard among women ; George has been. George has done things which I could not have done."

Lady Killshannon began to cry. "I don't know what to say at all. I'll go to the priest about it."

"I must request you to do nothing of the kind," said Lord Killshannon. "I'll not have my domestic affairs talked over to any priest who was ever born. If you think that the girl will reform him,—I speak to you as a woman,—let the thing go on; but I will not have an unsexed priest consulted."

"She is a Catholic," said Lady Killshannon, "and all Catholic women make good wives. After all, you know, we have some sort of a religion; even Protestants like George may be sound somehow, though it is difficult to see how."

Lord Killshannon, who was rather a warm Orangeman, repeated, to his pillow, the great toast to William III., and having relieved his mind in that way, said—

"If we keep the girl here, she is safe; if, on the other hand, we send her away, she would not be safe. As Christians, Kate, let us see that the girl comes to no harm. Does she love George?"

"I should say that she worshipped the ground he walked on."

"Well and good. The girl shall not be wronged. Only mind, Kate, I forbid you to say one word of this sacred confidence to the priest. If I find out that you have done so, I will throw him into the Shannon. When does George come?"

"The day after to-morrow."

How well the Duchesse d'Avranches remembers that day. She will say now that her life began on that day, and ended on the day when she faced Lord Hill. She knew O'Brien was coming, and she took the two little girls, her charges, down by the shores of the lake. Loch Corrib under the western sun was like a sea of glass mingled with fire. The pretty little Irish children played together, and mingled with the little bare-legged swarm of peasant children around them. She only looked at the long road by the lake, and wondered when *he* would come. Lady Kathleen O'Brien, Lord Kill-shannon's youngest daughter, came to her barefooted, loaded with lilies, and with a long story. "Indeed and indeed, she'd been into the wather herself—yes, indeed, but young Paddy O'Rafferty, he wint in furder "—(these young ladies never dropped their brogue, even afterwards when they came late into London society)—"and Paddy O'Rafferty got her the flowers, and was stung on the calf of his leg by a bum-bee. And she wanted sixpence for Paddy O'Rafferty." On the other hand, Lady Nora O'Brien was creating a violent disturbance with young Rory O'More because he had given her only forty rushes for twopence instead of fifty. The affair heated itself to that extent that Lady Nora, a strong girl of eleven, seized Mr. Rory O'More by the hair of his head, and thumped and banged him until he cried for mercy. Poor Miss Martin separated the combatants, and rebuked Lady Nora severely for calling young Rory O'More "a little thieving limb of Satan." Lady Nora, however, was not to be overcome, and was stating her wrongs to the world and kicking Miss Martin, when Lady Kathleen, having dropped her lilies, darted into the affray, bit Miss Martin on the hand, and then boxed her sister's ears. Her conduct seems to me an excellent example of what is called an "armed neutrality."

Miss Martin was still laughing when she felt a hand on her shoulder. She looked up. It was Captain O'Brien.

"Kathleen and Nora, will ye never be good amongst you? Here, ye gossoons, run away in a hurry" (to the village children): "and here's a penny apiece for all round to buy apples. Kathleen, pick up your lilies and kiss your sister, then run away home to the Castle and say I am coming. Miss Martin, stay with me, and I will lead my horse."

"I had better go with the children," she said in a low voice.

"No," he replied in a whisper, "I want to speak to you."

The two children ran away quite reconciled, and George O'Brien and Dora Martin were alone by the shore of Loch Corrib. She walked to the right of him, and he had his horse's bridle over his left arm. The moment they were alone he passed his right arm round her waist, and said suddenly, without any preparation—

"My darling, my love, my life, I have tried to keep away from you, but I cannot. Will you be my wife? I am not virtuous, but you can make me so. In God's name, Dora, save me from my present life, and make me to lead a better one. Dora! Dora! take me as I am; unworthy as I am, take me and save me."

It was all she wanted. She laid her head on his bosom, and told him how dearly she loved him, and that if she was worthy of his love she would share her life with him.

When I think of this man, I feel as if I should like to write in red ink. She turned in her unutterable happiness and looked back upon the lake, while he held his arm round her waist and covered her hair with kisses. No storm came up from the dim Atlantic to lash the water into spray and send it driving over the hills. The lake was almost like a mirror, and the pretty little Irish children were paddling about in their fathers' boats. " Let our life be like the lake, my darling," she said. " In our profession we shall have storms, but let us love one another, and I care not. The lake is often calm, always beautiful, and I love it for ever because you spoke to me on its shore."

" Dora," said O'Brien, " you would not have me quit my profession ?"

" I ! I wish my husband to be marked as a coward now, when our armies are beginning to hunt the French out of Spain ! No, love. Sailors' wives have to wait and hear the blast shaking the window-pane ; surely a soldier's wife can do the same."

" Dora, will you marry me at once ?"

" If you desire it ; but why ?"

" I expect that our regiment will be ordered to Spain in three months."

" Oh ! that's sudden. But have it as you will."

It was as he wished. That good couple Lord and Lady Killshannon made no objection, in fact hurried matters forward, for the long European quarrel must soon end one way or another ; no military man's life was worth sixpence, and in case of a failure of heirs the whole estates of Killshannon would go to the O'Briens of Bally Errol, a most intolerable thing. The pair were married in a fortnight, and in five months from that time Captain O'Brien was killed in the assault on St. Sebastian.

She was with child by him, and that probably saved her mind. The studious care and attention which she received from Lord and Lady Killshannon could not be over-rated. When the baby was born it was a bitter disappointment to them, for it was a girl, and the estates must go away from them into the hands of the seditious and truculent O'Briens of Bally Errol. *She* did not care, she had had one gleam of happiness. Her loved one had died the death of a hero and she had her little girl. She would be true to him, and would meet him in heaven.

What induced Lord Hill to consent to that piece of monstrous folly? When our men were being dragged by their heels to the trenches a large number of souvenirs were taken from them, and by one officer a perfect collection was made. At the peace Lord Hill let it be known by letter that at a certain date any relatives of the deceased (named) might have these souvenirs by applying at the War Office. Mrs. O'Brien had a letter to this effect, and in her widow's weeds went to the War Office on the day named, attended by Lord Killshannon.

The wild Earl, who was as gentle as a woman with women, told his sister-in-law that he wished he was on any other errand in the world, but they were shown up into the presence chamber among many others, and there sat the great and terrible General himself, two sergeants behind him, and all the relics on the table before him. Having bowed Lord Killshannon and Mrs. O'Brien to a seat, he called on the next claimant, a very old woman.

Hers was an easy business. She had only to take a battered old Prayer-book which had been found on her grandson's body at Talavera. She was in workhouse clothes, and said that her grandson would never have 'listed, but that Maria Jones married the sawyer. Lord Killshannon, like a true Irishman as he was, at once gave her four guineas. When she had curtsied herself out, Mrs. O'Brien's case was taken on.

Mrs. O'Brien sat in front of Lord Hill, and raised her widow's veil. She was quite calm, and Lord Hill said—

" Madam, in your deep affliction it must be some consolation to know that your husband fell like a true and splendid soldier."

" My lord," she said, "*cela va sans dire.*"

" You recognize this, Madam ?" he said, putting a chain and locket before her. "And you recognize this handwriting ?"

"I recognize both : that letter is in my husband's handwriting, and the chain and locket were given to him by me. The locket contains my portrait and my hair, as you will see."

She opened the locket and looked at it for an instant. Then yell after yell went ringing through the room, the screams of a desperate woman ; and she threw the chain and locket in Lord Hill's face.

The dog had been false to her two months after they were married. The portrait in the locket was not hers, but another woman's : the hair was not her hair—it was the black hair of a Spanish woman.

CHAPTER XVI.

SOME GAMBLING.

Mrs. O'Brien (Duchesse d'Avranches) told Lord Oakshott once, that after the interview with Lord Hill and the scene of the locket her soul died. Lord Oakshott argued with her —logically, I think—that such could not be the case, because nothing of the kind had taken place. She then said that she had not a soul to be saved : and then Lord Oakshott argued with her that she still might have a soul which —well, might go the other way. She, like a sensible woman, saw Oakshott's argument in the right way, and changed the subject to that of the Duc d'Aumale.

In spite of the boy's having turned out a girl, as Lord Killshannon put it, Lord Killshannon made an extremely handsome settlement on her, with her wife's entire consent. " Any money," said Lady Killshannon, " that we can keep from the O'Briens of Errol, should be kept ;" and so Mrs. O'Brien found herself rather handsomely off. She went to live in France, for what reason I am unable to understand. Perhaps to forget herself.

The poor woman had seen her father murdered by the Irish, and then from another Irishman she had received the bitterest wrong which a woman can receive. She fled to France cursing the nation, and later on began cursing the English as heartily as ever she did the Irish.

She had two great vices : savage, unthinking vindictiveness, and gambling. We have heard something of her vindictiveness already, but the habit of gambling was her only relaxation for many years. I do not mean for one instant that she ever demeaned herself by sitting down to a playtable at Ems, Wiesbaden, Homburg, or saintly Aix-la-Chapelle. She gambled keenly in stocks and shares. Granby Dixon, who knows everybody's business except his own, says that at one time she was worth £80,000, and that at that time she was living *au troisième* in the Rue Picpus, to be near her daughter in the convent.

" She was the woman, sir," said Granby to Lord Oakshott, " who wrote that article in the *Revue des Deux Univers*, on the influence of priests on women. Veuillot and About were both down on her like a thousand of bricks : Veuillot for her religion, About for her facts. As she had at that time, when we were all young, no religion, and knew no facts, she got the worst of it. Michelet had a turn at her, but she beat *him.*"

Would you mind, Granby Dixon, telling the rest of Mrs. O'Brien's story to Lord Oakshott? It would take a great load off my mind if you would. Granby Dixon is by far the best gossip in the world, and I know him. Lord Oakshott is said to be a poetical noodle; of that I can say nothing, because I do not know him except as a common acquaintance. I should be inclined to say that he is by no means a noodle, and as for the accusation of poetry, I will allow, however unwillingly, that he is a third-class poet.

We had much better listen to Granby Dixon than to your humble servant. I did not like that £4,700 over the election for Bournemouth, but Granby *can't tell a lie.* So I think we had better let him tell the truth about Mrs. O'Brien to Oakshott, and leave the responsibility on his shoulders. Because, do you perceive, she might drop in to lunch with either of us, and I would sooner that she beat up Granby's quarters than mine.

"In the first place, sir," says Granby Dixon, "the woman, although an extreme religionist, has no religion. The last, or possibly the last but three of her follies, was her taking to Spiritualism. In due course of business they raised a spirit called Ahamercoth, who shied the coal-scuttle out of the window. She confessed this to her priest, and the priest, being puzzled about the name of the fiend, and thinking that it sounded as though it came from the wrong side of the house, told her that she had committed mortal sin by raising *a* devil, if not *the* great old devil himself. She paid ten pounds, and went *en retraite* for six weeks; after which she declared herself bored, came out, and told the whole story to me.

"The woman's head is wrong. I asked Monseigneur Drew about her. He is a very clever woman's priest, and knows hysteria when he sees it. He shook his head about her. 'I can't do anything with her,' said Monseigneur Drew. 'I have seen cases like hers before, I will allow, but they were in prisons and madhouses. I tell you fairly, Mr. Dixon, that I am afraid of her.'"

Granby continued: "The woman was utterly frightened and scared in her young womanhood. Her father was murdered before her eyes. Her husband was false to her, and she bore all that without going mad. In my opinion she is far too clever to go mad.

"Well, she has been gambling these twenty years, with more or less success. I have no idea what the woman is worth at this moment, but it may be £100,000, or it may be sixpence. She sent into the House for me fifteen years ago, and asked me into her brougham. As I always do what I am asked, I got in. Before we started she asked me if I had any money: I, suspecting chloroform, said that I had my cheque-book only. She said: 'That will do. You will have to lend me fifty pounds, for my fool of a lawyer will not trust me, and I have not five pounds in the house. You will make four hundred pounds by this journey, you little man. Do you know that Gargentrino has won a great battle, and that the Arcuela Loan is up to seventy-six?' I said, 'Drive like blazes,' which order she gave to her coachman. We ran over a man and killed him ; the coachman was fined. At least we did *not* kill him, now I come to remember, because we only knocked him on the pavement ; and the coachman was not fined either, because Mrs. O'Brien gave the man five pounds. The old girl was perfectly right, sir ; I lent her fifty pounds, and made four hundred.

"I gave her the office about the Arizoba Polholyvirgin, and also about the Popocatapetl Sulphur, so what the deuce the woman is worth at this moment I can't say. I went out of these things with about a thousand pounds in my pocket ; she, a very strenuous and obstinate woman, would stay in. I judge that she sunk at least four thousand pounds in the crater of Popocatapetl for brimstone. She had quite enough of her own.

"Women are all fools at business ; they have not enough calculation to be anything else. I went in at Popocatapetl shares at once simply for this reason. I knew that there was brimstone there, because I had read Prescott ; and I knew that if they did not find brimstone there, we should *get* some brimstone from somewhere else, which would do quite as well in London. So I took shares. Brimstone was produced at the board in London, and shares went up. I sold out. Whether the brimstone came from Popocatapetl or not I am unable to say, and don't care ; I rather think not. You say that this is immoral, Oakshott : it is not more immoral than horse-racing. Don't be a fool. I don't think that the brimstone came from anywhere else than Battersea ; therefore I had a commercial right to sell out. Is not that logic ?

" Well, however, Mrs. O'Brien could not be induced to sell out at all. She told me that she believed that the brimstone *had* come from the works at Battersea, but still shares might go a little higher. There she was, your woman all over: she wanted to screw the last penny. In a week Popocatapetl was not worth a rush. She was in, and I was out. The woman was what all women are in business —a fool.

"Well, she was a fool in a very different way—a very great fool. I always thought that she had no heart whatever. I found out my mistake."

At this point the narrator is obliged to break off with Granby Dixon's narrative, and take it up further on. If Mrs. O'Brien was dead we could tell the whole truth; but then Mrs. O'Brien is *not* dead, and might wait on either of us to-morrow for a little conversation. The story goes (I of course don't believe a word of it) that Mrs. O'Brien, before she became Duchesse d'Avranches (which she never was), proposed marriage to Granby Dixon, offering to settle on him £8,000 of £100 shares in the Acapulco Railway (then at £11 10s.). Granby Dixon did not see his way to it. Let us resume his own narrative: he is a married man now :—

"The most beautiful thing about her was her intense love for her daughter. Her daughter, Lady Oakshott, Arthur's wife, was the only being she ever loved in her life, save O'Brien, who so cruelly deceived her. Before I ever was connected with her in business I knew this, because she lived in the Rue Picpus, close to the convent, and I went to see her there.

"She was there to be near her daughter, she told me. The nuns had got up a little Mystery, and her daughter was going to act in it. Gentlemen of good repute, who gave so much to St. Vincent and who were introduced by the mother of one of the young ladies, might go. I, Granby Dixon, make it a rule to go and see everything, so I went to see *that*.

"There was not much to see. In fact, it was near being rather a stupid affair. One whom I never name with my hat on, was supposed to have passed up into Jerusalem to his death. Two Marys, the Virgin and she of Bethesda (Mesdemoiselles Antoine Florèque and Eugénie Cartel), passed over the stage looking for his footsteps. They could not act at all, Oakshott. They were very beautiful, as most French girls are, but the Bavarians would have beaten them at acting. They did not feel their parts at all, and I said so.

"These two Marys passed on. They were followed by a stolos of priests and choristers with banners. Then every light but one was turned down, and we awaited the last Mary, Mary Magdalene.

"At last she came and all was hushed, save once or twice I heard a gasping sob among the audience. She was bare-armed, in a simple tunic. I never shall see such a sight again. First of all there was the transcendent beauty of the girl, and then there was her incomparable acting. The two good Marys had *looked* for the Saviour's feet; the priests had passed on with music, not caring. This Mary Magdalene came slowly forward and *felt* for the sacred footsteps with her long, thin, white fingers.

"Then she burst out suddenly and took us all by storm, singing, in a magnificent soprano—

> 'Dirige, dirige, Jesus, oro,
> Semper sequor, peto, ploro.'

So she went on with that hymn, and when she put her hands to her head and sang —

> ‘ Date panem vobis, vobis ;
> Date frustra panis nobis, nobis,’—

I fairly put down my head and made a fool of myself. I did the most unlucky thing in my life. I said to Mrs. O’Brien, ‘ Your daughter is the finest actress in the whole world.’ Well, I did not think much of what I had said at the time. She went on in the half darkness feeling for the footsteps. At last she lost them: she stretched her white, bare arms abroad for one instant like a cross, and then she fell heavily, a heap of ruined beauty.

“ How those French can act! The other two Marys came in and stood over her, and Mdlle. Eugénie bent over her. The other two girls could net *say* their parts, but they could *group*. I have never seen anything more beautiful than that group of the three Marys. I wish that Meissonnier or Gerome had seen it. Two fools, with no notion of the situation, standing over the finest actress which the world has ever seen, sir, who lay with her head in the dust of abasement, and one arm stretched out along the floor to feel for the footstep which she believed was lost for ever !

“ Well, Oakshott, Mrs. O’Brien’s affairs did not go well that year. I had warned her about the Tehuantepec Loan, but she held on, and, as a matter of course, lost. Killshannon told me that she tried to borrow £700 from him, and that he did not see his way to it. She asked me for money that year, and I told her what was exactly the truth, that I had not got any to spare : I never have. However, three months after the Mystery at the Picpus, that most unhappy lady, your cousin's wife, Lady Oakshott, was put on the stage by her own mother at the Variétés, with a salary of twelve hundred francs a week.

"That is the truth. I don't think that Lady Oakshott is a clever woman myself. I think that she is a magnificent actress, but I think she is a fool. You, being in love with her, think differently. What did she do to make her fortune? She came on as Hermongilde; she came to the foot-lights, spread out her hand, and said, '*Les pas perdus.*' She saved the play, I allow, and it was a hard play to save; but the woman is such an utter fool and such a splendid actress, that even Paris never found her out. I swear to you that Lady Oakshott does not know what she is talking about half the time she is acting. The last time I ever saw her play was at St. James's Street, and at the passage 'Non! non! Flori-don!' she put no emphasis on the second 'non!' She is, however, a glorious creature, and a good creature, and, though not wise, she is the best mechanical actress in the whole world.

"You might have won her, Oakshott. You and that black-guard Arthur fell in love with her at the same time in Paris: we know all about that. I believe that she would have chosen you, for she is entirely incapable of really loving any man. Don't scowl, because that is not in argument. She might at this moment have been the Countess if you had not exasperated her mother.

"This article I cannot varnish. You and the old woman, though you get on very well at times, seem to act and re-act like vinegar upon nitre; she hates you exactly like poison. If you had never quarrelled with her, things might have been very different, and you might have married the cleverest actress and the greatest goose in all Europe. She has actually submitted to your cousin Arthur; she would have bullied you.

"Arthur got the woman through her mother's influence. If I speak coarsely, I speak truly. Arthur spoke fairly to the old woman; you never were civil to her. I am glad that it is as it is. Now I go on to another matter.

"While Arthur was away you gave that woman protection. You need not speak; I can say all which you are going to say, and say it better than you can, for unless you are savage you cannot speak a hang. You made a fearful mistake there, Oakshott, and all the king's horses and all the king's men will not put your character or hers right. I know that you are perfectly innocent, because you have told me, but the world and your cousin Arthur do not believe it. You have made a very great fool of yourself. *You must always remember that the world will believe in anything except innocence.*"

Lord Oakshott doubted that.

"Fudge!" said Granby Dixon. "Now you are making yourself ridiculous about this boy. He is not your son (for you cannot lie). Why on earth do you make this fuss about the boy?"

"He is his mother's son," said Lord Oakshott.

"The Lord lighten_thee," said Granby Dixon. "Have you made your will in the boy's favour?"

"Yes, and I got it witnessed at Comfrey's here."

(This will was the "Thanatos and Mnemosyne" will, the will which Mrs. O'Brien desired to get.)

"Go down to Oakshott to your boy," said Granby Dixon; "I am sick of you. Or stay—can you get in a wax to-night?"

" Over what ?" said Oakshott.

" Alderney fortifications."

" Who is speaking ?"

" Lord Merthyr," said Granby.

" I think that he will exasperate me sufficiently ; but I have no facts."

" Come away, and I'll give them to you. A row will do you good : then go home and eat bread-and-butter pudding with your boy."

They were two hours over papers, and Lord Merthyr was wholly unconscious of what was hanging over his head. Lord Oakshott was perfectly ready for him on any point : but Lord Merthyr happened to hit him in a raw place, to Granby Dixon's intense delight. Lord Merthyr went on about the Alderney fortifications, allowing their utility, but finding fault about their expense. Lord Merthyr said : " These fortifications were begun by an enterprising Government, but have been carried on by a Government utterly deficient in the points of economy and of that feeling for national honour which is so necessary to us at the present time." Lord Merthyr had spoken very well up to this point, but after this most lamentable breakdown he fell an easy prey to Lord Oakshott. Lord Oakshott once distinguished himself, with what result we shall see. I think that if Lord Oakshott had taken a vow at the shrine of the holy Januarius to write no poetry for ten years, and had kept it (which is quite another matter), he would have made a very good debater.

Lord Balmerino saw him on his legs as soon as Lord Merthyr was down, and like a cunning old boy he sat still. Lord Merthyr had had the extreme stupidity to allude to the General Cornish Mining Company in his speech, and to say that he supposed that when the other party was in power, some arrangement would be come to similar to that of the now famous Company for which Lord Oakshott had paid every penny.

Lord Oakshott arose in his wrath, while Lord Balmerino sat and laughed. Lord Oakshott spoke very well and very clearly. He pointed out that the other party had begun the fortifications, and that during the few opportunities which the other party had had for getting a vote for them, they had demanded forty thousand pounds less than the objectionable party, so that not only were they responsible for the votes for the original proposition, but they were also responsible for starving them. It so happened that a noble lord who was in an under office at this time, had lately gone entirely to what Mr. Mantalini calls " the demnition bow-wows." Lord Oakshott politely alluded to him (indirectly) in this language :—

" Like some bankrupts who have degraded their order themselves, and humanity by their vices, who have swindled their sisters out of their marriage portions, their mothers out of their dowry; who have left their paternal towers to crumble to the earth; these men, who live in gambling-houses on the Continent, while the hare couches on the hearthstone where they warmed themselves in infancy—these, I say, my Lords, are the men who taunt us with want of patriotism."

There was a general rage on the other side of the House. Lord —— said to Oakshott, " You are in for it again, old fellow ;" and Oakshott said, " I suppose so, but I don't care a——*wicked word.*" In point of fact, Lord Oakshott was in for it ; but he got out of it by flatly contradicting everybody, while Lord Balmerino sat and laughed at him.

It was one of the turning-points in his life.   He was called
to order no less than four times in the gossiping debate
which followed.   Such a scene, said the Lord Chancellor,
had never been witnessed in the House of Lords before.   It
ended by a solemn rebuke given by the Lord Chancellor to
an infuriated Oakshott; but meanwhile he had exhibited
such powers of debate, and such rapid powers of reply, that
a certain great lord from the Lower House went away and
wrote him a letter.

He behaved very badly indeed.   Granby Dixon told him
that he was ashamed to be seen speaking to him.   The
Prime Minister, however, conceived a very violent affection for
him.   You will see in the following chapter how it happened
that Oakshott was not in office for many years, but was
saved to us to write that beautiful poetry which we all admire so much.

He followed Granby Dixon's advice.   He went home to
Comfrey's and went to bed.   He was in a very excited state
of mind, and once, waking up in the night, he thought of
getting up, taking a hansom, and going down to the House
of Lords to have some more of it.   It was then, however,
four o'clock in the morning, and so he had to content
himself by swearing that he would have another go at
Merthyr, on some subject or another, the next night.   He
rose early, and found two letters on his breakfast table.   I
must be allowed a chapter for those two letters.

CHAPTER XVII.

LORD OAKSHOTT'S FIASCO.

" DEAR OAKSHOTT,

" You showed such splendid powers of debate last night, that I am forced to ask you to join us.

" Your temper is very bad, but that will improve under the responsibility of office.   I like temper in a free lance, but when you are in office a gentleman like you will be sure to remember that exhibitions of temper compromise a man's colleagues;   and a man's colleagues are bound to back him up.

" I do not know anything of your business capacities, but your name will now stand high for chivalrous honour.   Will you come into harness as Under Secretary for the Colonies; soon, I hope, to be moved higher up ?"

" P———."

That was the first letter.   The second was—

" MY DEAR LORD OAKSHOTT,

" We have had no poetry in our Magazine from you for three months.   I don't happen to admire your poetry as much as some do, but our people admire it very much.   After your awful behaviour in the House of Lords last night I can expect nothing new, but surely you have something for me in your portfolio.   Please send me something.

" Very faithfully,

" J——— P———."

Lord Oakshott was a most business-like man.   He

answered the two letters at once, and sent them off by the next post ; *but he put them in the wrong envelopes.* So "J. P." got this letter :—

"My dear Lord,

"I have been hit rather heavily under the fifth rib, and at the same time I have had to pay away sixty thousand pounds. I don't see my way to office for a month or two. Pass me over this time, but come to me next. I will work for you like a horse.

"Oakshott."

J. P. set down Oakshott as a madman. Meanwhile the Prime Minister went into his study to look at his letters before he went down to the House.

There was one which he clutched at ; a great envelope with a large crest, and a sprawling "Oakshott" written in the corner. "By Jove," said the Prime Minister, "I have caught this boy. I will make a man of him. There are the makings of a Prime Minister in him. I dare say he will re-fuse this time, but I will get him another time. Stanley never spoke better than he did yesterday ; it reminded me of Disraeli and O'Connell. I wonder what he says."

And the astounded Prime Minister read as follows, Lord Oakshott's answer on the proposal of office :—

" My eyes are set on thine own eyes, darling
    Are thine eyes set on mine ?
  Over my head the chattering starling
    Sings in the bright sunshine.
Tell me, sweetheart——"

(It must be remembered that for at least a quarter of an

hour the Prime Minister thought that this language was addressed to *him.*)

'——art thou weary
Of the wild world's strife ?
Place thy head on my bosom, deary ;
Come and be my wife."

I will go no further in this poem. The above is quite enough. Still, explanations are necessary. J. P. had written to Oakshott for poetry. Oakshott at once dived into his portfolio. He was a most methodical man ; he always docketed his poetry (he did the same with his will). He came across a poem which was docketed

" Mine eyes are set," &c.,

and he sent it off to J. P. Now, the really pretty song, " Mine eyes are set on thine own eyes, darling," had not been written two months, but the balderdash which he intended to send to J. P., but by an accident actually sent to the Prime Minister, *was a thing which he had written at Eton when he was twelve years old.*

But will you contemplate the position of the Prime Minister? He met Granby Dixon in the tea-room that night.

" Dixon," he said, " you know Oakshott better than any one."

" I think so," said Granby.

" Is he mad ?"

" He is pretty mad," said Granby ; " not so mad as you or I, you know, but very mad. Not quite mad enough to get on : there is where he fails."

" Dixon, will you move ?"

" Yes, at an increased salary.   What is it ?"

" Under Secretary for the Colonies."

" Why did not you ask Oakshott ?"

" He is such a lunatic.   I did ask him, and he sent me a copy of verses, for which he ought to have been birched.   I can't trust him."

" I think you are making a mistake," said Granby ; " he is a hundred times the man which I am.   However, I am with you.   I never put by a good thing in my life.   But do think twice about Oakshott.   The man, with all his folly, is a man of genius, power, and go ; and we want such men. With the exception of yourself and one other, whom have we ? I am a needy man, but, I think, an honest one.   Think twice before you pass Oakshott over for a third-class man like me.   D———, at his best, was not better than Oakshott last night.   O'Connell was never better.   Think of what you are doing, and think how much we want our hands strengthened in the Upper House."

The wise old Irishman looked down on Granby, and he said—

" I can trust you, but I can't trust Oakshott.   A man who is so little a man of business as to send me a copy of silly verses when he is asked to take a prominent place in the affairs of the greatest nation in the world, is not to be trusted. You are an honest man, Dixon, and have spoken well up for your friend against your own interest.   Do you accept ?"

" I should like to ask Mrs. Dixon whether I was behaving honourably by Oakshott."

" I cannot wait for Mrs. Dixon's decision.   Yes or no ?"

" Yes, then," said Granby.

Granby Dixon saw Oakshott that night, and told him everything.

"I congratulate you," said Oakshott. "I don't think that I would have cared about office. I want to get away to my people and to that boy. What is this nonsense you tell me about my sending a poem to the Prime Minister?"

"You sent him a copy of verses by mistake, I suppose," said Granby.

"I dare say. Well, that is just as well as it stands. I am out of political life at present. But, Granby, is it not much better for me to go back to my estate and my people? Did I not leave the devil's hoof in the House of Lords last night?"

"You certainly did."

"Would it not be better for me to hold myself in reserve? To make them feel that there is a man in the background who can come cranking in on them at any moment; is that, I say, not better than fribbling one's self away in endless explanations as G—— does?"

"You will be forgotten."

"Why not? I shall have all the more power when I force them to remember me."

"You will lose your powers of debate."

"Fudge, dear Granby. I will fight my farmers over their treatment of the labourers. That will keep me in good form. For what *is* debate, after all? It is only the argument which sense brings against stupidity, or stupidity against sense. I assure you, Granby, that you can find no better training for debate than at a market dinner. It is very like the House of Commons with all Liberals excluded.

No; I shall go down to my people : my heart is with them, and I do not see why my body should not be there."

" Yes, you lunatic."

" Before you married Mrs. Granby, did you ever feel a wild mad hunger in the heart ?"

" Yes," said Granby.

" All gone now," said Oakshott.

" No, worse than ever. That precordial anxiety of which you speak is worse than ever. It has doubled itself. I was a single man once, now I am a double man : two lives, do you see ?"

" What should you do if Mrs. Granby were to die ?"

Granby looked very steadily at him, and then he made the motion of putting a pistol to his head. " I could not do without her now," he said.

" And yet you have no children," said Oakshott.

" No," said Granby. " And when a man or a woman casts out with his wife or her husband on that account, set down that man or that woman as a humbug. The most affectionate couples I have ever seen were childless couples."

" Can they take my boy from me, Granby?"

" Of course they can if you make it worth their while. Do you know, Oakshott, that you are behaving very fool-ishly ?"

" I have long known it."

" Why the deuce could you not have fallen in love with some other woman ?"

" Don't know ! why did you fall in love with Mrs. Granby ?"

" Well, you might have taken up with some other boy, at all events."

"No other boy would have had her eyes."

" Well, as you are politically dead for some years now, and as I have got your place, I will tell you something.   I will give you a piece of good advice.   Go down to Oakshott and marry your dairymaid.   You will get into trouble, or get her into trouble, if you do not."

The accumulated stupidities of Lord Oakshott rendered it necessary that he should retire from public life.   The next night in the House of Lords, Lord Barum regretted that he did not see his noble friend Lord Oakshott in his place.   Lord Barum, a " Rupert of debate," went on to say what he would have done with his noble friend if he *had* found him in his place.   Granby Dixon says that although he is not a rich man he would have given one hundred pounds to have Oakshott at his throat.

Oakshott was quietly sleeping at Henley-on-Thames while the infuriated Barum was denouncing him.   He read of all in the *Times* in the morning, but he said, " What does it matter ?" and he told his groom not to bring out the horses, and then he wrote his celebrated Ode to Park Place, which begins—

> " Three tall pine-stems aloft on the down ;
> Three white chalk cliffs over the town ;
> Three tall cedars, black and dark ;
> Three young bathers naked and stark——"

Every admirer of his knows this poem.   There is no need to quote it further.   There are certainly no cedars close to the house at Park Place, and the bathing-place is a quarter of a mile from the town.   Yet his admirers think it a very beautiful poem.   For my part, I think that the end is even

more beautiful than the beginning, but there is no accounting for tastes.

CHAPTER XVIII.

WHIPPLE AND CLARK MAKE AN ATTEMPT TO PUT THINGS RIGHT.

OAKSHOTT's life for a short time after this was very pleasant.
Of course he would tell anybody who would listen to him,
that his life was overshadowed by a great sorrow; and indeed, one night in his tower he discussed with young
Horsley, the poet of these parts, the best means of com-
mitting suicide. The butler looked at the whiskey decanter
the next morning, and understood why he found young
Horsley asleep on the library sofa. He also understood
why young Horsley insisted that the library was his bedroom, and insisted on that theory until the contrary one was
made clear to him by palpable facts. Then young Horsley
told the butler that any one would have thought he had been
drunk the night before : and the butler thought that such a
supposition was by no means improbable.

With his fishermen and his farmers Oakshott got on very
well, and though he chose to believe himself miserable, he
was intensely happy. In one of his innumerable wanderings
he met a young dairymaid, a very pretty girl, without her
shoes and stockings on. He first of all fell in love with
her : then he went home and wrote a poem about her :—

> " Thy feet are set amidst the grass,
>   With lilies round them blowing ;
> And as I lie and see thee pass,
>   I watch them coming—going.

> "To kiss thy feet were Paradise ;
> To kiss thy lips were heaven :
> No girl can match my own dear love
> In Dorset or in Devon."

I have not reprinted the rest of this poem.

Things were rather dangerous with him at this time. He debated with himself whether or no he should ask this girl (whom he had only seen but once and never spoken to) if she would marry him. On finding, however, from Mrs. Prout, his housekeeper, that the young woman's banns had been read twice in church, and that she was going to be married to a young butcher on the following Monday, he wisely stopped short at the poem.

He led possibly a foolish, but most certainly not an unhappy, or indeed useless life. When all is said and done, fourteen thousand acres is quite enough for one man to manage. He put his heart entirely into his work, and he did splendidly. Once in the year, at Christmas-time, he bloomed into hospitality, and had in the county, and all the county's daughters (who knew nothing whatever about " Thy feet are set amidst the grass, with lilies round them blowing"). The county, although universally voting him a lunatic, were very civil to him. One great orb had not yet been hurled into space, and that orb was the Countess of Oakshott. The Americans say that every young American woman is proud because she might be the mother of a future President. Every young lady in Dorsetshire felt that she might be in her own person the future Countess of Oakshott, with six or seven times the income of the President, and every chance of her husband ending his life as Prime Minister of Great Britain and Ireland, if he only got a good wife. Everybody was extremely civil to him.

But the children were a puzzle to them. Dickie they understood, or thought they did. Dickie was the reputed son of Sir Arthur, but there was a very dark story about that. The truth was obvious: the boy was Oakshott's son; no man ever showed such open tenderness for a child who was not his son,—that difficulty could be got over quite easily. But who, again, was the little girl Dixie, who came down to dessert with the little boy? Who was she? Mrs. Prout's niece forsooth! Quite so.

In fact, our good Oakshott got what you might call a patriarchal character in the county. They did not mind it a bit, but they looked on him in the light of a patriarch. Still, Dixie was a puzzle to them. It was evident that Dickie was Ishmael, but there was no biblical parallel for Dixie.

Now let the truth be told. I never made out, and Granby Dixon never made out, who this pretty little girl Dixie was. Granby Dixon says she is exactly like Oakshott, which is not true. Mrs. Prout says she is her niece; if so, Mrs. Prout must have had a sister about forty years younger than herself, which is barely probable. The county have made it out that she is Lord Oakshott's daughter. I am inclined to disbelieve that. Then some say that she is Sir Arthur's daughter; the story I am telling will entirely disprove *that*.

I think that you will find the real truth to be this. The child was some distant relation of Mrs. Prout's. Oakshott wanted children about the place, and he told Mrs. Prout, his mother confessor, so. She, I conceive, killed two birds with one stone. Something had happened in a distant branch of the Prout family which had no business to be in the world at all. The mother of the child so far regarded the respectability of the Prout family as to die ten months after the child was born, at the age of nineteen. Nothing was said about the matter, save that Mrs. Prout told two or three friends that the girl had done her duty by her family, and that she forgave her, but that if my lord ever discovered the truth, he would assuredly kill and slaughter the father of the child.

The child was five years old when she came to Oakshott, just before the arrival of Dickie. Lord Oakshott, rambling through the library, heard a noise which he at first mistook for the cooing of the innumerable pigeons outside, but, coming to the hearthrug, he found a beautiful little girl lying on her stomach and looking at the pictures in a nearly priceless missal of his which she had extracted from the shelves by means of the ladder.

"And who are you, little flower?" he said.

" Dixie Prout," said the little girl, rising and putting the book under her arm. Then the child made him a little curtsey and added, " I know who you are."

" Who am I, then ?"

" Lord Oakshott, because you look so kind. I want you to give me this book, and I want you to take me to see the trout in the ponds."

" I will give you a prettier book than that," said Lord Oakshott ; " but now we will come and see the trout."

So Oakshott took to the child ; and that is all that is supposed to be known about the matter, officially, at Oakshott. The grooms know perfectly well that the child was the daughter of a gentleman in Devonshire, but Lord Oakshott neither knows nor cares ; he has his Dixie, and that is all he cares about.

Dickie and Dixie made most excellent friends of one another, and Oakshott thought that the very least he could do was to attend to their education. He thought three days, and then he did what he always did in a difficulty—he wrote to Louis Brogden :—

" I want the best tutor and the best governess out of London. I have here° two young souls, and I want to see into what I can shape them."

Young Brogden wrote :—

" I will get you the best tutor and the best governess in London. I feel strongly on the point, for you say you have two young souls and wish to shape them. Without experienced assistance you will make both of them as great fools as yourself.

" You have simply ruined everything by this mawkish nonsense. You might have died Prime Minister.

" Pay in to us £4,000. Your creditors are pressing under the impression that you are in Queer Street. Why on earth can't you come back and show ?"

Oakshott laughed very much at this letter. In a very few days he got a second letter from young Brogden :—

" I have found you a perfect jewel of a governess. She was nursery governess at the Duke of Ballyroundtower's. Since then she has been teaching mathematics. Her father was Archdeacon Clark, and she is a dragon at mathematics, and will undertake to make astronomy plain to the meanest capacity. But, to stop joking, the Secretary at the College of Preceptors says that we have snapped up the cleverest woman in England dirt cheap—£150 a year ; but she has been overworking herself, and she wants rest. Don't argue about mathematics with her, or she will give you $x + y^{nth}$ in the eye."

" Well," said Oakshott : " so I am to have a horse's godmother quartered on me for ten years. I don't care. I have given up caring. When she begins her hanged mathematics, I shall go up to the tower and write verses. I wish that Brogden had found some one else. I know the woman exactly : with a nose like a horse, and spectacles like turnip-lanterns. I really think with Horsley that suicide is the best remedy."

But he did not do that. Being in a terrible fright himself, he determined, like a real old feudal master as he was, that his servants should share not only his joys, but his terrors ; not only his hopes, but his fears. He frightened them all out of their wits by telling them (through the butler, who was called "Seneschal" at Oakshott) that a lady of high position and attainments was coming down to superintend the education of Miss Prout, who was the adopted heiress of Oakshott. She was, he said, to be treated as the lady of the house in every way.

There were two—nay, let us say *three*—facts in what the butler told Mrs. Prout which demanded an immediate explanation from Oakshott. She knew when he was alone, far from all hope of assistance, and she went into the tower to him at half-past eleven. She laid her housekeeping keys on the table before him ; she put down her housekeeping books, and gave him warning that day month.

Lord Oakshott, who was by no means deficient in re-sources, immediately took the books and the keys and put them on the top of the fire. Mrs. Prout shrieked and tried to get at them, but the more she cried out, the firmer he held her wrists and kissed her. When she was exhausted she sat down, and begged him to pick the keys out of the fire with the tongs. Oakshott, looking on this as the captain of a man-of-war looks on the hauling down of a flag—as the sign of victory, in fact—picked her keys out. She clutched at them and burnt her fingers severely, but she stuck to them like an Englishwoman.

" I want to ask three questions," she said ; " and the first is, Is she respectable ?"

" If any one heard you ask that, you old fool," said Oakshott, " we should be in the Court of Common Pleas for libel. She is as high a lady as any in the land."

" Is she to be put over me in the housekeeping ?"

"She has nothing to do with it, Prout ; how very silly you are. You must keep house, and keep it well too."

" Is it true, as you have told the butler, that you are going to adopt Dixie ?"

" It is certainly true, Mrs. Prout. Do you think that I would send to London for a governess for her at this fearful expense ? Now, give me a kiss and go, my old girl, and don't be a fool again."

" Ah, but if you were to marry the woman that is coming !" said Mrs. Prout.

" Heaven save the women, what fools they are !" said Oakshott. " Am I in the least degree likely to marry an old frump in spectacles who teaches mathematics ?"

This appeased Mrs. Prout, and so, when the new governess arrived at the Castle the next evening, all was in readiness for her. She was to dine *tête-à-tête* with Lord Oakshott, and he rather thought, in consideration of the tremendous intellectual powers of Miss Clark, that he would make the best of himself and do homage to her. He put on his Star and Riband of the Bath, and stood waiting by the library fire.

A sound on the gravel told him that the awful woman had come. She was not very long dressing ; "strong-minded women never are," he said to himself. The door was thrown open, and Miss Clark came towards him under the lights, almost the most beautiful young lady he had ever seen. One fault in her face—it was a little too square ; perfectly dressed, with the air and carriage of a refined young lady.

He growled to himself, "This is too bad of Brogden ;" but he said to her—

"I am delighted to make your acquaintance, Miss Clark."

"Well, as to that, my lord," she said, turning her beautiful bright intelligent face on his, "some say yes, and some say no. We shall get on very well, because I like your poetry, and I will not bore you with my mathematics. For the girl you have me ; for the boy you have Mr. Whipple. Mr. Whipple is not yet arrived.

Lord Oakshott then and there fell in love for about the fiftieth time in his life, though he never was in love with any woman save one. It is not quite true, however, to say that Oakshott *fell* in love—he never was out of it. He entertained Miss Clark at dinner, and the butler wanted her to have some of his Chablis. She said " No," and added, to Lord Oakshott, " stimulants are the greatest blessing in the world when you want them. I don't happen to want any now ; this air of yours is as good as wine. Now, my lord, as I have finished my dinner, I will go to the children and begin my charge."

It was now nine o'clock, and she departed, Oakshott holding the door open for her. Immediately after the post came in with a letter from Brogden :—

"DEAR OAKSHOTT,

"I sent Miss Clark down without appealing to you. Miss Clark is so very well known that I wonder at her coming for that salary. With regard to the tutor, Mr. Whipple, you should never have hesitated. He is, however, coming, and I could tell you why.

"He will be with you to-morrow morning, third class. If I were a Fellow of All Saints, I would travel first. He is an exceedingly proud man, you know; and were I not behind the scenes, I could not have got him for you at all. I never served any man as well as I have you. You have only repaid me by a seat in Parliament. *Oakshott, I am going to ask more of you.* But I never kiss and tell. Whipple likes riding ; take a led horse over to the station for him.

"L. BROGDEN."

"I am like Issachar," said Lord Oakshott: "I am always stooping between two burdens. I want to do my duty and please every one. And the worst of it is that I am *not* a strong ass. I don't believe Issachar was. I'll do what Brogden asks me—I don't know what it is, but I'll do it. I can't commit burglary for him ; I should die of fright."

However, the terrible tutor, this Fellow of All Saints, was due at ten, and so poor submissive Lord Oakshott had four horses out by nine : two for him and his groom, and two for the Fellow of All Saints and *his* groom. Of course they were late at the station (Lord Oakshott always was). The tutor had been waiting a quarter of an hour.

Lord Oakshott went up to him at once, but he had not time to speak. Mr. Whipple said—

" Lord Oakshott, I believe ?"

Oakshott said " Yes."

" I thought that you or some of your people would have been here before. I have been kept waiting for a quarter of an hour."

Lord Oakshott answered, " Let me look at you."

Whipple set his face. It was a perfectly beardless face, but, as Oakshott saw at once, a very good one. He was very ugly, whereas Oakshott was very handsome. Oakshott looked at him, or rather *down* on him, for a few seconds, and then said—

" Take off those ridiculous spectacles, and let me look at your eyes."

Whipple did so, and Oakshott saw the grand magnificent smile, which some of us know so well, come mantling over his face. Whipple spoke first.

" Oakshott," he said, " you will do."

" And I think that you will do also," said Oakshott. "Come, mount your horse and hold your tongue."

" A thing I never did in my life," said Whipple.

" Why have you come to *me ?*" said Oakshott.

" In order to be in the same house with Miss Clark," said Mr. Whipple, promptly. " If you don't know that, it is Brogden's fault. I am engaged to be married to her."

" But why don't you do so ?"

" Because I have no money."

" You have your fellowship."

"Which drops when I marry."

"I see," said Lord Oakshott.   "Do you know that I have been in love with Miss Clark for twenty-four hours, and that now I must get out again the best way I can."

"Everybody always is in love with Miss Clark," said Mr. Whipple, "but she is never in love with any one but myself. I want to know——"

"What?" said Oakshott.

"I want to know about my cub.   Is he good?"

"How can you tell with a child?" said Oakshott.

"I want to tell you that I can't raise my hand on a child or beat it," said Whipple.

"You are wrong there," said Oakshott.

"I know, but I can't do it."

"Then don't.   I cannot either ; but I am an ass."

"Not such an ass as you show yourself in your poetry," said Whipple.

"What jolly rows you and I will have up in the tower," said Oakshott.

"What do you do there?" said Whipple.

"Write poetry, and keep a light burning."

"I have heard something of this rubbish.   Don't plague me with it, like a good soul, as every one knows you are. To change the subject : The man who owns this land ought to be hanged at his own door, as a warning."

"I own this land," said Oakshott.

"Then you ought to be hanged at your own door for a warning.   Come into this cottage : it is one of yours."

"Come into this one," said Oakshott, turning his horse's head up a lane.   "Why, you very stupid man, I have been extinguishing these very foul brutalities to which you extremists object.   Do you know one result which I have arrived at by building new and well-ventilated cottages, like this one before you, in contrast with the fever-hole in the hollow below?"

" No," said Whipple.

" I'll tell you, then.   The children may or may not grow up so healthy, though I cannot eliminate scarlet-fever on clay; but the old folks in these new-ventilated cottages go off like rotten sheep.   You must keep old folks warm if you want to keep them alive."

At this point a groom came swiftly up to Oakshott with a note.   Oakshott read it.   " Whipple," he said, " go on with my groom.   Here is a note from a dying man, and I must go. Go to your charge."

" Has your dying man done a good day's work?" said Whipple.

" Ah, God only knows what a good day's work he has done."

" Then let him die.   What higher honour could come to him?   Let me come with you, and see the grandest spectacle in the world, a labourer going wearied home to take his wages.

" 'Fear no more the heat of the sun,
Nor furious winter's rages ;
Now thy long day's work is done,
Home thou goest to take thy wages.' "

Who is the man that is going to heaven ?"

" Our Rector."

" Let me come with you," said Mr. Whipple.   " To me there is something splendid in seeing a good soul pass from earth to heaven.   Oakshott, it does every man good to see another man die."

"In war it brutalizes," said Oakshott.

"Do not believe it," said Whipple. "No men are more reverent than sailors, who live amidst death."

Oakshott and Whipple drew up before the Rectory, and handed their horses to the grooms. One of the grooms asked if the Rector was ill : Lord Oakshott told him he was dying. The boy burst into tears, and Mr. Whipple pointed his finger at him, and said to Oakshott, "That is the thing you Whigs wish to destroy, and when you have destroyed it, may God help you, for man cannot."

The Rector was very bad indeed. Whipple took possession of the room, and put Lord Oakshott on one side. He asked the nurse a question, but the nurse could not answer it. He then fetched the housekeeper, who knew where the sacred vessels were, and——all was done.

The Rector's last words were, "Take care of these sheep ;" and Oakshott said, "I will, by heaven !"

They got on their horses again, and trotted away homewards.

"He will be dead before morning," said Whipple.

"Next tide," said Oakshott.

"Do you believe such rubbish as that ?" said Whipple. "The man will go when God calls him."

"He has been going for a long time, said Oakshott; "and I have got a successor for him."

"That is the worst of patronage," said Whipple. "I don't say that it has not worked well on the whole. But take an extreme case. I know nothing about the agricultural labourer, and yet, if I flattered you and fawned on you for a year or two, you (not a very wise man) might put *me* in."

"That is exactly what I am going to do," said Oakshott.

"You are mad. I know nothing about the matter."

"I can instruct you."

"Instruct me possibly in some nonsensical sentimental folly, but influence me—never."

"Nonsense," said Oakshott. "£800 a year and Miss Clark: and, moreover, £200 a year for looking after my cousin's boy. Who is a sentimental fool now?"

"But you know nothing of me."

"I have my pocket full of testimonials to your character," said Oakshott. "I have only read one, from the Archbishop."

"I have done nothing but quarrel with you since I met you," said Whipple.

"We will continue the quarrel up in the tower," said Lord Oakshott. "I like a man who pitches into me."

"Lord Oakshott, you are very mad."

"I know; that is what the Prime Minister says. The Rector must go. When he goes, you move down here and marry Miss Clark. Lord, man! there is more real work to be done here than there is at Westminster. I have been in love with Miss Clark for a day, but I desire Miss Clark to continue her engagement with Dixie, and I expect you to continue yours with Dickie."

Whipple, when he got to his bed that night, wondered whether or not he had taken a situation in Bedlam. At the end of his cogitations, before he went to sleep, he came to the conclusion that he had done nothing of the kind, but that Lord Oakshott was the most sensible fellow he had ever met. For $800 + 200 + 150 = 1,150$. And one could almost live in a ruined Paris on that, though, if one were married, things might be different. Such an income, however, was enough to tame even the savage Whipple into matrimony. As for taming his tongue, that unruly member of Whipple's will never be tamed. He " gives it" to Oakshott just as badly now as he did the first day he ever met him. The only person who can in the least degree do anything with him is his wife, and she cannot do much, for she is afraid of him. The only person in the Oakshott household who has utterly beaten the whole lot of them is Dixie. She is Crown Prince of Prussia, Crown Prince of Saxony, Frederick Charles, and Von der Tann all in one. I don't happen to be afraid of her, because I sit and laugh at her. The odd thing is, that Dixie does not hate me for doing so.

Brogden wrote to Oakshott when Whipple was appointed to the living, almost civilly. He said that he was going to ask for it for Whipple, but that Oakshott had anticipated it.

Mr. Whipple married Miss Clark three weeks after he got the living, and moved to the Rectory. Brogden protested strongly, but Oakshott said that Mrs. Whipple was far too pretty to remain in the house with him, and that he was glad she was gone for the sake of his peace of mind. He then paid great attention to a fisherman's daughter, and in fact wrote five poems about her (" Marie," " Elize," " White-foot," " Tangle-hair," and, the most beautiful of all, " Thine eyes are like the summer's sea "), but the young woman would not have a word to say to him, and married a common sailor, who went away leaving her in the family-way, and was drowned off Cape Horn.

Granby Dixon, walking with Lord Oakshott, once saw her. " Granby," said Oakshott, " that young woman might have been Lady Oakshott had she given me the slightest encouragement."

"And she gave you none?" said Granby.

"No, she married a common sailor."

"What a sensible young woman," said Granby.

"Now she is going to marry another," said Oakshott.

"Better and better," said Granby. "I wonder if you will ever get any one to marry you. I wouldn't, I know that.—I say, Oakshott——"

"Well."

"Brogden was too clever by half over that Whipple-Clark business. The present position of affairs is absolutely monstrous."

"I do not see why."

"Well, look here: you are paying two people for consecutive time, and they are not giving it to you."

"They give me eight hours a day with the two children," said Oakshott. "They could do no more if they lived in the house."

"Nonsense," said Granby. "The fact of the matter is that they are four hours each at the Rectory, and after that they are no better treated than young savages, except in the fact that young savages, as a rule, are not under the protection of a noodle like you, to make them ill with cake. At what time were the children home last night?"

"Well, they lost their way."

"That is no answer to my question," said Granby Dixon.

"Well, I am afraid that they were not home till nearly ten."

"You are *afraid* they were not. What do you mean by that?"

" That is mere *façon de parler."*

" Hang *façon de parler:* you know that they were not home till ten."

" Well, I do know it, Granby."

" Then why do you not say so?"

" Don't bully," said Oakshott.

" I won't, old man, but you do exasperate me at times. Have you heard anything of Mother O'Brien lately?"

" No."

" Mind me, Oakshott," said Granby, sharply. " That woman will strike sudden, and strike hard. And she is going to strike."

" But she can have no case against me. I made her shares right for her out of my own pocket."

" Oakshott," said Granby, " you are one of the most talented men I know, but one thing you are utterly ignorant about, and that is women. You fall in love with about sixteen women in a year, but you know no more about them than a boy of fourteen. Innocent and just yourself, you fancy that every innocent woman is just also. I tell you that women have not the rules towards men that men have towards one another, and I tell you that an angry woman knows no law. She has no more pity than a wild beast."

" But," said Lord Oakshott, " I have been always so gentle and so pure among women. I have been chaffed about my behaviour to women at my club."

" That does not matter," said Granby. " Mrs. O'Brien, the *soi-disant* Duchesse d'Avranches, believes that you have misguided her daughter. I'll tell you the plain state of the case. I was at the restaurant in Regent Street last week, the Burlington—the only place, by-the-by, in London where ladies and gentlemen can sit in the same room at their meals. The Duchess was there, and she came suddenly to my table, and she said in French, ' Tell your dear friend Oakshott that the hammer is over his head, and will fall when I please. It will fall soon.' "

" But the woman can do nothing," said Oakshott.

" An angry woman can do anything," said Granby. " Where does Dickie sleep ?"

" I think he is sleeping with Mrs. Prout."

" Why don't you take him to your own bed, and see him into it at eight o'clock every night ?"

" Oh, hang it," said Oakshott. " I am devoted to Dickie, but I don't think I could go the length of having the dear little beggar in bed with me."

" Don't say that I did not warn you," said Granby.

" I will certainly do nothing of the kind," said Oakshott.

That night Dickie came home and set to work at his lessons. He had been three hours coming from the Rectory to the Castle, a distance of 500 yards. He gave up his lessons and went to bed. He did not seem to have been asleep long when he was waked by a light on his eyes. Two strong hands were put round him, and he found himself in Lord Oakshott's arms.

" Is it a fire, my lord ?"

" No, but I am cold in my bed, and I want you to warm me."

They lay together that one night, and the next day came the catastrophe of the white primroses.

For Mrs. O'Brien was very like Napoleon I. ; she struck first, and then talked about it afterwards : whereas,

Napoleon III. and Gambetta talk about it first, and then fail in striking.

She utterly believed that Dickie was Oakshott's boy. She utterly believed that Oakshott had misguided her daughter. And so to stab Oakshott she determined to destroy a soul; which soul was in the body of her own daughter's son.

Well did Granby Dixon say, "You do not know of what an angry woman is capable."

CHAPTER XIX.

THE ADVENTURE OF THE WHITE PRIMROSES.

It was an absolutely forbidden thing, and therefore most delightful. Eve would never have eaten the apple had she not been forbidden; and Adam would never have touched it if she had not persuaded him. Dixie wanted the white primroses, and she got Dickie to get her some of them. What became of Dickie for his sin we shall know hereafter. As for what has become of Adam's posterity for *his* sin, is a matter which we shall never know. We can only say that we are suffering still.

Dixie, like Eve, knew of the apple, that is to say, of the white primroses; she therefore egged on Adam, represented by Dickie, to go and get her some of them. She did not want them particularly, any more than Eve wanted the apple, but she thought that she might get Dickie into mischief, which would create variety, and so she gave him much the same advice as Partlet gave Chanticleer in the Canterbury Pilgrims; that is, to make an ass of himself, and come and tell her how he felt afterwards. That is what Eve did to

Adam. I have known the thing done since on many occasions, but now the woman always swears that the man did not make an ass of himself in the way she directed, but in a low and foolish manner peculiar to the male sex.

Dixie, however, wanted the white primroses, and they only grew in one place—at Morley Moat. Lord Oakshott had expressly forbidden him to go there. He would let the boy go to sea or cliff, but he forbade him that one place; so the boy Dickie made a purpose to go there. Lord Oakshott would put him on horses, would let him swim with the servants, would do everything he could to make a man of him, but he had a sentimental feeling about Morley Moat, and forbade it to the boy.

At one time there had been a Grange there, an appanage of the unmarried sisters of the Oakshott family for a long time. The story about its ruin was a very sad and terrible one. Lady Florence Oakshott in 1745 was notoriously for the Stuarts. She went to France and crossed to Scotland. No one knows what followed; it is totally impossible to say. The story is too wild and dark for human imagination, but it runs among the peasantry like this. She was in sole possession of Morley Grange, and after matters were settled at Carlisle she came back to Morley Grange, and stayed three weeks; after which she left, and was never heard of again. The peasants say that shortly after her departure the dead body of a new-born child, with the decapitated head of a young man with a long black beard tied round its neck, was found in the moat. For my own part, I do not believe the story at all, because I do not see how you could tie a man's head round a baby's neck; and, moreover, Mrs. Prout's account of the matter is in the last degree vague, though she believes the story; and, indeed, I believe that Lord Oakshott has persuaded himself of it now, in fact ever since he wrote his poem—

> " In this darkness of death,
>   In this terror of pain,
> I must draw one more breath
>   'Till I ken thee again.
> Thy head high on rampart,
>   My soul deep in hell,
> I will climb up and ken thee,
>   The winds will not tell."

This is one of the passages in Lord Oakshott's poems to which I object from its entire improbability. He presupposes the possibility of a young woman, far gone in the family-way, swarming up a pole above the gate of Carlisle, taking her lover's head from the top of it, and going off successfully. Granby Dixon urges that such an incident is extremely unlikely. Granby urges that probability should be insisted on by the critics. Granby admires Lord Oakshott's poem immensely, as he does Keats' " Pot of Basil," but he thinks them both very improbable. In Lord Oakshott's poem, Lady Florence drowns her baby in the moat by tying its father's head round its neck. How this could be done without putting the father's head in a cabbage-net, Granby cannot see; and Oakshott says not one word of the cabbage-net. Oakshott says—

> " A band round the father's throat,
>   A band round the infant's chin ;
> Away in the night to the moat,
>   And toss them lightly in.

> "The lilies will rock and toss
> Under the wind-driven rack,
> Beneath the sedges and moss,
> And I will come lightly back."

When Granby Dixon was getting Lord Oakshott's poems through the press for him, he found that this last line had been originally written—

> "And the ducks will waddle and quack."

It is a small matter, but posterity, particularly in America, is very particular to have every detail about great literary geniuses like Lord Oakshott; so Granby has betrayed his confidence. I only say that he nails his colours to the mast in saying that Lady Florence could not have fastened the dead Stuartist's head round the baby's neck without some arrangement similar to a cabbage-net. It stands to reason.

Lord Oakshott chose to believe in his poem, however, and he is not the first man who has done so, neither will he be the last. So Dickie was forbidden to go to the moat.

The moat was a very beautiful place. There are at least two moats similar to Morley Moat, one at Cheshunt in Hertfordshire, and one at Shortgrove in Essex. Moated granges like Shortgrove, Cheshunt, and Morley, generally lie far away from great high-roads. These moats were made four square, round much older buildings, for the sake of protection, by the second-class gentry. As life became more secure, a grange, almost always of Tudor or early Stuart architecture, grew out of the older building by its destruction. I think I could prove this in one instance, at all events, by pointing out random cut stones from a probably

Norman keep, worked in with brick, certainly not later than James I.   However, that is a matter which need not be discussed.   The eldest unmarried lady of the Oakshott family always lived at Morley Grange, and bored herself to death in the company of her younger unmarried sisters and nieces, until the horrible *fiasco* of Lady Florence took place in 1746 ; after that the unmarried Oakshotts refused to go near the place.   The Lord Oakshott of the time hired it of his sister, who took a house in Holborn.   He put all the poor relations into it with liberal allowances, for he had an eye to business, like the rest of his family ; but they all quarrelled among one another, and deserted it.   They took his allowance, but most emphatically declined to live there at all.   Collectively they fought him on the subject, and, as the odds were ten to one, they gained.   The poor relations, with one exception, departed.   They could not stand the Grange, and they said so.

To end Morley Grange, and make a finish of it as a habitable place, one young lady, a hopeless lunatic, insisted on staying behind.   There was no provision for lunatics in those days, and Lord Oakshott thought that she might be as well there as anywhere else.   She was a Miss Edith Oakshott, and I have seen her portrait.   The other day, on a rather careful examination of Bedlam, I met a young lady who was painting blue rabbits on a brown, black ground.   I really thought for a moment, being in Bedlam, that I had come on Edith Oakshott of 1747, in the flesh ; the lady in Bedlam was so uncommonly like Edith Oakshott's portrait, and her pictures were so fearfully like Edith Oakshott's samplers.

The doctor muttered to me, " Take care of her, keep behind me," and I did so, at the same time thinking about the old story ; of this Miss Edith Oakshott, whose portrait I had seen, and whose story I had from Mrs. Prout, whose grandmother was the very old woman left alone with her in the Grange. I said to this doctor, " Have you any attempts at incendiarism ?" He pointed to the barred fireplaces.

This Miss Oakshott, the last of the poor relations, quietly, and with cunning diligence, got every rag and stick she could, piled them about in the most clever manner, got out Mrs. Prout on a trifling errand, set the Grange on fire, and burnt it to the ground. One ruined gable only remains, and the remnants of a flagged walk coming down to the moat through the overgrown copsewood to a ruined iron gate between two pillars : and if you will go to that gate at seven o'clock on Good Friday night, and call three times, Edith Oakshott will come out of the ruins and let you in ; but you will never come out again. This fact I have on the very highest authority. Mrs. Prout, a most respectable woman, and now a licensed victualler in her own right, told it to me ; and if any fisher-boy in the port dared to deny it, he would have his head punched on the spot by his father.

To be business-like, Morley Grange is still an appanage of the unmarried Oakshotts. It carries with it a farm of 769 acres, exclusive of the island. It is at present held by Lady Jane Oakshott, aged sixty-seven, whose intellects are said to be disturbed. It is alleged that she appeared at Mr. Spurgeon's Tabernacle the Sunday before Easter, with a palm branch (a five-shilling one) in one hand and a lighted candle in the other. She says that she told the man to drive to Farm Street Mews ; he, on the other hand, declares that she did not, but said " The Tabernacle." Lord Oakshott advised the man to plead drunkenness, but this the man refused to do. The fact is that Lady Jane is very queer in her religious opinions. The young man who does the sermons for " The Universal Pulpit " told me that he had seen her in pretty nearly every place of worship in town. Every one knows that she was publicly received into the Roman Catholic Church at Paris in 1864, and that three weeks after she made a public recantation at Geneva.

It is a very lonely, haunted spot, and few people would care to be near it after dark. Sometimes the last ruined gable, which rises above the surrounding copsewood, is illuminated by strange fires, which frighten the belated children. One can account for this, however, by means more simple than supernatural means. Morley Moat is a rather celebrated haunt of gipsies, and the Oakshott family have protected the gipsies ever since the following little incident happened, according to Mrs. Prout.

Ethelbert, afterwards Lord Oakshott, had been ill for six months with the tertian ague, and the thought that he was dying. The doctors had given him over, and so they sent for the witch. The witch told them at once to send for the Italian doctor, Agaccio, in London, and he was fetched down express at a vast expense. The worthy doctor went into the keep and raised the devil, who gave him directions and departed. The doctor at once went out and caught a young gipsy man, and performed the operation of transfusion on Ethelbert. As the blood went from the young man's arm into Ethelbert Lord Oakshott's, the latter at once began to speak Romany, and to the day of his death could do the *Hokany baro* with the best gipsy of the lot. The young gipsy man, however, fell dead at the bed-side, and ever afterwards walked on the north terrace, on Good Friday, after three years. Such is Mrs. Prout's account of the matter ; and she says, moreover, that that is what makes the Oakshotts so rambling in their habits. This account may seem to some minds improbable. I argue that nothing is improbable with an Oakshott, and, moreover, that a hundred things more improbable are attested to by the perfectly respectable people who go pilgrimages to Lourdes.

Miss Prounce, however, has quite another story to tell. She says that Lord Ethelbert's mother had no milk, and that a gipsy woman was fetched in a hurry to nurse him. Whichever story is true, this is perfectly certain : if you go to Morley Moat, you are pretty sure to find gipsies there ; and, moreover, the head of game on that estate is so large, that Lord Oakshott says, laughingly, that he shall discharge his keepers, for that well-treated gipsies are the best preservers in the land.

When Dickie went there, there were no gipsies at all. He rather wished that there had been some, for he liked them very much. Their extinct fires were all around the ruined gable, though there was no trace of them in the flesh. An odd-coloured handkerchief, such as they wear, was left, strangely enough, and Dickie stole it and put it on.

Then he got the white primroses, and then he crept down to the water's edge.

No one seems exactly to know what occurred. A little girl, who happened to be lurking on the other side of the moat, said that Dickie was washing his feet in the water, and that the hazel-boughs beside him were parted by a gipsy who beckoned to him. He put on his shoes and stockings and went up to her. And that is the end of him for the present, so far as Lord Oakshott was concerned.

CHAPTER XX.

DICKIE'S DEATH.

How utterly puzzled we all are about death. It is useless for any one to deny it—we are totally puzzled. From John Henry Newman we get the " Dream of Gerontius :" going to the other end of all belief, we get " The Four Boards of the Coffin-lid," from A. C. Swinburne. We would give the very highest praise to both poems, but we most emphatically object to them, because they give us no information whatever, and leave us exactly where we were before.

" Sir," said one great man to his flunkey, " the object of poetry is not instruction. Simple instruction and description, such as one gets in poems of the Scotchman Thomson's poems, are not poems at all. Poetry, sir, should be written to expand the λόγος, not to instruct the ἐπιθυμία."

What follows on death? Can any one tell us? The answer is a most emphatic " No." Father Newman tells us one thing in exquisite language ; A. C. Swinburne gives *his* opinion in the most terrible language; Mr. Tennyson gets sentimental over it, and beats all the others :—

> " High up the vapours fold and swim ;
> Above him broods the twilight dim ;
> The place he knew forgetteth him."

Lord Oakshott, on the other hand, evidently believes in the extinction of the human soul after death :—

> " The wind shall not whisper in thine ear,
> Though the priest's hell be near.
> Thou wilt not ask for the priest's heaven ;
> The sleepers who will awaken are but seven.

The above lines were written by Lord Oakshott as the epitaph on a drowned sailor. If it mattered, which it does not, the Vicar (Whipple, his own man) found a young man cutting them on a tablet, and carried them off to the Bishop. The great case of Regina *versus* Oakshott arose in the end out of this. Oakshott insisted on erecting his tombstone to the drowned sailor, with these verses on it, without a faculty. The Bishop had him into the Arches at once, and then he got a faculty in a sly and secret manner, and so got the Bishop into the Common Pleas for taking his money under false pretences. Both suits were quashed, to the tune of about £4000 a side, but the tablet is there to this day, in the north aisle.

It occurred, however, to the Vicar (Whipple), who had £1100 a year for a population of 450, and was consequently rich, to take the matter before the Judicial Committee of the Privy Council. The Lord Chancellor gave judgment, with the concurrence of the whole court, that as the lines were absolute and perfect nonsense, the defendant Oakshott was absolved from blame, and the appellant must pay his own costs. So the Vicar after all got the worst of it.

We now, however, return to our question. Neither Mr. Tennyson, Dr. Newman, Mr. Swinburne, nor Lord Oakshott seems to have any idea of what becomes of the human soul after physical death. Will they put their brains together and tell us what becomes of a human soul after moral death? Is there no heaven or no hell in this world? Is there no quality of soul which will carry one through all temptations to a certain future? I know not, but I know that down in the East of London I have seen such beautiful love, tenderness, and kindness among people who are for all intents and purposes dead, that I think these people's souls must be immortal.

From the moment that Dickie followed the gipsy away from the moat *he* died. He was far too young to have had any impression made on him by Mrs. Prout, Lord Oakshott, or any of them.

When the child was cast into hell, the appearance of his body was very beautiful.

What was the quality of the soul? It is that to which we must look. *Per ambages*, we must follow the boy whose soul, thanks to Mrs. O'Brien, might be burning while Lord Oakshott was fiddling.

" Where are we going ?" said Dickie.

" Down to the shore, sweetheart," said the gipsy woman.

" We shall be there late," said the child. " It is a long way."

" Yes ; but I have something to tell you. Your father was drowned."

" Yes," said Dickie, " that is quite true."

" Well," said the gipsy woman, " you are not afraid of death."

" No," said Dickie. " I am not afraid to die. You know Cranmer was afraid at first, and then he was as brave as any one. As for Ridley and Latimer, they were top sawyers."

" I did not mean, were you afraid to die, but were you afraid to see a dead man ?"

" Why didn't you say so, then ?" said Dickie.

" I am going to show you one."

" Are you ?" said Dickie. " Well, I dare say he won't hurt me. I am afraid of no living man, let alone a dead one."

She walked the child down to the shore, and there was, in the little hut on the beach, the body of a young sailor who had been drowned the day before. Her object was to frighten the boy, but in this she most signally failed.

The young man lay quite quiet, as if in sleep. He was a young man with a brown face and a light-coloured beard. Dickie went straight up to him, kissed his beard, and then strewed the white primroses on his face.

That was the last of the adventure of the white primroses, until they turned up years afterwards. They were strewn on the face of a dead sailor.

But the gipsy woman said, " Rot the child, he is afraid of nothing. That woman O'Brien knows nothing."

Then the gipsy woman said, "Are you afraid of ghosts, my dear?"

Dickie, who had learnt low language from the fisher-boys, used it with regard to ghosts.

"You don't believe in them, then?" said the gipsy.

"Not a bit," said Dickie; "but I should like to see one."

"I will show you one," said the gipsy. "Come into the wood."

Dickie kicked and scratched, but she was too strong for him. She bore him away into the wood. The child said at last—

"You are stealing me, and I will not be stolen. I will stab you with my knife. You are as bad as Semiramis. Let me go."

The next moment a handkerchief was over his face. A faint sweet smell in his nostrils, and he knew nothing of what passed.

"It was the only chance left," said the gipsy woman;

"the little rogue would have roused the neighbourhood.
God bless Dr. Simpson for inventing chloroform."

CHAPTER XXI.

MR. DENNIS.

WHEN Dickie awoke he began thinking, but found that he
could not think reasonably. He thought of cheese, and
could think of nothing else. Therefore he said to himself,
"I am not awake at all, and so I had better go to sleep
again,"—a most illogical argument, which he at once brought
to a most practical conclusion. He went to sleep again.

Then he dreamt that he was broad awake, and that the
gipsy woman was giving him laudanum out of a bottle. He
(in his dream) kicked that woman violently in the stomach,
aud then he awoke indeed.

"Lie quiet, you little devil," said a hoarse roupy voice
beside him. "Lie quiet, or begorra I'll strangle you."

Another voice, a woman's, close by, said, "Leave that
kid alone, you busnacking bogtrotter.

"He's kicked me in the back, and me spine will be black
and blue in the morning," said Dickie's neighbour.

"Keep the child warm, you fool," said the woman's voice,
"and don't jaw at him, or I'll come and take him away from
you, and I'll put my ten commandments on your face if you
don't do as I tell you."

"Shure, Mrs. Stanley, you asperate yourself widout cause.
Would ye like to be roused from yer sleep by a kick in the
small of your back yerself?"

"Shut up—go to sleep, and keep the child warm," was

the only answer the honest travelling Irish labourer got. Then there was silence.

The man, with that exquisite tenderness towards children which is common to all Irish save those who have been debauched by long residence in English towns, said in a whisper to Dickie—

"Are you cold, darling?"

"Yes, I am cold," said Dickie; "but you said you would strangle me, and you called me a little devil. You had no right to call me a little devil, because I am a very good boy; and if you strangled me, you would go to hell unless you repented of it afterwards."

"It's only a way of talking," said the Irishman.

"It's a very bad way," said Dickie.

"Will you come inside my coat and be warm?" said the Irishman. "A little darling. I've five boys the same age as yourself."

"That can't be true," said Dickie, now thoroughly awake. "You may have five boys; and as it is rude to contradict, I believe that you *have* five boys, but at the same time, sir, don't you see that they could not be the same age as myself? Unless, indeed," said Dickie, reconsidering, "Mrs.——what is your wife's name, sir?"

"Mrs. Dennis, of Cork."

"Well, sir, if Mrs. Dennis of Cork had had five twins at once, the thing might be possible. As it is, I do not see how you can have five boys all my own age."

"But," said Mr. Dennis, "if she had five twins there would be ten of them, whereas there's only five. So you must be wrong."

Dickie knew he was right, but he was wanting to set Mr.

Dennis right also. He was beginning to think about this when Mr. Dennis pulled the boy to his side and covered his coat over him. The warmth of Mr. Dennis's body was extremely pleasant to Dickie, and under the cape of his coat they could whisper to one another perfectly. Mr. Dennis had been very savage on being awakened from his sleep by Dickie, and I am on the whole glad that it was not Mrs. Dennis who kicked Mr. Dennis on the back, and woke him. He might have punished her for doing so. But although we read every day of the savagery of the lower Irish in our towns towards their women, yet I do not find that the very worst Irish are as savage to their children as the very worst English or Scotch. The worst Irishman is softened by the sight of a child. An extreme political economist might say that this is very natural, seeing that the Irish bring a great many more children into the world than they are prepared to provide for. That is a matter of detail; I only know that I never knew an Irishman who did not take kindly to a child ; and if I found a child who would not take to an Irishman, I should think very little of that child.

We are much more prudent than the Irish. We are mediocre in our vices. If it were not for the London, Glasgow, and Liverpool Irish, we could knock off about £30,000 a year in the pay of police magistrates. But look at their domestic purity at home : it is greater than our own. Some say that it is because they are mainly Roman Catholics ; to those gentlemen I would point out the domestic morality of Brussels and Vienna. The domestic morality of the Irish has nothing to do with their creed : it is as great at Londonderry as it is at Cork. Purity is a noble national instinct with them ; they habitually make the most outrageously foolish marriages ; they bring children into the world whom they cannot support, and then they go to America and abuse us ; and the Americans are bound to believe that they have got a terrible case against us, though they have never found out what on earth that case is. The Scotch have a worse one, a far worse one.

Dickie, however, when he was under Mr. Dennis's coat, found that he could talk in whispers. Mr. Dennis said, " Don't speak out loud, love, or Mrs. Stanley will hear ye."

Dickie put his little hand out and found Mr. Dennis's whiskers ; then he passed from his whiskers to where his moustache would have been in those days, but which was only a mass of two-day-old stubble. However, he found his mouth, and he laid his finger on it. Mr. Dennis kissed his finger, and the compact between the poor deserted child and the poor savage was complete.

Dickie drew his body up and whispered in his ear—

" Are you a gentleman ?"

" No, dear ; I am an Irish reaper, but the old woman was in the straw, and I came over on the chance of grass-cutting."

" Will you help me ?" said Dickie, " because I'm stole."

" Hush, and I guessed as much," said Mr. Dennis.

" Where are we ?" said Dickie.

" Among the gipsies," said Mr. Dennis.

" I want to get back to the Castle," said Dickie.

" What Castle, and where is it ?"

" I don't know. I think it is Oakshott Castle, but I can't tell. And I don't know where it is."

" What county ?" said Mr. Dennis.

" I don't know," said Dickie. " That woman gave me

something which has made me ill. Will you help me, instead
of calling me a little devil ?"

"I'll help you."

" Go to Earlie of Oakshott Castle, and tell him the truth ;
that is all. Don't tell him a lie, because he beats people
who tell lies. Have you got any money ?"

" Divil a rap, or I shouldn't be lying in a gipsy tent."

" I had some : I wonder if the woman has taken it from
me."

" Whisht, pretty one ; never mind the money, though
indeed it might come convanient."

" Here it is," said Dickie ; " here is the half-crown—take
it."

" I don't like to take it," said Mr. Dennis, " but I'd best.
I'll lave ye me outside coat to keep ye warm ; so there's a
bargain. I'll find the way to my lord, and ye shall be back
to the Castle in three days. But listen to me. Be civil to
these gipsies, for we are in a rough country ; and if it was
worth their while to murder you, they'd do it—at least this
lot would. How long is it since you left home ?"

" Last night," whispered Dickie.

" Poor child," said Mr. Dennis : " do you know that you
have been muddled for four days with opium, or some devil's
diversion, and that they have only allowed you to come to
your senses now ?"

" Is that so ?"

" That is the truth, my pretty boy. Shake yourself together : you have brains and pluck for twenty. You ought
to have been an Irishman."

" Where are we, then ?" said Dickie.

" On Blackdown, between Somerset and Devon," said Mr.

Dennis. "Roll yourself up in me coat. I'll get away, and be back with my lord just now. Oakshott?"

"Yes, that is the name of the place, I think."

"I'll find him. Keep with these people till I come back. There'll be a shindy as I go, but take no notice. I can't leave them without"—(I can follow Mr. Dennis no further at this point)—"of Geordie Stanley before I go. He said that a gipsy was as good as an Irishman. Good-bye, pretty boy. Keep yourself warm."

Dickie always declares that poor Mr. Dennis did exactly what he said he would do by Mr. Geordie Stanley. I think Dickie is right. The gipsy lay in front of the tent on the grass, with his back towards the Irishman. It may be urged that Mr. Dennis *stumbled* over the gipsy; it may have been accidental, or it may not have been—I am not here to decide ; I only know, *teste* Dickie, that the gipsy roused the whole camp, and told them that Mr. Dennis had done to him the very same· thing which Mr. Dennis had told Dickie in private confidence he intended to do.

The moon being high, and every one being wide awake about the row, it was absolutely necessary that there should be a fight. Dickie realized for the first time that he was in a low gipsy tent, because, jumping up at the alarm of war, anxious for his champion, he started the whole arrangement, and brought it down on the top of him. In his desperate struggles he not only brought down his own tent, but carried it on him like a garment, plunging violently. It so happened that Mr. and Mrs. Stanley were in the next tent, and so he chanced to alight on the pair of them just as they were arousing themselves to see the fight. There were only four blankets to make the two tents ; consequently Dickie understood why Mrs. Stanley's voice had been so audible, and possibly other domestic quarrels with which we have nothing to do. It was certain, however, that his head ached violently, and that his kind bedfellow and friend the Irishman was going to fight.

A grand *bouleversement*, which consists only of a married couple, four blankets, a few bent sticks and a boy, is easily arranged. Mr. Stanley had got on the *necessary garment*, so there was nothing to be said about *him*. Mrs. Stanley had got on nearly as much as she generally had, which was not much. Dickie had put on the tent, having forgotten Mr. Dennis's coat in the heat of the moment.

Then the fight began. The gipsy tore his shirt off, but the Irishman fought with every rag on his back, save the coat he had given to Dickie. I think that fighting is very brutal, but no one can deny that it is very beautiful. We are, after all, the sons of our fathers. I suppose that a more respectable set of men than the present bench of Bishops never lived. Ask the most saintly and respectable whether he has ever looked on at a fight ; has seen the steady glare of the eye in the attacked and the attacker. You ask any Bishop if he has not seen it : not one will deny it, and three-quarters of them will say that they have *done it themselves*. In our "rough island story" there are few men who would deny the game of what the French call "*boxe*." Even Justice Shallow, a most respectable man, allows the soft impeachment.

The fight which was to decide Dickie's life was all against our gallant Irishman. Had the gipsy kept his clothes on, the matter would have been settled in a very few minutes ; for Mr. Dennis's brother had come home from America to fetch his grandmother to Illinois, and he had shown Mr. Dennis one or two dodges in rough-and-tumble fighting, which had better be told to the police, and not given to the general world. Mr. Dennis found himself fighting a stripped man, and he was to a certain extent puzzled, because the gipsy fought very well.

Mr. Dennis "got it" on the right of his left eye, and generally over his countenance. On the other hand, the gipsy "got it" under the ear three times;—it was really beautiful. No murderous rapier rattle of old times, no rascally pistol duel of modern times, could be finer. When men fight like boars or dogs over a private quarrel, you will find that that nation is in the ascendant. For example, take France!

This duel had, however, as sad a termination as that between M. Victoire Noir and the Prince Pierre Buonaparte. The fact is that honest Dennis lost his temper, and the gipsy was getting the better of him. The gipsy was stripped, which was a puzzle to Dennis, but Dennis saw that the gipsy's deltoid was sufficiently developed to give a hold to his hand. He clutched the naked deltoid with the hair underneath, pressed the point of his elbow on the gipsy's nose, and down went the gipsy to avoid that horrible click in the neck which tells you that your man is dead.

The gipsy avoided *that;* but Mr. Dennis went much too far. As the gipsy went down for the last time, Mr. Dennis made a grand mistake. He turned out his heels, consequently drew in his knees, and fell on his man. You had better fire a loaded revolver at a man than do that: it is death, for no man ever survives it.

Mr. Dennis had gone too far, and when the gipsy was

picked up he was dead. "Rupture of the colon and liver," said the wise Coroner.

Mr. Dennis was tried at Exeter for murder, but it was brought in manslaughter, and Mr. Dennis, poor fellow! was relegated to twenty years' penal servitude. I am very sorry for Mr. Dennis, but that same thing happened, and it is likely to happen to any gentleman who drops with his knees close together on the abdominal cavity of another gentleman. Only, don't you see, that in the confusion Dickie marched off, to find his way back to Oakshott; and the communication which was to be made to Lord Oakshott by Mr. Dennis was never made at all.

I speak a trifle too fast. Two years after Lord Oakshott got a letter from Perth (West Australia), which was endorsed "Henderson." The letter was from Mr. Dennis, and it told him that the writer could tell him everything about Dickie. At this point we must part with Mr. Dennis for ever. He was, however, faithful to his trust. He could not have told Lord Oakshott anything in particular, but he promised Dickie, and the poor fellow tried to redeem his promise. Why can't we make Dennis, and such men as he, love us? I fear they are not permitted to do so. At the day of judgment it will go hard with those who separate Great Britain and Ireland. Every nation has found them out. We found them out centuries ago, and called them sinners; now they are saints, though their language is not exactly saintly.

CHAPTER XXII.

THE RECTOR.

NOTHING would have been more supremely easy than for Dickie to have gone back to Oakshott; but two or three things were in the way.

He knew nothing about east or west, and he went west instead of east : that is one way of accounting for his conduct.

He was not very well, having been dosed with chloroform.

He did not exactly wish to go back to Oakshott Castle for a day or so : he rather wanted to see the world for himself.

Below Blackdown there are rabbits, and some hares. And although the hares are foolish things, and run away from you, yet if you creep through the copse-wood you can see the rabbits ; and the rabbits wash their noses with their fore paws, making believe that they have water, which they have not. It is, however, most amusing to lie among the flowers and watch the rabbits. And when you are tired of the rabbits, there is the Rector catching trout out of the Otter in the most scientific way. He lands a very large one, and as he takes the hook out of its mouth he says : " The Reformation, my brethren, was emphatically necessary. My brethren, before the Reformation, Rome was practically (not theoretically) the most Erastian of all the Churches. I beg of you to attend to me. Gregory VII. was both Erastian and Arian. Child, what are you doing here ?"

" I was listening to what you were saying, sir," said Dickie.

The Rector was in the depths of confusion. He had been talking to himself, and he had no witness but Dickie.

He could not for the life of him remember, on the spot, what he had been talking about.

"Which is the way to Honiton, please, sir?" said Dickie.

"Just across that field into the main road, my child," said the abashed Rector. And Dickie went away for a time. The Rector was glad, for he had been caught composing his sermon—a thing he hated.

Dickie from this time was lost to the knowledge of all who had hitherto loved him. But he had got into new hands.

.

CHAPTER XXIII.

GRANBY DIXON ON DICKIE'S DISAPPEARANCE.

"YOU must remember," says Granby Dixon, "in the first instance, that the memory of a child is a very dangerous thing to depend upon. Children do not remember names very well, and frequently misquote them. I had an argument with Dickie on this very point, urging on him that he was a perfect fool not to ask to be carried back to Lord Oakshott. He answered that he did so. Then the truth came out for the first time. He remembered that he had been accustomed to call Lord Oakshott 'Earlie.' If that is so (and I never knew Sir Richard tell a lie), that will account for a very great deal which otherwise would not be accounted for. The child, I fancy, wished to wander, and he either forgot Lord Oakshott's name or mispronounced it.

"The present Sir Richard tells me that even then he had that very odd instinct of *hoarding* money which he has now. He had, he says, eight shillings which the gipsies never discovered. With this money that mere child evidently wandered to Dartmouth. Whether he begged by the way he cannot remember. He says that he sold his clothes to an old Jew at Sidmouth, and had others in exchange. This seems to me to account for the undoubted and easily proved fact that the child got to Dartmouth without being stopped. I don't think that there is any stronger proof of the truth of Sir Richard's narrative than that. It stands to reason: a pretty boy in good clothes would have been arrested five times over. He tells me that he held two half-crowns and a locket in his mouth, while he bargained with the Jew for other clothes. The Jew thought he had an impediment in his speech. I can understand it. Dickie has proved himself capable of anything, dear fellow.

"Now cannot we account for Dickie's story, which at first seemed to me improbable, in this way? The child was most certainly dosed with chloroform, and heavily frightened. That will entirely account for matters as far as they have gone. Before we come to the Crediton business we shall see more reasons for Dickie's behaviour.

"On one occasion I was being driven into the Bight of Benin (nearly opposite the melancholy Gaboon, the home of the gorilla) by a westerly wind; and a swallow came on board, and perched on the maintopmast rigging. As the business was none of mine, I naturally took a great interest in it; and soon as prayers were over (it was Sunday) I went up into the rigging and had an interview with that bird. When I asked him why he had flown 150 miles to sea against the wind, he only preened himself, and gave no more answer than Dickie could. You cannot get a reason from children or fools. On one occasion, a Sunday afternoon at sea, we let all the parrots and cockatoos loose, not seeing that the skylight was open. They all flew out, went straight to leeward, and were drowned like Pharaoh's host in the Red Sea. I calculate that Jamrach lost fifty pounds over that business. There was a cockatoo who swore so magnificently that he was worth at least fifteen pounds. The birds did not know what was good for them any more than Dickie did."

One word more about Dickie. Granby Dixon says that he is the best fellow he ever met. "He has been in a great many places where he should not be—we all have—but you will always find him true, honest, and high-minded ; that is to say, a gentleman."

CHAPTER XXIV.

OAKSHOTT AND GRANBY DIXON IN CONSULTATION.

" Ho !" said Granby Dixon, coming into the hall at Oakshott. " So you have lost your boy."

" Yes, he is gone."

" And you can't get any news of him ?"

" Not a bit of news. I am awfully sorry for the boy. Don't joke about the matter; I feel it very sorely. You men of the world care for nothing."

"You do us wrong there," said Granby. "I care for you. You are the only entirely good man I ever met. I, however, want something of you, and I will give you something in return."

" Give me the something in return first, then," said Lord Oakshott, "and then I will tell you whether I will do what you want."

" No," said Granby, "I am not to be outdone in generosity.　I will make you promise to do what I want first, and then I will give you your *quid pro quo.*"

" What do you want, then ?"

" I want you," said Granby, " to come up to town and speak on S——'s side about the overcrowding of the milliners' girls at the West-end."

" Oh, I can't," said Oakshott.　" 'There is young Cecil ; he will do it quite as well."

" Cecil happens to be in the House of Commons," said Granby.　" We want a sentimentalist in the Lords, and you really must come up and varnish the article for us."

" What is the matter with the young women ?" said Lord Oakshott.

Granby Dixon gave him a perfectly true account of the West-end milliners during the season, without the least exaggeration.

" I'll be hanged if I stand that," said Oakshott.　" I'll go, and I'll make hay.　Have you got the Reports ?"

" Yes ; we will go through them after dinner.　You must have the exact report of the number of cubic feet of air, and must be altogether posted up.　You are a good fellow : I would not have bothered you if we had not wanted you. Do you mind doing something else ?"

" In for a penny, in for a pound," said Oakshott.

" Will you take the chair at the Homeless Children's dinner ?"

" Most emphatically I will," said Lord Oakshott. "Where is my Dickie now ?　Homeless Children !　*I* will make them a speech.　Are you connected with it ?"

" Yes."

" Put me down for five hundred pounds, if you please."

"Oakshott ! Oakshott !"

"Yes. If you hesitate, I will make it a thousand."

"Well, I can't refuse, though you do nothing like any one else.—Great heavens ! what is this ? Oakshott, have you ghosts in your house ?"

It was only Dixie. But the awful beauty of the child, coming suddenly on Granby, actually scared him. He gave two glances—one at Oakshott, and one at the child—and he shook his head.

"No," said Oakshott. "She is Mrs. Prout's grand-niece."

" I thought for an instant——"

" But you see that you are wrong. I wish it was so, Granby, for I am all alone in the world."

" Why need you be so ?"

"Fudge ! You know."

" Come here and have some fruit, my pretty one," said Granby ; "you look tired."

"I have been to the moat after Dickie, and I go every day. He went there to get me the white primroses, and he never came back. And George—that is one of our gamekeepers—says he was stolen by gipsies."

" Go on the lawn with your fruit, my love," said Lord Oakshott : and the child said, " Yes, Earlie," and went.

" I never saw such beauty as that," said Granby.

" Our fisher-folks breed very high beauty. So I must go up to town and make a speech ?"

"Indubitably."

" What is to become of my poem ?" asked Lord Oakshott.

"Say some of it."

Lord Oakshott repeated several stanzas, and Granby said—

"You can't possibly publish such rubbish as that, you know; they will send you to Bedlam," said Granby. Lord Oakshott submitted it to me some years after, and I was obliged to confirm Granby Dixon's opinion. Oakshott was a genius: a true genius; and when he gave his mind to writing nonsense, he wrote much worse nonsense than anybody else; no one ever came near him.

"Is it very bad?" he asked, quietly.

"It is *awful*," said Granby. "I never heard such rubbish in the whole course of my life."

"Well, I will come up and speak," he said. "Now give me your *quid pro quo*."

Granby gave him a letter from his cousin, Sir Arthur :—

"DEAR GRANBY,

"Is it absolutely true that my fool of a cousin has lost this boy? I have every reason to believe that I was utterly wrong in my suspicions of my cousin, and that the boy is my own. Still I will not write to my cousin at present. I should have to confess obligations; a thing I never do but once, and I have done it. If the boy is gone, Mother O'Brien knows something about it: tell my cousin that. And tell him also this, for he is a good fellow, hang him. I know some very queer emigrants here. I know that he has committed some gross indiscretion with the Carbonari or the Cammoristi, and that he must not go on the Continent. Two men, Borichi and Bellini, are looking for him."

So ended the letter.

"Is the last part true?" said Granby Dixon.

"Well, I am afraid it is," said Oakshott.

"An affair?"

"Yes, I am afraid it was an affair."

"Did you behave well?"

"Well, no one behaves well in an affair."

"But with regard to money!"

"Oh, yes. Trust me for turning my pockets inside out."

"Who was she?"

"The sister of Bellini."

"Why the devil did you go with those people at all?"

"I don't know," said Oakshott.

"You never *do* know, it seems to me," said Granby, with great irritation.

"Well, they seemed to me interesting people. They were such thundering rogues."

"You are incorrigible," said Granby. "Did you have a child by this woman?"

"A child!" said Oakshott; "bless the man, no. The young woman is as virtuous as your mother. I asked her to marry me, but there was another young man she liked better, —that is all."

"Did you have any quarrel with the Cammoristi?"

"Well, no. Only I was a sworn member, and in the heat of debate I told a full House of Lords what their objects were. There was not much harm in that."

"That is the matter: I suppose that you will have your throat cut. What do you lunatics want, then?"

"I don't exactly remember at this moment," said Oakshott; "I have got it all upstairs somewhere. I know it began with equalization of property."

"You mean that Oakshott Castle is to go?"

"Theoretically," said Lord Oakshott. "Why not? I sold Drumstone to pay Arthur's debts."

"About the Monarchy?" said Granby.

"Oh, I would sell Oakshott (if I could) to save the Monarchy. I swore by that when I took my seat in the House of Lords. We must keep *that.*"

"But you Carbonari and Cammoristi desire to destroy all monarchy."

"Do not malign us, my dear Granby. We assist Imperialism everywhere by talking far greater nonsense than any one else, yourself included. Pray leave us alone."

"You are not such a fool as you seem, Oakshott. Let us return to sense," said Granby.

"I am sorry for that," said Lord Oakshott.

"Why," said Granby.

"You have been talking the nonsense," said Oakshott. "See here, however, I will make a fool of myself. Do you think that Mother O'Brien knows where the boy is?"

"I can't think what you want with the boy. Come to London, and I will get you a dozen fine wives."

"Thanks, I don't want a dozen; one would be enough. I was going to propose to a dairy-maid the other day, but her banns were asked twice, and she married a young butcher. I wrote a poem about her: shall I repeat it?"

"In heaven's name, no!" said Granby. "You will end by marrying Mrs. Prout."

"Will you have me, Prout?" said Lord Oakshott, for Mrs. Prout was at the other end of the room.

"No, my lord," she said; "it is bother enough keeping your house, without keeping a fantastic, half-witted creature like you."

"They all turn from me," said Lord Oakshott. "Even Prout refuses me. But Granby, old boy, what do you advise about Dickie?"

"D——n Dickie! but I will tell you. Mother O'Brien is in London—in Park Lane. Come and match your wits against hers. In spite of all your folly, you are the cleverest man I know. You can find out what she knows in ten minutes."

"I will do so."

"That's like yourself. Do make the best of yourself. Remember that if our late conversation were reported, you would probably be sent to Bedlam."

"Let me recite to you another poem," said Lord Oakshott.

"If you do, I will shy this cigar in your face," said Granby.

"Let us get on with these statistics about the girls, then," said Oakshott. "I wonder if one of them would marry me."

"She would be a precious fool if she did," said Granby.

They went out on the lawn as soon as Granby had unpacked his blue-books. Lord Oakshott sang—

> "Thy feet are set amidst the grass,
>   With lilies round them blowing."

Granby listened.

"How well you sing, Oakshott. What a pity it is that you don't sing other men's sense instead of your own nonsense. After all, there was no one like old Ben Jonson."

"That was the best thing he ever wrote," said Oakshott.

"By far," said Granby.

"Why," said Oakshott, "I wrote that myself to the young woman who married the butcher."

"I have heard the air before," said Granby.

"'Drink to me only with thine eyes,'" said Oakshott. "Or will you have your claret out here?"

"Let us go into these statistics, you fantastical Spaniard."

By twelve o'clock Oakshott was sufficiently well posted up, and at eight o'clock in the morning he went off with Granby to town.

CHAPTER XXV.

AN AFTERNOON PARTY.

COMFREY was utterly amazed to see him. He was under the impression that he was a thing of the past. Not at all ; here he was, just as fantastic as ever—in fact, considerably more so. He had rooms on the ground-floor—he would go no higher—and, while preparing himself for his speech in the House, showed his old low tendencies by walking out with his hands in his pockets, and standing with his legs very wide apart, in the middle of the street.

M. Thiers was upstairs on the first floor, and the mere existence of M. Thiers was a pet objection of his; so, casting about matters in his mind, Oakshott succeeded, at one o'clock in the day, in getting hold of a Punch and Judy show, which at some expense he induced to perform in front of his window, he sitting with the window open and applauding. Comfrey was furious ; but Oakshott was a good customer, having no town-house, and he only relieved his mind to the head waiter. When the performance was over, and Brook Street clear, Lord Oakshott went up and called on M. Thiers, and discussed the Punch and Judy with him.

Having satisfied his soul by making a fool of himself, he became rational. He dressed himself very carefully, and went to an afternoon party in Grosvenor Square, to which he was not invited.

Old Emily was very glad to see him, and told him he was late. As she knew that she had not asked him, and thought he was in Devonshire, she thought that she had better say that, and so she said it.

"I never got your letter," said Lord Oakshott.

"Well, as I never sent one," said the good old woman, " I do not suppose that you did. But I am glad to see you : I am *really* glad to see you. Come and have something."

" I *will* come and have something," said Lord Oakshott ; " I will come and have your advice."

" You shall have it, my dear; but I must attend to the good people. This party is more troublesome than Mrs. Sprowles. What do you want to know ? Quick—here are more people coming."

" I want to know where the Duchesse d'Avranches is."

" She is here."

" I should not be here if she were not likely to be. Advise me."

" Deal with her like a snake that wants money. If you want anything of her, you must pay." This was in a whisper; then came, " How do you do, my dear Lord P. ?"

Lord P. was perfectly well (he always was). He turned to Oakshott and said, " What a pity it is that you are a poet. I wish we could trust you on business."

" Pray never do that," said Oakshott. " I paid my cousin's debts the other day—sixty thousand pounds ; and now I am going to match my wits against a woman's."

"Lord help you," said Lord P. "What woman?"

"The Duchesse d'Avranches."

"She sits there," said Lord P.: "just glance towards her, and talk earnestly to me. Talk about the weather and the crops, but glance at her—I know why. Do you want a hold on her?"

"I have it, and she has one on me."

"Why have you come to town?"

"To speak to-night."

"Good. I can never forgive your fearful *fiasco*, but I wish you entirely well. Your impertinence to me was very bad ; it was a *mauvaise plaisanterie*. You should not play foolish jokes on a man of my position. Now that I have given you a scolding, go and fight your woman ; and if she is in any way *difficile*, ask her when she is going to Vienna."

There was no time to ask for an explanation. And Oakshott at that time did not entirely understand Lord P.: so he approached the Duchesse d'Avranches rather unprepared for battle.

She was, however. She hurled her cavalry at him before he had time to speak.

Oakshott at once formed square with amazing dexterity, and took the defensive.

"What have you been hearing of me?" she asked.

"Nothing."

"I saw you and P. talking together, and you were talking of me, for you glanced towards me."

"Your name was scarcely mentioned. He only wondered why you never went to Vienna."

"I answer," said the Lancashire woman, "Because I dare

not : because I am a spy. Answer this : If I dare to go to Vienna, will you dare to go to Naples ?"

"Most emphatically not," said Lord Oakshott, laughing so loud that every one looked round. " I should have a knife in my ribs in five minutes. My dear soul, don't talk like a lunatic. Fancy my going to Naples."

"I wish you would get me an ice before you play your next move," said the Duchesse. " I like a game of chess or whist like another. Fetch me an ice, and then move your next piece. Stay half a moment, Oakshott, before we begin to play. Please consider that this is a perfectly friendly game. I don't rank your wits high ; but if I was younger, I would marry you."

" Oh no, you would not," said Lord Oakshott. " Do not think it." So he went for the ice, and came back laughing.

" Now," she said, "you move next."

" Well, as I have emphatically refused to marry you, I in a general way want to know what you have done with Dickie."

" I got him stolen by a gipsy."

" *Exactly* ; but what have you done with him ?",

" Check to my king," said the Duchesse. " How about Gipp's Land Gold Mining Company ?"

" Pawn move," said Lord Oakshott. " Well, H—— and P—— wrote to me overland to say that they had struck stone at eighteen ounces to the ton, and I have bought in to the tune of eight thousand pounds. I expect they will rise sixty per cent. ; if they rise to forty, I shall sell out. If you buy in, don't hold on too long, because this quartz is apt to be too flashy and deceiving at the surface. The Great Vic- toria at the Avoca holds out, but all do not."

"Thanks," said Mrs. O'Brien. "I will make my next pawn move. We are playing for the boy. Lake Superior Copper?"

"How much do you hold?"

"Four thousand; I bought at sixty."

"Sell out. It won't go higher for some years. It is at a hundred and thirty-five."

"You would not hold on?"

"*I* have sold out," said Lord Oakshott. "Now your next move."

"I want a good thing," said Mrs. O'Brien.

Lord Oakshott rubbed his nose with his hat, and then he whispered to her. No person but those two ever heard the dreadful secret. Mrs. O'Brien said years afterwards, when she was living in state in Rutland Gardens: "My dear, it was young Brogden who gave the office to Oakshott to get out in time. Oashott stayed in and paid his shot like a man—I will say that for him. He was, however, only slightly dipped; but when I got the office, *I*, as an unprotected female, came out."

After the dreadful secret was told, Lord Oakshott said: "Check your queen. Where is Dickie?"

"Oakshott," she said, "you are a good man; and I tell you fairly that I don't know. Your innocence is completely established in my mind. I tried to get that boy taken from you because I thought that you had wronged my daughter. I do not think so now. I do not know what has become of the boy."

"Woman," whispered Lord Oakshott, "if you lie to me, I will ruin you. I will smash everything you are concerned in, if I sweep a crossing."

"I won't lie to you, Oakshott. The gipsies lost the boy; and he is wandering about on the face of the earth."

CHAPTER XXVI.

THE RECTOR AGAIN.

How did Dickie get to Crediton from Dartmouth? It was a very singular journey, most singular in such a mere child; but he got there, and he can remember a great deal about it. It is a most remarkable thing that he remembers more about it as time goes on.

Among the ships at Dartmouth he met the sailors, and he lived with them for some time. He was only a little beggar. Sailors are often little better; and he was popular among them. They petted him, and he grew to love them. They called him "the little gentleman," a thing which Dickie always denied.

"I am a fisherman's son," he always said, when they called him a gentleman. And indeed, after some of them had seen him bathing, there was no doubt that he was a fisherman or sailor's son. His body was tattooed all over, actually with large designs on parts of the body which are not generally seen even at Eton unless a boy is bathing. Oakshott's fishermen's sons were a very rough lot, and would tattoo a man anywhere if he gave them the chance. However, Dickie was so far tattooed that he passed for a sailor's boy.

He wanted to go to sea, but he was far too young. He showed his capacity for going to sea in a most emphatic manner, however.

There was a great gale from the south-west; every ship in

the offing had got in, save one brig with her foretopmast gone. She could not make the harbour, but was trying to claw off. It was a hopeless business; she would be on the rocks in half an hour. The lifeboat was brought down; and the men, answering to their names, went into her. The last man who went into her was the coxswain, and he never came out of her again alive.

No one else chose to see Dickie get in; every one was quite blind; but in he got. When they were launched, an easy thing in smooth water, he appeared between the coxswain's legs, and said " Shove away !" The men all laughed; and as it was evident that they could not put Dickie back, they let him go on.

· It was pleasant enough while they were in harbour; but when they got outside it was not so agreeable. The boat slopped herself nearly full three times, and Dickie had not a dry rag on his body. However, he liked it: there is no accounting for tastes.

He sat between the coxswain's knees; after the boat had emptied herself the third time, they approached the wreck.

She was on the reef; she had struck, and the sea was coming over her in great cascades. There was no chance of saving her; the only chance was to save the men. That would have been easily done, for the water was not very rough on the lee of the rock. Suddenly, however, the mizen-mast came down on them, and killed the coxswain.

Dickie was not hurt, and he did not know at all that the coxswain was dead. He thought that he was only stunned. The men left their oars and cleared the wreck of the mizen-topmast.' During this time the boat had drifted some hundred yards to the leeward. There was no hope of salvage, and an easy way home before the wind.

But there arose a cry on the night wind which made every sailor look at his brother sailor. As I said, the hope of any salvage was gone ; but they heard the men calling for help on the rocks or on the ship, they knew not which. The coxswain was stunned, and they had no commander. " We must go back to them," was the general agreement ; "but who will take the helm ?"

" I will do that," said the child. " I am very strong ; and I have steered a boat. I have steered Earlie's boat often and often."

" Let the child do it," said the oldest of the crew, a Methodist. " God is abroad on the storm. Let the child do it. Give way all !"

They gave way, these splendid fellows, and Dickie took the helm. They got up once more under the lee of the reef, and they got their men off. It was not discovered that their coxswain was dead until they got into Dartmouth. But dead he was, struck on the head by the mizen-mast. He was dead beyond all doubt.

There was an inquest on him, and the verdict on him was that he met with an accidental death while performing his duty—a most proper verdict. But, unfortunately, the Coroner had on blue spectacles, and they frightened Dickie out of his life.

" This, sir," said the commandant of the coastguard, " is the gallant boy who has covered himself with honour by taking the lifeboat in under the reef."

That was all very well, but it by no means accounted for the blue spectacles. Dickie said so in fact.

"I don't care about steering a boat, but I am not going to be put here and exasperated by an old fool in blue spectacles."

The sailors all laughed.

"Boy! boy!" said the Coroner, "do you know to whom you are talking?"

"I don't know, and I don't care," said Dickie. "I only know that I am not going to be bullied by an old fool like you. I am only afraid of your spectacles, not of you."

The sailor interest was very strong, and the Coroner was afraid of it. "Child," he said, "what is your name?"

"I don't know," said Dickie, "because Dickie is no name at all. What is yours?"

"Augustus Algernon Jamieson Clark," said the Coroner.

"Then you must have had three godfathers," said Dickie. "Look here, sir, I want to speak to you. I am a poor little fellow. I am older than Earlie thinks I am, but not so very old. I know *that.* If you will let me go this time, I will promise never to go on board of a lifeboat again."

Murmur among the sailors.

"We shall get nothing out of this witness," said the Coroner.

Dickie was dismissed, and sped out of the town.

He had been frightened, sadly frightened. Knowing nothing of criminal procedure, he was under the belief that he was in some way on his trial, and the child thought that he was flying from justice. One thing is certain, however; the boy was much older than Lord Oakshott conceived him to be. It is wildly possible that Mrs. O'Brien and Lady Oakshott know more than they choose to tell us.

Granby Dixon, in his loose and improper way of speaking, told me the other day that he would give a hundred pounds, from sheer curiosity, to know Dickie's exact age. His theory is that Sir Arthur was married whole years before it ever was announced, and that Sir Richard (Dickie) is several years older than he claims to be. Against Lady Oakshott's character Granby says not one word. Let us, however, follow Dickie.

Knowing about the world a good deal, I always found some people turning up in unexpected places. As far as my knowledge of the world serves me, I think that the people who turn up in the most unexpected manner are officers of Engineers, officers of Artillery, and parsons. You are never safe with these three classes of men, for you meet them always when you least expect them. Probably, however, your parson is the man who astonishes you more than the Artillery or Engineer officer. Busnack, of some college in Oxford or Cambridge, gets his degree, gets ordained, and has a curacy. He is lost sight of. Years roll on, and he is only a pleasant memory to you; when one day you are riding through the bush, all alone, thinking of the old college, and you meet a bevy of black fellows, running like mad, with spears and torches, ready to be lighted at dusk. You naturally ask if it is the Governor. No, it is only the Bishop. And here comes Busnack along among the acacias, riding with an apron over his stomach. The old boy has developed into an Angela Bishop.

No such change, however, had passed over the Rector of Dickie's acquaintance. He had merely got the living of Crediton, and that is the reason why Dickie came across him once more.

Dickie sped away, as he thought, with an avenging angel after him. A coroner in blue spectacles is naturally alarming ; to the child's mind he was utterly terrible. Dickie had some money, and he had kept his locket carefully concealed, always putting it in his clothes before he went to bathe. The child was not absolutely ill-provided for a few days ; the sailors had made him many little presents since the life-boat adventure. He was by no means afraid of his adventure, and had bread and cheese at Totness.

Then he began to see the river in its magnificent beauty : he had seen no stream like this before. This was like Abana and Pharpar, better than all the rivers of Judea. The boy had hitherto only been used to chalk downs, and to the bright streams which came from their interior or invisible channels. Now, for the first time, he saw a river-bed from the surface. Every trickling tiny lade, every foaming brook, told its own story : and the story to Dickie was, "My darling, we are hurrying to the sea ; we cannot stay and speak to you."

The flowing river himself talked always to the boy, and, though angry just now, was always kind to him. There had been a great deal of rain on Cawsand, and the river was hurling itself dark brown round Benjay Tor. The river said to him, "My little love, I cannot stay to speak to you now ; you must come to me again."

Between the granite rocks, out of the dark brown water, there leaped a sheet of silver three feet long. It was not a trout, for Dickie knew trout : and he wondered what fish it could be. The fish wanted to go up one place, and Dickie clambered over the rocks with a view of helping it. The fish was very much exhausted, and Dickie took it out to rest it, which showed that he had not studied natural history very much. It was very easy to take the fish out of the water. I have seen a lady take one out, when it was trying to get up.

Dickie stroked it, as if that was any good. A voice in his ear said, "Put the fish back."

Dickie obeyed ; he always did. The fish made a fresh rush at the stream, and then got over. Dickie saw his black tail go up over the top of the waterfall. Then he turned to see who had spoken to him. It was a very curious gentleman indeed, dressed in grey, very pale, and very hoarse. Dickie, though sharp enough, could not make him out. He settled in his mind that he was either a poet, a novelist, or a journalist. He was not any one of them : he was an escaped convict from Dartmoor Prison. Dickie thought that he was an eccentric gentleman of those parts, possibly of large property.

"Could you tell me sir," said Dickie, "what the name of that beautiful fish was ?"

" It was a salmon of twenty pounds, my child. Will you answer me a question ? What money have you ?"

" I have eleven and sixpence," said Dickie.

"Will you give me five shillings."

"Yes, sir, certainly."

"God bless you, my child," said the convict. "I could have taken it from you, but I cannot do a mean action. I am an honest man, my boy, though I am an escaped prisoner."

" If you are an escaped prisoner," said Dickie, "you should go to Earlie. We have the Castle full of them sometimes ; that is all I know."

" Who is Earlie ?" said the convict.

" I can't tell," said Dickie. "My head is all wrong.

Here are the five shillings. They misguided me, you know, and I can't remember anything. I can't remember Earlie's real name to save my life. But he had some other name than Earlie before they gave me that stuff, I warrant you."

The convict left the child, having taken his money. The child sat by the snarling river for a time, and then went upwards.

He thinks that he slept at farmhouses, but it is emphatically certain that his memory was at this time completely gone. I think that he must have crossed from the valley of the Dart to the valley of the Teign, for he most emphatically says that he went up through Gidleigh Park before he got to the summit of the awful Cawsand.

When he got there the poor little fellow lay down to die. He was beaten out all round. He was actually going to sleep, when he heard some one saying, " Hein! Hein! But this is not a Britannic fortification after all."

Dickie knew the next voice perfectly well; it was that of the Rector whom he had seen fishing on the Otter, in furious anger.

"You have the whole thing before you, Count. I will not trust myself to say anything more."

The Rector had a *spécialité* about Dartmoor which he worked a little too hard. He had a great Brittany authority as his guest, the Comte de Coutances. This Comte de Coutances led him the life of a dog. He denied Grampound, and utterly turned up his nose at Drewsteignton. They fought so furiously that it was reported at Crediton that the Rector's housekeeper slept with a loaded gun in her room. The Rector said that the Dolmen at Dol was no Dolmen at all.

But this was after they found Dickie. I cannot go into the argument. What is more to the purpose is, that they were wrangling at the top of Cawsand, and that their wrangling was stopped by finding Dickie.

(Granby Dixon got a ship sent to inquire into the matter about the Dolmen at Dol, because Jones, R.N., had nothing to do, but had influence. On the whole it was the cheapest plan, because his coal bill was so heavy that he has never had a ship since.)

" Here is something which will stop our quarrel," said the Frenchman. " Here is a boy dying."

It was only too true : the boy was very near death. He was lying under the Cairn when they found him, and they carried him down to the Rector's dog-cart.

The Rector took him home to Crediton, and, moreover, took great care of him. He recognized him, and was more and more puzzled by him. The boy was a mere ragged little rascal, still he seemed a gentleman.

There is one thing to be said, however : you could never have *made* a gentleman of Dickie. He was *born* one.

One of the most gentlemanly young fellows I ever met was a chimney-sweep. I told him that his manners were very good, and he said, "Yes, sir, we get licked into that, *the same as the young gents do down the river there at Eton.*" Spicer most likely ate with his knife, and committed all sorts of small faults of which he could have been cured in a week ; but he could never say a coarse word to a woman, or a hard word to a child. How many gentlemen can say that?

I must, however, follow Dickie. He met the Rector, and the Rector was very good to him. Dickie desired entirely to run away, but he hurt his foot, and the Rector got possession of his person for weeks. But the Rector was a severe man, and put Dickie to work in the garden, which Dickie did not like. He and the Rector had many conversations on this point. The Rector found him digging one day, and the boy began—

" Earlie never made me dig ; I don't like it."

Said the Rector, " Earlie, whoever he is, should have made you dig ; idleness is the worst thing in the world for boys. You were late at church yesterday."

" I *hate* church : Earlie never went."

" Earlie was a wicked man, then," said the Rector.

The boy broke into a fury of passionate tears. " Earlie was a gentleman. He was not a common parson like you. He lived in a castle, and for my part I love castles better than parsonages. I am a nobleman."

The Rector was half inclined to believe the boy. " Who *is* this Earlie ?" he asked.

" Why, he is Earlie ; he is the Earl of something."

" Cannot you remember of what ?"

" No, I cannot remember at all. Dixie and I never called him anything but Earlie. But he lived in a castle by the sea, and Mrs. Prout lived with him."

The Rector smelt a rat. The child was the illegitimate child of some nobleman, and Mrs. Prout was that nobleman's mistress.

" Boy," he said, " the misfortunes of your birth shall not cut you off from my kindness. Will you behave well ?"

" No."

" I shall have to beat you if you do not."

" I shall kick you in the gaiters if you do.'

" Have you read Mrs. Sherwood's ' Infant Pilgrims,' which

I lent you ?   Did you read about Inbred Sin, who went with the children ?"

" Yes."

" What did you think of *him ?*"

" I thought he was the only fellow worth a halfpenny among the lot.   I wish *I* knew him—what fun we would have !"

" Did not the examples of the other children strike you ?"

" I was sorry they killed Peace," said Dickie, leaning on his spade.   " But the other two were utter duffers.   As for Humble Mind, he was a muff, and if I got him here I would punch his head.   Inbred Sin is the one I should most like to imitate.   I'd bet he could swim, and I'd bet Humble Mind couldn't."

The Rector was utterly aghast.   He only found time to say—

" Can you swim, then ?"

Dickie solved that matter by dropping his spade and pitching himself head over heels into the Rector's carp-pond, which was close to them.   The pond was from ten to twelve feet deep, as the Rector well knew, and full of water-lilies. The boy went down, and did not come up again.   The Rector kicked off his shoes and dashed in after him.

He swam about with his head out of water, but no boy. At last, at the further end of the pond he saw some lily-heads move, and he swam towards them.   He found the boy had been lying on his back laughing at him for about three minutes.

When they were dripping on the bank together, the Rector said—

“You must not play such tricks, sir.”

“Why not?” said Dickie.

“You have spoilt me a new suit of clothes,” said the Rector.

“Why did not you stay on the bank, then?” said Dickie.

“Because I could not see a boy like you, hard-hearted and unconverted, launched into eternity, without making an effort to save him.”

Dickie’s face flushed up. “You are a good man. You are not so good as Earlie. When I come into my property I will make Earlie give you a living, or make you a Bishop. In our bay our grooms can swim, and also our footmen—miles out. When I find Earlie, you shall come and see us swim. You must not take off your clothes before the others, because you are a clergyman ; and Earlie cannot, because he, being in the House of Lords, has to attend to etiquette.’

“What is the name of your bay?” said the Rector.

“Oakshott.”

“What is the name of the man you call Earlie?”

“Why, Earlie, you silly man. I am very cold, and must get my clothes off.”

The Rector took him in, and accounted to his housekeeper for the state they were in, in the best way possible. Dickie was of course put to bed, and when he was in bed with a warm posset, the housekeeper came and aired her mind to the Rector.

“John saw what happened,” said the old woman, “and so it is no use to prevaricate. The little devil tried to drown himself, and you fished him out. He is a little gipsy, that one. He is not only tattooed on his left arm, but all over, in figures which I believe to be heathenish, on his——" say arms and legs.

"Have they punctured the child's arms?" said the Rector.

"Come and look for yourself," said the housekeeper. " There is a ship in full sail on one arm, and a lighthouse on the other."

"The child must have been among the sailors," said the Rector.

"That don't matter to me," said the housekeeper. "You come and look at the child's body."

The Rector said not one word.

"Ah, you want to exasperate me by silence, do you?" she said. "I won't have the little villain in the house, I tell you. I have not been here so many years to be put out of the way by a little varlet like that. That fool John let him have the nozzle of the garden hose to-day, and I came out to look at the flowers, and he turned it on me. I was wet——"

And the good lady went into details which only old age can justify; and she ended by saying that she would not stay in the house one moment longer, if the little wretch remained there.

The Rector lit a cigar, and then said—

" Mrs. Dickson."

" Sir to you."

"Would you have the goodness to pack up your things and get off, Mrs. Dickson?"

" Do you mean it?"

"I do. I am going to be married, Mrs. Dickson, and my new wife has a temper of her own. As you have once more used language to me which I disapprove of, I think we will part, if you please."

She went without one word. She had made a good harvest out of the Rector, and she guessed that he was going to be married; but she had bullied him so long that she had thought that she might bully him longer. She was quite unprepared for this.

Women will bully men until some fine morning they find a hitherto perfectly submissive man, who throws all past relations to the wind, and balances his book inexorably. Men will bully women until some fine morning they find, not a submissive wife or sister, but an angry woman overstating her case. And an angry woman overstating her case is not a very pleasant thing to deal with. Bullying is the most fearful mistake on the face of the earth.

As a general rule, as far as my experience goes, men will stand more of it from women than women will from men. When a *gentleman* like the Rector gets over-bullied, he simply states his case. When a man, not a gentleman, gets over-bullied, he recriminates. That is a great mistake: the weapon of a man is his tongue; the weapon of a woman is absolute silence or perfect acquiescence. No woman ever found out this except the late Mrs. Shandy, and *she* was the creation of a man.

The Rector, however, was by no means what the Americans call a "one-horse power" any longer. A beautiful woman had accepted him, and he cared no more for all the old catamarans in Europe, than he did for the plagues of Egypt. He knew that Mrs. Dickson would play him some trick or another, and looked to his wife to defend him. Meanwhile he had got the name from the boy, and he took down the

" Peerage and Baronetage," looking up in both the name of "Oakshott."

As he read, his memory came back. He nearly remembered the whole thing. He had heard it talked about at All Souls. Lord Oakshott was the poet and lunatic. This Sir Arthur Oakshott was the baronet and swindler whose debts Lord Oakshott had paid. Some Fellow of All Souls had told him of it. By heavens, it was Granby Dixon! He opened the window and called his groom.

" James, you took my note to Lord Haston's this morning ?"

" Yes, sir."

" Who was there ? You saw all the grooms, I suppose ?"

" Yes, sir. There was Mrs. Caston, Mr. Belsher, the Sheriff, and Mr. Granby Dixon, staying in the house, and——"

" Get the brougham ready," said the Rector.

He drove over to Lord Haston's to a dinner which he had declined. Granby Dixon had been called to London on important public business, but Lord Haston knew enough to assure him that Dickie was the boy of whom Granby Dixon had been speaking, and who was lost.

He went home, and up to the garret in which the boy slept. He intended to turn the key, but the key was already turned.

He unlocked the door and went in. The bed was empty, and the window was open.

CHAPTER XXVII.

DICKIE AT THE POLICE COURT.

A BOY, whose head reached very little above the dock, was brought before Mr. Hall at Bow Street, charged with having no visible means of subsistence. The case excited great sympathy, for the poor child had only just been brought from the hospital. Inspector Brown said that he thought he had better bring the case here. The boy had been six weeks in hospital. The boy had seen a child lying in the road in a street in the Seven Dials, and the little hero darted forward in front of a butcher's cart, and had thrown the child on the footway; saving the child, but getting knocked down and being stunned himself. Police-constable Moriarty saw the thing happen, and was rebuked in Court for saying that "Be Jabers, he was a plucky little divil entirely." The house-surgeon of the Charing Cross Hospital said that the boy had sustained a most severe concussion of the brain, and that his life had been in extreme danger. If the child received proper care and attention, there was nothing to prevent his doing well; the child was singularly well-grown and handsome, and from the child's habits and from the few clothes he had left when the accident happened, it was quite evident that he had been delicately brought up. One of the first things which the boy had asked for was a tooth-brush.

"Unhappily, however," the good surgeon continued, "that has happened here which occasionally does happen. The boy has entirely lost his memory."

" What is your name, my child ?" said the magistrate.

"I don't know, sir ; indeed I don't. I can't remember anything at all before the hospital."

" Poor little fellow!" said the magistrate. " Will he regain his memory, doctor ?"

" It is very improbable ; he is so very young. He will form new associations and new impressions, and he will practically begin life again. I recommended this course in the first instance. A boy who is a hero at nine cannot be sent to a workhouse or a reformatory. He is a most gentle and grateful little fellow also ; and he cried because he could not remember his prayers, but the nurse has taught him new ones, which shows that his mind is not affected, only his memory."

The boy was told to stand down, and he did so for half an hour, at the end of which time he was put in the dock again. Two young ladies, who did not seem to have done their hair lately, politely making room for him, and going out, he heard one say to the other, " Two months ain't much, Jess ; don't round on Bill :" and the other said, " No fear ; good-bye, old girl." Then the boy found himself behind the spikes agian, and a gentleman in a state of violent perspiration in the witness-box.

" I have come as fast as I could, your worship."

"So I should conclude from your personal appearance," said the magistrate, good-humouredly. " Your feet are swift to do good. Well, can you manage this boy for us?"

"Oh, yes, your worship. Would the gentlemen of the press be kind enough to say a word for me? I am the superintendent of the Home for Houseless Boys in Orman Street. We take in any boys we can catch. We will take this boy with pleasure. We try, gentlemen of the press, to find out which way their talents lie, and then we develop them. Would you say, your worship and gentlemen, that we are not rich, and that we live from hand to mouth?"

"My poor boy," said the magistrate, "will you go with this gentleman?"

"I had sooner," said the nameless boy, "go with the doctor and the nurse, but I will go with this gentleman if you tell me; I was told always to obey orders."

"Who told you?" said the doctor, sharply and keenly, hoping for some one glimpse of memory. The magistrate also leant over "with parted lips and straining eyes."

"I don't know," said the boy simply. "Somebody told it to me before I died. I have been dead, sir, you know; and doctor and nurse brought me to life."

"Can you remember nothing, my poor child?" said the magistrate.

"There were the white primroses, and I should not have gone for them."

"Who sent you for them?" said the magistrate.

"I don't know; I can't remember."

The magistrate called the doctor to come to him while he had his lunch. Meanwhile the boy was once more taken away, and the gentleman waited.

"Is this imbecility, my dear sir?"

"No; loss of memory," said the doctor. "The boy says he was dead; practically he was. The boy is bright and sharp enough, and will probably grow into a very fine fellow. Do you believe in the immortality of the soul?"

"Certainly."

"Immortality involves eternity, and if you believe in a

future state you must believe in a past one. How much do you remember of your past state ?"

"Very little : only sometimes I know that I have done the same things and uttered the same words previously."

"We all know what that is," said the doctor. "That boy is in the same state in which we are. He can't remember anything except the white primroses, which is very strange."

"Can he read and write ?" said the magistrate.

"Not one word or one sentence," said the doctor. "But he has been *taught*. He holds a pencil or pen as well as you or I."

"Let us have him in here," said the magistrate, "before I go back to my filthy drudgery."

The child was brought in, and the gentleman from Orman Street came also. The boy was a singularly beautiful one, but with a slightly vacant expression. He spoke first.

"If you please, sir, I should like very much to go with this gentleman. Through him I feel sure that I should find my way to——"

Here came a hopeless look, sad to see ; and the boy burst into tears.

"This is a splendid case," said the doctor. "Winslow, Tuke, and Bucknill must all see this case. Now, my pretty boy, sing to the magistrate the first verse of the hymn which the lady visitor taught you in the convalescent ward."

The boy folded his hands, and sang the first verse of a hymn with exquisite pathos and power. The voice of the boy was so strong that it was heard in the witness-room, in a place where few sounds were ever heard, save oaths, recriminations, and foul talk.

" There is no imbecility *there*," said the magistrate, wiping his spectacles. " Sir, I thank you for taking the boy; he may go."

" You have a country establishment, have you not?" said the doctor.

" Yes, doctor."

" Send him there. I want his lungs to expand. Good-bye, my pretty fellow. Here is half-a-crown for you. Good-bye."

The boy cried very much at parting with the doctor, but the good gentleman got him a very fine bun, and he went along quietly enough.

CHAPTER XXVIII.

DICKIE AND THE RIETONS.

THE boy went away with the gentleman, and it so happened that the gentleman was going to take charge of the country establishment with his wife, having, so to speak, served his time in Orman Street; and so our boy was but a short time there. When the gentleman and his wife moved, the boy with no name went with them.

Let me pause to say one word for the London charities. As a matter of course there should be no charities, but there are such things, and Granby Dixon accidentally has had to examine one half of them in a semi-official manner. In every one of them he finds the same man: a bright-eyed, pleasant man, doing the work of a slave for love, with a salary little over that of a so-called working man. He could name these men by the dozen. They get but small recognition, and are not, as a rule, long-lived. He says that he could mention two very peculiar types of them, but refrains from doing so. They, as he said before, work for love. Our gentleman was one of these, and his wife backed him up most loyally.

Such couples are often without children. They do an immense amount of good in the State, but the worry attendant on their work generally prevents the woman from having any children. Our couple, however, had one child, just of our boy's age, and it so happened that not only did the two children fall in love with one another, but Mrs. Ribton fell in love with our nameless boy.

The simple and gentle couple went before the Board of Directors and told their story plainly. Ribton did not deny that Mrs. Ribton was going to have a child again, to their great surprise, but it might be a boy or a girl for anything he knew. Mrs. Ribton had taken a great fancy to our boy, and he wished the consent of the Board to Mrs. Ribton's adopting the boy.

The Board hemmed and hawed a great deal, but at last concluded most wisely that it was no earthly business of theirs, and so consented. *The consequence was, the boy was never advertised.*

Mrs. Ribton was confined far too late in life, and at too long an interval. The consequence was puerperal madness, with all its horrors. The baby had to be kept from her, and our boy and little Ribton, sleeping together, used to hear her yelling and raving, until she was taken away to the Surrey Lunatic Asylum.

The baby died. Our boy and little Ribton continued to sleep together until a terrible event occurred. Mr. Ribton,

who always slept in the room with them, had been to see
Mrs. Ribton in the Lunatic Asylum. When our boy woke
in the morning he went to rouse Mr. Ribton. His bed was
covered with blood, and our boy ran away crying for help.
The poor fellow's last view of his mad wife had been too
much for him. He had quietly made away with himself.

Then there was a complete change : an old military
officer came as manager, and Georgy Ribton got a pre-
sentation to the Bluecoat School. (He is now second
master of the Todmorden School, and there is nothing to
prevent his becoming a Bishop.) Our nameless boy was
thrown amongst the other boys, with the solitary name
which the gentle, kind Ribtons had invented for him,—
" James Richardson."

Granby Dixon said to me once, "Why does God plague
such good people so ? I cannot think. I went to see
Mrs. Ribton to-day, and afterwards went to the Opera.
N—— was on in *Lucia di Lammermoor.* When the last
scene came she could scarcely sing to my mind. The difference between real madness and feigned is so great.
Sometimes it seems to me that God is cruel."

I repudiated the proposition with utter scorn. But the
man who made it to me did not seem convinced then.
He has come into my way of thinking since. God is never
cruel. Even when you are rebellious, He is kind.

A case like Mrs. Ribton's is a great puzzle. As I have
no solution to offer with regard to such cases, I will offer
none. The case of an overworked governess in Bedlam,
who had been trying to keep her mother out of the workhouse, and had gone mad from overwork, was a great puzzle
to me. It seemed to arraign the justice of God. The case

of Mrs. Ribton again is a frightful puzzle. A life given to good works: a woman who had saved endless boys and girls from worse than death,—and the reward in this world a strait-waistcoat, and a howling, yelling devil, uttering blasphemies and impurities from between the pretty lips which beforehand had only been open to preach the Gospel and bring souls to Christ.

Horrible! Yes. Go to Bedlam and see for yourselves, and you will find that I am not telling untruths. From some strange affection which touched the brain, Mrs. Ribton was changed from a gentle woman into a howling, hopeless lunatic.

Still every bud and every flower tells one to hope. And we do hope.

CHAPTER XXIX.

LORD OAKSHOTT WRITES ANOTHER SONG AT A WRONG TIME.

I BEG of you to understand that Captain Aston, poor Ribton's successor, was by no means like Ribton. Any one could have made a fool of poor Ribton. The whole Board of Admiralty could not have made a fool of Captain Aston, R.N.

Granby Dixon got him this place when he was Under Secretary to the Admiralty. Granby would have given him the *Chichester* herself to get rid of him, but he was not fit for the *Chichester*, and the commander of that ship had been doing such noble work that all England knew of it. Captain Aston was a very needy man. The place was worth £300 a year; and Granby, by subscribing for my Lords £100 to the institution in Orman Street, in reality had a great deal to say about the nomination of Captain Aston. As for Granby's manœuvres, I have nothing to do with them at all.

It is emphatically certain, however, that Granby got Captain Aston this place. That Captain Aston accepted it, and that a fortnight afterwards he met Granby in St. James's Street and offered to pull his nose for twopence, is a matter of history. It was very sad : it happened in front of Crook's Club, and all the members came out to see the fun.

The thing was quite wrongly reported in the newspapers. Lord Edmondbury and Sir Harry Mallory saw the whole affair. They agree in saying that Granby had the best of it, and that Lord H—— was wrong in asking him to resign. Aston made an effort at our dear Granby's nose, whereupon Granby got hold of *his*—a most magnificent Wellingtonian nose (whereas you might have missed Granby's in the dark). Mutual friends interfered.

The upshot of the matter was that Captain Aston, R.N., refused to keep his appointment; and, moreover, that Granby Dixon emphatically refused to give up his. Said Granby Dixon to Lord H——, " I won't resign. The beggar told me in the public street that he would pull my nose, and I pulled his. You gave me that place for him, and that is the last thing I will ask you for; but resign— never !"

The whole affair was unutterably absurd. It was not the first time that Granby had committed himself. He never could be trusted with high office, clever as he was. It was one thing with him one day, and something else the day after. Matters, for example, were just mended between Granby and Captain Aston. They had, in fact, only parted (the best of friends) about ten minutes, when Granby, who drove very badly, got emptied out of his cab at the Piccadilly corner of Bond Street, and cut his face, so that he was unable to show at his office for a month.

We must, however, return to Captain Aston, nearly as unlucky a man as Granby himself. He had had four ships ashore in his time, and the wreck of the *Incomparable*, with Captain Aston's heroic conduct in refusing to leave the ship until every man was gone, is one of the brightest pages in our naval history. Captain Aston was accustomed to say that he would sail any of her Majesty's ships, from somewhere beginning with an H, to Hackney. But he never did it. There was a party against him at the Board, and he never was allowed to sail his ship from either place. But for all this it was perfectly notorious that Aston was an old fool : he had immense interest, however, and it was necessary to shelve him. Granby managed that ; and Captain Aston wanted to pull his nose for doing it.

Aston had one great *spécialité*, however ; he was one of the finest amateur musicians in Europe. No sooner had he taken possession of the school than its character was changed. In Ribton's time boys were advanced for general good conduct ; in Aston's time they were advanced for music. Captain Aston never got another ship, and was ultimately made Governor of the Gaboon. His single-handed encounter, when he had only a knife, with a gigantic gorilla, bigger than himself, will be remembered by every one. Also the paper which he wrote for the Physiological Society, proving that the roar of the gorilla was four notes lower than Lablanche's lowest note—making, in fact, less than 15,000 vibrations per second. The gorilla scratched him in the most pestilent manner on the face, and tore that sainted man's trowsers off his body. When he came back to England, Granby Dixon openly expressed his wish that the gorilla had won. "Fellows like that," said Granby, "have no business to turn up again after they have been properly provided for. If a man is sent to the Gaboon, he is expected to die. If he comes back alive, he swindles the nation. That fellow will not die, Oakshott: you mark my words. That fellow and his gorilla will live long after we have been bored into our graves."

"The gorilla is dead, at all events," said Oakshott.

"You are so awfully green," said Granby Dixon, pettishly. "The gorilla was never alive until Aston killed it. That stuffed gorilla will get him a first-class colonial appointment, and the sooner he gets it the better I shall be pleased."

"The man does not annoy you," said Lord Oakshott.

"Here's a pretty fellow! Here is an hereditary legislator! Why, when I was down with the fever at Dijon, I left word with Louis, the waiter, that if a gentleman of the name of Aston called, I was too ill to see any one. I awoke from a feverish slumber, and found the brute reading the Bible by my bedside. He said that he had come to nurse me, and had brought a young man to help him."

"What did you do?" asked Lord Oakshott.

"Well, I am afraid that I swore dreadfully," said Granby.

"That was a pity."

"He had none on me. I got rid of him by accepting the services of the young man. Oakshott?"

"Yes."

"That young man was fearfully like you before you got old and ugly."

"Thanks," said Oakshott.

The above conversation is antedated by some years. We must now return to Captain Aston, as he was at Croydon before the gorilla business.

Dickie says now that he was a good fellow but a sanctimonious old prig; and that he took the gorilla to be the devil, and consequently fought him. Dickie also says that when Captain Aston was attacked by the gorilla he was playing the fiddle in a wood, and that the gorilla took the fiddle from the Captain and ate it before the Captain went in at him. This is obviously fiction; still it is perfectly certain that the Captain could play the fiddle very well, and also that he killed a gorilla.

Dickie, who should know, says that Captain Aston was the best and cleverest instructor in music that he ever met. He was very kind to all the boys, but he liked Dickie the best of all. (This, you must remember, was long before the gorilla ate his fiddle, and scratched the trowsers off his legs.) The boy James Richardson took a great liking to the cornopean, and became a great hand, or rather mouth, at it.

When the boy seemed fifteen, and a well-grown, beautiful boy, Mr. G—— happened to come round recruiting for his band. Mr. G—— was very much struck by the boy's playing, and spoke to Captain Aston about it. They were both devoted to music, and they spoke confidentially.

"Captain Aston," said Mr. G——, "that boy plays very well. You must give him to me. He must be a grenadier, that boy."

"G——," said Captain Aston, earnestly, "you shall have

the boy, of course. But listen. The boy is too good for you. He has a voice."

"H'm, hem," said Mr. G——; "then you have been injudicious in making him work at the cornopean. How old is the boy?"

"I don't know; but we will have him in."

Dickie was sent for. "You are going into the army, sir," said Mr. G——. "Has the boy's voice changed, Captain Aston?"

"I cannot in the least degree say," said Captain Aston. "It seems to me a rather fine tenor."

"Oh! we get plenty of fine tenors before fourteen, who turn out utter rubbish afterwards. Take off your clothes, sir."

Dickie did so. Mr. G—— looked at him, and then examined his chest. Then he whispered to Captain Aston.

"The boy is, as you see, a man; he is over sixteen. Boy," he continued, "put on your clothes."

Dickie obeyed.

"Now," said Mr. G——, "I want to hear you sing."

"Sing——" began Captain Aston.

"Let the boy sing what he likes," said Mr. G——.

Dickie began—

> "Drink to me only with thine eyes,
> And I will pledge with mine."

Mr. G—— was very much startled, but he did not show it. He only said, "Can you drum, you boy?"

"Get your drum, boy," said Captain Aston.

The boy came rattling along the passage with it in a few

minutes, and drummed like a Frenchman, till he was told to leave off and go away.

"What do you think of his voice?" said Aston.

"One of the finest voices in Europe."

"Is it safe?"

"Lord bless you, the boy is seventeen if he is a day, with a chest which would fill La Scala. The voice is safe enough; I will answer for *that*. The only fear is, with his cut of head, that he will marry too soon."

"What shall you do with him?" said Captain Aston.

"I shall send him to the King of Bavaria, and then he will get in with Wagner. I think that will be the plan. Do you know anything about the boy?"

"He came here from the police court," said Captain Aston. "I suppose he is some one's son, but we can find out nothing."

"He is of a fine stock," said Mr. G——, "whoever his father was."

"Are you made of money?" said Captain Aston; "because, if you are, you may lend me some, which I will solemnly promise not to repay. You talk about sending this boy to the King of Bavaria. Who is to find the cash?"

"Why, Oakshott, to be sure. He is absolutely certain, in an affair of this kind."

"I think I should like to know him," said Captain Aston.

"That is not very easy," said Mr. G——. "I only get at him through Granby Dixon and Brogden. He has gone out of all society, and has locked himself up at Oakshott with a girl."

"Improper?"

" Not a bit of it. The man is mad, and is writing an epic poem. You know the story."

" Not I."

" Lord Oakshott had a boy by his cousin Sir Arthur's wife. Sir Arthur, when he went to smash, left the boy. Lord Oakshott lost the boy, refused to marry, and has adopted this Miss Prout, one of the greatest beauties in the world. The county, the most particular county in England, have taken her up, and she will be in society in two years. Oakshott believes that he will get his boy again, and I am certain that he will send this boy to Munich."

"There are fools and fools," said Captain Aston. "I wish he would send *me* to Munich."

"Well, I won't argue. I will take the boy, Good-night."

The correspondence below followed :—

" My Lord,

" I have discovered a tenor of such surpassing excellence that I wish to ask your lordship if you would find the funds to send him to Munich or Milan.

" The voice is perfectly safe. I have seen the boy's chest. I should say that he is nearly eighteen. The voice is very well cultivated, but the boy has a genius of his own. I hope that you will help me. I have taken him into my band, but he is too good for us. I wish that you would see the boy.

"D. G."

The answer was :—

" Dear G——,

" I cannot possibly come to town to hear your tenor. I send you a crossed cheque for a hundred pounds, and I beg of you to tell the young man to take more care of his money than I have ever done. It would be a glorious national victory if we could get another tenor like Sims Reeves. Tell the young man to expand his chest, and to drink no wine except Beaune. When he wants another hundred pounds, of course, if you desire it, he can have it.

"Would you be so kind as to set this song for me?

"OAKSHOTT."

I see no particular reason why Lord Oakshott's song should be lost to posterity. So here it is :—

> "King Rose he went a-wooing
>   Among the garden bowers,
> When autumn winds were strewing
>   The shed leaves of the flowers.
> But the Lily said, 'I am dying,'
>   And the Hollyhock said, 'I am dead,'
> And the Larkspur, 'I am sleeping
>   With the grave mould over my head.'
>
> "'No bride for me,' said bold King Rose ;
>   'No bride in this garden fair ;
> No bride for the flower who has kissed the Vine
>   And toyed with the Jessamine's hair.
> No bride for the Lily's lover,
>   No bride for the Eglantine's friend.'
> And Death, as he walked in the garden, said,
>   'Too late—this is the end !'
>
> "But the Aconite said, as she raised her head
>   From the death mould over the Lily,
> 'I will be true to the darling love,
>   And foolish old Death is silly.
> Kiss me at noon on Christmas Day,
>   And I will marry thee ;
> Then we'll see what stupid old Death will say
>   At the match betwixt you and me."

> " When Christmas Day was come and gone,
>   The Aconite was there ;
>   But the gentle touch of the dead red Rose
>   Was no more in the Jessamine's hair.
>   And Death laughed loud at the dead red Rose,
>   Looked down through the frozen snow :
>   ' Oh, Aconite sweet, thy love and I meet,
>   For thy love is dead, I trow.'

> " And Winter whispered, ' Die, my love,
>   Thy love is false to thee ;'
>   And sweet Spring murmured, ' Wait for the Rose ;
>   They lie to thee and to me.'
>   When the Rose arose from his winter's sleep,
>   With the Lily and Larkspur fair,
>   He looked at the flowers around his feet,
>   But there was no Aconite there."

Granby Dixon does not, for his own part, agree with the indiscriminate praise which has been given to this poem by one review of undoubted eminence and respectability. Neither, on the other hand, does he agree with another review, equally eminent and equally respectable, when they say that it is " outrageous rot." " All poetry must of necessity be absolute nonsense," says Oakshott; "but Granby Dixon does *not* see that mine is worse than the average. In point of fact, Granby Dixon says it is *above* the average."

The public must judge between Granby Dixon and Lord Oakshott, because Granby Dixon says in the Emporium that although it is balderdash it is not worse balderdash than ——'s poetry. They have quarrelled over the matter. They always do. Old Colonel B——, the father of Crook's Club, says that he is in the position of M. Thiers or the late Lord Nelson. So long as you do not fire on her Majesty's flag, you may say and do what you like. The two men would quarrel continually, but neither would let any one else say one word.

One can never be comfortable with people in this world. Granby Dixon and Oakshott have both come down on Colonel B—— because he wrote the last sentence. He pointed out to them that it was the ministerial policy; and then they said that he talked nonsense. He cannot be brought to see it. He maintains that there are strong analogies between M. Thiers' position at Versailles and Nelson's at Naples. No one else, that he can find, sees it, however.

D. G. sent the boy Richardson to Italy. He went there as the *protégé* of Lord Oakshott, the beloved of both the Carbonari and the Cammoristi. Of his adventures we shall hear some day. The good Earl was well remembered. Indeed, he kept his memory green by large donations towards Italian unity: and as for this James Richardson, he kept him supplied with money most handsomely, not for one moment dreaming that it was his own Dickie.

I extremely regret to say that I must drop your acquaintance for seven years. It is a long time, but we shall both get over it. Two Prime Ministers got over it, and Lord Oakshott got over it. Also I may mention that Sir Arthur Oakshott got over it uncommonly well; though I can hear nothing about his preparing to pay back the £60,000. Dixie got over it, and so also did Dickie. It seems rather a pity that Lord Oakshott was so busy with his song that he had not time to ask for an interview with his *protégé.*

CHAPTER XXX.

AFTER SOME YEARS.

"Now," said Granby Dixon, "we are all undone together."

Lord Oakshott was in bed and asleep, and he cursed Granby Dixon by his gods.

"What the deuce is the matter *now?*" said Oakshott.

"Your cousin has come home."

"I always knew he would," said Oakshott. "Where is he?"

"He is in Park Lane."

"Why the devil did he not come to see me?" said Oakshott.

"Why, you know," said Granby. "I suppose he did not like to."

"It is extremely probable," said Oakshott. "I have known the same kind of feeling before, myself. When I make a mull of a poem, I don't like to come near you or S——. What has the —— said to my poem?"

"That it is the greatest rubbish ever published," said Granby.

"Good," said Oakshott; "I shall succeed in literature. This looks promising, being cut into by the ——. I am gaining an audience. J. P. paid me fifty pounds last week on condition that I would not publish a novel, the MS. of which he had in his possession. I am getting on, my dear Granby."

"Do put on your breeches and talk to me," said Granby.

"Why breeches?" said Oakshott, getting out of bed. "The 42nd wear no breeches, and I have followed men of that regiment up the steps which connect the old town of Edinburgh with the new, and I can only say that the kilt is quite as becoming and quite as proper as our absurd breeches."

"Do not be so fantastic, Oakshott. Do knock your brains together," said Granby.

"Ding yer harns thegither," said Oakshott, putting on his trowsers. "Well, and so Arthur is come home?"

"Yes, and has been home for some time I believe."

"Lord love the man," said Oakshott, "he is always at some trick or another. And so he is at old Mother O'Brien's, in Park Lane. Do you think I had better go to him?"

"No."

"Why?"

"You would see her in all probability, and you had much better not."

"So she is with him still?"

"Yes. He is ill-using her badly, I am afraid. Let her come to my wife, Oakshott; she will be safe there; let her come to my wife."

"What?" said Oakshott.

"I wish you would let her come to us. I don't like to say it, but she could get a divorce on the grounds of *sævitia*."

"Have that woman dragged into a Divorce Court," growled Oakshott. "Go and rouse up Arthur, and leave me to sleep. Criminals sleep before they are hung."

Granby went straight to Sir Arthur's residence. Several

windows were lighted up, though it was one o'clock in the morning.   Granby was at once admitted.

Sir Arthur was sitting in the dining-room and smoking a cigar.   He seemed almost to *expect* Granby Dixon.   He said, " You come from Oakshott."

" I have been with him."

Sir Arthur was very little changed ; Granby says that he could have picked him out among two dozen other criminals at the Old Bailey, had there been any necessity for identifying him.   Granby had all kinds of things to say to the man, but his unabashed impudence was too much for him.   He only said—

" I beg your pardon, Sir Arthur, I saw that the house was lit up as I came by, and" (he dared not say I wish to speak to you about Lady Oakshott) " I came to ask if you would meet Oakshott as if nothing had happened."

" Most certainly," said Sir Arthur.

" H'm ; is this true about the Idaho Diamond Fields ?"

" Yes," said Sir Arthur.   " *Is Oakshott in it ?*"

" Yes ! to the tune of £10,000, I think."

" I am glad of that.   All his money is as good as gone then.   I am safely out.   Are *you* in it ? "

" Yes."

" Ah, it's too late to get out now.   I would have saved *you*, because you are not a very significant person.   I would put you into a good thing or two.   I have no particular animosity towards *you*.   I give you my word of honour as a gentleman that we spent four thousand pounds, hard cash, in scattering the diamonds about exactly where fools would find them.   Then we had to buy off the Indians.   Of course, dear Granby Dixon, I did not personally superintend these little matters, any more than I originated them. Of course I was not the prime mover in the whole matter. Of course I did not clear out first, and (as I find) leave you and Oakshott in. (I repeat that I am very sorry for you.) Of course I did not ride 2500 miles homewards to find Oakshott installed with my wife and his illegitimate daughter at my own fireside. Oh, of course not!"

Granby said "The devil!" which was improper, because there was a lady in the room, standing behind him. He was not aware of it until Sir Arthur said—

"Lady Oakshott will confirm every word which I have said: there she is, confound her!"

Granby rose and confronted her.

"There she is," said Sir Arthur. "There is the great saint: there is the woman who had her first boy stolen, and who let her second die." (Sir Arthur put this in words impossible to repeat.) "Now she has gone to the priests. Look at her. See what I am tied to for the rest of my life! Look!"

He turned and looked as he was told. He saw before him a grey woman, with the majesty of unutterable sorrow upon her face.

The majestic expression of sorrow will make the meanest face beautiful. In this case it was reflected on a very beautiful face. Granby felt as though he were looking on one of Fra Angelico's saints. He thought of Mrs. Granby, and wished that she had been there, for his anger was rising.

"Who is this gentleman?" she asked in a very quiet voice.

"Granby Dixon," said Sir Arthur; "the most infernal tittle-tattle in Europe. That is what he is,"

"I wish for your orders, Arthur."

"Go to bed. Where have you been?"

"To midnight mass only."

"Yah!"

"I wish this gentleman to witness that I obeyed you. Arthur, love is gone between us, but even for the sake of your own prestige you might treat me better than this."

"Go to bed now," said Sir Arthur, "or I will put you to bed in a way you won't like. You are going to Rickaby's party to-morrow night, mind."

So she went. Then Granby rapped out suddenly—

"In taking my leave, Sir Arthur, I beg to inform you that you are the worst scoundrel I ever met. If it would in any way suit your convenience, I will be at Boulogne the day after to-morrow."

"A little pot is soon hot," said Sir Arthur. "My dear, I couldn't see you at twelve paces, while I should be a perfect target for you. Never mind duelling,—I'll give you a good thing. Wade in for the Bolivia and Chili Main: it is a thundering swindle, but I can float it. Don't tell Oakshott about it, or he will blow the gaff in the House of Lords. He is getting too sharp for the best: that is what makes me feel so delighted at letting him in for £10,000 over the Idahos. Now go home and go to bed, you good little man, and don't in future talk about shooting at a man twice your size, because it is cowardly."

Granby got home at what Dixie would call "immeasure-ably tall hours." Mrs. Granby, a heavy sleeper, never knew when he came to bed. But in his sleep he was so persistently saying "Chili and Bolivia," that she woke. She thought, though not a jealous woman, that they were the names of two young ladies whom Granby had met at a party. She punched and shoved Granby till he was awake, and then he explained the matter to her. He asked her should he go in for the Chili and Bolivia.

She expressed her opinion in the most emphatic way. "Granby, my love, keep clear of Sir Arthur and Lord Oakshott; they are a pair of gambling swindlers; and in my opinion Lord Oakshott is the very worst of the two."

A pretty character for a poet! The author of "King Rose," "Thanatos and Mnemosyne," and various other poems, was never a favourite with Mrs. Granby Dixon. She said that when that man (meaning Oakshott) was in question, she never knew whether she stood on her head or her heels. Even when Oakshott wrote the song beginning

"My friend's wife is mine own wife,"

and dedicated it to her, she repudiated it with scorn, and said it was like his impudence. On the present occasion she told Granby that he had woke her up (*she* had punched *him*), and that she should be quite too tired to go to Rickaby's party and see the meeting between Lord Oakshott and Lady Oakshott. Granby was rather glad.

CHAPTER XXXI.

PREPARATION FOR RICKABY'S PARTY.

RICKABY was a very noble fellow: some said he was a German Jew. Two things, however, were absolutely certain: he had done splendidly at Cambridge, and he had accepted office, knowing no more about the work of the office than the man in the moon,

Granby Dixon was ferociously virtuous over the matter. He was Secretary in that office now, and had hoped to be Minister. Not at all. Rickaby was pitchforked in as First Lord, and Granby was left swearing.

"The fellow knows nothing about the details of his office," said Granby Dixon to Lord Oakshott.

"Yes, but he knows about ships," said Oakshott. "His father had fifty ships, and he has sixty."

"I don't care about that," said Granby Dixon.

"I do," said Oakshott; "I think that it is well to put one of your leading merchants as civil First Lord. I don't say that the man could actually *sail* a ship; I would not trust him to sail my yacht; but at the same time he knows more about ships than you or I do. He has been brought up among ships."

"That is all very well," said Granby Dixon; "but I don't see my way to it. The head of the greatest navy in the world ought to be a sailor."

"Just a moment ago you would have undertaken the post yourself, and you are no sailor. You were sick a month ago, when I took you round to Lulworth in my yacht."

"That is all very well," growled Granby Dixon; "but I have been passed over, and I hate being passed over."

"*I* have been passed over," said Oakshott.

"Yes, *you*," said Granby; "but you are so horribly rich."

"But you are not poor, Granby."

"Thanks to you, old fellow, I am not," said Granby; "you made a fine fortune for me, and why on earth you never made a greater for yourself I cannot understand. You are such a splendid financier. It is an astounding fact that a man who writes such rubbishing poetry, and publishes it, should finance so well."

"Genius, my dear soul, genius. I have made £280,000 in two years."

"I heard that it was £500,000," said Granby Dixon, "and that is nothing in these days, you know."

"Lies! lies! lies!" said Lord Oakshott. "The question is, are you going to this man Rickaby's party to-night, or rather his wife's party?"

"Most certainly," said Granby.

Lord Oakshott had not been in town for several years. He was out of England for four years, the principal part of which he spent in America. Dixie had been his only companion. He had only come to town now for a certain purpose. Dixie must be presented at Court, and Dixie was so presented by the Duchess of Ballyroundtowers.

The most august person in the world, if I humbly dare say such a thing, knows nearly everything in English society. She knew, for example, that Lord Oakshott was an extremely talented and fantastic person; she knew all about that. She knew that Oakshott had lost his cousin's boy, and that he had adopted his housekeeper's niece, Miss Prout. The good Lady of Lipworth had given Miss Prout such a character that the most august person in the world was not only eager to receive her, but was very anxious to do so. The greatest Personage in the world had her wish.

The great Lady looked steadily as she saw the mass of maiden beauty and jewellery which came before her. It is a way which the greatest Lady in the world has.

Dixie was horribly frightened. She thought that the great Lady was angry with her; she found out that this was by no means the case. A round foreign Princess came down and talked to her after she had made her poor little courtesy.

"My dear," said the round Princess, "has any one told you how beautiful you are?"

"No, your Royal Highness," said Dixie. "No one has told me at all. Am I so pretty, then?"

"You are very beautiful, my child!"

"I am glad of that, because it will please Earlie to know it," said Dixie.

"Who is Earlie?" said the round Princess.

"Lord Oakshott."

"*I* know," said the round Princess, "be sure. You would like to come to the concert, would you not?"

"I like fine times," said Dixie, "and I expect that the concert will be a very fine time. I expected very much that this muss would have ended in a fizzle as far as I am concerned. I mean that I should be an entire failure. You don't think so, do you?"

"No, you are a great success," said the round Princess; "but what *are* the meanings of muss and fizzle?"

"Well, Princess, I expect that it is what you would reckon up as tall Canadian. The American girls always talk company language in society; but we Ontarians, why, we air the English language till the starch is out and you can see through the fabric."

"I was not aware that you had been in Ontario, my dear."

"Oh yes, Lord Oakshott took me there for four years. We lived with his brother Sir Arthur for some time before we went South. I was only a child, and so I learnt this way of speaking: that, you understand, was before the Apache war. I can speak company language if I choose, but I don't mind you, and the other comes natural. Can you tell me, dear madam, who the old woman is who is

going up to the great Lady now? I mean the old woman
with the gold slush lamp on her head, and the eight-day
corn leaves toppling over her nose."

I am informed by Miss Hicks that the lady in question
was Lady X——. Her head-dress was the admiration of
every one. She had a gold coronet, surmounted by maize
leaves. The Empress of the French, who seldom adopted
anything, adopted that, and christened it the "Chevelure
Hiawatha."

The kind round Princess told her who the great lady with
the slush lamp and the eight-day corn leaves was; and
Dixie said, "Law! Why, she is one of the greatest ladies
in Europe. They don't figure up that style in the States.
I saw Mrs. Lincoln; why, she was no more to look at than
I am. Our Governor-General's wife, however—she *was*
fine. No posts and rails about *her*; no, *sir.*"

Dixie was dismissed kindly by the round Princess. Lord
Oakshott put her in her carriage, and then went along the
Mall with Granby Dixon.

"You have spoilt that girl, Oakshott," he said.

"I very much doubt that," said he.

"She talks slang."

"What slang?"

"American slang. She did so the other day. She told
me that you were going to send her to the Queen's Pow-
wow, and that Lady Ballyroundtowers had got a fifty-dollar
scalp for the occasion."

"It is only prairie talk," said Oakshott quietly. "They
talk like that about the lakes. Though, mind you, Lady
Ballyroundtowers' wig (scalp, *Dixie* calls it) cost more than
fifty dollars."

"I want to have a long talk with you, Oakshott," said Granby.

"What the devil about?" said Oakshott. "What have I been doing? It seems to me that every one always wants to have a long talk to me. I am talked to death. Before you begin, may I ask you if you know G—— S—·—, the architect?"

"Yes; why?"

"Because I want an introduction to him. Dixie wants Oakshott Abbey restored : and he is the most honest of all our architects in the way of art."

"That will cost a great sum, Oakshott."

"With the entire restoration of the Abbey, the rebuilding of the cloisters, the building of the new clergy house, and the endowment of the establishment, it will cost about £120,000."

"Are you mad?"

"Yes. But Dixie sketched out the scheme, and I am going to carry it out. It is a most lovely scheme ; and the best of it is that I have the money for it. The restoring of the Abbey will come to about £20,000, the other buildings about £25,000, the new grammar school about £20,000 ; as for the endowment of the old gentlemen, I must see to that."

"The old gentleman !" said Granby, thinking that he meant the devil and was mad at last in earnest.

"Ah, the old gentlemen," said Lord Oakshott. "Those old parsons are not fairly treated. Dixie and I agree on that point. A lunatic with a long nose said to me the other day that if capital was not put to nobler uses it would be forbidden to exist by labour. What the deuce would become of labour in that case I did not ask him, because I was perfectly sure he did not know. I, however, am going to make a home for old parsons and their wives. I am going to have a splendid school, in which these old parsons shall teach, assisted by their wives. The service in the Abbey will be such that it will not in any way offend High Church, Low Church, or Broad Church. The sons and daughters of reduced clergy are to be admitted free. I have also provided a graveyard."

"But what are these people going to teach?" said Granby, now fairly aghast.

"Plain sewing, grammar, tent-stitch, the Catechism, and (if the Archbishop will allow it) dominoes. Now, don't take me up before I have finished, Granby. You say, ' Why dominoes ?' "

"I said nothing of the sort," said Granby.

"Well, you meant it, then ; will *that* do ?"

"I did *not* mean it," said Granby.

"Then shall we pretermit dominoes ?"

"That," said Granby, "does not depend on the Archbishop at all ; it depends on the Bishop."

"What, Sarum ?" said Oakshott.

"Sarum," said Granby. " He is a very High Churchman, and he will send you and your dominoes flying, if you don't mind."

"I will send him some peaches," said Oakshott.

"That would be no use," said Granby. "I wanted to have a long conversation with you ; you evidently do not desire one, for you have been talking nonsense ever since we left St. James's."

"I have not said one word of nonsense," said Lord Oakshott.

"Well," but surely all this humbug about the Clergy Home and the £120,000 *is* humbug."

"Not a bit of it," said Lord Oakshott, entering Comfrey's Hotel.   "It is every word of it true.   By-the-by, did I ask you to dinner to-day?"

"No."

"I am losing my memory, I think," said Lord Oakshott. "You were asked here to dinner at half-past four; you must dine with me, and you will find three covers laid—continental hours."

"American, you mean.   Go up, you lunatic; go up."

Lord Oakshott went up and dressed.   Granby sat down to dinner without dressing.   They had fairly begun when Dixie came down.

If you think that Dixie *came* into the room, you are utterly mistaken; she was *shown* in by the head waiter. The door was opened, and Miss Prout was announced. Granby Dixon rose at once, for he had never seen anything like it in his life.

She was dressed in light-blue velvet fringed with old lace. But over her blue velvet went wandering strings of opals, set in gold.   Her sleeves were open to the elbow, and round each elbow hung the price of a small Indian campaign. Granby had seen much, but he had never seen anything like this.   He gasped.   "Such women as these," he said to himself, "upset empires and drive men mad."

It is noticeable that Mrs. Dixon was at Swanage, a watering-place which he highly recommends, although he never, by a curious conjunction of circumstances, happens to have been there, and never means to go.   Oakshott says that no one has any right to praise a watering-place unless he has never been near it.

Dixie's hair was very short, in close curls, and if her beauty was describable I would try to describe it. I think that I will leave it alone, if you please. The portrait of her by a great artist is a humbug, like the painter.

"Earlie," she said, as she took her soup, "the good Princess says that I am so pretty. Is that the truth, Earlie?"

"*I* don't know," said Lord Oakshott; "I have been bothered with you too long to care. Don't, whatever you do, get it into your head that you *are* pretty, because then you will become insufferable."

"No, Earlie; only the Princess said I was, and I should like to be pretty."

"Why?"

"To please you, Earlie."

"Would you like to marry me, Dixie?" said Lord Oakshott.

"Who do you think would ever dream of marrying *you?*" said Dixie; "I won't. Mind, I am going to marry some one, but you may rest assured that it will not be *you.*"

"Why not?" said Oakshott.

"You are too good for me," said Dixie; "and you write too much poetry. None of it will sell. Ah! it is all very well; you are frowning at Mr. Dixon, but I won't marry you. If Mrs. Dixon was dead,' I would marry Granby to-morrow. Do you think that you could get rid of Mrs. Dixon and propose to me, Mr. Dixon?"

"I would not have you at all," said Granby Dixon.

"*Quite* right. Same here," said Dixie.

"Dixie," said Lord Oakshott, "I want you to leave off the old prairie slang."

"All serene," said Dixie.

" But that is not leaving it off," said Oakshott.

" Yes it is, old hoss," said the outrageous Dixie. " I have done with it, though it comes pleasant to my tongue.　You will never hear another word of it from my mouth.　You cut upstairs presently, and fie yourself out for Mrs. Rickaby's Pow-wow."

" Dixie !" said Lord Oakshott.

" Well, hoss," said Dixie.

" You said you would not."

" Well, then, I won't ; only if you don't go up and rag out, I will kick up the most immortal old tar river Jerusalem breakdown ever you heard.　Molasses to a pine-apple !　I'll burst the railings of your lot."

She turned from the table, and then she came back and threw her beautiful arms round Lord Oakshott's neck. " My darling Earlie," she said ; " why do I vex you like this?　I will never say one solitary prairie word again."

" Don't say as much as that, my sweetheart," said Lord Oakshott ; " only in English society they do not like it."

Dixie kissed him and left the room.

" Is that real American talk, Oakshott?" said Granby, when she was gone.

" Oh dear, no," said Oakshott ; " nothing like it.　The American ladies and gentlemen are very much like our people, only they talk a little through their noses, and never, by any chance, leave off talking.　The girl has picked up a phrase here and a phrase there, but it is nothing like American.　You should have heard her talking to the Indians in Colorado in their own language."

" Indians ! Colorado !" said Granby.　" Have you been there ?"

"We have not only been there, but we have come back again. By-the-by, do you think that Mrs. Granby would like a few scalps for her drawing-room chimney-piece?"

"I don't think so," said Granby.

"Well, it is a perfect matter of taste. Only I killed one of the chiefs of the Apaches, and took all the scalps out of his belt. I thought Mrs. Granby might like one."

"Not at all," said Granby. "Mrs. Granby would like very much to hear about Macador Silvera."

"Out!" said Oakshott. "What the dickens ever put you in? Out to-morrow!"

"Are you going to marry that girl, Oakshott?" said Granby.

"Marry Dixie!" said Oakshott. "Are you going to marry your own daughter?"

"Why, no," said Granby. "But you are very young, Oak-shott. Chivalry is chivalry. At the same time you must remember that you are scarcely old enough to be the girl's father. The world will talk, if you don't mind."

"Hang the world!" said Lord Oakshott. "Look you here, Granby, my oldest and most faithful of friends. I am swindled by my cousin; well and good. My cousin takes away from me the woman who ought to have married me; well and good. I take my cousin's child; Mrs. O'Brien gets him stolen to spite me, believing that her daughter was his mother by me, and then Mrs. O'Brien entirely loses him; well and good. I am left utterly alone in the world, and I take up with this girl, the only being, save yourself, who ever loved me or understood me (you don't understand me, Granby; you have not the brains). I adopt this girl. Why not? I am as incapable of doing her a wrong as I am of killing you with that poker. And now you say that the world will talk about our relations! If the world has come to that, I repeat my previous observation, that the world may be hanged. I think you will allow that in matters of this kind there is no appeal from the Court."

"Well, it has never made a mistake yet," said Granby.

"And I tell you," said Oakshott eagerly, "that boy of my cousin's is not dead. I tell you, Granby, that that boy is not dead, and he shall marry Dixie."

"Oakshott !"

"Yes."

"Will you make me a promise ?"

"No. Promises are like pie-crusts, made to be broken."

"May I implore you to consult me as to the identity of this young man ?"

"Yes, certainly; I will promise that. I will give you my word about *that*."

"If you do not you will have some wretched young man foisted on you."

"I am not a fool," said Lord Oakshott.

"I doubt it," said Granby.

"Rubbish," said Oakshott. "We poets are far cleverer than you are. I tell you that Dickie is alive."

"How do you know ?" said Granby.

"I dreamt it," said Oakshott. "You know that all dreams dreamt before midnight come true. You know as much as *that*. Come."

"Go on, in Heaven's name," said Granby.

"Don't fidget and kick," said Lord Oakshott; "it is not manners. I want to tell you my dream. I dreamt that you were an infernal old ass."

" That dream has come true," said Granby.

" It *came* true before I dreamt it," said Oakshott.

" Well, about the rest of the dream ?" said Granby.

"I dreamt that my cousin was coming home from America. I principally dreamt that because I had a letter from him a considerable time ago to say that he was coming. I dreamt also that I had managed his estate for him so well that he could come back a rich and powerful man. I dreamt that every one had forgotten everything, or had chosen to forget everything, including my honesty to him."

"Old boy, don't be silly. No one will forget your be-haviour."

"Granby ! Granby ! I tell you that black midnight sinner, my cousin, has forgotten that. *He knows where that boy is !*"

" Earlie, you are mad. If he knew where the boy was, it would be to his interest to tell you."

" Interest!" said Lord Oakshott; "he has no interest. He is a perfect soulless devil. I have spoken with Bucknill, Tuke, and Connolly about such cases. They say they occur now and then, but that they are rare."

"Go on with your dream, Earlie."

" Yes, I will go on with my dream. I dreamt that Arthur came back. I dreamt that he knew where this boy was, and refused to tell."

" But the boy is his son, not yours," said Granby.

" That is true, but he wants to plague me."

" I see," said Granby ; " go on."

" Well, then, I dreamt that things are not fit nohow you could put them."

"That is American," said Granby. " Is that all you dreamt before twelve o'clock ?"

"That is all," said Oakshott, "that I dreamt before twelve o'clock."

"Anything after twelve?" said Granby Dixon.

"Yes; I pulled out my watch, and then it was a quarter-past twelve. Then I went to sleep and dreamt that you were a liar, and were false to me."

"That dream shan't come true, anyhow," said Granby.

"I know that well, true heart," said Oakshott.

CHAPTER XXXII.

LORD OAKSHOTT'S CASE AGAINST THE WORLD.

"OAKSHOTT," said Granby Dixon, "I want to know many things. I want to tell you that I love you above all men alive. But I wish to ask you questions. First, why did you go to America?"

"To see my cousin, Sir Arthur."

"Quite so. Why did you buy property in Ontario?"

"Because it paid."

"Do you notice that you are not answering a single question which I ask you?"

"I did not notice it myself," said Lord Oakshott. "I have sold out in Ontario, and I have netted eight per cent. Are you angry with me that I did not let you in for a good thing?"

"Not at all. I only wanted to know why you went to America at all."

"As I have told you—to see my cousin."

"You were four years in Ontario," said Granby.

Granby had got nothing to say, and so he uttered this astounding platitude. To which Oakshott replied—

"Quite so—there and elsewhere."

The dead-lock was so utterly absurd that both men burst out laughing.

"Now, come, Oakshott, tell me what you did in America."

"Well, as it is no possible business of yours, Granby ; and, as I have no earthly right to speak on the matter to you, I have, of course, the greatest pleasure in telling you everything."

" Don't be fantastic, Oakshott."

" I am not. I tell you the simple truth. It is no business of yours, and so I am going to tell you the whole story. Fantastic, quotha ! Is Lady Goram fantastic ?"

" Certainly not."

" Well, she came here to me and told me the whole of the relations between herself and her husband, and said that that girl left the house, or she did."

" What girl ?"

" I have not the wildest idea," said Lord Oakshott.

" What did you do ?"

" I did not do anything at all. I never uttered a word. I might have been brought in as a co-respondent. But I think that it is rather a fantastic thing for a married woman to come to a bachelor with her troubles, merely because that bachelor has written some rather twopenny poetry bearing on the relations between man and wife. She had read my ' Heloise and Abelard,' don't you see ?"

"No."

" Let me repeat it to you."

"Certainly not. You have promised to tell me about America."

"I will. Granby, are you in the Grand Turk Railway?"

"Yes."

"I came out this morning at three premium. I call it the railway from Constantinople to Easter Monday. It will pay when we are both dead, but not before. You had better go out the first thing to-morrow morning; my secession will send them down."

"Thanks," said Granby. "Now, old boy, after giving me a thousand pounds or so, let us have the whole American story. It will take some time."

"It will take three seconds. I wanted to see that woman, my cousin's wife."

"Oakshott !"

"Granby !"

"Oakshott, you had no right to do that."

"Why not? You see your cousin's wife."

"But I am not in love with her."

"Who said that I was in love with Arthur's wife ?"

"No one."

"Then there is another dead-lock in the conversation, but I will go on to spite you."

"You have been going on for half an hour," said Granby; "now go on for good and all."

"Do you believe in the immortality of the soul ?" said Lord Oakshott.

"Yes, confound you, I do."

"Well, I wish that you had said that you did not," said Lord Oakshott. "Because, if you *had* done so, I would have kept you here another hour before I gave you twopennyworth of news. What is your opinion about the meeting of people who have loved one another after death?"

"It is not revealed," said Granby, trying to avoid swearing.

"My dear fellow, you have not learnt the mere grammar of your religion. Lots of things are not revealed. You have no sense."

"If you had any sense," said Granby, "you might have been Prime Minister."

"If you had any sense, you might have made as much money as I have," said Oakshott; which was unfortunately true, and so Granby had not one word to say for himself.

"You want," said Oakshott, "to hear the whole truth about the American expedition."

"I do," said Granby.

"I was bored," said Oakshott. "Every one bored me except Dixie and yourself: you never bore me at all; you are as great a goose as I am. Then I was in love with my cousin's wife, which you say is improper. Then I wanted to make some more money, and I thought that I could do so out of the Yankees. I did so. I tell you fairly, Granby, that, keen as they were, I could find there no intellect keener than my own."

"Yet you went a fool's errand after a woman," said Granby.

"That is true enough," said Oakshott. "Granby, do not be so bitter with me. I can take foul scorn from any man, and hurl it back in his teeth. From you, the only man I really love, it is death to me. I am as incapable of injuring Arthur's wife as I am of injuring yours."

"Don't be pettish, Oakshott."

"I will not. I pray your forgiveness. I will tell you everything, even to the last. I went to America. I was followed by a telegram asking me to stand for Chairman to the Perth and Brecknock Railway."

"I know the line," said Granby, laughingly: "you accepted the nomination and stayed in America. Was ever any one like you?"

"I accepted the nomination, and I am *heavily in it now*. I worked for them there like old boots. I was followed to America by all kinds of reports with regard to my wealth, which is great, and my power of finance, which is greater. I wonder who sent those reports."

"If," said Granby, "you had not taken to write that rubbishing poetry, we might have done much better."

"Do you think it rubbish, Granby?" said Oakshott anxiously.

"I don't think it *all* rubbish," said Granby Dixon. "I told you that you must not publish some of it. I don't know one end of a poem from the other end. But that thing about Eros and Psyche was improper balderdash."

Granby wondered why Oakshott laughed till his face was as nearly red as it could get.

Say that the thing was improper balderdash. It at all events was never published. We leave it alone; we say nothing whatever about it. We only wish to put the man of the world face to face with the genius. The man of genius, Oakshott, went on :—

"You never will know how I was dipped, Granby. I was frightfully dipped. I had to look round the world for the greatest commercial fool in it. I tried the most improbable people. I began with the Dutch."

"Good Lord!" said Granby.

"You may well say 'Good Lord!'" said Oakshott. "I could not get a penny invested in Holland. They *are* awful fools, those Dutch ; they know the colour of good gold, and they won't risk it, not even to England. Well, Granby, I tried the Belgians. They were no use at all ; they were as keen as myself. But I *did* the Dutch after all."

"How ?" said Granby.

"I bought into the Luxemburg Railway at 75. In one month, when the French took it, I sold out at 150. I *did* the Dutch."

"Go on with the catalogue of your crimes," said Granby.

"Well, I tried France," said Oakshott ; "but France's money was all locked up. It is my opinion that the French keep their money under their beds."

"I should be glad to get to America," said Granby.

"That will come in time," said Oakshott. "My dear, I did a great thing. I got money out of Prussia."

"Nonsense, Oakshott."

"I *did*."

"You would get blood out of the devil, then," said Granby. "How did you do it ?"

"I decline to answer that question," said Oakshott. "I *did* it. Then I looked round the earth for the greatest commercial fools. I thought of the Americans."

"And of your cousin's wife," said Granby.

"I took Dixie," said Lord Oakshott, "and I looked at those Americans. They are just as green as grass about money matters. A Scotch student is a match for the whole nation."

"Earlie !"

"Yes, Granby."

"I wish you would be more moral, for you talk like a betting man."

"The world has chosen to turn against me, and I have chosen to turn against the world. The world has left me nothing except Dixie, yourself, and my place in the House of Lords. The world has not served me well, and God has ill-treated me. I defy Him. There is a law which governs *Him*, the law of right and wrong. I abide by that."

"Oakshott, you talk like a poet, wildly. You must bow your head to God."

"I will not," said Oakshott.

"He will *make* you," said Granby.

"That is priest's cant," said Oakshott.

Granby was going to give a somewhat angry reply, when Dixie was in the room with her blue velvet and opals.

Granby and Oakshott had been uncommonly near a quarrel. Dixie had no idea about it. But if she had stepped between the fallen and unfallen angels she would have stopped a quarrel.

CHAPTER XXXIII.

RICKABY'S.

"Are you ready, Earlie," she said, "for Mrs. Rickaby's?"

"No."

"You ought to be."

"I dare say! Granby, will you come?"

Granby Dixon rose and rang the bell. A footman appeared.

"Send Lord Oakshott's valet here, and tell him to get me a suit of Lord Oakshott's clothes," said Granby.

"Then you *are* coming, Granby," said Dixie.

"Does it appear to you at all reasonable to let Earlie go out by himself?"

"My darling Earlie! why not?"

"You do not think Earlie silly, then?" said Granby.

"He is silly in goodness," said Dixie; "but then all good people are silly. For example, yourself. I like the First Lord's parties—at least I think that I shall like them, for this is the first I have been to. I love sailors, and we shall have plenty of them. Sailors always dance well; Earlie does not dance well. I am going to have a fine time of it, I promise you."

"Dixie, you promised," said Lord Oakshott.

"What, about American?" said Dixie. "Law, I forgot. Now, Granby, we are waiting, and we will trouble you to trot upstairs and rag out."

"You are perfectly incorrigible, Dixie," said Lord Oakshott.

"Well, Granby will be perfectly incorrigible if he don't fix on your store clothes and cut away smart."

Granby did so, and Dixie, who was in one of her moods when no one could do anything with her, complimented him on the rapidity of his toilet. She said not one other solitary word to him until they got to Mrs. Rickaby's. She had been presented at Court, and so, by a process of mind entirely her own, she conceived that she had a right to present every one else. She marched up to Mrs. Rickaby and saluted *nez en air*. Then she went down the room, collared Granby, and presented *him*. Seeing that he was Secretary to the First Lord, it was rather unnecessary. She behaved in the most splendid manner, however, and her beauty lit up the room. The sailors admired her greatly. "Who is she?" they said.

Society replied that she was Lord Oakshott's adopted daughter.

The sailors scarcely saw their way to that arrangement, because sailors, rather free on some points, are rather particular on others; but when Society told the sailors that the Court had received her that morning, the sailors fell at her feet. The sailors were all nearly mad about her, and she might practically have commanded the fleet at this moment, but——

Rickaby and Mrs. Rickaby had lived a short time at Dresden and at Ems. They came home quite determined to revolutionize the hours of English Society. This was their first attempt.

In Dresden you dine at four (or did—the Prussians have altered many things). At Ems, again, in domestic parties one dances at seven, and men and women who can sing are asked to sing between the dances. The Rickabys tried to introduce this custom, and they began their party at half-past eight.

Dixie Prout could sing, and could sing uncommonly well. She had not the wildest idea that she was going to be asked to sing. She danced with two sailors, and then she leant against a door with Miss Flora Herries. The girls talked to one another, as good girls will.

"Do you feel any pride in your beauty?" said Miss Flora with that singular outspokenness which distinguishes the three children of Lord Charles Herries.

"I have no one to admire it except these sailors,"

said Dixie. "But tell me, Miss Herries, am I so beautiful?"

"You are incomparable," said Flora. "But always think, my dear, what a gift and what an influence God has given you in your beauty. You might be the wife, for all you know, of one of the rulers of the world. We are the most powerful people in the world. An Englishwoman should choose carefully and wisely."

Mrs. Rickaby came up to the two young ladies, and she said—

"You sing, I think, Miss Prout?"

"I sing very well," said Dixie. "You know Miss Herries, I think?"

"I know Miss Herries perfectly well," said Mrs. Rickaby.

"I thought you did not, from your way of looking at her," said Dixie. "Do you want me to sing?"

"I should be much obliged," said Mrs. Rickaby, rather wondering whether the girl had gone mad.

"The obligation is on my side," said Dixie; "I like to be admired."

She was taken to the piano by Mrs. Rickaby. Mrs. Rickaby had every possible song in the world ready for her, but she would petulantly have none of them. "If you please," she said, with her usual civility, "I will have none of this stuff. I am going to sing a song of Lord Oakshott's which has been set by a young Italian. I don't think that he is an Italian, though, because he was one of our drummers once."

"Have you got your music, my dear?" said Mrs. Rickaby.

"Not I," said Dixie; "I don't want any music for Earlie's songs."

So she sang Oakshott's "River." The words may be poor, but Riccardo's setting is absolutely splendid. No one who has ever heard it will forget the way in which Dixie sang it.

> " From the left to the right of the river,
>   Where the slow stream is sundered in twain,
>   I watch for my loved one for ever,
>   In vain and in vain.
>
> " From the right to the left of the river,
>   I watch for ever and aye :
>   The willows toss and shiver,
>   The boats go by.
>
> " But at right or left of the river,
>   I watch from dawn to eve.
>   That boy shall come to me never,
>   I wait and grieve."

Dixie sung this nobly. One lady was affected to tears. Granby turned on Miss Flora Herries almost savagely.

"That is some of Oakshott's performance, which young Riccardo has set," he whispered.

"You need not pinch me, Mr. Dixon," said Miss Herries, laughing.

"I beg a hundred thousand pardons," said Granby, entirely shent (for he had caught Miss Flora by the wrist) : "but Oakshott is so utterly foolish. There is nothing the matter with him but he puts it all in poetry."

" That is scarcely logical, is it ?" said Miss Flora, laughing. "Granby," she said, suddenly—"forgive me, everybody calls you Granby—who is that splendid young man who is behind her ?"

"I do not know," said Granby. " Hush, Miss Herries ; the people are calling for an encore."

Dixie had finished splendidly. There was a general murmur in the room. A few people not exactly used to the society of those times said, "Thank you," which was not the best of manners then. Mrs. Rickaby was rather uncertain herself what to do, but she thanked Dixie in set terms. A certain gallant admiral, however, formally requested Dixie to sing her song over again.

She flashed her beautiful eyes in his face, and saw that it was Lord L——. "I would sing a hundred thousand songs for any cabin-boy of the *Agamemnon* or the *Retribution*," she said; and then she suddenly grew pale. For there was a youth beside Lord L——, as tall as he, who was looking at her. She felt deadly cold, but she turned round, and set to her work again.

The encore was a failure. Her hand had lost its touch on the keys, and when she came to the line—

> "That boy shall come to me never,"

her voice passed nearly into a sob.

"Forgive me, Signorina," said some one behind her; "you tried to turn to a minor key at that passage. I set that song for Lord Oakshott, and I am particular about my work. Would you allow me your hand for one moment?"

Dixie, without looking round, allowed him to take her right hand. His hand was a very strong one, and grasped her fore-finger almost roughly as he guided it to the black key which she should have struck.

As he did so a white primrose fell over her jewelled little finger on to the black keys, and lay against the mahogany which reflected it.

She rose suddenly. "Lord L——," she said, "would you get me some water? I have been singing too much."

Lord L—— would have got her sulphur out of the crater of Popocatapetl if it would have done her any good, but the young man Riccardo said: "Allow me, my lord; I am a professional musician, and I know that great exertions like this bring on faintness with ladies. Would you mind her quietly, while I go?"

Lord L—— agreed entirely to this arrangement, and stayed with Dixie. He thought the singer was a very well-behaved young man. He watched him to the door. As he approached it, it was thrown open, and the servant announced—

"Sir Arthur and Lady Oakshott."

Riccardo made a bow, and was proposing to pass Sir Arthur Oakshott in order to get Dixie the water. He unfortunately blundered among three ladies, and nearly upset the eldest just as she was being announced.

"Mrs. O'Brien."

The door was once more shut before he could get to it. It seemed to him that Miss Prout might die before he could get the water. He turned and saw her talking comfortably to Lord L——; so he was in no great hurry now. Also he saw that she had his white primrose in her hand.

The door was once more opened in his face, and a spectacle was presented to his eyes which caused him to forget all about Dixie.

"Lady Kathleen and Lady Nora O'Brien," shouted the footman. And Riccardo reeled before these ladies. He had never seen anything at all like them in his life.

These two ladies had been left with an impoverished

estate in the west of Ireland. They were very rigid Romanists, and they had taken to themselves a special priest, a Galway man, with a face like a bull-dog and a heart like a lion—a man who ought to have had a wife and a dozen children, if virtue and honesty is to be propagated. These three noble souls had found matters wrong in the west of Ireland, and had set to work to make them right. They would not have done much at that if it had not been for a certain friend of ours. But they had, during this time —keeping entirely out of England, or even Dublin—developed into two of the most alarming middle-aged ladies which the world ever looked on.

They had put a nephew in the navy, and he had greatly distinguished himself. They had to come to London on Chancery business. Their nephew, Captain O'Dowd, had got them an invitation to the First Lord's party. So they burst on the astonished house of Rickaby. We may laugh at them on earth, but God will not laugh at them in heaven.

The old silk, the old lace, the old jewels which they had kept by them, would have bought half the things in the room. But they were put on in such an astounding fashion. They had pinned and hooked all their property on themselves, and Oakshott said that it pleased him, because they thought themselves far finer than any one else, which was the object of Society.

Lady Kathleen had understood that the hair was now worn long behind, and so she had put on a kind of outrageous and improbable wig behind her head, which Granby christened as a "mare's tail," after a certain famous cataract in Scotland, though it was not white, but of that strange colour one gets in artificial hair. Lady Nora, on the other hand, had gone in for the front part of her head, and had covered herself, nearly down to her nose, with ringlets. Still, fearful guys as these were, there were many women in the room who would have given a joint of one of their fingers for a yard of their lace.

What does it all come to, this fashion? Could a dandy, one of the terrible fighting dandies of 1820, walk the streets now? Fancy the beautiful Marie Antoinette showing at a party. I should like to see Beau Brummel try to walk down St. James' Street now. These good Irish ladies were only, like Fluellen, the man whom Shakespeare loved, "a little out of fashion."

"The top of the morning to ye, Mrs. Rickaby," began Lady Kathleen, in a brogue which Father Prout would have considered extremely passable. "We should say the evening, I doubt; but ye said from nine to one, so the morning will do as well. This is me sister, Lady Nora."

"To be sure," said Lady Nora; "the handsomest woman in the county Tipperary, the boys say. Sisther, have you got a pin about you? for I have a feeling exactly as if my wig was coming off."

After a careful examination of Lady Nora's head by Lady Kathleen, such was discovered to be the case.

"Ye had better take it off altogether, sisther," said Lady Kathleen.

"Sure and I think so," said Lady Nora; "and what I put it on for I don't know, sisther."

Lady Kathleen removed Lady Nora's wig, to the speechless astonishment of the splendid assembly; and then most people drew their breath. There stood before them the most beautiful middle-aged Irish lady that any of them had ever seen. The beauty of an Irish lady surpasses that of any lady in the world; but as a general rule they do not *last* as well as English or Scotch beauties, but go off like the Americans or Australians. Lady Nora's beauty was one which would last a long week after death. When Lady Kathleen had adjusted the yellow-ochre-coloured cap over her sister's hair, she gave her a slap and turned her round. "Sure I thought I was dressing a gossoon," she said.

"And it is many a one you have dressed at your own cost, me darling," said Lady Nora. "What are ye doing with me wig?"

"I'll put it on the top of the piano, to be out of the way," said Lady Kathleen. (She did so, and they went away and forgot it. They sent for it next morning by a Commissionaire, but it never was found.) "Now, Mrs. Rickaby, if you introduce us to your company we will be obliged."

Mrs. Rickaby was very sharp: a Minister's wife *has* to be. She said there was a keenness in Lady Nora's eyes which she did not at all understand.

"The French Ambassador."

"Scotch, Irish, and French against these English," said Lady Kathleen in beautiful Irish French, which a friend of mine told me once was the prettiest foreign French talked.

"I do not think that she would get on without the English, Mademoiselle," said the French Minister, gallantly.

"Well, I suppose that we must let them exist a little longer," said Lady Kathleen.

"The Austrian Ambassador."

The Austrian Ambassador probably wondered whether these two marvellous ladies could speak German, or whether

he should have to air his English against their Irish. He
had no audience, although Lady Kathleen wanted to consult
him heavily about the potato rot. Before she had time to
make more than half a " gintale" curtsey, Lady Nora had
seized her by the wrist and said, " There he is !"

" Who ?"

" Oakshott."

" The holy saints make his bed !" said Lady Kathleen :
and so, leaving the Austrian Ambassador to take care of
himself, she bore down on Oakshott, and sat on Granby
Dixon, whom she had not noticed, but who was sitting beside Oakshott. Lady Kathleen, having discovered her
mistake, shoved him out of the way, whereupon Lady Nora
sat upon him with the rapidity of lightning. However,
Granby only moved to the other side of Oakshott, and said
to Dixie, who came up—

" Those two Irishwomen have sat on me one after the
other."

" Why did you not get up ?"

" Because I mean to sit by Earlie. What have you got
in your breast ?"

" A white primrose."

" Who gave it to you ?"

" The young man Riccardo."

" Do me a favour."

" Yes, Granby."

" Hide it from Earlie."

" But I never hide anything from Earlie."

" Hide this : I ask you most particularly. Why are you
so pale, Dixie ?"

" I have been frightened," said Dixie. " I have seen a
dead child,"

" Did the Sisters of Charity show it to you ?" said Granby.

" No," said Dixie; " here is the dead child." And she showed him the white primrose.

" Well, now listen to me, Dixie : don't let Earlie see that."

This conversation was carried on out loud with the greatest ease, because Lady Kathleen and Lady Nora were somewhat loud, not to say obstreperous, in their recognition of Lord Oakshott, whom they had never seen before, but who had sent them £5000 for a scheme of theirs in the west of Ireland. The scheme was a good one as it stood, but Oakshott, as they frankly told him, would only see his money back in heaven, to which place, as Lady Nora remarked, he could never go unless he turned Roman Catholic. Lord Oakshott demurred to this, saying that he did not care for his money; it had gone into the soil, and therefore by all rules must come out of the soil in some shape, either into the pockets of labour or capital. Lady Kathleen said that he would find his treasure in heaven; and Oakshott pointed out that, as he could not possibly go there according to their own showing, he could not find it at all; and supposing that he did not die for forty years, how would interest be charged ?

They argued with him very strongly. He let them. He was masking his battery all the time. Three people had their eyes on him, Mrs. O'Brien and Sir Arthur and Lady Oakshott.

Arthur Oakshott had been watching Mrs. O'Brien, and Mrs. O'Brien had been watching *them*. She tried to cut the line of the fleet first, and Oakshott saw her preparing. He manœuvred in the most masterly way. He said suddenly to the two old ladies—

" Go up and keep Mrs. O'Brien away from me for an hour. Do you know who is here ?"

“No,” said Lady Kathleen.

“Sir Arthur Oakshott.”

“Good heavens !”

“Yes : keep the O'Brien away from me until I have talked to him. Don't quarrel with her, and never think one moment about the rubbishing money.”

Lady Kathleen and Lady Nora made such particularly lively times of it for Mrs. O'Brien, that she never turned up until the awful interview was over. Captain O'Dowd had his ship, and it could not be taken away from him under three years; but if Mrs. Rickaby had known that he was going to bring his lunatic aunts to her party, he would never have trodden a plank of her. They were sorry about Earlie's money, these two old ladies, and they had scores to settle with their old governess and aunt, Mrs. O'Brien. They chose to settle them at Mrs. Rickaby's party : a fact which Mrs. Rickaby avenged in bed on her husband, who had nothing to do with the matter in any way. He, when his wife began to snore, slipped out of bed, roused his private secretary, and at once sent orders to the Admiralty that the *Anadyomene*, Captain O'Dowd, was to coal at once and proceed to the West Coast of Africa for three years—an order afterwards rescinded.

So O'Dowd did not gain much by bringing his aunts to Mrs. Rickaby's party. They *left* him forty thousand pounds. O'Dowd went into Parliament on it, and the way he mangled the Admiralty is a matter of history.

Meanwhile, the two old ladies had made a clear field for the meeting of the cousins.

“You had better go away, Dixie,” said Oakshott. “Granby, stay with me.”

CHAPTER XXXIV.

MOTHER AND SON.

"You have been long out of England, Arthur!"

"I have been very long away.   Here is my wife."

So Lord Oakshott looked on his love, his only love, again.   His love for her had nearly died years ago, but the meeting in Canada had unhappily revived it.   His love had been for Dixie and Dickie.   But as he looked on her he loved her again, with a mad passion of fury such as only a poet can feel.   He thought that he had loved her boy; he had written endless poems about her boy.   Now he knew that he loved *her*, and no other.   Her boy had looked him in the face twice or three times that night, but he did not know him.   He thought that he loved Dixie; it is possible that he did.   But when this grey, bent woman came before him he knew the great mystery of a great, eager, possibly incoherent heart, given away once and for ever.

Where was all his half-inarticulate poetry now?   The best of it only fit to be the dirt under her feet: and she a bent, grey woman.

She had aged fearfully; she looked as old as Lady Nora, who was old enough to be her mother.   Yet she was beautiful still, possibly more beautiful than ever.   Oakshott said hoarsely, as he stood before her—

"Let me hear your voice once more, Lady Oakshott."

She spoke very low: "Your recollections of me cannot be very pleasant."

"My recollections of you," said Lord Oakshott, "have always been extremely pleasant—among the most pleasant of my life."

Granby Dixon says that a flash of hatred passed between the two cousins' eyes at this moment. I say nothing about the matter, because I was not there.

Sir Arthur said, "Oakshott, I suppose we shall meet as friends?"

"We *must* meet as friends, most certainly," said Lord Oakshott. "Will you call on me to-morrow?"

"I shall be happy."

A footman came up and said, "Miss Prout's carriage stops the way, my lord."

"Ask Miss Prout to go down. I am going home with Mr. Granby Dixon. Or stay, I will see her in. Will you wait an instant, Granby and Arthur?"

He turned, and a splendid though beardless young fellow confronted him.

" I know that you are busy with your parliamentary duties, my lord," said the young man. "Will you let me see Miss Prout to her carriage?"

"Surely," said Lord Oakshott. "Why, you are the young gentleman, Riccardo, who set my poor silly song so sweetly. I thank you. Would you tell Miss Prout that I shall not be long, but I have parliamentary business."

The young man stood in the centre of the group. Suddenly Lady Oakshott put her hand on his shoulder. "I want to ask you a favour," said Lady Oakshott.

"Surely."

"Give me that flower. What is it? I have been so long in America that I do not know."

"It is a white primrose, Madam," said the young man, looking into his mother's eyes without the slightest recognition. "I always wear them."

"Why?"

"Ah, that I cannot tell. I must run after Miss Prout."

Nothing more was said, except from Lord Oakshott to Sir Arthur. He said: "Come to-morrow at ten, for Granby, the plague of my life, wants me to speak in the House of Lords at four."

Granby and Oakshott got their coats in the hall, and walked home through the streets smoking. Lord Oakshott spoke first.

"That cousin of mine has been ill-treating that woman his wife."

"That is most obvious," said Granby. "He looks a greater cut-throat than he did when he went away."

"Granby," said Oakshott, "do you sit up reading very late at night?"

"Yes, I have to."

"Do you keep a lamp burning?"

"I don't see how I could read and write without it."

"Do you ever let your light go out before daylight?"

"Certainly."

"I intend to put my light out before daylight, some day."

"Oakshott, you would never do such a thing as that."

"That man has aged that woman twenty years."

"Yes, but you would never do such a thing as you speak of. I would burn your Castle down first. I would, by heaven!"

"You may burn my Castle down," said Lord Oakshott; "but you can't force me to keep my lamp burning."

CHAPTER XXXV.

FACE TO FACE.

TEN o'clock in the morning was the hour when the cousins were to meet. Sir Arthur arrived at that hour exactly, and found Lord Oakshott walking up and down the breakfast-room, smoking, with a breakfast-table laid. Smoking before breakfast is considered by some reprehensible, but Lord Oakshott did it, and Comfrey permitted it—(he had been so used to foreign dignitaries that he did not mind it, though he declared on his death-bed that the story of his having cooked a pug-dog for the Chinese Ambassadors was entirely without foundation)—so Lord Oakshott smoked his cigar in peace.

"Good-morning, Arthur," said Lord Oakshott.

"Good-morning to the head of the family," said Sir Arthur.

"Your boy *is* dead, then?"

"Yes, my boy is dead."

"Arthur, I am very sorry; on my soul I am very sorry."

"I believe you," said Sir Arthur; "you are weak enough to be sorry for anything."

"Come, speak more gently than that, Arthur; you may want my help some day. Where did the boy die?"

"In Tennessee."

"Of fever?"

"Of ague."

"I am very sorry. You will eat breakfast with me, Arthur?"

"I shall be most happy to have breakfast with the best man in the world," said Sir Arthur: "more particularly as I have not been to bed all night." So the breakfast was brought in, and they sat down.

"What have you been doing all night, Arthur?"

"Following your occupation—gambling."

"I don't call my game gambling, Arthur," said Oakshott, sitting down to the breakfast-table. "At least it is gambling, with a difference. You don't mean to say that you have been at the real thing?"

"Yes," said Sir Arthur, laughing; "I *have* been. I have lost a hundred and fifty pounds. My dear Oakshott, the *real* thing is humbug, and I don't see any fun about it. It is chance. You and I are two of the greatest gamblers in the whole world, are we not?"

"Well, we are."

"Did either of us ever lose a hundred and fifty pounds on a chance?" said Sir Arthur.

"You lost £60,000, Arthur," said Lord Oakshott.

"Yes, but then I knew you would pay that on sentimental grounds. That was no chance at all."

"Arthur! Arthur!" said Lord Oakshott; "do you know what people would call you if they heard you talk?"

"They would call me an infernal scoundrel, I think," said Sir Arthur.

"What has made you so wild, Arthur?"

"Bad blood, I suppose," said Sir Arthur. "But I want to pay you back that money you paid for me. I will do so at once. The Austrian Government have guaranteed five per cent. on the Trieste dock works."

"You will let me run away," said Lord Oakshott suddenly, ringing. "May I tell Granby Dixon?"

"Not till you have finished your own business," said Sir Arthur.

Lord Oakshott was away for one hour and ten minutes. When he came back he found Sir Arthur reading the *Times.* He looked up and said, "Have you done it?"

"Yes; thirty thousand at fifteen."

"You have told your man to be quick," said Sir Arthur; "because it will be all over the town this evening."

"The thing is done," said Oakshott, impatiently. "I have brought you here a receipt for the whole of the money I paid for you. When I was safe I told Granby, and he is safe by now. That is all about the matter. I have signed a cheque, payable to you and order, for a thousand pounds."

"Hand it over, Oakshott."

"Only on one condition—that you answer truthfully to my questions."

"I will swear that," said Sir Arthur. "Have you got a cigar?"

Lord Oakshott gave him one.

"Now give me the cheque. Mind, I swear."

Lord Oakshott gave him the cheque also. There was a spirit-lamp still burning under the coffee-pot, for the waiter had re-supplied it; and Sir Arthur deliberately rolled up the cheque, lit it at the spirit-lamp, and burnt it in lighting his cigar.

"Now I will tell you all about it, old man. We have had an explanation or two before by letter. We are face to face at this very moment. I love her, and she loves you; also you love her. Consequently I hate you. Why, in the devil's name, did you come to America?"

" Have you ill-treated her, Arthur ?"

" Yes, beaten her. Down in Illinois I was hunting one of the Tapansoca ring, and I told her to be civil to the man ; and she wouldn't be civil to him ; and I beat her. And the Illinois magistrates wouldn't take a fine. They gave me two months."

He held his head down as he said this ; otherwise he might have taken the awful warning in Lord Oakshott's face.

" What else did you do in America ?" said Oakshott.

" I speculated, and that is the country for speculation. I am worth £80,000 now."

" Arthur," said Lord Oakshott, " we are certain about the Trieste business ?"

" Quite certain."

" Well, we will talk no more now. You are a cleverer man than I am at gambling. I will sell out of the Euphrates Valley, and I will put the whole of the money into your hands for re-investment."

" That is a pretty strong trust to a man who hates you."

" You said that I was the best man in the world."

" I hate best men. Still give me the money; I will use it well for you."

" I will do so. But now, do you know anything of your boy Dickie ?"

" On my knees before God, Oakshott, I know nothing at all."

" You see, we are both interested," said Lord Oakshott. " Your estate is cleared, your forgeries are forgotten by all but me and young Brogden. I have been a fine steward for you. You can take your place in the county—nay, with your talents, in the country. My property goes to you, and you will be the Earl: with your talents you might be Marquis. I shall not marry. Your boy is dead. All we want is an heir."

"Why will you not marry? I thought you would marry Miss Prout," said Sir Arthur.

"Marry Dixie! why, the man is mad," said Oakshott.

"I suppose you will marry no one but my wife," said Sir Arthur.

"My dear soul, I must murder you first," said Lord Oakshott. "Arthur, it gets late, and I have to speak in the House of Lords at a little after four. I want a few more words with you. When am I to give an account of my stewardship?"

Said Sir Arthur, good-humouredly: "I will go down to Poole to-morrow and inquire into your defalcations. I am sorry that you will not accept repayment from me, Oakshott."

"I have accepted it, Arthur, by what you told me about Trieste."

"Yes, and then have practically returned it to me by putting it in my hands in ten days. The moment you found that I had ill-treated that woman who is my wife, you in reality gave it to me back again."

"Arthur, I will not take money from you. All that is realized in this transaction must go to you, and I will make up the balance. Now go away."

And Sir Arthur went to his place, as he found Oakshott dangerous.

Young Horsley, the Dorset poet, is making a collection of Lord Oakshott's speeches, like those of the late lamented

Prince Consort. Granby Dixon, when he heard that some one else was preparing his poems for the press, and young Horsley his speeches, said that he did not know which was the greatest fool of the two. He did not mean the late Prince Consort and Lord Oakshott; he meant some one else and young Horsley. Some one else argued with him and used language. Some one said that Oakshott's poems were worth preserving. He said, " But the speeches!" Granby may sneer, but some of Oakshott's speeches were quite as good as *any* one else's. Lord P—— ought to have known, and he said that if Oakshott had a head on his shoulders which did not always turn hindside before, he could have been one of the finest debaters of the age. In the end Granby took the poems in hand, as he says, to save the world from Bedlam.

I think that he was an able debater. (I object to disagreeing with Lord P——.) I think that he was one of the ablest debaters ever known. If you desired to gather his sentiments on any one point, he would at once turn to with a will and tell you more about some other subject than you ever knew before. For example, if you asked him (he knew a deal of astronomy) about the rings of Saturn, he would tell you at once about the tides in the Pacific. Granby tried that in answering Admiralty questions in the absence of the First Lord, but the sailors would not stand it.

Though young Horsley is editing his speeches (Oakshott has not done speaking yet), I shall take the liberty of editing one—a very short one.

He met Granby Dixon by the Abbey, and he said—

" Granby, I shall put the light out some night. He has been ill-using her again."

That is the speech I wished to edit.   Horsley may take
the whole of the rest.   Oakshott, under his fearful temptation, made that speech to Granby Dixon.   One speech he
made which I will not edit.   He said to the empty air—

" The dog shall die ; he has lived too long."

CHAPTER XXXVI.

OAKSHOTT IN BETWEEN THE DEVIL AND THE DEEP SEA.

GRANBY DIXON'S idea was that Oakshott might get his oar
in about four o'clock ; but things were otherwise arranged.
It so happened that Lord Oakshott never got his oar in at
all in the debate in which he was wanted to speak.   At five
there came on a perfectly innocent-looking question, about
the Grand Turk Railway.   It was a very innocent question ;
it was only a question amounting to this : " Whether her
Majesty, in case of war, was prepared to guarantee the
neutrality of the Grand Turk Railway."   Oakshott had a
lot of money in it, for he had deceived Granby, and he did
not want to lose it.   So he at once, instead of minding the
business he was set on, thought about his shares.   He had
not been in the House five minutes before he saw that Lord
Roversdale was dead against the Grand Turk Railway.   He
looked round to see who was there, whom he knew.   He
saw no one but the Archbishop, and so he stepped over to
him.

He explained matters to the Archbishop, who listened
carefully to him, and then told him, Oakshott, that his dealings in the matter of the Grand Turk Railway savoured
strongly of the mammon of unrighteousness.   The more

Oakshott pointed out that the railway was intended to Christianize the East, the more did the Archbishop, a very sensible man, point out that commercially the thing was a swindle.

Oakshott knew it. He had determined to sell out; as shares were above par, he would make a great deal of money by this, for the Grand Turk Railway at one time, when he bought in, was a laughing-stock in Europe. He had resolved to sell out at once, but he would put his shares up by to-morrow morning. He had told Granby Dixon that he had sold out, and had told that kind little man to do so, but in fact Oakshott had not entirely sold out. He hungered for a few pounds more.

Meanwhile Lord Roversdale was pounding the Grand Turk Railway to bits. He did so, but he had not the facts and figures about it which Oakshott had. Oakshott rose after him—Oakshott, the very cleverest financier of the day. The House of Lords listened. Oakshott demolished Lord Roversdale utterly, so utterly that even Granby and Sir Arthur would have bought in the next morning, unless they had heard from Oakshott that he had sold out. His peroration was very fine :—

"Railways create commerce; they create civilization. They engender new wants, new thoughts, and, what is more valuable than all, new ideas. They engender new wants : they supply them. They engender new thoughts : they supply them by books and newspapers. They engender new ideas : and they supply them by the circulation of ideas," continued Lord Oakshott. "These are, however, very trivial matters. I recommend them to your Lordships' House. Most of the best railways, such as the Illinois

Central, started on the path of civilization, and paid small dividends at first. They created civilization, and they are paying. I say about this scheme as I would say about a hundred others, give no guarantee. Cast your bread upon the waters, and you will find it after—— after things get fixed up—I mean developed."

This speech of Lord Oakshott sent Grand Turks up, and some sold out and made money. But people had a belief in American finance in those days, and the concluding Americanism convinced them. They knew he had been in America, and they bought.

However, as far as we are concerned he was in an abominable humour with himself. He did not like the business at all. When all was said and done, Lord Roversdale was an honester man than he. Yet Lord Roversdale laughed at his best poem (Granby has not given you that; Lord Oakshott objected). Lord Roversdale stood up there and spoke God's truth about these swindling schemes, while he, Oakshott the gambler, did not speak the exact truth. Oakshott knew well that he had quite the power and brains of Lord Roversdale : he knew that he could beat him, or any man, in financial debate. Yet he wished that he was Lord Roversdale, with his magnificent honesty. That man, Roversdale, owned many racehorses. He, Oakshott, had never owned one. Yet the wretched welshers who hung about race-courses always knew that they could depend on Lord Roversdale to run square. Those poor dogs, with their lives in their hands, could trust Lord Roversdale. How could Granby and Sir Arthur trust him—after to-morrow ? for he had as good as lied to his own friend Granby—for Granby's good, doubtless; but he had been false.

He thought of these things as he walked home over the Park to Comfrey's. But he said to himself, "I will do it."

He was in Piccadilly, and was gaping about him, when he felt a hand on his shoulder, and a voice in his ear said, "Oakshott!"

He turned. It was Lord Roversdale. "Oakshott, have I offended you?"

"I do not think so; I have offended myself. If you have offended me, I entirely forgive you."

"Oakshott, I am older than you. I want to speak to you very seriously. You must come among us again."

"I am not fit to come among you."

"Nonsense, you are one of the best men we could have."

"One of the best men!" said Oakshott. "I am going to sell out of the Grand Turk to-morrow morning, and make twenty-five thousand pounds."

"We can do nothing with you," said Lord Roversdale; "P—— said so."

"I can do something for myself, though," said Oakshott. "I can cut my own throat, or another man's."

"About a woman?" said Lord Roversdale.

"Yes."

"So I thought. If you ever come to your senses, come to us. You are a good fellow. Are there not other women in the world?"

"Not for me, Roversdale. Good-bye."

CHAPTER XXXVII.

MURDER.

WHEN he got to his hotel, the head waiter met him. "I beg your pardon, my lord, but I have taken a great liberty."

"I am used to that," said Oakshott. "Where is Miss Prout?"

"Miss Prout, my lord? She went away with Lady Kathleen O'Brien to dinner with Lady Hainault."

"I forget—I forget—quite right. And what liberty have you taken?"

"The Duchesse d'Avranches came, my lord, and she said that she would wait here till you came home. I told her that you had to speak in the House of Lords, but she would take no refusal. I put her into the little room."

"You did quite right," said Oakshott. "Will you lay covers for two at dinner?"

"Have you spoken, my lord, or do you go back?"

"Yes, I have spoken : I remain at home."

It was dark now, and he took a candle from the slab. The man, from some instinct, did not follow him upstairs.

He had a deadly feeling in his heart. There were some countries in which you could do murder and escape.

He went into the little room and put the candle on the slab. He saw no one at first.

Then something which looked like a black ghost moved on the sofa and stood upright. Oakshott trembled; he saw that it was Mrs. O'Brien. She was in black velvet.

She came to the point at once ; it was her way.

I confess that I would rather not write the scene which

follows. It is very short, and *aposiopesis* would only confuse the reader.

"Oakshott," she said, "that hound, that dog, has been beating my daughter."

"I know it," said Oakshott : "he told me himself."

"Will you let him live ?"

"No."

"How will you kill him ?"

"In a way never to be detected by law."

"Sure ?"

"I think pretty certain."

"Oakshott, I hated you at one time, and believed you to be a rascal. I love you now."

"You were quite right in believing me a rascal," said Lord Oakshott, "for I am going to do a very singular act of rascality to-morrow morning. Are you in the Grand Turk Railway, Mrs. O'Brien ?"

"No. Should I buy in, dear ?"

"By no means. The thing is a rotten humbug. I have made a speech in the House of Lords this afternoon which will put shares up in spite of Roversdale, for our people are fools. I am going to sell out."

"Sharp practice," said Mrs. O'Brien.

"I am only a gambler and a poet," said Oakshott. "I am a very good gambler, and a very bad poet. Now, Mrs. O'Brien—I never call you Duchess—come to dinner."

The Duchesse d'Avranches declined dinner. She went out. She had lied to Oakshott, for she *was* in the Grand Turk, and she departed to make her arrangements for the next day. When she and Oakshott parted, they had murder in their minds.

CHAPTER XXXVIII.

SAVED.

OAKSHOTT sat down to dinner alone, and determined to eat and not to think of anything. There was whitebait, and he liked that, and was beginning to eat it when the head waiter came in and brought him a card.

"Signor Riccardo."

"Show him up," said Oakshott.

And up he came. The pleasantest, handsomest, most gallant young man you ever saw. I have not kept my secret very well, and I do not see the use of keeping it any longer. In the very best plays you always know the truth if you are a good playgoer. Riccardo was Dickie of the white primroses. But Oakshott was not in the least degree in the secret.

"You set a song of mine the other day," said Lord Oakshott. "You set it very well. The words were very bad, but the scanning was good enough for setting. But sit down to dinner with me, and we will talk."

"Is it right that the singer should sit with the patron, in England?" said Riccardo. "I ought surely to sit with your servants. Still, I take the great honour from my dear patron. I shall love you for ever."

"I don't quite understand you, Signor Riccardo. A man like you is fit for the company of princes."

"Do you not know, then? I am the little drummer boy whose fortune you made with your money."

"Dan G——'s boy?"

"Exactly."

"God has sent you to me, lad. I will not do it."

"Do what, dear lord?" said Riccardo, pausing in his dinner.

"I mean merely that the light shall be kept burning, and that I will leave my money in the Grand Turks."

Riccardo had long known that all poets were mad, so he assumed that Oakshott was as mad as the rest of them. This misguided young man, not having a sound English education about him, admired Lord Oakshott's poetry, and set to music as much as would scan. When it wouldn't scan he altered it. Oakshott never discovered it. If you were to make Oakshott an apple-pie bed, he would apologize to the chamber-maid, and say that he got in at the wrong end by mistake.

Underlying all Oakshott's gentleness and good humour, there was a substratum of potential ferocity. In Edinburgh, the other day, I had nearly the finest bulldog in the world licking my face and taking biscuits from my mouth. At one word from her master she would have taken me by the throat, and one of us must have died. I should have had to kill the dog. The dog, properly treated, would try to kill any enemy of yours at which you set her. The boldest burglar would never dream of facing that dog. The boldest swindler was afraid of Oakshott.

Yet he was gentle to tenderness with Riccardo. "I like pretty things about me," he said, "and you are a pretty thing. You are making much money, are you not?"

"I am making a grand fortune, thanks to your generosity," said Riccardo,

"I am glad of that," said Oakshott. "I am very glad of that. I wrong people by winning my money, but I like to do good with it. Will you do me a favour? Will you set a song for me?"

"With deep pleasure; what is it?"

"Rubbish as usual, but there is lilt enough in it to go."

"Can I hear a verse?"

"Yes. A young couple of ours was blown all the way to Cherbourg the other day in a fishing-boat. The husband then went on a coasting voyage (for they were very poor), and he left her with our dear friends the Mantalents at Cherbourg. She was with child by him, and when he came back to her she had a bouncing boy. They were in great danger of their lives in returning, and somehow we heard nothing of them for six months. It is a simple story enough, but it struck me as pretty. I will give you the song after dinner. At present, however, I wish to know your history."

"I think that is very easily told."

"Then tell it. To begin with, where were you born?"

"You puzzle me there, dear patron; I do not know."

"What do you first remember?" said Oakshott, seeing his way to a new poem.

"These things," said Riccardo, pointing to some white primulas in his button-hole.

"Nothing beyond?" said Oakshott.

"I am utterly confused, Lord Oakshott. Did you ever steal anything?"

"Apples," said Oakshott, slowly and thoughtfully; "treacle, jam, cream to any amount, and, on one occasion, a sovereign! In my speculations I have robbed and plundered widows and orphans no end, but I never actually *stole* any larger sum than a sovereign. Would you continue your recollections ?"

"Well, I made a terrible robbery at some time or another, I can't think when. It must have been before the white primroses."

"Where did you get the white primroses ?"

"On the banks of an enormous river, miles wide. Trees hundreds of feet high on both sides. And a woman ten feet high, who got me to go away with her."

"Americans," said Lord Oakshott. "This was an American river ; probably the Missouri."

"I think not," said Riccardo. "I went away with that woman, and I kept what I had stolen."

"How ?"

"It was in my mouth always when I thought they were likely to take it from me. See here."

He took a five-shilling piece, laid it on the palm of his hand, and then passed his hand quickly over his face : the five-shilling piece was gone, but he went on talking just the same.

"I learnt that from—from—I can't remember. I have not taken too much wine, Lord Oakshott, have I ? I never do. But I thought that the devil was in the room, or something."

"The devil *was* in the room, boy, until you came in and turned him out. Go on. He is not here now, by any means. We poets and musicians excite ourselves unnecessarily. I am a poor poet, but I have my dreams. You are a splendid fellow, and have no doubt stronger ones."

"Yet I am not given to it. You looked at me, and my memory seemed to go back. Forgive me one hundred times."

"Granted one hundred thousand times," said Oakshott. "Now about the thing you stole, and which you kept in your mouth in spite of every one. Can you show it to me?"

"No, Lord Oakshott. I have it round my neck, but I would much sooner not show it. It is the miniature of a boy set in diamonds."

"What is it?" said Oakshott to *himself*. "I wonder who it can be."

"Well, after the white primroses," Riccardo went on, "you pretty well know everything : drummer, bandsman, and the whole of it.——My God !"

Dixie had opened the door between her room and the dining-room, and had appeared suddenly to Riccardo. She had come from her dinner, and had dropped her chaperone on the road. She had robbed the conservatory of the house where she had been of white primulas, and she held them in her hand.

"I know what you are doing, Earlie; you are getting Signor Riccardo to set those verses for you. See, Signor Riccardo, I also have white primroses. Give me yours, and I will give you mine. I dreamt of you last night, and I dreamt that you swam a great river to get these for me. Did you ever swim a river ?"

As she said this the same fixed look came on her face as came on Riccardo's. "I swam the Po once, Mademoiselle, but not for you. It was for another young lady."

"Faithless," said Dixie. "Earlie, I am going out no more to-night."

"How did you call his lordship?" said Riccardo, suddenly.

"Earlie,"

"Well, may we interchange primroses, Mademoiselle? The name rings tones on my ear."

"Americanisms apart, I love you for saying that, Signor Riccardo. Did you ever know a man with a timber leg?"

"Dixie, you are talking slang," said Lord Oakshott.

"Well, I will not, then. Did you ever know a man with a hickory leg, Signor Riccardo?"

"That is just as bad," said Lord Oakshott.

"Then we will go into California," said Miss Prout. "Did you ever know a man with a whipstick leg, Signor Riccardo?"

By this time Riccardo had time to speak. "No, Mademoiselle," he said.

"Earlie has a whipstick leg," said Dixie. "Earlie gambles; Earlie does things which I hate. Yet Earlie is a good and generous man."

"What have I done, sweetheart?" said Lord Oakshott.

"You told me to bull when I should have beared," said Dixie, "and I have lost twenty pounds."

Riccardo rose to leave the house, because he had his professional engagements to attend to. Lord Oakshott happened to leave the room for a few minutes, and Riccardo and Dixie Prout got on very well together.

There was suddenly a violent hammering at the door, and Comfrey opened it, or, to be more correct, one of his waiters did so. Two men in helmets rushed upstairs and into the room; and the foremost of them cried out, "Oakshott, there is a splendid fire; come away!"

No Oakshott was there. Riccardo happened to be speaking very earnestly to Dixie as they came in. He may have been rather close to her, or he may not. It is, however, perfectly certain that as Riccardo faced them they both stood still.

Riccardo watched them very carefully. The foremost of the pair was a bull-necked, bull-headed young man, who looked as though he could love, fight, and die like a gentleman. Riccardo thought to himself, "You are no fool either. I would go to the devil after you. You will do !"

The young man who stood behind the first young man was much taller. He had a long beard, which mixed with the strap of the helmet. They both stood still for a moment, and then the tallest of them said—"We came for Lord Oakshott : is he here?"

"I will call him in a moment," said Riccardo.

The bull-headed young man said, "I thought you were he at first."

"I am Riccardo the singer, your Highness," said Dickie.

"You are very like him," said the other young man, who happened to be a duke. "Call Oakshott. Tell him that there is a great fire, and that we can get a helmet for him."

Oakshott was brought at once. He had been promised the great treat of being scalded and scorched long before. On his being put to the test he emphatically declined, and said that he would wait until his own house was on fire.

"I will go," said Riccardo; "I am sure you will let me come with you."

And he went with the two other young men.

CHAPTER XXXIX.

RICCARDO'S DISASTER.

THE fire was a very fine one indeed. The first personage got scratched on his nose, and the second personage got

his head broken by a brick while he had taken off his helmet
to wipe his forehead. Riccardo got up a ladder to rescue
some one who turned out to be purely imaginary : he, however, was allowed to have performed prodigies of valour.
He was severely burnt in his trousers ; which, so to speak,
shows that he was fairly under fire, though he declares that
the fire was under him. When I visited him in bed, I
noticed that he could lie on his right side or his left, but
never on his back ; so I suppose that his theory of the fire
having burst suddenly out of the second floor window while
he was on the third, and its having taken him in the rear, is
in the main correct.

A much sadder thing than burnt trousers befell Dickie,
however. As he was coming down the ladder, he found
that his shirt was on fire in the very place where the flames
from the second story had caught him. Trying to put the
fire out with his left hand he let go with his right, and, falling
eighteen feet, not only knocked down the second personage,
but broke his own leg.

He was, by the orders of the first personage, carried round
to Lord Oakshott's apartments, as he exhibited a strong
objection to go to St. George's Hospital.

No one was there but Dixie, for Oakshott, having been
asked to go to the fire, had gone for a walk on Westminster
Bridge, on his new principle of never doing what he was
asked. Now, Dixie had seen a great deal in America, and
was not in the least degree afraid of a man. Dixie had seen
a dead man or two in her time, so she was not in the least
degree afraid of a live one. She had him in, and made
the fireman and the policeman lay him on the sofa ; then she
sent a waiter for a surgeon.

Dickie was not exactly moaning, but giving that curious grunt which the bravest men give in their agony. Dixie knew the sound well. She had seen a few things in Colorado which would frighten most people. She was not in the least degree frightened now. She got her scissors and cut his trousers up above the ankle; then she got some cold water and a towel, and bandaged his leg; meantime the waiter held the candle and looked on in wonder.

If he had been her brother, he would not have wondered at all; but he was most obviously not her brother. He held the light, wondering. Then the doctor came, and he pronounced compound fracture, which meant, as Dixie well knew, six weeks in bed.

She waited until the doctor had done, and then she waited for him in the outer room.

"You have got him to bed?" she said.

"Yes, Miss Prout; into Lord Oakshott's bed."

She at once rang twice for the chambermaid.

"Lord Oakshott will want another room to-night," she said; "let it be on this floor, if you please, because he will wish to watch this sick gentleman."

"You are accustomed to sick-beds, I perceive, Miss Prout," said the doctor.

"Well, no," said Dixie; "I know very little of anything except wounds and accidents. I know very little of real sickness."

"You know about wounds, then?" said the doctor.

"Why, who should know better?" said Dixie, with the entire belief that the lunatic expedition of Lord Oakshott to Colorado was perfectly well known in England. "I have *had* to know. Why, doctor, when the Apaches and Commanches hooked together against the stars and stripes, we were like a rotten pumpkin against a Newtown pippin for odds. We thrashed them, though, and will thrash them again. If you ever wade in West, doctor, don't you care one bit for Creeks or Blackfeet, but you mind the Commanches and Apaches. I took my scalp to Court the other day: if they had known how near it was being hung in a wigwam, they wouldn't have liked it quite so much."

"I have heard of Lord Oakshott's travels in America," said the doctor.

"I suppose you have," said Dixie; "we never talk of them."

"I was not aware that you were with him."

"I am not aware that it was any one's business to know," said Dixie. "However, we were there together; and in spite of Apaches and Commanches, we may go there again. Earlie and I are not like other people : we are different from other people altogether. Earlie and I go where we will, and do as we choose. I for my own part think that that is the privilege of riches, and Earlie is very rich indeed."

"Earlie is——" said the doctor.

"Lord Oakshott," said Dixie.

"Ho! I see," said the doctor; but he did not see one bit, for all that he said so. "You will see to the cold bandages," continued the doctor, for Dixie had said nothing at all.

"Yes."

"You had better let me send you a nurse."

"I hate nurses," said Dixie.

"Well, a Sister, then?"

"I don't see, myself, what we want with a Sister; but

perhaps you had better send one. I will watch the young gentleman until she comes. Good-night."

The doctor thought this a strange arrangement, but he departed to a Home near by, and sent a Sister off post haste.

CHAPTER XL.

DICKIE'S NURSES.

"How is he, Miss?" said the Sister quietly, as soon as she had taken off her wimple and come to the bed.

"I don't like him at all," said Dixie in a matter-of-fact way. "He won't hold his hand still for me to feel his pulse: and he is wandering also. There is something more than a fracture, I fear."

Certainly this young man was very ill, and entirely out of his mind. He faced the Sister very humbly, but to Dixie he always said, "Kiss me, darling."

"That is the way he goes on," said Dixie. "I don't like it. I tell you fairly, Sister, that I *don't* like it."

"My dear," said the Sister, "he does not mean any harm."

"Any harm!" said Dixie; "I don't suppose he does; I should think not. I mean medically. He is going to have a serious turn of delirium."

"He is delirious now," said the Sister.

It was perfectly evident. The poor young man was utterly beside himself with pain; they could do nothing with him at all, for he kept crying out that his back was broken, and that he must kiss Dixie before he died.

Dixie said to the Sister, "I had better kiss him, I think;"

and the Sister said, "It would be much better." So she kissed him.

"I wish Earlie would come," she said, and then sat and waited. Her kiss had quieted this young man for a time, and they thought he was dying.

"You have been used to this, I see, Miss Prout," said the Sister.

"I! Oh yes! In the Indian war in Arizona we had much worse cases than this—bless you, much worse. I was with Cousin Marie then, and I used to help her to nurse the men. In Arizona there was a young man just like this, who insisted on kissing me and Earlie before he died. That makes me superstitious, you know."

"Who is Earlie?" asked the Sister.

"Why, my father, Lord Oakshott," said Dixie.

"How came you in the Indian war in Arizona?" said the Sister.

"It was some speculation of Earlie's," she answered; "some silver mines, I think. He made money, I know, because he gave me diamonds, and took me to Saratoga, and I hate Saratoga as badly as I do Brighton."

"You do not care for pleasure, then," said the Sister, as Dixie thought with ulterior religious views, for Dixie by all accounts would be made horribly rich by the mad nobleman.

"Oh yes, I do, though," said Dixie: "I do most mortally like to be fine. I want to go on the stage, but Earlie won't stand that."

"But you are religious, my dear," said the Sister.

"Of course I am; all good women are religious," said Dixie.

" And all good men," said the Sister.

"I don't know anything about *that*, not being a man my-self. Earlie is a good man, in my opinion, but he is not considered a religious man. He will spend hundreds of thousands of pounds on the Church : you know he intends to do so ; he is going to restore our Abbey ; but I can do anything with him except make him go to church when he does not want to. Why, here is Earlie !"

In fact, Lord Oakshott having, for no earthly purpose which any one ever discovered, taken a boat at Westminster stairs and gone to Rotherhithe, had now reappeared. That a young man lay groaning heavily in his own bed was not a matter of the smallest surprise to him. It was rather a nuisance, certainly, because he wished to compose a song on the Thames at midnight. It was never written, as far as I can find. The only fragment of it which I can find consists merely of the lines—

> " I floated on the stream at the midnight hour,
> And I ——"

We cannot find any more. It is a terrible loss to literature, no doubt, but our readers will be spared it. He declares that he wrote it all out at Baden. If he did, he left it there, or lost it ; we can find no trace of it at all.

CHAPTER XLI.

SISTER CAMILLA.

LORD OAKSHOTT approached the bed, and looked at the young man. Then he said, "Dixie, leave the room ;" and Dixie did so.

" My dear Madam," he said to the Sister, " what do you think of this case ?"

" It seems going very badly; " he cannot lie on his back." Lord Oakshott suggested reasons.

" More than that," said the Sister; " he cannot lie on his left shoulder."

" Let me raise him," said Oakshott, " while you pull his shirt down.   I need not tell *you* to be gentle."

They got him up and pulled down his shirt.   Under the left shoulder was a large splinter of wood as long as your hand, which the doctors had unfortunately never observed ; it was the splinter from the side spar of the ladder from which he had fallen.

" Sister, go and send for the surgeon," said Lord Oakshott hurriedly.

The Sister did so.   She was not gone more than a minute. When she left the young man, he had a thin gold chain round his neck.   She only saw his back, but it was perfectly evident that something hung on his breast suspended by it. When she came back, the chain was gone.

Oakshott had turned the young man over in bed.   I have seen a dead man in his coffin look twenty years younger than he was when he died.   And some say that people who are very ill sometimes look younger.   I only know that Lord Oakshott, when he turned the young man over, saw in his haggard features no less a person than the lost Dickie.

He saw it now for the first time ; but round Dickie's neck was hanging a gold locket, very small, but set with diamonds. He remembered what Dickie had said of it, and he knew how to open it.   He did so.   It contained a portrait of himself as he was at eighteen.

He had found the boy at last, but how?   The boy was to him only the mother's son.   He loved the boy now as he had always done ; but now he had a gentler passion for the mother, and a murderous hatred towards the father.   The innocent old times were gone for ever.

The Sister came back.   "Madam," he said, "I will wait until the operation is concluded ; then I will go elsewhere."

"Whither?" said the Sister quietly.

"I cannot tell," said Oakshott ; "what does it matter?"

"It matters this much," said the Sister : "you have the look of Cain on your face, and so I wish to know where you are going.   Oakshott ! Oakshott ! I knew your face so well once, that I know now that you are angry."

"Why do you call me Oakshott?" he said, growing pale.

"Look at me !" said the Sister.

Oakshott looked, but shook his head.

"You do not know me?"

"No."

"I am Camilla Borichi.   You loved me once, and I think that you wronged me.   I think, though, the world, our little world, forgave you and said no, for the time."

Oakshott fell back against the wall.   From every quarter of the heavens his sins were coming on to his devoted head. While he had been writing fribbling poetry, speculating, and making sharp speeches in the House of Lords, the consequences of his actions had been developing themselves like dragons' teeth.   They were coming on him now with a vengeance.   His head was hot, and his speech thick.

"Camilla ?"

"Yes. Hush, now ; we do not know who is listening."

"I should not have known you."

"Be quiet. You are watched, and your life is in danger How did I come here to-night, do you think?"

"I do not know."

"I lied. I have been watching you and yours night and day. When I heard that there was an accident in your house, I said that the young man was a Romanist, so that I might get into it. I tell you, Oakshott, as you live by bread, that I care nothing about the young man at all. What was that which you have taken from him?"

"Only a picture of myself, which he stole. This young man is my cousin's son."

"And *her* son," said the Sister.

"Yes," said Oakshott, "and *her* son."

"Oakshott, our time is short," said Sister Camilla. "Do you love her?"

"Yes."

"Then mind Sir Arthur, for he has put the Cammoristi on you. In God's name, mind yourself. What will have you made?"

"I did not make any; I wrote a song instead. I saw it the other day."

"Like you," said Sister Camilla. "Then all your property will go to Sir Arthur."

"I suppose so; but I am dazed and stunned."

"Here are the doctors," said Sister Camilla. And in one moment she was the decorous Sister of Charity.

The operation was very tedious and long, but successful. The young man was laid on his back in bed again, and the doctors were congratulating one another, when the lunatic Lord Oakshott did one of his most lunatic acts.

He said to the Sister of Charity: "Camilla, one kiss.

The world is closing round me. The consequences of my own actions are now reaching me."

The Sister, to the astonishment of the doctors, said—

" Oakshott, if you see that, and will act upon it, you are safe still. I will kiss you."

" I see it—I see it all now. I see what I ought to have done, and I see that I have not done it. Kiss me, and let me go."

" Whither?" said Sister Camilla.

" To the hell which I have created for myself by negligence," said Oakshott; " a hell of misery and still possibly of crime."

So he passed out, leaving them wondering what he meant.

And as he went along he kept saying to himself, " After all she loved him. For her sake and for her son's sake, No !"

CHAPTER XLII.

WORSE THAN MURDER.

THE House of Commons sat very late that night, and so he was sure of young Brogden, who was the sort of member that would sit the seat of his trousers out if there was the remotest chance of his getting his oar in. Oakshott told the doorkeeper that he wanted Mr. Granby Dixon and Mr. Brogden when they were disengaged. As it appeared that Mr. Granby Dixon was engaged in a violently acrimonious and personal debate, and that Mr. Brogden was to follow him, Oakshott wandered into the House of Lords, and took his place.

It so happened that Lord Roversdale had got on to the

railway business again, and had been pitching into (I hope
that is not vulgar) several noble lords, not one of whom by
a singular accident happened to be present. On Lord Oakshott's appearance Lord Roversdale instantaneously saw his
quarry, and said that, seeing the noble lord in his place, he
would presently ask him—something or another, but something very disagreeable, on a matter of detail.

Lord Oakshott immediately rose. "My lords," he said, "I
am not prepared for debate to night. I have had a heavy
blow, a very heavy one. On any other night but this I would
engage in battle with my friend Lord Roversdale, but I think
that I am addressing you for the last time."

Then he walked out of the House.

He was scarcely in the lobby when Lord Roversdale had
his hand on his shoulder.

"Oakshott, what is this ?"

" Ruin !" said Oakshott.

" Financial ?"

" No, domestic."

" Can I do anything ?" said Lord Roversdale.

" Yes, you can blow my brains out," said Oakshott.

When a man tells you that the only thing you can do for
him is to blow his brains out, you naturally consider that his
affairs, whether domestic or pecuniary, are in a bad way. Lord
Roversdale therefore left Lord Oakshott, with a parting shake
of the hand.

Granby Dixon and Brogden were in the passage of the
House of Commons now. They both looked at one another
as Oakshott came up.

He looked fearfully wild ; they both noticed it as he came
to them. Granby said—

"Oakshott, what have you been doing?"

"Nothing as yet," he said. "I have found Dickie, and I wish to make my will."

"Oakshott," said Granby, "you promised me that you would not do anything without consulting me."

"Well, I will not, then. I only want Brogden to make my will; and I want you to witness it. Come in here; I know this hotel,—we can have a quiet room."

Under the belief that he was in one of his mad moods, they went in with him. He did not seem to be mad at all. His lips were very dry, and he called for some soda-water. "Will you listen, Brogden?" he said.

Brogden wrote down his last will and testament.

"I leave everything of which I am possessed to the young man now lying at Comfrey's Hotel, in my lodgings, under the name of Signor Riccardo, who is my cousin Sir Arthur's boy."

"Oakshott!" said Brogden.

"With the exception of the following legacies," said he, savagely. "To Miss Prout I leave £50,000; to Mrs. O'Brien I leave £10,000; to Granby Dixon £10,000."

"I am no use here, then," said Granby; "I can't witness the will."

"The waiters can do it," said Oakshott. "That is all."

"I will have this knocked together for you by to-morrow morning," said Brogden.

"You will do it now, if you please," said Oakshott. "I made one will before, which I opened the other day; and I have told Mrs. O'Brien where I secreted it. What fun it will be when she tries to steal it and finds it better to put it back."

They dared not speak to one another before him. It had to be done, and it was done. The landlord of the house and one waiter were the witnesses. Then Granby said to him, "Where are you going, Oakshott?"

"To a place where you will never go," he answered—"to hell! You will never see me again, old Granby—never, never more. Oh, my dear old Granby, after so many pleasant years, to part with you for a woman! Granby, try to think kindly of me; God only knows how I love you."

Brogden knew nothing of tragedy, so he was very much surprised at what followed. In an instant Granby Dixon had seized Lord Oakshott's arm.

"*Oakshott, is it done?*" he said.

"No. But he has beaten her again."

"We had better go, Brogden," said Granby quietly. "Good-night, Oakshott. I shall see you to-morrow."

And they went away.

CHAPTER XLIII.

THE BLACK NIGHT.

PEOPLE generally go to bed at night, and so it is by no means improbable, as regards the reality of fiction, that Mrs. O'Brien was in bed. At all events she was, fiction or no fiction; and all her servants were in bed also, when there came a terrible knocking at the door.

Not a soul moved. Mrs. O'Brien thought that it was the woman who lived next door, and who could upset a decision of Lord Ponsance's by getting into her husband's house. The cook thought that it was fire, but having smelt down the stairs and found no smell, thought that it was a drunken man who would leave off soon. The rest of the servants slept the sleep of the just, until the fourth round of the knocking.

Then the servants began to think that something was the matter. The second housemaid at once departed through the dormer window to the top of the house, and wandered about on the roofs of the neighbouring houses in her night-gown, until she was dexterously rescued by a fire-escape. The cook lay in bed and yelled, but the page (a singularly clever boy) put on his trousers and thought of opening the door. He not only thought of doing it, but he did it.

In front of it he found Granby Dixon. "Confound you, you young monkey, go and rouse your mistress, and tell her that Mr. Granby Dixon is here and must see her at once—instantly."

Granby went into the dining-room, and the boy went up-stairs. In three minutes Mrs. O'Brien was with him. She spoke first :—

"Granby, are they off?"

"No."

"Thank God !"

"Let us thank God when we are through it. What new thing does Oakshott know to-day?"

She bared her arm to him,—there was ecchymosis all over it.

"The devil !" said Granby.

"Arthur has beaten my daughter savagely to-day, and I got these wounds in defending her. Oh God ! Granby—save us, save us ! We have no hope but in you. I only came home to sleep for a few hours. She will go to Oak-shott, and then I will hang myself."

Granby leant against the mantelpiece for a little time, and then he said —

"You know that Dickie is found?"

"No."

"I feel certain of it—never mind why," said Granby. "Can we utilize his love for Dickie?"

"I think not. If Dickie is found, Oakshott's love for my grandson would only the more embitter him against Arthur. What shall we do, Granby? Only save my daughter—for she, even she has turned on him, and she will go to Oak-shott, and then Arthur will kill him."

"Oakshott will kill Arthur if we do not take care," said Granby. "Duchess, do you know that Oakshott loves her?"

"My dear," said Mrs. O'Brien, "I know it to my cost."

·"Does she love him?"

"That is a curious question to ask a mother about her married daughter."

"I dare say," said Granby ; "but answer it."

"Yes."

"Ho! Can you think of any way by which we could get rid of Sir Arthur?"

"Yes."

"I was only joking," said Granby.

"I was not," said Mrs. O'Brien. "I will get rid of him fast enough—I have determined on that."

"Madame ! Madame !"

"Yes, and Monsieur! Monsieur!" said Mrs. O'Brien. "His new yacht I beg of you."

"I know nothing of that about which you speak, Mrs, O'Brien. I only want to save a terrible scandal,"

"I also," said Mrs. O'Brien. "The beast has abused her again, and if I was near him I would put a knife in his heart. Then I should be hung, and she would be free to marry Earlie; but there shall never be a scandal about our family. Granby!"

"Yes, Mrs. O'Brien."

"Go and knock Arthur up, and see if she is gone."

"God bless an Irishwoman for wit," said Granby.

"Granby," said Mrs. O'Brien, "go to Oakshott afterwards. I don't think that she will have gone straight to him—I don't think it, my dear. It never was in our family."

Granby said "Good-bye," and went. He had his own opinions, and he went to Oakshott first.

The night porter admitted the Secretary to the Admiralty at once. He took a chamber candlestick, and he went into Lord Oakshott's bedroom. He was in bed, alone.

"Oakshott," said Granby, "you are contemplating a terrible crime. Think."

"I have thought," said Oakshott. "God has behaved badly to me, and I defy Him."

"But think of her."

"Think of her! When do I ever cease doing so? Her face was black and blue this evening."

"Then you have seen her."

"For one instant I forced my way in. I told her that I had found her son."

"Oakshott, if she comes to you, send her to my wife."

"I will do nothing of the kind," he said.

"Will you not pause?" said Granby.

"No, certainly not. I have made up my mind. I

am going to make a widow of her, and then ask her to
marry me."

" But, Oakshott, that is villany."

" Is it not villany to strike her in the face ? Now go,
Granby ; I have parted with you once before ; this must be
the last parting. Remember that there was once a fantastic
fool called Oakshott, and that he developed into a scoundrel and a murderer. I thought that boy had saved me,
but I have relapsed. I am no longer fit company for
honest men,—go."

The good-natured fellow went at once to Sir Arthur. He
was shown into that gentleman's study directly, and found
him in all the confusion of packing, among gun-cases,
portmanteaus, and what not. His first words to Granby
were—

" I see you have come ; I expected you. Tell Oakshott
that I cannot find a friend in London, my character is so
infernally bad. I shall be at Cherbourg in less than a week,
where I know plenty of French officers who will act. Have
you seen her ?"

" Who ?",

" Lady Oakshott. I suppose she has gone to him in pre-
ference to her mother ; for, to tell you the truth, my dear
Granby, that mother of hers, with all her affection for her,
led her the devil's own life, and made uncommonly lively
times of it for me. She forced Marie on to the stage against
her will, and she was always coming between us. After
railing at Oakshott for years, she turned in his favour ; it is
all one now. The world need know nothing at all about it
unless you cackle ; but the fact of the matter is, that there
is another lady in the case now, and that Mrs. O'Brien, our

dear duchess, found it out, told her daughter, and there were tears. Tears exasperate me, and I lost my temper and came to a physical explanation with Lady Oakshott. The old woman interfering, I gave her some of it for herself. Lady Oakshott has been gone five hours. Do I understand you that Oakshott has sent no message?"

" None."

"I wish he had, because then I could have chosen my weapons. It will be the same thing in the end: he must die before he marries that girl, because I have pressing need to be Earl of Oakshott, and this is a justifiable plea for making myself so. As to the poor old beggar, I really bear no malice; I don't think that he is worth it in any way. Granby, you study human nature, and I wish that you will explain this to me. I was very fond of that woman until very lately. What has maddened me is, that I always knew her heart was with him and not with me. I know his plan perfectly well: he wants to kill me and marry her; I intend to kill him and be Lord Oakshott. Has the old fool made a will?"

" Yes, in favour of your son."

" Well, that is not of much use."

" You know that your son is found?"

" I heard something of it from my valet. When he forced his way in to-day, he told her so, I believe. Some young cub. Who shall prove his identity? He can't leave the entailed property away from me, and it would be a question with me whether it would be worth my while to bother about the real estate. Let that be. Now I must really ask you to go, for I am for Southampton by the first train to-morrow morning. Good-night."

Granby Dixon was so appalled by the man's cool rascality, that he left him without telling him that he had seen nothing of Lady Oakshott. Then he went to Mrs. O'Brien again, and thence once more to Oakshott. The poor lady had been heard of nowhere at all. In the grey of the morning, when the sparrows began chirping, the three— Oakshott, Granby, and Mrs. O'Brien—were sitting together, pale and haggard.

It was a fearful case : each of the three knew what was in each other's mind, but none dared utter it.

Oakshott sat deadly pale, biting his lips, his hair dishevelled and his dress disarranged : he was such a terrible sight to look on, that the other two preferred to cast a stealthy glance at one another sooner than encounter his dreadful stare. He cowed them both.

Mrs. O'Brien's love had been rather feline, but she loved desperately well, with all her faults. She looked at Granby with the muscles in her face panting and throbbing, as though with a thirst for the water of tears which would not come.

Granby's face expressed nothing but profound sorrow and alarm ; he was, however, the first to speak after the meeting.

" The unhappy lady," he said, " has been terribly tried, and we must look facts in the face and prepare for the very worst. My last hope was that she was gone to Mrs. Dixon, but such is not the case. It is totally impossible to say where she has gone."

" She is my daughter," said Mrs. O'Brien ; " and has very properly gone to the river."

There was a dead silence for a minute. Had the three known what was in store for her, they might have wished that it were so.

This unhappy lady had been so terribly ill-used that we cannot calculate on her mind being perfectly balanced. Her natural course was to go to her mother, and had she done so everything would have been perfectly right. She has gone somewhere else. I can only travel over that ground ten times over. She was heavily bruised on the face, and, when she left Sir Arthur, was wild in her demeanour. She would most certainly be stopped by the police ; that is our hope.

"If," said Oakshott hoarsely, "she is found again, I will let that wretch live to complete his crimes."

"And —— ?" said Granby.

"No," said Oakshott.

"Well, God send you better thoughts," said Granby hurriedly, for her mother was present. "I wish you would tell me this. Was she ever mad in America?"

"He says she was, but his mouth is full of lies. There was enough to drive an ill-used woman mad among those whooping devils."

"I wish you would tell the truth about that American business. They say that Miss Prout dressed in man's clothes."

"I won't tell the truth further than this. Lady Oakshott and Miss Prout are the two most pure, excellent, and noble ladies in the world. Lady B—— did the same."

"Well, the hour is come to act, and we must rouse the police at once. We have used our own powers as far as we can. I for my part have very great misgivings."

There was a short pause, and they heard the sound of rather hurried steps in the street : they passed the door and then returned, but at so long an interval that Granby, with some strange instinct, waited hat in hand before he started on his errand. Granby told me a long time after that the steps were like those of a naval officer walking fast on his watch to warm himself.

The footsteps paused at the door, and they looked at one another. There was a cautious ring at the area bell. Mrs. O'Brien's boy, who, finding that there was mystery and trouble in the house, would have died sooner than go to bed, and had indeed been listening all the time, answered promptly.

They heard a man's voice at the door, and heard him ask for Mrs. O'Brien at once. They all three stood together, and Oakshott said, "The end has come now."

A tall, brown-faced man entered the room—evidently a sailor. Granby and Mrs. O'Brien knew him, but Oakshott did not. Granby held his breath, and got hold of Oakshott's arm, and whispered "Hush ! By heaven, it is O'Dowd !"

"It is a bad time to call on a lady, Mrs. O'Brien, especially on a lady so little known as yourself: but the fact is that I was ordered to the West Coast of Africa for three years with my first ship, in consequence of my aunt's wig coming off at Mrs. Rickaby's party. So my engineer (we are among friends) knocked a crack in the bottom of one of his pistons. Though passed in steam in the first class, I can't tell how he did it. I had to put back, and it will take two months to mend ; so I got leave to go and see my aunts at Croydon : I went to Lady Kathleen and Lady Nora O'Brien."

"Hope !" shouted Granby.

The astonished sea-captain looked at the Secretary with mingled feelings of deep awe and profound wonder. With a view to avoiding the West Coast, he was very particular indeed.

" And we were sitting at supper last night, when there came a knock at the door, and when it was opened in came Lady Oakshott, and said, ' Kinswomen, I have come to you for protection. Take me in and send some one to my mother, to tell her that after his usage of her I should only bring more trouble on her head from him if I went to her. Ask her to come to me.' "

Granby was the first man to recover his presence of mind : he dashed at Captain O'Dowd, seized him by the throat, and rocked him to and fro.

For a young captain on his promotion to be seized by the throat and rocked to and fro by the Secretary of the First Lord is doubtless complimentary, but it is also puzzling. Captain O'Dowd had a strong idea that Granby was drunk ; but when Granby shook his fist in his face, and asked what he meant by talking about the West Coast of Africa, it became plain to him that Granby was mad. When Granby began laughing to prevent himself crying, he began to think that there was method in his madness.

" You shall never go to the West Coast while I live," said Granby. " O'Dowd, my dear fellow, look at him with his arm round her, and she crying on his breast. Think of the sus-picions which poisoned her life ; think of her terrible tempta-tions ; think of her wasted life ; think of the hell from which you have saved us this night ; and think that if there is one spark of gratitude in Oakshott or in myself, you will feel the power of it. You have done better by this night's work than if you had won fifty brilliant frigate actions. You shall go to the Mediterranean."

Captain O'Dowd was very glad to hear it, and determined to get married before he went to sea, which would give him a month's honeymoon. As for all the things which Granby told him to think about, he knew absolutely nothing about them, but determined to consult his aunts. Moreover, he determined by hook or by crook to get another invitation for his aunts to Mrs. Rickaby's next party, and make them wear their wigs. Those wigs, after all, seemed to have brought luck.

CHAPTER XLIV.

THE MEETING AT LAST.

LADY OAKSHOTT, as we see, had never gone to Oakshott at all. She had fled, but she had fled to her quaint, good, Irish aunts.

This act of hers occasioned what is called by Granby, who told me this story, " the poker watch." Lady Kathleen and Lady Nora sat up alternately all night with the drawing-room poker, determined to inflict summary vengeance on Sir Arthur, should he appear. He never did. Had he done so, Father Moriarty would have been ready for him. They had a still more dangerous enemy, however, in Oakshott.

I believe that his intentions were not good : I am afraid so. He wanted her to come away with him, and he went to see her. He was received by Lady Nora.

" The top of the morning to you, my Lord Oakshott," she said. " And so you have proved Dickie's identity, and left him and Dixie your money. Don't alter your will, and there will be a match with them as sure as you're born, pretty lovers."

" Lady Nora, I came here to see Lady Oakshott. Can I see her ?"

"If I had my way, you would only see her through convent bars," said Lady Nora; "but Kathleen is sentimental, and she and the good father have consented. I'll send her down."

In that little room there was a more terrible tragedy going on than in most others. Oakshott was left alone.

Mad with love, mad with hate, he was still waiting to propose one crime and execute another.

The room was nearly dark—there were only two candles in it. He paced up and down.

There was a rustling of silk in one corner as she came in. His heart went short and thick, and his mouth was dry. His life had come into the room. Women cannot understand this; *men* can.

"My darling, I am come for you."

"Oakshott, you must go away."

"After so many years?"

"Yes."

"Do you hate me?"

"Oakshott, you know that I love you."

"Could you come to me if he were dead?"

"Yes, but not if he died by your hand. If you were to kill him, directly or indirectly, I would never see you again. You have found my child?"

"Yes; not one kiss for that, my darling?"

"Not one."

"May I kiss your feet?"

"No."

"It is not much to ask."

"But it is too much. You must go. Where is he?"

"At Cherbourg with his new yacht."

" Now you must go," said Lady Oakshott.

" Yes, I will go," said Oakshott ; " but you must make me a promise, or neither of us leaves the room alive."

He put his back against the door.

" I know that you love me well enough to kill me," she said ; " but what is the promise ?"

" That you will never take vows."

" I certainly shall not," she said ; " you may depend upon that."

" Good-bye," said Oakshott.

" Oakshott, one word more. You told my mother and Granby Dixon, on that black night when I ran away from him for the first time, that if I was found you would spare him."

" Well, I did."

" You swore it. Will you break your vow?"

" If he were dead, would you marry me ?"

" Emphatically, no. I would not bring such sorrow and misery on you. I tell you, Oakshott, that I am not to be trusted—look me steadily in the face."

He did so.

" Edward," she said, " he has led me a hard life, but I have led him a very bad one ; he was never sure of me since that night."

" Forget it, in God's name."

She set her mouth and made a sound so low that it could scarcely be heard by the listening Lady Kathleen, who had her ear at the key-hole the whole time: a sharp double movement in staccato, probably in C, but ending with the wild wail of the Coyote. It was the Apache war-cry. Oak-shott covered his ears,

"Forget! forget!"

"I cannot. I have never been safe since that night. See what Arthur has had to suffer. Will you spare him for my sake, Edward?"

"Yes, before God I will." And so they parted.

Lady Kathleen, who slept with her sister, inquired of Lady Nora, as soon as they were in bed, "What devil's devarsions they had been up to amongst 'em in America." Lady Nora hoped the saints might make her bed, and that she might die in it. Lady Kathleen deponed that she had heard Lady Oakshott trying to raise the devil, but that Lord Oakshott stopped her. There was no peace, she said, for a religious woman among these English, and the sooner they got back to a decent and civilized country, like Galway or Connemara, the better: in which sentiment the other sister emphatically agreed.

CHAPTER XLV.

OAKSHOTT AGAIN.

DICKIE had got quite well. Dixie was tired of London, and Mrs. O'Brien rather thought that she would like to see Oakshott Castle; in consequence of which Lord Oakshott made a move in his own fortress, and took not only Dickie and Dixie, but Mrs. O'Brien herself down to Oakshott.

It so happened that the Lord of Lipworth had a very particularly grand party at this time, a fact for which you will see the reason of mentioning directly. Lord Oakshott got his own party to Poole, and then made the brilliant discovery that it was blowing a gale of wind.

The firs were tossing and tearing, the sea lavender was bending, and the sea aster was nearly torn up by its roots. A drive over to Oakshott did not seem a very pleasant matter. He went to look at his carriage, and found that his coachman had brought a waggonette.

"We shall be blown out of it, Sam," he said.

"The Lord of Lipworth is here, my lord," said Sam, "and he is going to face it."

"Where is he, Sam?"

"In the Nelson room, my lord."

Oakshott at once went in.

"My dear Cardinal," he said, "what brings you out in such weather?"

"I came to fetch Lady Oakshott from the train," said his Eminence: "how shall we get home?"

"Has Lady Oakshott gone to you, then?" said Lord Oakshott.

"Not at all. I wish that she had. She is by no means likely to come to us. She refuses vows. Oh, here she is."

So she came in, grey, beautiful, magnificent. She gave Oakshott a smile and said not one word, even of common civility. But the smile was worth all words.

He knew that she loved him, but would not sin for him, not if he were to lie cold and dead at her feet. He refused to believe all reports about her intellect. One thing only, as he thought, divided this man and this woman—the life of a worthless hound.

"I will get his Eminence to drive us over to Oakshott soon," he said, "for I very much want to see my mother."

At this moment the window, a French one, blew open, and the lock of it cut her sharply on the forehead : she was stunned and dazed for a moment, and in that time Oakshott had put his arm round her waist, and had said, "My darling, are you hurt?"

She put him quietly away. "The wind is blowing very heavily," she said, "and I am not much hurt. Your Eminence, we had better drive home through it."

His Eminence, who was a discreet man, had not noticed the small indiscretion which Lord Oakshott had committed. He would have been most awfully angry if he had seen it, but he was looking at the weather, out of another window than that which was blown open.

"It is the greatest gale for forty years," he said.

(It always is the greatest gale for forty years; but, in the name of heaven, why forty?)

Lady Oakshott stepped out of the room and had an interview with her mother, not long, and by no means important. Then the two carriages started over the down.

At Dixon's bars they were to separate, and then his Eminence was very much surprised.

"Cardinal," said Lady Oakshott, in a whisper, "will you let me go to my mother?"

"But to *his* house?" said the Cardinal.

"Yes; I want to go to my mother. I am fearfully ill."

"Go then, but never leave her."

"No; depend on that, Cardinal."

She got into the Oakshott carriage, and nestled beside her mother.

No one of the Oakshott party wondered at all. She had met her mother, and it was natural that she should go with her.

CHAPTER XLVI.

AN UNWELCOME FRIEND.

OAKSHOTT drove. Dickie and Dixie nestled together to keep away from the wind, you will understand. They got over the down very well, and when they saw the tower Oakshott said—

"I will keep my light burning to-night. Mrs. Prout has been doing it lately; I will watch up there to-night."

"You will have a windy night of it," said Mrs. O'Brien.

"Well, it *is* a gale," said Lord Oakshott; "and," he added, taking out his little barometer, "it is going to blow harder."

There was a very pleasant dinner in the hall; then Oakshott went up to his tower and smoked.

The wind was wilder and wilder. They all said that it was the worst gale for forty years (the usual forty). It was certainly the worst for three. Oakshott sat in his tower and smoked, with the light burning.

Part of the room was very dark, and Oakshott heard a movement in it. He smoked on.

There was a flash and a crack of a pistol. Oakshott had heard the click and had moved. The bullet went into the wall; in another moment he had Borichi by the throat, and was holding him down. Borichi struggled terribly, but Oakshott managed him. In the struggle the light was overthrown, and the room left in total darkness.

" Borichi, you have tried to kill me."

"You seduced my sister."

"You lie ; she is as pure as your mother."

"Will you give word, Earlino ?"

"Yes."

"Then kill me. I was wrong. But kill me yourself, Earlino. Earlino, dear, do not let them *hang* me. We loved one another once."

"Yes."

"Earlino, kill me yourself."

"Why did you try to kill me ?"

"Earlino, the Cammoristi are against you, but Sir Arthur used his influence to have me set on you."

There was a flash of light in the darkened room, and a shivering of the windows. The coastguard had fired. There was a ship in the bay.

"Borichi," said Oakshott, "will you earn your life ?"

"Yes."

"Then get up. You were the finest swimmer in Naples. Come and save your life."

"I will do so, Earlino."

Another shot from the coastguard.

"Then come, we must haste. Can you find your way ? How dark it is ! Take my hand. Mind the steps. This is an awfully dark night for our bay."

They passed swiftly down into the dining-room.

"Two shots from the coastguard," said Oakshott. "Out all hands. The gentleman and I had a little difference up-stairs. He is going to do wonders for me."

Dickie looked at him. "Why, that is my friend Borichi, the tenor. He was in the——"

"Psh ! Psh !" said Borichi ; "we are assassins who go

to war, are we not? My lord is one of us, and has escaped execution. Let us go out to this ship, then; if I have failed in one thing, I may succeed in another."

It was not very far to the beach, and they were soon there—Oakshott, Borichi, Mrs. O'Brien, Lady Oakshott, Dickie, and Dixie. The fishermen were walking up and down, wondering where *she* would come on shore. For SHE was there in the bay, fighting for her life—she a tortured and desperate ship, in her last agony.

To some English people ships are like human beings; to others they are no more than wood. This ship was a mere beautiful schooner of 250 tons, and she was making such a noble effort to claw out to sea, that every fisherman saw that a real genius was in command of her.

" I am sorry," said old Prout, "that your lordship has put your light out to-night, the first time for so many years. If she could have kept that light in a line with St. Albans, she might have got inside the reef."

Oakshott looked at his tower. The light, the old beacon of his fishermen, was out, and the tower stood dark against the rising moon.

In his struggle with Borichi the lamp had been overturned. Truly, his sins and negligences were coming on his head now.

The pretty little ship could not do her work. The sea, her perpetual enemy, lifted her over the reef, but the terrible crack which the sailors heard told of her doom. Her diving and plunging were over for ever. She sunk inside the reef, and she sunk at once. The men were swimming and drowning, and then three or four men came out like heroes.

Lord Oakshott, Dickie, Borichi, and two fishermen were in the water at once. The poor little thing of a schooner knocked about a deal of wreck as she went to pieces. Lady Oakshott and Dixie stood on the shore with the fishermen's wives.

In the midst of the violent breaking of the waves, in the midst of the awful confusion of the wreck, Oakshott got hold of one man and held to him. The wreck knocked them about, and Oakshott's man got a terrible blow on the head. Oakshott held to his man as long as consciousness lasted, but at last, when he was practically dead, he and his man were washed on shore together.

The fishermen's wives gathered round them, but they were parted by Mrs. O'Brien, Lady Oakshott, and Dixie.

"Two dead men, my ladies," said an old fisherman's wife. "Our dear lord is one—but who is the other?"

A scream went through every one's head. It came from Lady Oakshott. Before her, clutched shoulder to shoulder, lay on the sand, Oakshott, who should have been her husband, and Arthur, who *was* her husband.

A sailor examined them. "I fear that they are both dead," he said to Lady Oakshott and Dixie.

CHAPTER XLVII.

THE RECONCILIATION.

THAT very remarkable young lady, Miss Prout, emphatically called the sailor a stupid old thing, and had both Sir Arthur and Lord Oakshott carried into the inn.

"They are neither of them dead, I tell you," said Dixie impetuously. " I ought to know a dead man when I see one ; I have seen more than all of you put together. Keep their heads up as you carry them. Lady Oakshott, you attend to Sir Arthur—*you* know how ; I will mind Earlie."

The simple sailors had seen a great deal of this kind of thing in their time, but they now witnessed something they had never seen before.

Lady Oakshott they had known in old times : she was now a grey, bent woman. Dixie Prout they had known also : she was now a brilliant and splendid beauty, who, it was said, had been carrying everything before her in London. The greatest lady in the land had recognized her.

But here she and Lady Oakshott were ordering them all about, and showing a knowledge of details of which they knew nothing at all.

That Dixie Prout might know something about nursing was one thing to them, but Lady Oakshott was a still greater puzzle. She had been a lady, her mother was a duchess (as good a duchess as any of them, they thought), and here she was hurrying to and fro, and giving the most extraordinary directions.

Neither Sir Arthur nor Lord Oakshott was dead, as it very soon appeared. They were put in different beds, and they both recovered. The fishermen who were crowding into the room heard Dixie Prout and Lady Oakshott talking.

" Dixie, dear," Lady Oakshott said, " see if any one can scrape some lint. Arthur has got a scalp wound, and it goes on bleeding."

" Get a cobweb, some of you fools," said Dixie to the fishermen. " Riccardo, here you are ; get a cobweb,

Dickie, and ice—never mind what—Sir Arthur may bleed to death."

Dickie, with the dexterity of the nation with which he had been bred, dashed upstairs and found any number of cobwebs in the maid's room. That young woman, being of nervous temperament, had interned herself, so to speak, at the first mention of disaster. Seeing from under the clothes a very handsome young man in the bedroom, on the top of a chair, clawing wildly at the ceiling, she conceived that her room had been invaded by a lunatic. She therefore (I think most properly) yelled three times at the top of her voice. Dickie fled with his hands full of cobwebs, and everything would have gone right had the young woman kept in bed.

She did nothing of the kind. She was mortally determined that no one, let alone her sweetheart, should ever have it in his power to say that a young man had been in her bedroom and that she had not resented it. She burst out of bed, wrapped the bed-clothes round her, and pursued Dickie, screaming violently.

She never got into the room into which Dickie had passed. The fishermen's wives got hold of her and took her back to bed. She was obliged to confess, when she was quiet, that the young man had not offered to say a word to her.

When Dickie got in with the cobwebs, Lady Oakshott was sitting on the bed and holding Sir Arthur's head up, wiping it with a wet rag.

" Thank you, sir," she said, as she put the cobwebs on Sir Arthur's head ; " you may have saved his life for aught I know. His life is very dear to me, more dear than you can tell."

Dickie, who was at the other side of Sir Arthur, said—

" Mother ! Mother ! don't you know me ?"

" Mother ! Know you ! Yes, I know you as Riccardo the singer."

" I should know you among ten thousand."

" I do not know you," she said hurriedly, with fluttering hands. "I had a little Richard once, but he is dead, or worse than dead. Your voice is not his, your face is not his. Look into my eyes."

Dickie did so.

" Yes, they are his eyes, but you are not he."

" Daughter !" said a voice from behind.

" Yes, mother."

" That boy is your boy. Oakshott and I can prove it now."

Mrs. O'Brien touched her daughter on the shoulder.

" That is your son."

" Mother ! Mother ! you would not say such a thing if it were not true."

" My daughter, no."

" I will believe it, then. Hoop ! you devils of Commanches. Put your arm round your father's neck and hold him up. Dickie ! Dickie ! you must try to love me !"

" I love you now, mother. God only knows how I love you."

Sir Arthur had revived most wonderfully. He knew nobody, but he asked to go to sleep, and they gave him some stimulants and let him go.

Then Mrs. O'Brien, Lady Oakshott, and Dickie were left by his bedside.

"I know you now, Dickie," said Lady Oakshott. "Come and lay your head on my bosom."

Dickie did so. The poor lady said nothing at all to him, but seemed pleased that his head should be there. The wind roared round the house, and Mrs. O'Brien watched her daughter with great anxiety. Lady Oakshott, who had been so keen and so shrewd at the beginning of the evening, now seemed dazed and stunned. Sir Arthur awoke.

"Arthur !"

"Yes."

"Do you know me ?"

"Marie, my darling."

"Kiss me." And he did so.

"I give you all I have left, Arthur. I give you the remains of my intellect."

"Marie, I have been dead."

"And I am going mad."

"Marie, be still : I have much to say to you."

"And I to you, but it must be said in Bedlam. Arthur, while my intellect lasts, will you promise me two things ?"

"Yes, if you will stay with me."

"Will you forgive Oakshott ?"

"He put his light out, and tried to drown me."

"His light went out by pure accident."

"Do you say that he was the man who got hold of me on the wreck ?"

"Yes."

"You are wandering again, my poor girl !"

"I am not," said Lady Oakshott.

"I know you never sinned with him, and that boy is mine. Try to find him."

" He is here. We have found him," said the poor lady.
" My mother and Oakshott will give every proof."

" Let me see the boy." Dickie bent over him. " Marie, I
have behaved badly to you. I have led you a life fit to kill
a woman. Marie, my darling, let us live more happily together in future."

" Yes," said Lady Oakshott.

Mrs. O'Brien, with her keen quick eye, had watched matters, and was getting terribly anxious. Her daughter, Lady
Oakshott, was fluttering her hands about in a strange way,
and when her husband said probably the first kind words he
had said to her for some time, she saw a stare in her daughter's eyes which she did not at all like. There was silence
for nearly a minute, during which the unhappy lady continued to button and unbutton the breast of her gown very
rapidly.

They say that a bird may light on the lower end of an
Alpine snow-drift and bring down the whole avalanche. It is
a trite old figure, used a hundred times, and possibly a perfectly untrue one, but let it serve once more. I cannot
answer for such stories. I can answer, however, for the (I
believe permanent) madness of a woman which was caused by
a sudden and ill-considered order of Frederick Charles two
years ago. A thing very much similar occurred now.

There was a shivering of the window glass. The coastguard had fired. There was another ship in the bay.

Lady Oakshott heard it. She rose, and from that moment
her intellect left her for ever. She had refused sin with Lord
Oakshott, and she knew well that the rest of her life was
doomed to the man who had beaten her and ill-treated her.
The few kind words he had said to her were nothing : she

had heard those words before. She had nursed her husband kindly and well. When the gun came, she rose and asked if Oakshott was alive.

" Yes, dear," said her mother ; " and doing well."

Bang went another gun.

" That is from Fort Commorin," said Lady Oakshott. " Save your scalps, ladies—save your scalps and your virtue. These are not Apaches: these are Commanches—they always come from that side.   Arthur, the creeping devils are upon us.   I tell you that that was a gun from Fort Commorin."

Dixie was away from the other bed at once. " Lady Oakshott," she said, " there are no Commanches here."

" Who is this ? Dixie—child, you are a fool. You remember that night ?"

" I remember it very well, Lady Oakshott. I do not think any one is likely to forget it."

" Where is Big Bear," said Lady Oakshott. " He was here last night ; he was here to-day.   Let us go and find him, or get to the fort."

" Lady Oakshott," said Dixie, " you are all abroad. Please be quiet ; Earlie is recovering."

" Earlie !"

" Yes ; Lord Oakshott.   Do not get excited."

" Is Oakshott ill ?"

" Yes.   Come away."

Dixie had her on one side, and Mrs. O'Brien on the other, by now ; they got her outside.   Then she began crying, " Edward, Edward, make for the fort !"

" Lady Oakshott," said Dixie, holding her among the wondering fishermen, " there is no fort. We are in England. All that hideous time is past—past for ever. Please remember that there are no Commanches here. Why, Big Bear was killed; you must remember that. Oh, thank God! here is Granby Dixon. Mr. Dixon, Lady Oakshott has lost her mind; pray help us."

"Yes. Is Oakshott dead?" said Granby.

"No. Help me with Lady Oakshott."

"Commanches! Commanches!" screamed the unhappy lady. "Where is Big Bear? He is here."

Granby told me this. The terrified fishermen had parted right and left, and Lady Oakshott cast off her mother and Dixie, and with her hair down stood alone.

"In one instant the whole quiet little village rang with the horrible staccato of the Apache war-cry. Then her mother got hold of her and got her away in one of the Oakshott carriages to Sir Arthur's house. From that time she practically disappeared. The poor woman was mad.

Granby Dixon says provokingly odd things, and although he is the soul of truth, one wonders where he gets them from. He says that on one occasion, in a war between the Apaches and Commanches, Arthur was on one side and Oakshott was on the other. He says (in private, that is to say at his club) that "Big Bear" was no other than the Right Honourable the Earl of Oakshott. This does not in the least degree fit with poor Lady Oakshott's exclamations, as I pointed out to Granby himself.

He said, "No: I see; it does not fit. My theory must be wrong. Did you ever see Miss Prout in a low dress?"

"No."

"Nor ever will, sir. She has got a bullet wound on the left shoulder, and she can't show, sir. She always wears a high dress. Now will you have the goodness to tell me what those two lunatics were at in America?"

I confessed my total and entire inability to give him one solitary hint.

"I don't see my way to it, sir, at all. Arthur was up to no good, and Oakshott was up to no very great harm, possibly; the least said the soonest mended. You turned up the other night, like a regular stormy petrel as you are. She gave the Apache war-whoop in the street."

"Could it not have been Commanche?" I said.

"Not in the least, sir. One of the sailors, who had been well in the Apache country, told me that she gave the whoop as well as an Apache. Depend upon it, sir, that those two cousins were at one another's throats, one with the Commanches and one with the Apaches, until Uncle Sam interfered between the two nations."

"It seems to me not only improbable, but impossible," I said. "What *object* had they?"

"Have you got any money?" said Granby.

"No."

"Same here, at present. If you had, you might go into Eroba Silver. *They* found it."

"The*y found* it?"

"Yes. I don't know which of them actually found it, but they were both there together."

CHAPTER XLVIII.

THE WAR-CRY.

LORD OAKSHOTT'S revival was less pathetic and less tragical in every way than that of Sir Arthur. He sneezed a great deal, and then he asked for Dixie.

"I am here," she said.

" I want Granby Dixon."

" He is in London."

At this time Dixie was called away to the scene at the other bed which has been given above; no one remained with him but Mrs. Prout.

" Prout," he said, " I shall never die in my bed."

" No one ever thought you would," said Mrs. Prout.

" You ought to be glad of that," said Lord Oakshott.

" Why ?"

" Because I am in it now, and therefore I shall not die. Prout, tell me, is the man I saved alive ?"

" Yes, bad luck to him.   Richard has gone up to the top of the house to get cobwebs to plaster his head with. He had better have gone to your brains."

" Thanks; I like compliments.   Ask the name of the man I saved."

" It is Sir Arthur."

" Arthur !"

" No other," said Mrs. Prout.   " You can leave your tenantry for four years, neglect every duty, and then drown yourself for a creature like that.",

" Nonsense. Arthur is not a bad fellow, not half a bad fellow, Prout.   I wished to kill him, certainly, but that has all been washed out of my head.   Is Marie with him ?"

" Yes, and her mother too."

" That is good.   Prout, see that he is taken to Oakshott, not to his own house."

" Why should he not go home ?" said Mrs. Prout.

" The house has been uninhabited for so very long, and it always *was* damp.   No, he must go to Oakshott Castle."

" Very well, my lord," said Mrs. Prout.

" What noise is that?" said Lord Oakshott. " Tell the boys not to howl like that."

Alas! it was Lady Oakshott giving her wild Indian cry in the street.

She repeated it, more clearly and more terribly than before; it was unmistakable now.

Both men were out of bed in an instant, leaning on their dripping clothes with trembling fingers, and staggering as they did so.

Prostrate as they were before, two mere heaps of humanity, they had a preternatural strength now. It was very odd that both these men had been sane five minutes before. Oakshott knew that he had saved Arthur's life, and Arthur scarcely realized it. Arthur only half knew what had happened to him: that his son was found, and that his wife was in the first stage of hysterics. Though both of them were perfectly sane a minute before, they were both mad now. Granby Dixon's theory of their having been against one another does not quite hold good: from what followed, they were at all events together once.

" Commanche! Commanche!" cried Sir Arthur. " Oakshott! Oakshott! see to Marie and Dixie. Where the devil are the carbines?"

" In the rack," said Oakshott; " I cleaned them when you were snoring, you fool. Look alive. Marie and Dixie, get your revolvers ready. I'll shoot you, my dears. There is one chance for Big Bear; he is not beyond the creek yet. I'll give it mouth."

He sent the Apache war-cry ringing through the rafters. It was answered feebly from a distance. It was the last ever heard of the unhappy Lady Oakshott.

Thereby proving that Oakshott was not Big Bear, but that some one else was. "What the deuce those four were up to in America," said Granby Dixon often, "I *can't* make out. They discovered the Arizoba Silver Mines, however, and so I have no right to inquire."

As I have not the wildest idea about what those four did in America, I am perfectly unable to assist Granby Dixon in any way whatever.

CHAPTER XLIX.

"DE MORTUIS NIL NISI BONUM."

DIXIE had just seen Lady Oakshott into a carriage with her mother, when she heard the Apache war-cry ring out from the little inn. The poor child had been entirely upset by Lady Oakshott, and she lost her nerve. Among the wondering fishermen she cried out suddenly, "Oh God! the Commanches are on us!" and rushed indoors. She lost her head quite. It was dark, and she had been frightened.

"Give me the revolver, Earlie."

Once more the war-whoop sounded through the village, and Oakshott took her in his arms.

"The Commanches, Earlie! Arthur, kill me, kill me. Whoop again, dear; Big Bear is close by."

Oakshott did so.

"Is Bedlam broke loose?" said Granby Dixon, walking into the room as if he had just come down St. James's Street. "Sir Arthur, will *you* give us a howl? because, if my memory serves me rightly, you have a good voice, whereas Oakshott can't sing even his own poetry."

"My Granby. Why, where are we?"

"Well, you are at Oakshott at present, you will be in Bedlam soon."

"We must be all out of our minds," said Oakshott.

"There is no need to say that," said Granby. "What the dickens were you making that row about?"

"It was only the 'Pache war-cry," said Sir Arthur, looking extremely foolish.

"Oh, you have been there too, have you?" said Granby. "You are a nice couple. A few gashes on your heads might produce some sense."

"Never!" said Mrs. Prout.

"Your sentiments do honour to your head and your heart, Madam," said Granby. "Miss Prout, will you have the goodness to go home to the Castle, and leave me in possession here."

Dixie went.

"Now, Mr. Oakshott, perhaps you will have the goodness to retire."

Dickie was going at once, but Granby planted his back against the door until he heard the Oakshott carriage drive away; then he let him out.

"Now, you two lunatics," he said, "get into your respective beds and let us talk."

As neither of the men had one word to say for themselves, they did so.

A man in bed is at a fearful disadvantage. Either of them could have *killed* Granby; but they had been making great fools of themselves, and, moreover, were very ill; and, moreover, they were horizontal, and Granby was perpendicular—a wondrous advantage.

"I am going to give it to you two," said Granby.

Lord Oakshott turned sulkily over in his bed. Sir Arthur said, " I wish the Commanches had you."

Granby said nothing to this at all; he went on :—

" Now, you have been up to no good, you two, and I very much doubt if either of you will ever be up to much. What were you up to in America ?"

Dead silence. I must beg you to remark that Granby had at this time not the remotest idea that there was anything seriously wrong with Lady Oakshott; he would not have spoken in this style if he had known it.

" I ask, what did you two do in America ?"

Not one word.

" Now look here, you two," continued Granby : " I don't say that you are two good fellows—that would be a lie. Oakshott used to be a good fellow ; you, Arthur, are not a good fellow—you are a very bad fellow."

" Granby," said Sir Arthur, rising in bed, " if your father had left you a terrible legacy of hatred ; if your father had pointed out to you that the only chance for honour and fame was Oakshott's death, what would you have done."

" I should have immediately hit the old gentleman over the head with the fire-shovel," said Granby, not in the least degree discomposed ; " and if that did not bring him to his senses, I'd have banged his head against the wall."

" Your own father ?" said Sir Arthur.

" Yes, and my grandmother too. I know all about *that*."

" From whom ?"

" From Borichi. Do you think that you can truckle with such dogs and not be betrayed ? Oh, fool ! Do you know the name of the man who pulled you out of the sea to-night ?"

"I don't remember now, though they told me; I had my
head cut; it was one of the fishermen."

"It was Oakshott."

"Oakshott, is this true?"

"Yes," said Oakshott, rising in his bed.

"Would you have done it if you had known it was I?"
said Sir Arthur.

"Yes. Arthur, I thought I could kill you when you ill-
treated Marie; I could not, and I cannot. Only be kind to
her, for I do love her dearly. I cannot get at her, but I can
get you both. Arthur, try to be better. Remember how we
all stuck together when we had to cross the Commanche
war-trail. Remember the affair in the Ranche, when the
Commanches were on us. You say that I came after Marie:
that is perfectly true; she is a necessity to me, but I would
do her no harm. Arthur, let us be friends."

Granby Dixon made his recurrent murmur to himself:
"What the deuce *did* those four do in America?"

No answer will ever be given. If you ask Dixie, she
talks about the weather. One thing is certain. At a great
party a German professor asserted the theory that all the
Indian war-cries were in C in alto. Dixie at once, before
an astonished assembly, remarked—

"Molasses! It is not in C in alto at all. Here is the
Apache war-cry. I ought to know it, for it was *our* war-cry
at one time."

She rang it out in that very polite assembly. Those who
were round that great poet, Lord Oakshott, were very much
surprised. His lordship was talking in a drawing-room
voice with Lord Dumbledore and Lady Bumbee. When
Dixie committed her indiscretion by giving the war-whoop,
he started up and capsized Lord Dumbledore.

"Commanche! Commanche!" he cried. "Give the women their pistols." Society always allows poets to be mad. The society of London has withdrawn Lord Oakshott's certificate. In the first place, they say that his poetry is too bad; in the second, they say that he knows far more than he chooses to tell.

Lady Kathleen O'Brien says that this is true of Dixie also. Dixie showed scalps which an American officer's lady had given her, as a curiosity, to Lady Kathleen. The American officer had taken them at the death (by the American officer's own hand) of a terrific and awful chieftain, whom Dixie pleases to call the Swimming Opossum. As opossums never do swim, it may be conceived that this is a flight of fancy on Dixie's part.

We must, however, return to Granby Dixon and his two patients.

"What on earth is a man to do with two such fools as you?" said Granby.

"Put us in bed together, and let us talk it over," said Oakshott.

"That would be scarcely safe," said Granby; "you might throttle one another, or I would. Arthur!"

"Yes."

"Oakshott has saved your life to-night. The going out of the light was a sheer accident."

"I believe it."

"It came singularly from your own act. You set the Cammoristi on Oakshott."

"I did not."

"Will you forgive him?"

"Yes, if he will forgive me."

"I forgive you everything, Arthur," said Oakshott.

"Then say not one word more about it," said Sir Arthur. "Listen to me, Granby. I have been nearer death than ever I was before. My son is found, and something else has happened."

"What is that?"

"Lady Oakshott has tried to murder me."

"Arthur Oakshott, in heaven's name think of what you are saying."

"I loved that woman," he went on, "before Oakshott did. I never loved any other woman. She was mad twice while I was with her. I used repression with her, I will allow that. Edward called it ill-treatment. Edward!"

"I hear you."

"Do you remember the affair on the ford of the Colorado?"

"Yes."

"What did I do there?"

"You risked your life for mine, Arthur."

"Why did I do so? Was it for love?"

"There has been little love between us, Arthur."

"I did it out of bitter hate, Oakshott. I knew that Marie would go mad, and that if I died you would marry her. I reserved that fate for you, believing that I should know that I was avenged when I was in hell."

"Bedlam and Newgate!" said Granby Dixon. "We must have no such talk as this."

"Hush, Granby," said Sir Arthur; "your petty ways are not ours. Edward, I saved your life once, and you have saved mine to-day. We are square about that. For Borichi to say that I set the Cammoristi on you is an infernal lie, that is what it is. Edward, if I had been a mean assassin, I have had your life in my hands a hundred times. Why, at the passage of the Ortona I could have cut you over ten times. Bet your life, Dixie would never have known which way the bullet went, for she was wounded herself."

"That is true, Arthur," said Lord Oakshott.

"Now I want to make a pact with you, Edward. Will you promise not to marry Dixie?"

"Yes," said Lord Oakshott, "if you will make a promise that you will not marry your grandmother."

"I want to make another pact with you. If I die, you will not marry Marie."

"No, I won't do that," said Oakshott, firmly. "She *may* be mad, as you say, but if she was sane enough to go to the altar I would marry her. My dear Arthur, why so many words. We both love the same woman. I have treated her as a sister, you as a wife. You and I and Marie and Dixie have been through two Indian campaigns together. My dear fellow, if you were to drop any time within the next twenty years, I should ask Marie to marry me. Do let us be friends."

"Would you marry a lunatic?" said Sir Arthur.

"Lunacy is only a matter of degree," said Lord Oakshott. "For example, you and I are both as mad as hatters."

"Now we are coming to common sense," said Granby Dixon; "I thought that we had deserted it for ever."

"You," said Lord Oakshott, "are the most infernal noodle in creation; you go on with your petty *tracasseries*, and do really nothing. Grand rascals like Arthur and myself may become Prime Ministers. *You* will never be Prime Minister, Granby."

"I don't conceive I shall," said Granby; "and I might say the same of you."

"I don't know," said Oakshott; "I am a very thoughtful man. I have every qualification. I am of good family. I have great wealth. I could turn extremely High Church if I was wanted to do so. I don't care one hang for or against the Ballot. I am perfectly prepared to send the whole British Constitution flying in fragments into the middle of next week, and leave the other party to pick up the pieces. I should make a magnificent Prime Minister."

"Will you make peace with your cousin, Oakshott? You are getting in one of your fantastic moods."

"You would be in a fantastic mood if you had just pulled your cousin out of the sea. Yes, I will make peace. Arthur !"

"There is no quarrel."

"None, Edward. Granby, come here to me directly; my bed is all wet. Come at once to me."

Oakshott and Granby were with him at once, but it was too late. He gave one sigh, and died. An old wound, got in the Indian war, had burst, and he bled to death in a moment.

The wound was a singular one, but I cannot give the details. I can only say that I saw it, and would give the details to a doctor. Granby Dixon turned down the clothes. The bed was full of blood.

"That is the wound which he got on the passage of the Colorado, where he saved my life," said Oakshott. " It is the strangest wound ever known. Those Commanches, you know, sham dead, and——Dixie was wounded in the b reast there, and there was no one to look at her except Marie. Poor Arthur! Oh, my poor, dear Arthur! Such a fine fellow, Granby; such a noble fellow. We hated one another, Granby, but only over a woman—about nothing else in the world. If men can't hate one another about a woman, what the devil is the country coming to?"

"I don't know," said Granby. "Sir Arthur is dead, and you seem sorry for it. Had not you better lie down for a little, and have it over with yourself? Not sharing your sentiments, I shall do nothing of the kind."

It is a most extraordinary thing, but Lord Oakshott was very sorry. He *did* put his head in a corner and make a fool of himself. Why not? They had been boys together, and had loved one another. They had made the mistake of loving one woman: that is true.

Oakshott would have killed Arthur at one time to get at the woman, for he could not sin. Arthur, I most entirely expect, at one time compassed Oakshott's death. The Cammoristi story is by no means clear. Granby Dixon shakes his head about it. Let Arthur lie peacefully in his grave. Who knows the real truth about anything?

But here were two lives ruined for the sake of one woman, and that woman was a lunatic. How long will men follow women like this? The answer is perfectly easy.

Men will follow women to the death as long as they are helpmates for men. When they are frivolous and silly, they are mere toys, and an earnest man soon has done with them. Of poor Marie I know nothing: of Dixie I know much. I know this about both of them, however. Poor Marie followed her husband through everything, and Dixie followed Oakshott through everything. One woman, Marie, was treated like a dog or a squaw, and followed faithfully and truly. The other woman, Dixie, was treated like a daughter, but she followed faithfully wherever Earlie went.

CHAPTER L.

AMERICAN JUDGMENT ON OAKSHOTT.

"I WOULD give fivepence-farthing," said Granby Dixon for the fiftieth time, "to know what those four lunatics did in America. Why, young Lady Oakshott (Dixie, I mean) showed me a heap of sapphires which she says she got at some place with an unpronounceable name. She is going to have them set, sir; and she took out the largest, and she said to me, 'I held this one in my mouth when Earlie and poor Arthur were having that awful row with the Creek chiefs.' What have they been up to?"

Granby said afterwards that certain items in some famous Claims were those against Great Horse, Little Horse, Donkey, and Great Sheep. The claim was too absurd to go to Geneva, of course; but Granby says it was put in, and came in to Granby's office. *He* says that these people were represented as Indian chieftains, but the American Government insisted that they were British subjects, and that two of them were women. No one knows more about the matter than Granby, if as much. It is only known that Granby says that "Great Horse" was Lord Oakshott, that "Little Horse" was Sir Arthur; "Donkey" was Lady Oakshott (Dowager), and "Big Sheep" was the present Lady Oakshott.

Granby Dixon met a young American officer who confirmed this statement entirely. He said that they were with the Apaches, and that they made work for the Commanches to get at that silver. " Oakshott owns it now, you know," said the American officer, who happens to have been born in Pomerania.

" Has it all ?"

" Yes, he and his young cousin; they have every share. Don't you know about the Oakshotts ?"

" No ;" which was a partial lie.

" They came south-west. Well, Arthur had got his wife, and Oakshott had got his daughter. The two women were dressed like men, and they shared a tent together. When the grand skirmish came on, the women behaved as well as the men."

" What skirmish ?" said Granby.

" Why, the grand Commanche skirmish," said the American officer. " If you don't know, I am not going to tell you. Come, Mr. Dixon, you have done a few things in India, and not a few in Australia, which you decline to talk about. Civilizing nations must act, sir. You said a few words in the House the other day which did not please me at all. You asked where the North American Indians were. If I had been a member of that House, I should have asked you where the Australian natives were ; and so I tell you."

" I suppose that it is pot and kettle," said Granby.

" Yes, but you pots must not use language to us kettles. Your nation and ours are civilizing the globe. The English language is the language of the future. French don't assimilate, and the French don't spread. So, if we do one thing, and you go and do the same thing, don't sit on us."

Granby promised faithfully that he would not sit on the

United States. He said that he was not big enough to do it.

"Well," said the American officer, "I never went to what you English call Queer Street myself. But those four did on the prairie : they fired into American troops by mistake. That lunatic Oakshott is by far the greatest lunatic which your nation ever turned out. He wanted to take his daughter down the cañon of the Colorado in a dug-out."

Granby suppressed the fact that Dixie was not his daughter.

CHAPTER LI.

THE PARTY OF THE LADIES O'BRIEN.

THERE are parties and parties. It is within the bounds of human probability that that which was given by Lady Kathleen and Lady Nora O'Brien was one of the most remarkable ever given since parties were given.

Lady Kathleen and Lady Nora had taken a little house in Bolton Row. It was a furnished house, and so they had little to do except light up and provide the supper. Their good priest would not allow any dancing, because it was the vigil of what we in the English Church would call a "red-letter" Saint.

"Faix," said Father Tiernay, "they are late with them. There are some coming whom you never saw. Pull me coat down behind me, some of ye ; it is not tidy, somehow."

Lady Nora was contending with his coat when rat-tat-tat came the first arrival. They were all extremely proper at once.

The man threw open the door and announced—

"Lord Ascot."

Very grey, with a grey beard and moustache. Not well set on his legs. He knew Lady Kathleen and Lady Nora, but when he was face to face with Father Tiernay he did not know him at all.

"Charles Ravenshoe," said Father Tiernay, "surely you remember Tiernay."

"Tiernay the groom?" said Charles, who since his cousin's death had succeeded to the title. "We had Tiernay a groom once, and he went with us to the Crimea. I don't remember anything about Tiernay a priest."

"Do you remember nothing about a black hare?" said the Father.

"No, sir. I can remember nothing at all. My wife is not here, and I am all alone. I have come out to these ladies because they bid me. I can give no other answer. I can remember nothing unless I am at Ravenshoe."

"But you can remember the Light Cavalry charge, Lord Ascot?"

"To tell you the truth about it, my dear sir," said Lord Ascot, "my memory is utterly going. What did you ask me to remember?"

"The Light Cavalry charge."

"Well, you see, I got heavily hit. I got hit on the head, though I did not know it. You see, sir, that I am not bound to remember. I don't conceive that I am bound to remember. I have left the army. While you stay in the army you are bound to remember, but I have left the army."

"Can't you remember me, dear old boy?" said Father Tiernay.

"No," said Lord Ascot; "I don't think that I remember you at all."

"Well, but you remember my brother, who played the organ at Ravenshoe?"

"Yes," said Lord Ascot; "I remember the young priest who played the organ at Ravenshoe. But you are not he."

"Lord Oakshott and Miss Prout."

"How are you, Ascot?" said Lord Oakshott.

"I am well from everything except memory, Oakshott. I can't remember anything at all. I got a cut on the head in the Light Cavalry charge at Balaclava."

"You did nothing of the kind," said Oakshott. "Ascot, do you not remember the row with the Blackfeet?"

"No!"

"Don't you remember your falling down among the rattlesnakes, and not one of them biting you?"

"Not a bit."

"You were hit with a tomahawk by a Blackfoot, my good Ascot."

"I dare say," said Lord Ascot. "I only know that I cannot remember. I have wandered, you know, lately; and since my cousin Ascot died, and I have been in the House of Lords, I have never taken any interest in public matters. Who is that young lady?"

"Miss Prout. Let me present her."

Dixie looked at him. She believed what Oakshott had told her now. He had told her that on Charles Ravenshoe's face a shadow of sorrow had passed which would never pass away any more.

Dixie looked at Lord Oakshott. The same shadow was there, as there was in Charles Ravenshoe's face. She heard Lord Ascot say to him—

"Oakshott, your fate is the same as mine. You will re-

member everything you ought to forget, and forget everything you ought to remember.   I *can't* remember things.   I
don't remember about the Blackfeet a bit in the world just
now.   Look here, Oakshott.   I remember that we both were
fully prepared to go to the deuce after two women.   It would
be better that we were both dead, Oakshott."

"Ascot," said Lord Oakshott, "I have some one to live
for.   I can live for Miss Prout."

"Are you going to marry her ?"

"You are ridiculous.   I am going to marry no one at
all."

There was an interruption.   The servant announced—

"Mr. and Mrs. Granby Dixon."

The effect of the entrance of that glowing little fellow was
to bring Oakshott to sanity, and Lord Ascot to his memory.
That little fellow would have stormed a fort and apologized
to the wounded afterwards.   A most remarkable thing about
the man was that wherever he came bad temper fled.

He stood in the centre of the room before Lord Oakshott
and Lord Ascot; and he laughed without speaking.

"The two greatest lunatics in the world have met at last,"
he said—"Oakshott and Ascot.   You have been talking
nonsense, you two.   I see it in your eyes.   Tell me what
nonsense you have been talking, and I will help to the
best of my ability, you know."

"Granby," said Oakshott, very sententiously, "the most
extraordinary thing is that Charles and I have been together
ten minutes, and we have talked no nonsense at all."

"I say, Oakshott, that will not do, you know," said
Granby.   "This matter is impossible."

"I should have thought so," said Lord Oakshott ; "but

the matter is true, nevertheless. I assure you that we have talked no nonsense at all."

"If we could stop you from talking nonsense it would be an immense matter. I never knew you do anything else. But what has Ascot been saying?"

"He has lost his memory," said Oakshott.

"Ascot!" said Granby Dixon.

"Yes," said Lord Ascot.

"Come here to me," said Granby.

Ascot came to him at once.

"Sit down," said Granby Dixon. "You were in Italy, I think, lately?"

"Yes; my wife was ill there."

"Exactly. I want to know if you remember a certain Signor Riccardo there."

"Yes."

"Could you swear to him?"

"Certainly."

"Then your memory is not gone?"

"At times it is."

"Look here, Ascot. Did you ever pull a boy out of the water?"

"Yes, the same boy you mention—the young Riccardo. I did it on the Adige."

"Was there any mark on his body?"

"Yes; a mark on his fore-arm—a tattoo."

"You can swear to that?"

"Yes."

"And now," said Granby, "you talk of having lost your memory because you got dexterously tomahawked on the top of your head while buffalo hunting."

There was no necessity to swear to it at all ; no dispute was ever made; but Granby liked to be safe. It was perfectly evident that Lord Ascot could remember anything if he was properly asked to remember it. His mind was not gone, only in abeyance. If any one between the four winds of heaven cares about Charles Ravenshoe, they may console themselves by hearing the simple fact that he is quite well again, and that he had a long and affectionate interview with a friend of ours four months ago. In saying this I would also say that young noblemen and gentlemen may employ their time better by attending to their estates than by getting themselves knocked on the head by the clubs of the Black-feet.

The party went on most comfortably. The next announcement was—

"Mr. and Mrs. Austin Elliot."

They say that Austin Elliot has become a bit of a prig. Granby Dixon says that he always *saw* that coming. But then he hates Mrs. Austin Elliot like poison. I cannot conceive why.

Ascot, Austin Elliot, and that very curious old black-guard, Silcote, were standing together when there came into the room a very strange man. Young, yet grey, and partially bald. He was perfectly blind.

He was without an attendant. Oakshott saw him first, and went to him.

But he pushed Oakshott away. He did not know the feel of Oakshott's hands. In the darkness of his darkened eyes, he felt one man after another, and then he said suddenly—

" Austin, Austin, they told me that you were here."

It was Lord Edward Barty.

He felt his way to Charles Ravenshoe, now Lord Ascot. He said : "Those fantastic fools are coming. For God's sake prevent my laughing myself to death : take me to Austin."

Charles took him to Austin at once. "My dear," said Lord Edward, "I should like to hear those children again, but they are behaving so very badly. They are quarrelling in the hall."

It was perfectly evident. There was a violent squabble going on on the stairs, and the nearer the quarrel came to the drawing-room door, the more silent everybody became. Lady Nora and Lady Kathleen, backed by Lord Oakshott, prepared to receive the visitors.

The footman, as one who had relieved himself of a vast responsibility, cast the door open and announced—

"Miss Herries, Captain Herries, and Lieutenant Herries."

They were at it hammer and tongs. They had fallen out in the carriage because Flora had been too long dressing. They had (as Oakshott and Granby Dixon say) pegged away at one another all the way from Grosvenor Square to Bolton Row. Flora, however, was most perfectly self-possessed. She bowed to every one, and then she began on her brothers again.

"Lord Oakshott," she said, "my brothers are worse than the lower Greek Emperors. I beg of you."

"My dear lady, I do not know your *façon de parler*. What do you demand of me?"

"To bring my brothers to their senses."

"Miss Herries, I have lost mine long ago ; how can I bring them to theirs?"

" Well, there is a good deal in that," said Flora, emphatically. " I forgot you were mad. I beg a thousand pardons, but I totally forgot that you were mad. And I, who am so particular in my manners, to forget that you were a lunatic! I am sure, Lord Oakshott, that you will forgive me."

" A hundred times over," said Lord Oakshott.

" Do you like being mad ?" said Flora.

" I think I do, on the whole," said Lord Oakshott. " I think I like it."

" I should like to be mad very much," said Flora.

" Why ?" said Oakshott.

" It must be so nice," said Flora. " You have no responsibilities if you are mad. But you will marry some day, and then you will have responsibilities."

" Did you ever see any one you would like to marry ?" said Oakshott.

" No one except yourself," said Flora.

" Will you marry me ?"

" Certainly not," said Flora. " You are a notorious lunatic. I don't want to marry lunatics. For the matter of that, there are more than one of them in the world. Charles Ravenshoe, now Ascot, is an utter and entire lunatic. Good gracious, goodness me ! here is trouble again. You have proposed to me. I have refused you, and my brothers are raising Cain. I sometimes wish I was dead with those two boys. Such pains as I have taken with them too. It's enough to break one's heart."

" What is the matter now ?" said Lord Oakshott.

He might well say " What is the matter ?" Gus and Archie were at high words. Gus had taken hold of the cat in the hall, and Archie had most emphatically resented it.

The cat had clawed Captain Gus to the bone, but Captain Gus was holding high words with his brother about the cat.

"I got her first," said Archie.

"It is not true," said Gus.

"Listen to his language," said Archie. "He has told me that I told a story."

Flora immediately began :—

"I do not know why I am aggravated in this way, I am sure. I have been sister to Cain and Abel at the same time. And Abel is worse than Cain. Miss Prout, would you come and separate my brothers?"

The laughter was general. The Herries children were always laughed at and loved. Something followed, however, which is more important than the absurdities of the Herries children.

"Miss Prout," said Flora, "do try to keep my brothers quiet."

"I am not aware that it is any business of mine," said Dixie, "but I will do my best."

"Miss Prout!" she added, in a whisper.

"Yes, Miss Herries."

"Should you be very angry if Lord Oakshott should marry anybody?"

"My dear, it is the only thing I desire."

"But are you quite sure, Miss Prout? You must remember that you have the entire keeping of his conscience."

"There you are utterly mistaken," said Miss Prout. "Earlie's heart is by no means with me. Earlie's heart is with ——I will not say where."

"With some one else?" said Flora.

"I do not say that," said Dixie. "It is not with me."

"If it was with me, would you be very angry?" said Flora.

Dixie flushed up, red to the roots of her hair. Then she said: "Flora, this is all as it should be. I am going to marry Sir Richard Oakshott."

"That is grand," said Mrs. Herries; "that is entirely grand. "Does any one know it but myself?"

"Only a few personal friends, just now."

"I am so glad you are not going to marry Lord Oakshott," said Flora, with a curious mixture of sense and absurdity. "I am an old married woman myself, and I assure you that it never would have done. He is too old, and you never know what he will do next. He proposed to me this evening before I had been in the room five minutes."

"I hope you accepted him, Flora," said Dixie, laughing.

"Not I, my dear; I gave him a flat refusal on the spot. I did take a liberty when I asked you the state of your heart; you will forgive my poor little curiosity?" said Flora in her most irresistible way.

"Surely, Flora," said Dixie, with a kiss. Whereupon Flora relapsed into nonsense.

"You ask why I call myself an old married woman : my dear, I have been married to Gus and Archie ever since I was a child. I have been a mother to them."

This seemed slightly illogical, but Dixie let her go on her own way.

"What I have suffered with those boys no one will ever know. I gave them the best advice. I told them where they would go to, and no less than five times have I paid their debts out of my own private fortune."

"But that is incredible dishonesty on their part," said Dixie, looking very grave.

"It is true, however," said Flora. "First and last I have paid over four pounds for those boys, who treat me like Judas; sometimes (at least on one occasion) as much as seven-and-sixpence at a time. You remember that dreadful case of Archie being fined five shillings at Gosport for breaking a window at Portsmouth?"

Dixie had politely forgotten.

"*My dear, I paid the money and lent him half-a-crown besides.* Lord Oakshott behind us, who is listening to every word of the conversation in a not very polite manner, doubtless remembers it."

Oakshott bent over and whispered in her ear.

It was Flora's turn now to blush, and she turned her beautiful face on his. "When did you hear it?" she said.

"Only just now, from Louis Brogden. He told me that you were to marry his little brother."

"Am I worthy of him, Lord Oakshott? Will he forgive my little foolish fantastic ways? Try to make him love Archie and Gus, for there are no finer fellows in the whole world than my two boys. I brought them up, and I ought to know it."

(This, it may be remarked, was a fiction on the part of Flora which was respected even by her brother Gus, who was two years older than herself.)

"I should think that any one would love your brother, my dear, without your pleading," said Oakshott. "Now we have done talking nonsense, let us go to our two bridegrooms: they have been waiting long enough."

The young ladies knew perfectly well where the bridegrooms were, and were no doubt quite comfortable. Lord Oakshott, leaving them, came suddenly on Lord Hainault and Rickaby.

"Hainault," he said, "we shall have two happy marriages."

"One I know of. Flora is a noble creature, and I would not wish her better off; her husband will be in Parliament with a large income. I will give her all I can. I do not regret having no children of my own. Since my poor wife's death Flora has practically kept house for me. There are no two finer boys in the Army or Navy than those boys of mine, Gus and Archie, with all their quaint ways. What is the other marriage of which you speak?"

"My adopted daughter is going to marry Sir Richard Oakshott, my cousin."

"I am *very* glad of that," said Lord Hainault: "I am *very* glad indeed; because some absurd people said that she might marry *you*, and that would never have done at all, you know."

"Why not?" said Oakshott.

"Why, because it would have spoilt the whole romance of the thing. Your reputation depends on your high and chivalrous character, in spite of certain laches in the way of speculation. I do hope, Oakshott, that you will come into public business again. Your powers of debate are masterly —you have high authority for that. Give up poetry and gambling, and we will make a man of you yet."

"I am going," said Lord Oakshott, "to win the Derby on an entirely new principle. I am going to buy Achievement, and have a colt by Blair Athol; whereby, don't you see, I win the Derby. During the three years which it will take to

accomplish this, I shall not come near London, but give all
my time up to writing an epic poem, on a subject which I
have not selected yet, and with which I am totally unac-
quainted."

So he left Lord Hainault, and was caught up by his host-
esses. "Me darling," said Lady Kathleen, " see to this."

It was a cheque for £5,000.

"See," said Lady Nora, "we can pay you your money
back, and God's blessing with it. Our aunt Lady Lock Ree
is dead, and we can pay ye."

"Take back the money, dear ladies, and put it in the soil
again. Use it in clearing the Shannon of those weirs, and it
will pay ten times over."

"You are not such a fool as they make you out, at all, at
all," said Lady Kathleen. "We will have to spend it in law,
though, but we will help to redeem a county."

CHAPTER LII.

CONCLUSION.

DICKIE and Dixie tried their place at Shepperton, and
stayed there for a year: then they fled ; and where should
they fly to but to Oakshott, with the new-born baby in
Dixie's arms.

They could not stand Shepperton at all. Dreghorn
Castle, the most unutterably melancholy place I know, was
nothing to Shepperton. At Dreghorn Castle you can see
the lights of Edinburgh, but at Shepperton you could see
nothing at all ; still Dreghorn is distinctly suicidal.

What a change from Shepperton to Oakshott ! Fires in

every room lighting up the Castle, and a fire in the hall, which, when the door was opened, answered the lighthouse on the Needles. Mrs. Prout in lavender silk at the door, to catch the baby out of the gale of wind which periodically blows at Oakshott; Oakshott himself before the fire with Granby Dixon.

"My dears," said Lord Oakshott, "I knew that you would come to me sooner or later. I knew that you would never stand that place. When I got your letter, Dickie, I made all ready for you. Now get ready for dinner, you two; I have been at work all the morning: we dine in the hall."

When Dickie came down, Oakshott was there. Dickie was a little puzzled. He knew perfectly well that Oakshott had made some sort of bargain with Dixie, but she would not tell him what it was. A gentleman was introduced to him, and sat with them at the upper end of the table. He was a very nice gentleman, but he talked of nothing but wrecks and disasters at sea. At the lower end of the table, below the servants, were rough, brave-looking men, who came in humbly and sat down to their supper respectfully. They were common workmen, but of a very high class. Dickie was puzzled; Dixie was not.

"You see, my lord," said the strange gentleman, "that we have the boat nearly finished, and she will be here in a fortnight. With regard to the other boat, my lord, we will be as quick as we can."

An announcement:—"Mr. Stevenson" (dripping wet).

"We have got the last stone down, Lord Oakshott. We are above high-water mark, and shall be finished in a year. Bless the old Channel, she fought us to the last, but we beat her.　You dry-shift men at the lower end of the table, you are on to-morrow morning at ebb, you know.　I say, butler, tell them to see after the last shift, and get me some warm soup."

" Oakshott, what is all this madness of yours," said Granby Dixon, " for I have not had time to inquire ?"

" I made a compact with Dixie that I would restore the Abbey—you remember that plan ?　She has compounded with me for a lighthouse and two lifeboats, one here and one at Alum Bay.　The men who are sitting at the lower end of the table are workmen connected with the lighthouse, which Mr. Stevenson is building at my expense, under the directions of the Trinity Board."

" I see my way to the lifeboats," said Granby ; " but the lighthouse ?"

" Our fishermen have depended on the Castle light so long," said Oakshott, " that it had better be made permanent.　I am going to build it.　One lamentable accident happened because my tower light was put out while I was struggling for life.　I have missed doing much in the world, Granby, but my fishermen's sons shall not say that I did not do my best to guide them to their homes."

Some years after Lord Oakshott was having an interview with a great publisher about his epic poem, on which they both lost a heap of money.　The publisher asked Lord Oakshott if he would write a book containing his experiences in America.　Lord Oakshott immediately seized his hat and umbrella, bowed, winked, and withdrew.

THE END.